# SHADOWS OF NIGHTSONG

## Borgo Press Books by ROBERT REGINALD

*The Astral: Till the Day I Die * Avalon: An Historical Novel * The C.A.M.P. Cookbook * The C.A.M.P. Guide to Astrology * Charms, Spells, and Curses for the Millions * Color Him Gay: That Man from C.A.M.P. * The Curse of Bloodstone: A Gothic Novel of Terror * Darkwater: A Gothic Novel of Horror * The Daughters of Nightsong: An Historical Novel* (Nightsong Saga #2) *** The Devil's Dance: A Novel of Terror * Drag Thing; or, The Strange Tale of Jackle and Hyde * The Earth and All It Holds: An Historical Novel * A Family Affair: A Novel of Terror * Fatal Flowers: A Novel of Horror * Fire on the Moon: A Novel of Terror * The Gay Dogs: That Man from C.A.M.P. * The Gay Haunt * The Glass House: A Novel of Terror * The Glass Painting: A Gothic Tale of Horror * Goodbye, My Lover * The Greek Boy * The Green Rolling Hills: Writings from West Virginia* (editor) *** Green Willows: A Novel of Terror * Kenny's Back * Life & Other Passing Moments: A Collection of Short Writings * The Lion's Gate: A Novel of Terror * Love's Pawn: A Novel of Romance * Lucifer's Daughter: A Novel of Horror * Moon Garden: A Novel of Terror * Nightsong: An Historical Novel* (Nightsong Saga #1) *** The Pot Thickens: Recipes from Writers and Editors* (editor) *** San Antone: An Historical Novel * The Scent of Heather: A Novel of Terror * The Second House: A Novel of Terror * The Second Tijuana Bible Reader* (editor) *** Shadows of Nightsong* (Nightsong Saga #4) *** The Sins of Nightsong: An Historical Novel* (Nightsong Saga #3) *** Spine Intact, Some Creases: Remembrances of a Paperback Writer * Stranger at the Door: A Novel of Suspense * Sweet Tormented Love: A Novel of Romance * The Sword and the Rose: An Historical Novel * This Splendid Earth: An Historical Novel * The Tijuana Bible Reader* (editor) *** Twisted Flames * The WATERCRESS File: That Man from C.A.M.P. * A Westward Love: An Historical Romance * White Jade: A Novel of Terror * The Why Not * The Wine of the Heart: A Novel of Romance * The Wolves of Craywood: A Novel of Terror*

# SHADOWS OF NIGHTSONG

## AN HISTORICAL NOVEL: THE NIGHTSONG SAGA, BOOK FOUR

### V. J. BANIS

THE BORGO PRESS

MMXIII

# SHADOWS OF NIGHTSONG

**FIRST BORGO PRESS EDITION**

Published by Wildside Press LLC

www.wildsidebooks.com

# DEDICATION

I am deeply indebted to my friend, Heather, for all the help she has given me in getting these early works of mine reissued.

And I am grateful as well to Rob Reginald, for all his assistance and support.

# CONTENTS

**PART ONE** . . . . . . . . . . . . . . . . . . . . . 9

PROLOGUE . . . . . . . . . . . . . . . . . . . .10

CHAPTER ONE . . . . . . . . . . . . . . . . . .17

CHAPTER TWO. . . . . . . . . . . . . . . . . . .24

CHAPTER THREE . . . . . . . . . . . . . . . . .36

CHAPTER FOUR . . . . . . . . . . . . . . . . . .48

CHAPTER FIVE. . . . . . . . . . . . . . . . . . .57

CHAPTER SIX. . . . . . . . . . . . . . . . . . . .66

CHAPTER SEVEN . . . . . . . . . . . . . . . . . .76

CHAPTER EIGHT. . . . . . . . . . . . . . . . . .86

CHAPTER NINE . . . . . . . . . . . . . . . . . .96

CHAPTER TEN . . . . . . . . . . . . . . . . . . 105

**PART TWO** . . . . . . . . . . . . . . . . . . . 117

CHAPTER ELEVEN. . . . . . . . . . . . . . . . . 118

CHAPTER TWELVE . . . . . . . . . . . . . . . . 128

CHAPTER THIRTEEN . . . . . . . . . . . . . . . 138

CHAPTER FOURTEEN . . . . . . . . . . . . . . . 148

CHAPTER FIFTEEN . . . . . . . . . . . . . . . . . 161

CHAPTER SIXTEEN . . . . . . . . . . . . . . . . . 170

CHAPTER SEVENTEEN . . . . . . . . . . . . . . . 181

CHAPTER EIGHTEEN . . . . . . . . . . . . . . . . 190

CHAPTER NINETEEN . . . . . . . . . . . . . . . . 201

CHAPTER TWENTY . . . . . . . . . . . . . . . . . 211

**PART THREE**. . . . . . . . . . . . . . . . . . 221

CHAPTER TWENTY-ONE . . . . . . . . . . . . . . 222

CHAPTER TWENTY-TWO . . . . . . . . . . . . . . 233

CHAPTER TWENTY-THREE . . . . . . . . . . . . 241

CHAPTER TWENTY-FOUR . . . . . . . . . . . . . 250

CHAPTER TWENTY-FIVE. . . . . . . . . . . . . . 262

CHAPTER TWENTY-SIX. . . . . . . . . . . . . . . 267

CHAPTER TWENTY-SEVEN . . . . . . . . . . . . 277

CHAPTER TWENTY-EIGHT. . . . . . . . . . . . . 290

CHAPTER TWENTY-NINE . . . . . . . . . . . . . 298

CHAPTER THIRTY. . . . . . . . . . . . . . . . . . 305

ABOUT THE AUTHOR. . . . . . . . . . . . . . . . 320

# PART ONE
## SAN FRANCISCO, 1910

# PROLOGUE

The glitter of the salon paled when Lydia saw Peter appear in the doorway. He began speaking to someone he knew but kept looking around until his eyes met hers. When he smiled and started toward her, Lydia found she was not listening to what Willie Hearst was saying. Seeing Peter now made her remember the first time she'd met him in that tiny village somewhere deep inside China. As always, the sight of him started something stirring within her.

But before Peter reached where she was waiting, his wife, Lorna, intercepted him, her fan fluttering with irritation at his lateness.

Lydia averted his eyes and heard Willie say, "Lydia, you still make good newspaper copy. Why your name alone has that strangeness about it that is almost mystique. Lydia Nightsong... not a name commonly found in the telephone directories." He refilled Lydia's champagne glass and leaned back, hooking his thumbs in his waistcoat and puffing on his cigar.

When next she looked in that direction, Peter had moved off somewhere with his wife.

"But it's monstrous, Willie. After fifteen years your newspaper is still dragging my children and me through the tabloids on every anniversary of little Adam's disappearance. Can't it be left alone? Don't you realize what it does to the child's mother? April has never gotten over the shock of that terrible night." Lydia moved aside the glass of champagne, feeling the pain in her heart. "I'm afraid she will never recover, even if the boy is found one day. And neither will I."

"Lydia, I'm just a newspaper man, doing my job, same as you do yours. You happen to be a very beautiful, extremely wealthy woman with a glamorous past as well as a dazzling career in the cosmetic industry."

"Glamorous past? You mean disreputable, don't you?"

He shrugged. "A lot of people think there is no difference between the two."

"People are interested in me for only one reason: The Nightsong scandals. They delight in reading and rereading about them, and every time your paper prints something about my family some new lurid detail finds its way into the story, usually something manufactured in order to make the copy fresh. I do think it all very unfeeling, William."

He took her hand. "I realize the stories must hurt you deeply, my dear, but in all truthfulness, I only hope and pray they will be of some benefit. Look at it this way, Lydia. Fifteen years ago little Adam was taken from his crib by a person or persons unknown. His nurse had been heavily drugged and remembers nothing of that night, or at least refuses to remember. Not a single word has been heard of the four-year-old since. Each year we rake up the whole unfortunate affair because it just may be possible that someone will read the story—even after all this time— and come forward with a clue, some information that will help in getting your grandson returned to you."

"Yes, I suppose there is something in what you say, Willie, but...."

He squeezed her hand. "I know how hard it must be on you and poor April, but frankly, my dear, I am not doing this solely to sell my newspapers. I, too, like everyone else, want to do what I can. Contrary to what you may think about your followers, Lydia, they aren't interested in you purely for the salacious parts of your life. You are truly liked and greatly admired, my dear. You did things women all over the world dream of doing."

She glanced around the drawing room of the recently completed Hearst townhouse atop Nob Hill. The earthquake four years earlier had reduced the sprawling mansions on Nob Hill to rubble and the rubble had been reduced to ashes during the ensuing three-day fire. It had taken a very short time, however, before Nob Hill again glittered with new palaces. Some, like the Hearsts, preferred to change in favor of a more modern home—a townhouse, they called them; while others, like Lydia Nightsong, stuck to old ways and rebuilt in the same style as before. Hers was a stunning house complete with wrought-iron fencing, sloping lawns, turrets and cupolas and gingerbread trim. By Lydia's way of thinking, everything around her was changing so rapidly, so drastically, she wanted to hold onto at least a small piece of the past.

William Hearst's words were still with her as she climbed from the chauffeured limousine and started up the steps to her new mansion. She paused just inside the door and welcomed the silence that enveloped her. Nellie's footsteps approached from the servants' quarters.

"You shouldn't have waited up, Nellie."

"And when, may I ask, haven't I waited up for you, Miss Lydia? Did you enjoy the party?"

"I think I'm getting too old to enjoy parties anymore, Nellie." Her voice was tired.

"Too old, me foot! You still look like the young slip of a girl you were when I was a girl meself." She turned and started up the winding staircase. "I'll turn down your bed."

Lydia glanced at herself in the hall mirror. It seemed such a short time ago when she was young. Still, the years had been kind to her—at least so far as her appearance was concerned. Men still called her beautiful. Her red-gold hair had lost none of its brilliance and the several silvery strands that did exist only served as lovely complements. Her dark green eyes still held their sparkle and her skin was as smooth and soft as that day when she'd run from the Mandarin prince she'd been forced to marry in China. There were no lines that reminded her of that perilous escape to America with her daughter, April. But behind her she'd left the graves of her parents and more importantly, her infant son with whom Prince Ke Loo refused to part.

"That was thirty years ago," Lydia mused as she began removing her long white gloves.

She glanced at the staircase but didn't follow her housekeeper upstairs. It was rather difficult for her to get accustomed to the fact that her bedroom was no longer on the main level of the house. When rebuilding the mansion, April and Caroline succeeded in convincing her that it was far safer for her to sleep on the second floor, reminding her of that night the Dowager Empress had sent one of her assassins—who'd hidden himself in Lydia's bedroom—intent upon either killing her or taking her back to his Empress in China, where Lydia could be punished for stealing the Empress's personal scent. That scent that had made Lydia a huge fortune and had put her life in danger of assassination by Tz'u-Hsi's henchmen. That threat was past now. Tz'u-Hsi, the Dragon Queen of China, was dead and the infant Emperor Hsuan T'ung was on the unstable throne of the Manchu dynasty. If Prince Ke Loo did not depose his cousin, then the revolutionaries would.

She turned and made her way toward the small back parlor where a low fire was burning in the hearth. Overhead an electric chandelier gave a brightness to the room that Lydia did not like. She switched it off and clicked on the heavily shaded table lamp. She missed the oil lamps with their crystal prisms. Electric lights erased all the softness of a room. She missed the romantic shadows of candle and gaslight.

She seated herself in the chair by the fire and looked around the dim room. It was almost a duplicate of her favorite room the earthquake and fire had destroyed. The old memories were still here, though the furnishings were slightly different. She could almost picture Peter sitting across from her, smiling that enigmatic smile that she found impossible to resist. Her flesh tingled at the thought of how they'd made love. Her cheeks burned when she remembered the shameless things she'd done to him, the forbidden ways only desperate lovers made love.

"Peter," she sighed. He was a part of the Nightsong scandals, though he hadn't suffered as much notoriety. Perhaps it was because he was as important and powerful a man in San Francisco as Willie Hearst. A man with a respectable wife— so far as the public was concerned—and fine children. Lydia smiled, thinking what a field day the newspapers would have if they knew the truth about Lydia Nightsong and Peter MacNair— that one of her daughter April's sons was, in fact, the son of Lydia and Peter. Peter himself didn't know about Marcus. No one knew, except April and her one time husband, Raymond.

Raymond Andrieux was Lydia's husband now. Oh, how the gossips loved to rehash that old bit of gossip. A mother who married her own daughter's former husband.

Like so much of the Nightsong scandals, the truth was rarely told or known. She had had to marry Raymond or lose her entire cosmetic empire, and go back to being the poor impoverished girl who had come to America with only a small half-Oriental daughter and the clothes on their backs.

Lydia brushed a hand across her brow as if to try and dispel all the unpleasant memories. Hard as she tried, she could not think of too many happy memories, only those few stolen moments with Peter MacNair.

Idly, she picked up the large scrapbook that lay on the table beside her, the scrapbook she'd so fastidiously—and somewhat perversely—maintained for the past fifteen years. Carefully glued to the pages were every newspaper clipping, every memento of her life, her family—the Nightsong Chronicles, as she thought of the scrapbook.

She gazed at the sketch of the handsome little boy whose face appeared beneath the headline CHILD KIDNAPPED. It had been the first of the innumerable articles that appeared about little Adam's disappearance. And over the years the disappearance was kept alive by continuing articles that eventually brought to light every fact or supposition of the Nightsong family, especially the more lurid aspects of Lydia's life and the lives of her children.

She glanced through the articles, her eyes catching an almost forgotten incident, an incident she wanted desperately to forget.

"Mrs. Peter MacNair," Lydia read, "announced to the press this morning that the missing boy is in fact her grandson. Mrs. MacNair went on to add that she doubted very much if April Nightsong was indeed the child's natural mother."

That was one of the scandalous furors Lydia wanted to forget. The nightmare of April's rantings, the name-callings, the threats. April's retaliation; her accusation that it was Lorna MacNair herself who'd arranged for April's son's abduction; that if Lorna and Peter MacNair had not interfered in her love affair with their oldest son, David would be alive to prove whose child Adam was.

Little Adam disappeared without a trace, leaving April bitter and despondent and half-crazed. Lorna and Peter MacNair were still determined to have April legally declared an unfit mother and the child, when found, put into their custody.

Lydia's eyes rested on the account of how April had run away from her French husband, Raymond Andrieux, and fled to China with David MacNair, abandoning her daughter, Caroline, and newly born son, Marcus—the son Lydia had given over to April and Raymond in secret. Then there was the tragic news of David's beheading by the Dowager Empress, April's return to San Francisco, her refusal to acknowledge her legal husband and their ultimate divorce, followed shortly by Lydia's marriage to her former son-in-law, a marriage that had doomed any hope of her ever marrying the man she truly loved, Peter MacNair.

She slammed shut the book. The memories were too painful. She wanted to think of more pleasant things.

Her son, Leon, was coming for a visit. This time she'd try to convince him to stay, rather than returning to his Mandarin father and his political machinations in Hawaii. She closed her eyes and tried to remember what Prince Ke Loo looked like. She had never seen him after leaving China; she never wanted to see him and it broke her heart when Leon—Li Ahn, as his father called him—chose to return to his father's side after Leon himself had succeeded in escaping to America and in becoming more Western than any one born to her. Leon fell in love with America. There had to have been a reason for him to so abruptly decide to join his father and Dr. Sun Yat-sen in their proposed rebellion against the Empress. The Boxer Rebellion had been suppressed by international forces and now Sun Yat-sen was proposing to dethrone the child emperor and make China a republic, though Prince Ke Loo was fool enough to think that he would usurp the throne and continue the Manchu dynasty. Why Leon had wanted to embroil himself in that madness, Lydia could not understand.

Well, some goodness had come out of all that tribulation. At least April hated her less and was now living in the Nightsong mansion again. Caroline had grown into one of the most ravishing beauties in the city, very modern and independent. Marcus was almost twenty-one and had a passion for the new racing cars, which he tried to keep hidden from her.

All in all, she prided herself on having done a good job in raising the children. If only Adam could be found. She wondered where he was—or if he was.

# CHAPTER ONE

Far out in the English countryside, miles from London, Adam Clarendon sat astride Silverstreak, the new stallion his father had given him.

The stallion felt powerful and sure between his legs. Adam let Pamela race on ahead and watched her mount easily take the hedge and gallop off across Darthshire Clearing. She had lost her riding cap and her long raven hair flew wildly behind her. Adam saw the cap and reined up to retrieve it.

The day was dazzling, bright, and clear, with puffy clouds floating lazily across the pale blue sky. Somewhere in the stand of birches that bordered the clearing, birds chattered to one another. It was spring. Surely their songs were love calls.

He felt a familiar stirring inside him as Pamela slowed and turned her mare, trotting back to him, her young, full breasts jostling provocatively as she posted. She was breathtakingly beautiful. He felt his sexual excitement rise as he noticed the curves of her thighs, the full hips, the slender, soft line of her throat. He wanted to pull her from the saddle, rip away her clothes, and ravage her here and now on the grassy slope of the field.

He dismounted, adjusting his semierection, and picked up Pamela's riding cap. She sat astride her mount on the other side of the hedge, waiting for him.

"My cap?" she called, seeing it in his hand.

"Yes. I mustn't take you back looking all disheveled. What will people think?" he chided.

He put his foot in the stirrup, but as he hoisted himself up he felt a slight weakening of the cinch and stepped back down.

He heard the shot before recognizing it for what it was. Not until the searing pain ripped through his thigh did he realize he'd been shot.

Pamela screamed and spurred her horse just as Adam grabbed his leg and fell to the ground. "Adam!" The mare retook the hedge fast and clean. A moment later Pamela threw herself out of the saddle and rushed toward Adam.

"Darling," she cried, kneeling next to him. "What happened? I heard a shot."

"My leg," Adam moaned in pain.

A tight little scream caught in Pam's throat when she saw the blood stain that was rapidly spreading. Her first instinct was one of horror as she clamped a fist to her mouth. A moment later her common sense came to the fore.

"You're bleeding badly, darling. I'll have to bandage the wound before getting you home."

"Someone shot me," Adam said, not believing what had happened. Pamela tore off a broad swathe of the petticoat she wore under her riding skirt.

"Surely an accident."

Adam glanced toward the stand of trees that crowded the rise. Yes, surely it was only some careless poacher. He thought suddenly of Jeremy Slyke and wasn't altogether certain it had been an accident.

He watched as Pamela tore open the leg of his britches. The sight of the oozing blood made her stomach contract, but she concentrated on what had to be done.

The bullet had entered several inches above the knee and off to the side. It had gone straight through the fleshy part of the thigh and there was blood rushing from both entry and exit. She tied a tourniquet just above the wounds, slowing the bleeding and tore off another strip of petticoat to cover the holes.

"I'm afraid that will have to do for now, darling," she said. She bent closer over the makeshift bandage and her eye caught something dark and strange on Adam's thigh, just above the tourniquet. She spread apart the rip in his britches and stared at what at first glance seemed to be a bruise, but it had a definite outline and form. Two opened flowers—poppies, she decided—encircled by a ring of dots, had been etched on the skin. She looked questioningly at Adam but his head was thrown back, his teeth clenched in pain. He looked quite pale.

She had to get him back to Clarendon Hall and have his parents summon Dr. Griggs. "Come, darling, lean on me. I must get you home. That wound must be properly treated before it becomes infected."

With an effort she got Adam to his feet and tried to make light of his groans of pain. "Stop acting like a baby. You are not going to die yet, old boy."

He girded himself against the terrible ache that was spreading through his body, and pulled himself up into the saddle.

"Easy, Adam," Pamela cautioned when he started to canter off. "Walk Silverstreak. Those bandages aren't very expert, I'm afraid."

Twenty minutes felt like twenty years, but finally Pamela and Adam walked their mounts into the courtyard that fronted Lord Clarendon's country estate. In a flash Pamela was out of her saddle and rushing toward the arched doorway.

"Stay where you are, Adam," she called back. "I'll fetch the stewards to help you down and ring up Dr. Griggs."

From the minute Pamela burst into the library to interrupt Lord and Lady Clarendon's quiet conversation until Dr. Griggs came out of Adam's bedroom an hour later, Clarendon Hall was a flurry of worried activity.

"He's fine, just fine, Millicent," Dr. Griggs said to the ashen-faced Lady Clarendon. "The bullet went straight on through. He'll be uncomfortable for a while. I've given him something for the pain. Best let the boy sleep. I think he is more frightened than hurt. Insane poachers," he added with a disgruntled move of his hand. "They'll kill someone one of these days, if they haven't already."

Lord Clarendon looked from under his heavy brows. "Yes, poachers," he said almost to himself and with a quick glance at his wife. Like Adam, he wasn't convinced it had been the fault of a poacher. They hadn't had problems with poachers on the grounds for years.

"I'll be back tomorrow to look in on the lad. Pamper him," the doctor said with a smile. "It's the best medicine by far. In the morning he'll be boasting about his adventure, genuinely proud of his brush with death."

When Dr. Griggs was gone, Lady Clarendon turned to the almost forgotten Pamela Albright. "You poor darling, you've had a dreadful time of it. I can't begin to tell you how much we appreciate all you've done." She slipped her arm about Pam's waist and steered her toward the morning room. "Come have some tea."

"A glass of sherry might help calm your nerves," Lord Clarendon put in as he fell in behind.

Later, settled around the table in the morning room Pamela lazily stirred a spoonful of sugar into her tea. "I noticed," she started, rather hesitantly, "a strange marking on Adam's leg."

"Strange marking?" Lord Clarendon asked, sipping his sherry. He gave his wife a flick of his eyes.

"Yes. I had to rip open his britches. It was rather high up—on his thigh," she said, feeling the color rise in her cheeks. "I didn't see it clearly, of course, but it looked like a design—two open flowers."

Lord and Lady Clarendon exchanged hurried glances, glances that held an element of fear. After an awkward pause, Lady Clarendon said, "A rather unfortunate birthmark, my dear."

"It didn't look like a birthmark, Lady Clarendon. It was much too precisely drawn. I thought it more like a tattoo."

"A tattoo?" Lady Clarendon said in a silvery laugh. "Dear me, no, child. Why on earth would we have our son tattooed? It's a birthmark, nothing more." She smiled broadly and touched Pamela's hand. "But I do admire your marvelous imagination."

She laughed more merrily. "After all, child, Adam is hardly a common seaman. Aren't they the ones who tattoo their bodies, dear?" she asked her husband, looking most innocent.

When alone later in the library with her husband, however, Lord Clarendon said, "I don't like the idea of Pamela spotting that design on Adam's thigh, Millicent."

"It can hardly be kept a secret, Basil. After all, if the girl eventually marries Adam, which I believe is a good likelihood, she'd learn of the ridiculous marking soon enough." She leaned back in her chair. "I remember only too vividly the fright I got the first time I saw the design on Little Adam. Little Adam," she said, reflecting. "It hardly seems possible the years have gone by so swiftly. I can close my eyes and tell you every detail of that private railroad car we'd hired to travel across America." A sudden thought occurred to her and she looked over at her husband. "Any regrets, Basil?"

He hesitated, resting his elbow on his knees, his chin in his hands. "No," he said a little weakly. He let out a deep sigh and got up. "What we did was wrong, Millicent, but I am not sorry we took Adam home with us."

"What else could we have done, Basil? I still have the newspaper clipping about his terrible kidnapping and that awful mother who only seemed to want him back to use as a weapon for revenge on her husband's family. If indeed the man was her husband," she added scornfully. "The woman had abandoned her other two children. There was nothing to indicate she would not willingly have abandoned Adam for the right considerations. No, Basil," she said emphatically, "I could not in good conscience return that poor tyke to that awful Nightsong family or the equally ruthless grandparents."

"But we don't know anything except what was printed in the newspapers."

"The newspapers are usually impartial, Basil. Besides, you made discreet inquiries about both the Nightsongs and the MacNairs. You know we could never send Adam back into that environment."

"Yes, yes," he said a little impatiently. "I realize all that, my dear. The mother was a bad apple from the word 'go.' I'm only saying that we committed a crime in taking a child to whom we had no legal rights."

"I take full blame for any legal wrong we committed. Yet, if it were to happen again, I would do exactly the same. Oh, Basil, don't you remember the endless specialists I went to, always with the heartbreaking news that I would never bear you an heir without it taking my life? I wanted you to have a son, darling. I would gladly have died in childbirth to give you that son."

"You were always a determined woman, Millicent. I knew you'd never give up trying to bear me a child. That is why I went along with the idea of taking Adam. I'm as much to blame as you for any wrong we've committed." He began pacing. "It isn't the boy or Pamela's seeing the tattoo that's making me unnerved."

"What then?"

He turned and frowned down at her. "Who in bloody hell shot the boy?" He realized he'd yelled and ran his hands through his hair. "And we both know the answer to that one, Millie. Jeremy Slyke." He spat the name with such hatred Millicent's hands went to her throat. "Speaking of bad apples, he's the worst in the barrel."

"You're not implying that Jeremy actually tried to kill our son?"

"You yourself heard the threats he's made on too many occasions."

"All the more reason not to carry them out. If anything questionable happened to Adam, Jeremy would be the first one suspect. He'd never dare harm Adam."

"Jeremy Slyke is not particularly clever—or perhaps he is too clever. He's in love with Pamela and that type of man usually doesn't do without what he has his heart set on." A thought struck him and he started for the door.

"Where are you going?"

"I'm going to Jeremy's father and have my say."

"Basil," Millicent called. "Be sensible. Tom Slyke despises

you as much as his son despises Adam. He swore he'd shoot you on sight if you ever stepped foot on his land."

"Let him shoot away. Perhaps that will bring an end to this bloody revenge that Slyke feels he must have on us. It wasn't my fault our glass factory was favored with those government contracts. Is that a reason to want to kill us all? Mark me, Millicent, it's Tom Slyke who's been goading his son on and I intend to confront him."

The door closed sharply, emphatically. Lady Clarendon twisted her hands in her lap. Somehow she had the feeling that they had crossed some significant threshold, one that led to the end of everything.

# CHAPTER TWO

Lydia Nightsong paced angrily to and fro in her San Francisco office, her husband's letter crumpled in her fist. Raymond's demands had enraged her. The only balm for her rage was that Peter MacNair would arrive soon.

Lydia threw Raymond's letter into the wastebasket. He was ruining her with his disregard for money and his insane business deals were sinking Empress Cosmetics deeper and deeper into debt. Somehow, much as she disliked the idea, she had to convince Raymond to shut down the Paris offices and return to San Francisco.

Evelyn Clary tapped on the door and came into Lydia's office. "I'm off to lunch, love. Don't forget, Peter MacNair is due in about five minutes." She glanced at her long-time employer and noticed the new dress. "But I should know better than to have to remind you of any appointment with the dashing Peter MacNair."

Lydia felt the color rising and fussed with the set of her new coiffeur. "Don't be idiotic, Evelyn. It's just another business luncheon."

"From the first day you hired me, more than twenty years ago, lunch dates with Peter MacNair always cost you a new hairdo and a new frock." She studied the dress. "I like that, Lydia. The cut becomes you, even though I find it a bit tailored."

"It's all the newest rage in Paris."

She was wearing a short mauve taffeta dress with a jacket to match—the new two-piece fashion that was currently so chic. It had a tailored look that Lydia made as feminine as rose petals.

"It isn't exactly new, however," she told Evelyn, "and as for the hairdo, you know I always have Philippe do my hair every Thursday. Peter and I are simply going to discuss my possibly going into door-to-door selling, which has obviously been so profitable for MacNair Products."

"On the chance of sounding like a snob, Lydia, we both know Peter MacNair's cosmetics are inferior to ours, and his products belong door-to-door with five-cent magazines and peddling salesmen."

"He's coming out with a higher priced line that would compete with ours."

"He tried that once before with Lady Lydia, remember?" Evelyn's voice was like milk.

"Lady Lorna," Lydia corrected, "named after his wife."

"It was originally Lady Lydia. Remember, sweets, I'm the old dog who was in on all this from the beginning. You know, you should have married that man when you had the chance."

"You know why I couldn't and didn't. Without Raymond there would be no Empress Cosmetics—no me, no you."

"And look where Raymond Andrieux has led you. His letter this morning wasn't marked PERSONAL. I read it, of course, just like I read the financial reports Auditing sends down. We both know your French aristocrat and his aristocratic nose is pulling this firm to the brink of extinction."

"Oh, heavens, Evelyn, you needn't remind me. But without Raymond's nose, who else would reproduce Nightsong Perfume'? And without Nightsong we'd be out of business in a month." She let out a sigh. "Raymond has us cornered, Evelyn."

"I remember all those years ago when you stumbled upon Raymond Andrieux, the one man with a talent to smell a scent and know not only which blossoms a perfume contained, but how many blossoms, when the flower was grown, when it was harvested, and the composition of the soil in which it was grown. A Nez," she mused. "Not a particularly attractive title for a man with such unique talents."

"In the cosmetic business, Evelyn, as you well know, a Nez is as rare as peonies in winter and the most valuable asset a perfume manufacturer can have. He's the equivalent of a taster in a scotch distillery."

"There must be others with such a talent. You've stopped looking, Lydia, and I think it's about time you started."

Lydia turned toward the windows just in time to see Peter MacNair's automobile stop in front of the office building. "I don't know, Evelyn. I honestly am feeling very old and very tired. I would just like to settle myself and be left alone."

"You'd be content with inactivity for about two days. And as for being old, you're fifty-five, five years younger than me—and I certainly haven't stopped eyeing the tightness of men's pants." She gave a little wave. "Have a nice lunch. If you overeat and have to siesta, I'll understand." With a wink of the eye she swept out.

Lydia heard Peter and Evelyn greet each other and Peter mumbled something that made Evelyn laugh. A moment later he stood, hat in hand, framed in the doorway.

"Hello."

Her heart was beating so fast it actually hurt. She put her hand on her breast to try and still it. "Hello, Peter."

"I'm sorry we did not have the chance to see each other alone the other evening at the Hearst's." He grinned and came toward her. "But Lorna says that even though we weren't together you and I spent the entire evening alone."

"We did rather search each other out much too often with our eyes. Lorna has a right to be annoyed. I shouldn't provoke her as I do."

"I couldn't help wanting to be with you, Lydia. Just as I want to be with you now." He took her hand and pressed it to his lips. "You are still the most stunning woman I have ever seen."

"Your eyes are getting dim."

"Never. They're as sharp as razors."

Her smile was radiant. "I'm a fifty-five-year-old woman with a legal husband, though I haven't seen him for over a year and a half. My hair is graying, my waist is broadening, and my bones ache on wet, damp days."

"I still see you as that same frightened little girl in the bamboo grove halfheartedly fighting off that lout who wanted to get under your skirts."

"Halfheartedly?"

He laughed. "Truthfully, Lydia, I do believe you were as eager as he was."

"I suppose you're right, but it wasn't until you mistook me for one of your singsong girls and opened your hut's door wearing only what you'd worn when God brought you into the world that I became inquisitive."

He took her into his arms. "Obviously, you liked what you saw."

"Simply curious." The vision of him flashed across the backs of her eyes. How handsome he was, with sandy brown hair that spilled carelessly over his forehead and with eyes so brown they looked black when he scowled.

"Of course," she said, "I was shocked speechless. I had never seen a completely naked man before. I remember wondering where men concealed it when they put on their trousers."

Holding her close he gently moved her hand downward. "As you can see, I can't conceal it very well when you feel and smell and look the way you do."

The blood was rushing through her veins, out of control. Gladly she'd let him rip off her new dress, every stitch she wore, and take her here and now if he wanted to. He kissed her deeply, lovingly, and she felt herself wilting in his arms.

Somewhere outside the slamming of a door made them aware of where they were. Lydia reluctantly pushed him away and self-consciously patted her hair. "You've come to take me to lunch. I'm famished."

"So am I, but not for food, particularly."

"Peter, behave yourself. We have business to discuss. Afterward...." She let her sentence trail off.

"Afterward I have every intention of forcing myself upon

you," he said, again kissing her mouth.

With a sly smile she said, "And I have every intention of permitting it."

"You're a brazen hussy, Lydia Nightsong."

"And you're a scoundrel and a rogue."

"You judge me unfairly. I'm neither of those."

"You are both, and more," she said putting on her hat. It was a large velvet creation with a luxurious display of both ostrich feathers and ospreys. Also, she carried a muff, very large and purely ornamental. "A scoundrel because you are unprincipled and unscrupulous, and a rogue because you are dishonest and deceitful. I've been tricked by you too many times, Peter MacNair. I've never completely forgiven you for a number of odious things you've done that hurt me deeply."

"Surely you don't still blame me for bartering you into marrying that Mandarin? You'd have surely died of the plague or been killed if I hadn't forced you into his protection."

"No, I've long since accepted what you did as being for both our benefits." She paused, thinking. "I believe the most difficulty I had in forgiving you was when I learned you had taken my own daughter as a mistress."

"It was more the other way around. April merely wanted to hurt you by seducing me. Though I admit I wanted to hurt you also because of your marrying the Frenchman."

She glanced at him and saw the same strange cloud slip across his brow. She'd never in her life trusted him completely; she never would. Perhaps that had something to do with the fact that she loved him so desperately.

Outside, the mist hung thick and dank, obscuring the sun, but with Peter beside her it was, to her, the most beautiful of days.

He started toward his sedan but she tugged his arm. "Let's stroll to the Palm Court, darling. I feel like walking and having people see me with the handsomest man in San Francisco."

He grinned. "You were always one for giving my wife's attorneys lots of reasons for her to clean me out if she ever decided to divorce me."

"Lorna will never divorce you and you will never divorce her," she said with a note of anger and sadness. They started toward Union Square. "I resigned myself to that a long time ago."

"You're mistaken, Lydia. It just seems that whenever I'm in a position to be free, you aren't. I was prepared to divorce Lorna years back when you announced your engagement to Andrieux."

"Your wife will never let you go, and you are perfectly aware that I had no other choice but to marry Raymond. I'd be bankrupt today if I hadn't agreed to his demands."

"He's bankrupting you as it is, I understand," Peter said under his breath.

"What?"

"Oh, nothing. Gossip mostly. Raymond Andrieux is not exactly behaving himself in Paris."

"What have you heard?"

"As I said, it's just talk. But any nitwit can tell your Empress Cosmetics empire is in trouble simply by watching the stock market. Your price per share has fallen sixteen points in the past eight months."

Lydia bit her lower lip. She was tempted to confide all her problems to Peter, but experience had taught her to be cautious with him on business matters. Too many times she'd made herself vulnerable to this man and too often he'd taken advantage of her confidences. She loved him desperately, but love was far apart from business.

"A temporary problem," she said with a casual tilt of her head. "I've handled Raymond in the past, I'll handle him this time."

"I warned you about that snake."

"Raymond is my concern. He will not destroy everything I've worked so hard to build. I'll ruin him first."

He smiled. "You've become even more brazen, Lydia."

"Not brazen. Bold." She plucked a leaf from the hedge bordering the square and examined it as she would something completely unusual. "I suppose I've always been bold.

Back when Prince Ke Loo took me to his palace in Kalgan, I resolved then I would stay alive somehow. Then it was because I wanted revenge on you. That need to stay alive grew stronger and stronger inside me, but for different reasons. I survived that desperate flight from China, my uncle who'd raped and abused me, that sordid business with Walter Hanover when he tried to take everything I had. I'll continue to survive, believe me."

"He's dead, you know."

Lydia stopped, surprised. "Walter Hanover?"

"Yes. Last month. A heart attack in London."

"Heart attack? He deserved far worse. And what of his daughter? Kathy? Wasn't that her name?"

"She married some count or baron or something. Like her father, she deserved worse."

"Walter held claim to fifty percent of Empress Cosmetics. You bought that claim but you have never exercised it."

"I told you before, Lydia, I never will."

"Then why not give it back to me?"

"And lose my hold on you? I know you, darling. Your business acumen sometimes blinds you to the more pleasurable things in life." He gave her a suggestive glance. "You might kick me out of bed on impulse, but you'll never be able to kick me out of your corporate affairs."

His words only made her realize, not for the first time, that they were two of a kind and were made for each other.

The Palm Court was quiet and elegant. Peter and Lydia entered and exchanged greetings with the maître d'hôtel. Peter asked for an isolated table in a window alcove, and after they were seated and the wine ordered, Peter said, "I brought you here that first day, when we met again."

"After I escaped from the Forbidden City and Prince Ke Loo?" She shook her head. "No, it was the Crystal Room on Portsmouth Square. Unfortunately, that area has become a bit seedy. April gave up her flat there, you know? She's back living with me on the hill."

"Yes," he said a bit shamefacedly. "I've seen her a time or

two—always in the window. Doesn't she ever come out, or take her children for walks?"

"Children?" Lydia said, avoiding his question. "Caroline is twenty-two now and Marcus will be twenty-one next month."

He shook his head. "I must be getting old. I still think of my own son and daughter as children."

A terrible impulse made her want to tell him that Marcus was their son—hers and his. The waiter saved her by arriving with the wine, and by the time they'd finished the ritual of deciding upon lunch, the temptation was gone.

Peter sipped the wine approvingly. "And what of your son, Leon?"

"Still with his father, in Hawaii. He's promised to come on a visit very soon, if Ke Loo permits it. The Prince still insists he—and eventually Leon—will one day sit on the throne of China. Now that the old Dragon is dead, Prince Ke Loo is convinced the throne will be his, as soon as he gets rid of Dr. Sun Yat-sen and the child emperor."

"The Manchu dynasty is finished. China will be a republic within the year. Mark me."

"And what of your children, Peter?" Lydia wanted only to forget China and the dreadful Mandarin she'd been forced to marry, and all the reminders of that horrible woman, the Dowager Empress, who had maimed and beheaded for the sheer enjoyment of it.

Peter drained his glass and in an instant the waiter had refilled it. "Susan's in New York," he said.

"And very happily married, I understand."

"Yes, but still the same independent, headstrong girl she always was. Somewhere, fortunately, she found time to give me three very beautiful grandchildren."

"A girl and two boys," Lydia said.

He looked surprised.

"You never knew it, Peter, but Susan and I became friends several years ago. We keep in touch. She wanted to come to work for me once. I wouldn't allow it, knowing what a row it would have caused between Susan and you and Lorna. You and I weren't always friends, remember."

"Only too well." He didn't want to remember those times. "Susan's coming on a visit."

"Good. I'd love seeing her again, and the children, of course." The waiter arrived with the Dover sole they'd both decided upon. When the waiter had left again, Lydia asked, "And what of your youngest son, Efrem? Is he still working at MacNair Products?"

Peter's look soured. "Yes," he said simply. He started to say something, but thought better of it. Something was amiss with Efrem; what it was, Peter hadn't the faintest idea. The boy drank himself into bed every night and was interested in nothing except getting drunk and hanging about the shadiest parts of the city. Even Lorna—close as those two were—could get nothing out of the boy. Boy? Peter reminded himself. Efrem was almost thirty-five years old and still living at home. It wasn't healthy.

"The sole is good," Lydia commented, noticing that Peter seemed suddenly disturbed.

"Yes." He brightened. "It's dessert I'm looking forward to," he said, as he boldly touched the toe of her shoe with his foot.

"Peter." A smoldering fire suddenly burst into flames inside her. She squirmed slightly on her chair and felt a delicious warm wetness begin to flow.

"We are having dessert?"

She knew her cheeks were aflame. "Of course. Why do you suppose I chose today for our luncheon? The servants are off. Marcus and Caroline have forced April to go with them to a fair in Sausalito. The house is ours for the afternoon."

Half an hour later Peter and Lydia walked into the cool, elegant interior of her Nob Hill mansion. "You did a fine job in reproducing the old place, Lydia," Peter said as he looked around at the damask-covered walls of pale salmon, and the magnificent marble staircase that curved so gracefully up to the second floor. "I was always puzzled that you never wanted anything oriental in your furniture, not even a rug."

"I want to forget everything about the Orient. It has only

terrible memories. I'll have nothing Chinese in the house." Her eyes twinkled suddenly. "With one very important exception." She reached for his hand and hurried him toward the stairway. "Come. I've something new to show you."

Her bedroom was feminine, yet strong and definite in its muted tones of rusts and shades of autumn. One wall was dominated by towering windows, thinly hidden behind beige Austrian draperies.

"Voilà!" Lydia said with a grand sweep of her hand.

At first Peter didn't recognize the painting that hung impressively over a long, low chest. It took a moment before it came back to him. "Nightsong," he breathed reverently.

"I had it copied as closely as I could remember it. Is it right, Peter? You would know better than I."

A sudden stinging gathered at the backs of his eyes. "Oh, yes, Lydia. It's exactly right. I'd forgotten." He turned and gazed lovingly into her face.

"I hadn't," she said. "That small dingy shack you lived in is the only memory of China I want to keep alive."

"I only lived there because of that painting on the wall." He looked again at the picture that Lydia had reproduced on three panels. Set against a background of gold leaf was the branch of a plum tree in full blossom, and a bird perched on the branch, its beak open in song. High above was the slightest curved rim of the moon, as if it were waiting for a young couple in love. "I never knew who painted it," Peter said. "Some artist centuries ago, I imagine."

She came up behind him and pressed herself tight against his back, wrapping her arms around his waist. "The Nightsong painting isn't my only memory of your little hut."

He grinned as he turned to her. "I'd forgotten the painting; however, I do remember the rest of it."

His breath was sweet with wine and she sensed a need sweeping through her, the need she'd felt that night so long ago in that far off shack in a Chinese village. "Darling," she whispered.

He kissed her gently; as both their passions raced, the kiss became harder, more demanding. Lydia could feel the hardness of his love pressing against her thigh.

"Take me, Peter. I love you so. I need you so."

Swift, frantic hands stripped away clothing until nothing was between them but their nakedness.

"I love the feel of your body, so strong, so powerful."

"Hardly the same body that you had that first night, but I do admit," Peter said between the kisses he rained on her throat, her breasts, her mouth, "I keep pretty trim for an old man."

"Be quiet and make love to me."

Gently he parted her thighs. She reached for him and thrilled at his size, his hardness. Lydia fitted him to her and urged him inward. Slowly he entered, filling her with such exquisite pleasure and ecstasy the whole of her body exploded into thousands of stars. Her body moved in rhythm with his, her hands smoothed and caressed the muscular back. A drowning sensation crept over her as Peter quickened his tempo, sending her from one oblivion to another. Again and again spasm after spasm wracked her body as he pounded out his love, filling her to overflowing with his intensity.

"Lydia," he groaned as he moved faster, more violently.

She clung to him so tightly they were as one being, one soul.

"Peter," she cried as another eruption tore through her and her body throbbed and pulsed with the violence of her final orgasm.

They lay in each other's arms, aware of nothing beyond this moment.

Peter stirred, reaching for the pocket watch he'd placed on the night stand. "Damn," he said.

"What time is it?"

"Almost four."

Lydia sat up and began scurrying into her clothes. "The children will be home soon. You'd better leave, darling."

By the time they stood together in the foyer, anyone would have taken them for two very proper Nob Hill old acquaintances who'd just finished some business transaction.

"When will I see you again, Peter?"

"I hope before I leave for Europe next week."

"Europe?"

"Yes. I have to go to Ireland to see the Waterford people about a new flask I want them to develop for me. I'm coming out with a new scent—a little higher classed than my door-to-door merchandise, yet nothing that will match your Nightsong."

"Waterford doesn't manufacture flasks and bottles."

"I know, but they weren't deaf to my proposal. They're hurting, moneywise, I understand. The potato famine destroyed the economy."

"When do you leave?"

"Thursday next. Wait a minute," he said excitedly, looking into her beautiful eyes, "what's to prevent you from coming with me?"

"But...."

"Who would have to know? Couldn't it just be a coincidence that we found ourselves traveling on the same ship? It's the *Mauritania*, leaving New York on the twenty-third. Say you'll come, Lydia. Please say you'll come."

"Well...," she stammered. "I hadn't thought...."

"Please," he begged.

She hesitated, thinking of Raymond for no more than a minute. "Yes, of course I'll come."

# CHAPTER THREE

Bitterness and sorrow had aged April Nightsong far beyond her years. At thirty-nine April was an old woman. The brightness was gone from her eyes, stolen from her when her son had been stolen, leaving them misted with a kind of madness. She'd come from China to avenge her husband's death only to find herself a victim of her own vengeance. Now she was beaten and empty. She would gladly have died years ago, but her determination to find Adam kept her alive. Somewhere he lived and ate and slept, not knowing of the mother who'd loved him more than anyone or anything on earth. Adam was her heart, her very being. Not until they were reunited would she live again, April swore.

"There you are," Lydia said as April came into the sitting room. "Aren't the children with you, dear?"

The way her daughter insisted upon dressing bothered Lydia. April purposely accented the almond shape of her eyes, the yellow of her skin. She wore the clothes of China and was quick to remind everyone that she was indeed a Manchu princess. She wore too an expression that so reminded Lydia of that heathen empress and her tyrannic ways. Every time Lydia saw her daughter she wondered whether it might be best if little Adam was never found and returned to this half-mad woman, whose only reason for wanting him back was to place him in line of ascent to the Chinese throne.

Lydia knew better, however, than even to hint at this line of thinking, lest April fly into a rage. Adam was her son, as she was quick to remind anyone, he was tattooed as a Manchu prince, even the Empress herself had acknowledged him.

"Caroline met a friend," April answered her mother's question. "Marcus was with that Wilson girl. Why he wants to marry so far beneath himself I cannot understand."

"Amelia Wilson is extremely nice."

April did not agree, but did not condescend to argue. After all, what was Marcus to her? He was her mother's bastard—no part of her blood.

"You came home alone?" Lydia asked, disapproving.

"I am no child. And who would dare raise a hand against a princess of China."

There was a time when April had genuinely hated her mother. That hatred had since mellowed into indifference. She still remembered how Lydia had passed her off as a common servant in order that no one learn Lydia had a half-caste daughter, lest San Francisco society shun them. Lydia's perfume business came first, before even her own daughter. It still did, so far as April was concerned. April had resolved to make her mother suffer for all the hurt she'd caused. David would be alive today if Lydia and his father, Peter MacNair, had not intervened.

Where Lydia was ashamed of the Chinese blood that flowed through her daughter's veins, April prized it. She was, after all, a princess, and hadn't the old Dowager Empress broken ancient tradition and allowed April's son—a son with part Caucasian blood—to be accepted into the Manchu dynasty, branded on the thigh with the twin poppies and the circle of seeds.

April had kept a close watch on the present rebellion in China. The republic would only last for a short time. The people needed their royal rulers. They'd become too accustomed to dynasty rule to want anything else. The old Empress T'zu Hsi might be dead, but the Manchu Dynasty was far from finished. The infant emperor, Pu-yi, would hold on until Prince Ke Loo and his forces could again unite the country.

April wished Leon would write more often. She wanted to go to her father and brother in Hawaii and join their fight to put down the unrest in their native country, but the need to find Adam was even stronger than her desire to return triumphant to the Forbidden City as the exalted daughter of the great Ke Loo.

Lydia got up from the window seat and wandered toward the archway that led to her study. "I'm planning on taking the train to New York in a few days."

"New York?" April asked with little interest.

"Yes. I'm going to sail on the twenty-third for Europe."

"Oh?"

"I want to see Raymond. He's causing me all sorts of financial problems. I am not looking forward to our confrontation, but it can't be avoided." She felt uncomfortable, but her explanation wasn't a totally lie. She did intend having it out with Raymond, though the idea had not occurred to her until after Peter had asked her to accompany him.

"New York. The night Adam disappeared a train left San Francisco for New York," April said, speaking almost as if she were in a trance. "No one saw anyone get on board that train with a small child. The conductor said there were no children aboard, but of course he was lying. He was obviously in on the kidnapping. After all, didn't he quit his job and drop completely from sight a short time afterward?"

"April, please," Lydia pleaded. "Let it rest."

"I called that to the attention of the police and they said I was too suspicious of everyone." She turned her accusing eyes on Lydia. "I've even wondered if you weren't the one who took Adam from me. You and Peter MacNair."

"April, you know you are speaking nonsense."

"Maybe you are going to New York now because you have Adam hidden there."

As so often before, April broke into a flood of tears.

Lydia took her in her arms. "Actually, I was thinking of taking Marcus and Caroline with me, unless you'd like to come." She knew April would never leave San Francisco for fear Adam might be brought home and find her gone.

The young people burst into the house, raising a din. Caroline looked like her father, Raymond, dark-haired and green-eyed. She had a definite Parisian manner about her—the way she moved, the way she arched her brows, that typically French sensual expression. Raymond's titled background showed in Caroline's walk, in the use of her hands. She was a stunning woman dressed, as always, in the latest Parisian fashion.

Marcus was as handsome as any young man had a right to be; tall and muscular without being overly so. He wore his clothes well, which accentuated his perfect physique. He had also inherited his father's looks. His hair was ruddy brown, thick and wavy and a trifle shaggy by standard conventions; but he liked it that way. "It helps me to express myself," he always said, tossing his head and running his hands through his hair. Like Peter's, Marcus's eyes were brown and serious.

"Where did you go, Mother?" Caroline asked April. "Marcus and I were frantic."

"You had your friends. You didn't need me there."

Marcus said, "Well, you could have at least told us you were catching the ferry home. We were truly concerned."

April merely shrugged and walked out of the room.

"Well," Lydia said brightly. "Sit and tell me about the fair."

"It was most exciting, Grandmother," Caroline said. "There were all sorts of exhibits. Of course, it was very unsophisticated in comparison to the Pacific Exposition you let us go to in Seattle last year."

"But they had neat new automobiles," Marcus added. "Better and faster than those they had in Seattle."

"Which reminds me," Lydia said with a stern look. "I hear you are becoming much too interested in racing cars. I absolutely forbid it, Marcus. They are far too dangerous."

"What do you mean, forbid it? Why? Automobiles represent the future. One day there will be no such thing as horses and carriages on the streets."

"It's the high speed racing to which I object. You must realize, Marcus, that you are a man, not a boy who is free to tinker around with dangerous toys. One day you will be the one to manage everything I have built. I lost one grandson to kidnappers. I lost Leon to his father. I will not lose you to some ridiculous caprice."

Marcus started to speak, but Lydia stopped him cold. "I have said all that is to be said on the matter. You will, henceforth, content yourself to be in the grandstands. If I hear one word of your disobedience, mark me, Marcus, you will deeply regret it."

He jutted out his chin, and gave an angry toss of his head. "You have always done what you wished. Why can't I have the same privilege?"

"Placing your life purposely in jeopardy is hardly a privilege. Why would you, or anyone else, deliberately want to try to kill yourself? Are you suicidal?"

"Grandmother, you are living in the past. There isn't any more danger in automobiles than there is in riding a horse."

"Horses do not explode and spew out flames."

"But they can bolt and kick and throw a rider," Marcus argued.

"Marcus, I will not tolerate any notion on your part about racing those ridiculous machines and that is final."

He turned sharply on his heels and stormed out of the room.

Caroline smiled at her grandmother and slowly shook her head. "He'll do as he wants, Grandmother. You know he will. He's so much more like you than like Mother. The same determination, the same romantic ideas about the future that lies ahead. Don't be too hard on him. Racing is only a hobby that attracts him deeply. You only see the idle side of Marcus. You're always too occupied with Empress Cosmetics to see his serious side. He's extremely bright about economics and can argue down the best of them on President Taft's new policies." She laughed. "And you should hear his views on Teddy Roosevelt."

Economics? Politics? Lydia thought. "I never realized," she said aloud. "And perhaps it is about time that I did. I've been too involved with keeping the family's head above water to think of the family as individuals. I intend remedying that. I'm sailing for Europe out of New York toward the end of the month. The twenty-third to be exact. I want you and Marcus to come with me. We'll have a grand time and put no limit on when we'll return. What do you say, my dear?"

She hadn't intended to blurt out the invitation. She blamed it on her guilt. Peter would definitely disapprove, but that she would face when the time came.

"Europe," Caroline exclaimed, clasping her hands. "How positively delicious. Oh, Grandmother, I can't think of anything more exciting." She suddenly grew fearful. "But will Mother approve? You know how she refuses everything that might complicate efforts to locate little Adam."

"Little Adam is a grown man by now," Lydia reminded her, exasperated. "I do wish your mother would resign herself to that. She continues to cling to the idea that when she finally does find him, he'll still be four years old. She even has you and Marcus thinking the same way. Adam is almost your age, for heaven's sake. Sometimes I actually pray that Adam never be found. There has been so much bad blood over the entire incident. Locating him and bringing him back home would only result in a lawsuit that Lorna MacNair would immediately instigate."

"Perhaps little Adam...well, all right, not so little—but perhaps Adam won't want to return to San Francisco. Perhaps he's totally content where he is."

"Under the law he isn't his own man yet. Both your mother and the MacNairs could force him back. I only hope for everyone's sake he won't be found until he is legally of age and can make his own decisions. Your mother made terrible threats to the MacNairs. She raved about her need for revenge, how she held Peter MacNair responsible for his son's, David's, death. How she'd gladly strangle the child before their very eyes before relinquishing Adam to his MacNair grandparents. She was a woman possessed."

"She'd been through a horrendous experience. Being forced to watch the beheading of one's husband would surely unhinge any normal woman."

"I've no doubt that is true, but the fact is, she should never have left your father and run off to China with David. David was miserable there. He'd said as much to his father when Peter found him in Peking. David was going to try and convince April to come home, but everything was so complicated. She was still married to your father, married also by Chinese law to David. She'd abandoned you—and Marcus, and was expecting David's child." Lydia shook her head. " Your mother had tied herself into a Gordian knot. It was God's will that David died."

"Poor Mother."

Lydia rose from the window seat. "Yes, your mother has had a difficult life. I blame myself for a great part of it."

"You mustn't, Grandmother." She put her arms lovingly around Lydia's waist and hugged her. "But do you think Mother will refuse to let us go with you to Europe?"

"I mentioned it to her. She didn't seem particularly interested one way or the other."

"May I go and ask her?" Caroline asked excitedly.

"Of course. Speak with Marcus as well. And if April raises any objections you send her down here to me." She kissed her granddaughter's cheek. "Now I believe I'll tackle that work I brought home yesterday. Then I intend having a short nap, a long soak in a hot tub, and I'll see you all at dinner."

The upstairs maid told Caroline her mother was sleeping. In Marcus's rooms Caroline found him sitting at his study desk in the alcove, poring over a manual on the intricacies of the gasoline combustion engine.

"When are you going to remember to knock?" he admonished. "One of these days you're going to be shocked out of your skin when you find me lounging about in the all-together."

"I've seen your 'all-together', Marc, old boy. Believe me, it wouldn't shock anyone," she teased, tousling his hair.

"It shocked Rosemary Matthews," he said with a wink.

"Marcus! You didn't?"

He looked down at the manual and began studying the mechanical drawings again. "No, I'm only fooling. I just wanted to see if you could be shocked. I was beginning to think that all that women's suffrage business had turned you into a brother instead of a sister."

"Stop that. Just because we want to be treated on an equal plane to men doesn't change us into amazons."

"Mark me, Caroline. If you ever do get the right to vote you won't be satisfied with that. One day women will want to walk around the street in men's trousers."

"You just don't understand anything. You're like every other man."

"Women have their place; we have ours. Why can't you ladies accept that?"

She tousled his hair again. "Because men have more fun." She glanced at the manual. "What's that?"

"I'm thinking of building my own racing car."

"Racing car? You heard what Grandmother said."

"Sure, but after I get it built and take her for a spin in my new machine she'll forget all about her old-fashioned ideas. I might even get her to invest in building a whole new line of faster moving automobiles. Ray Harroun can get his Marmon up to almost seventy miles per hour. When the race track is finished in Indianapolis he says his new Marmon will easily go seventy-five."

"Ridiculous. No automobile can go that fast, or ever will."

"They'll go faster and I intend to build them. Me and Ray Harroun."

"With Grandmother's money, I suppose."

"If not hers, then someone else's."

Caroline looked at the manual again and put her lips close to his ear. "I know of a way in which you might start softening up Grandmother."

"What?"

"She wants us to go to Europe with her. An extended tour. No time limit."

Marcus was disinterested. "I can't."

"It would give you plenty of time to convince Grandmother

how safe automobiles really are. She's still an adventure-loving dear. And she always was rather partial to you, Marcus. You could convince her." She toyed with the hair at the back of his neck.

He brushed her hand away. "Why are you suddenly playing up to me? What do you want?"

"Your help in convincing Mother she should let us go to Europe with Grandmother. You know she won't, even though Grandmother thinks she will. Mother is so selfish about everything. She doesn't seem to care what we do and yet she never wants us too far away from her."

Marcus went back to his studying. "I'll do what I can, but I'm not going to Europe with you."

"Why not? It...."

He held up his hand. "I know all about coaxing Grandmother around to my way of thinking, but much as I'd like to go, I just can't."

"Why?"

"Because between you and me, Caroline, I am running away from home next month." He was grinning.

"Running away from home? To where?"

"Indianapolis, of course. I'm going with Ray Harroun as one of his mechanics crew."

"You mean working with all that oil and grease and dirty tires and things? You're mad."

"Mad as a hatter," he agreed. "But it's what I am going to do with or without anyone's blessing."

"Grandmother will disown you."

"You go to Europe with the dear love and keep her there for a few months. I'll be back by then and nobody, except Mother, will know I've been away."

"What do you intend telling Mother?"

"College project, something like that. I might even say I'm chasing down a lead about little Adam."

"Marcus, that's cruel."

"Who knows? Maybe Adam is really in Indianapolis."

"I don't like it, Marc."

Afterward, Caroline was tempted to tell her mother about Marcus's deception, but thought better of it when April scowled at her and said, "I do wish you'd act more like who you are rather than some store-window mannequin." She eyed Caroline's new dinner dress with disdain. "You should wear yellow, the imperial color of China. How many times must I remind you that you are the daughter of a Manchu princess?"

"Half-daughter." Caroline had long since gotten accustomed to her mother's rantings. "Besides, darling, yellow always makes me look sallow for some odd reason. I've never cared for it."

She touched her lips to her mother's cheek. "Don't be displeased with me, Mother. I'm aware of my royal blood, but we're in America where things like that don't matter. Look at Anne DeBoussard. Her father's a baron and he works on the Stock Exchange. Come on, let's join Grandmother and Marcus for dinner."

As they started down the staircase Caroline girded her courage. "Grandmother's going to Europe on the twenty-third. She asked me to go with her."

To her amazement April said, "Then go."

"Do you mean it?"

"Of course. You'll like Paris. I met David there at the Exposition." She was suddenly lost in old memories. "I wore yellow that night, with pearls braided into my hair. I was the most beautiful woman in the world. He told me so."

"You are still beautiful."

They entered the drawing room where Lydia and Marcus were having sherry. "Ah, there you are. Nellie was getting nervous about the dinner getting cold. She mis-timed the roast again," Lydia said with a laugh.

"Mother's agreed to let me come with you to Europe," Caroline gushed.

"Good. And Marcus tells me he can't go. Too bad."

As they went into the spacious dining room with its marble fireplace, gilt mirrors, and red velvet-covered walls, April said,

"Speaking of Europe, Mother, I read where an old friend of mine has been named charge d'affaires of the American Embassy in London."

It always surprised Lydia that April could so easily change from raving to rationality. "Oh?"

"Edward Wells. You remember Eddie. He helped me in getting little Adam back to America." She looked at Caroline. "Officially, little Adam's name on the custom's ledger is Adam Wells."

"Yes, Mother." Caroline had heard the same details repeated again and again over the years. "You told me."

"Look him up, Mother," April said. "You and Eddie will like each other. You're both very much alike. Neither of you have any scruples and you can't restrain yourselves from creeping into strange beds."

Lydia calmly tasted her soup and waited for Nellie to go back through the swinging door. "It must have been difficult—you and Mr. Wells."

An awkward silence descended. To alleviate it Lydia said, "I had a letter from Leon today." April frowned, annoyed that her brother hadn't written to her instead.

"Unfortunately," Lydia went on without seeing April's scowl, "Leon can't come for a visit after all. But the happy news is, Mei Fei married her Hawaiian beau."

"She married him months ago," April said smugly.

"Oh? I didn't know. I assumed from Leon's letter that the marriage was recent."

"My half-sister writes me often."

"Why haven't you mentioned it?"

"I don't have to tell you everything."

"Of course not, but Mei Fei is, after all—"

April cut her off. "Mei Fei is nothing to you. She is my sister." From out of nowhere an aching sadness swiftly throbbed in her breast. How she missed Mei Fei, Leon, even Ke Loo—anything and everything that reminded her of China. The tears came before she could stop them. April pushed back her chair and ran, sobbing, from the room. Upstairs she threw herself across the bed and cried into the pillows.

"Why, oh why is everyone happy?" she wept. She thought of her sister's rapturous letter. "Don't be happy, Mei Fei. It will only turn to pain."

# CHAPTER FOUR

Mei Fie snuggled close to her husband's naked body. She felt his hands, then his mouth on her breasts and breathed his name. "Tehani. Oh, my darling husband. How I love you."

The thatch of the roof rustled softly in the breeze that blew in over the lagoon. Tehani and his brothers had built the handsome little hut as a wedding present to Mei Fei. She loved its spacious, uncluttered rooms, its pure simplicity. She especially loved the quilted platform on which they slept and made love. Tehani's mother had made the silk covering, carefully cramming it full with goose down.

Somewhere out in the night drums were beating out a quick tempo, matching the fast beating of her heart as Tehani's bronzed young body moved over her, parting her thighs and fitting himself into her warmth.

"Mei Fie," he gasped as the heat of her body enveloped him. "Oh, my beautiful Mei Fei. I will never stop loving you."

They moved as one, swaying, clinging, kissing deeply, passionately. Their bodies rose and fell as their thrusts grew more frantic.

Their blood mingled, their minds fused, their bodies tangled together. Mei Fei twisted and churned beneath her beloved, her single hand raking the hard, corded muscles of his back.

Her other hand, the one carved of ivory, lay above her head where she knew Tehani enjoyed admiring it. He and his people believed her a goddess from some far off heaven—a beautiful goddess, half human, half precious stone.

"Tehani. Tehani," Mei Fei moaned as she heaved and thrashed, her eyes closed, shutting out everything except the intense pleasure he was pounding into her.

Tehani wrapped his arms around the soft, naked body of his beautiful goddess as she clung to him, milking him of every ounce of strength that bolted and gushed from his body.

"Mei Fei," he gasped, his teeth clenched.

"Yes, my dearest, yes," she cried as they climaxed together and felt themselves exploding across the deep darkness of the island sky.

When they awoke the dazzling sunlight shafted through the windows, bringing with it rainbows of color, orchid and pink, lush greens and golden yellows. The palm trees whispered high above the roof. Mei Fei lazed on the downy quilt and listened to the native boys scampering up the tall trunks to harvest the coconuts.

When she turned her head she found Tehani propped on his elbow, smiling lovingly into her face. "I like looking at you," he said.

Mei Fei giggled and covered her face. "I am a hag in the morning. Every woman feels that way."

He took her hands away, kissed the polished ivory fingers, then kissed her eyes, her mouth. Again his hand went across her waist and upward, cupping her breasts. He kissed her deeply and put his hand between her thighs, feeling her wetness, her renewed passions.

"No," Mei Fei cried and playfully pushed him away. "If I give too much of myself you will stop wanting me." She started to get up from the pallet.

"Never," he said grabbing her.

They rolled and laughed, their bodies steaming with new desire.

"Daughter!"

The voice froze the two lovers. A shriek caught in Mei Fei's throat as she curled against her husband to try and hide her nakedness from her father's angry eyes.

Prince Ke Loo stood just inside the door, his feet placed well apart to support his short, heavy frame. His fists were clenched on his hips. Slowly, the Manchu raised his hand and pointed menacingly at Tehani. "Lazy Hawaiian swine," he shouted. "There is work to be done. Get dressed. The boats are in the lagoon waiting to be loaded. Go!" He turned and stomped out.

Their mood was shattered. Mei Fei sighed and slipped into her muumu. Tehani took her in his arms. "Your father is right. I should be about my work. I take advantage of him; but, oh, Mei Fei, I hate so to be away from you even for an hour."

"How can you take my father's part? He hates us."

"He does not hate us. He is just disappointed that you defied him when you came with me to my parent's island and we were married under Hawaiian law."

"Prince Ke Loo has always frightened me," she said as she cuddled up to him. She looked at her sculptured hand of ivory and knew only too well how cruel and inhuman the Manchus were. But she was Manchu. She would be cruel if Prince Ke Loo did any harm to Tehani, she vowed.

"I must go," Tehani said. He kissed her quickly and hitched his lavalava about his waist. "I will be back for our swim." He kissed her again and was gone.

Several long-boats were beached on the shore of the lagoon. Bales wrapped in watertight canvas stood in a stack, waiting to be loaded aboard and taken to the rusting freighter that lay at anchor outside the lagoon.

"Leon!" Tehani called when he saw Prince Ke Loo's son coming out of the palm grove and start toward him. When they met they shook hands.

"I have seen little of you since your wedding, Tehani. And less of Mei Fei," he said, grinning. "Surely it does not take all your time to start a family?"

Tehani laughed. "No, but it is so enjoyable." He slapped his hand on Leon's back. "You should know, my friend. Your wife and little ones are well?"

"Very well. You must come to a luau we are having this

Saturday night."

Tehani shook his head. "You know we have been banished from socializing with your father and his family."

"Damn my father. It is my house, my luau. I will entertain whom I please."

Several native boys straggled onto the beach. Leon said, "Say you'll come—and bring Mei Fei, of course." He saw Tehani's reluctance. "Please. Believe me, I will handle my father. He will cause you no trouble. Come, we must load the longboats but please think about my invitation. Prince Ke Loo may be too involved with his teenaged concubines to even attend."

"I will think on it. Leon."

"Good."

As they worked, straining and sweating, the sun rose higher in the sky. Tehani and the others spoke little. When the last of the bales were loaded Tehani said, "In all the years I have loaded these bales onto boats I never knew what was inside."

"Trade goods," Leon said, disinterested. "Prince Ke Loo is what they call a 'middleman' for a merchant in Hong Kong."

"Why?"

Leon shrugged. "I am not much interested in what my father's business is here. In fact, if I had my way I would not be here at all." He put on the shirt he'd taken off earlier and began buttoning it. "I miss America so much it actually pains me. One day I will take my family and go back to San Francisco."

"Ah, but then your wife and children would miss their home here."

Leon had to smile. "True. I guess I am being selfish, but I cannot help the way I feel. How I'd love to go to a theater, see a lantern show, listen to a symphonic concert, dance a two-step. America is a marvelous place, Tehani. You would like it very much."

"I know it is not my business, Leon, but if you love America so much why did you come here in the first place?"

"Family reasons," Leon hedged. "I am the eldest son—Prince Ke Loo's only son."

"Ah yes, the revolution in China. Mei Fei has spoken to me about it."

Leon frowned. "She should not have. It is a Manchu affair. Don't speak of it to Prince Ke Loo."

Tehani laughed. "Me, speak to the great prince about anything? You know he wishes he would not have to see me, let alone have me speak with him."

The two men parted and Leon started back toward his house, not far from Prince Ke Loo's own sprawling house with its veranda of bamboo and Chinese furniture.

Leon wasn't in a mood to go home to his wife and family. The mention of America had brought back all the old, uncomfortable memories to haunt him. A hundred times he'd tried to convince himself that the affair with Efrem MacNair had been nothing but boyish curiosity and innocence. He should have returned to San Francisco long ago, regardless of Prince Ke Loo's threats. A nagging fear, however, persisted. It was this fear that had always made him cancel his promised visits to his mother. Efrem may not have outgrown the love he'd expressed, and returning would only rekindle something in Efrem that should have died years ago.

Leon shook his head, but he couldn't dislodge the image of Efrem's face.

When Leon emerged into the compound of houses he saw a strange, yet familiar Chinese speaking with Prince Ke Loo. He pushed the image of Efrem away and tried to remember who the man was. He knew the stranger but could not be certain from where. By the way the Chinese was dressed he was most assuredly not from America. The man wore palace garb, the silks and gold of Manchu royalty.

"Ah, Li Ahn," his father called. As Leon mounted the steps of the veranda he heard his father tell the man, "My son has americanized his honorable name and calls himself 'Leon.' " To Leon he said, "You remember Wu Lien, of course?" When Leon continued to look puzzled, his father clarified, "Our cousin. The Dowager Empress's most trusted advisor."

Leon had only been a boy at the time, but hearing his cousin's name, seeing the face, he remembered this brutal, conniving man who changed loyalties as easily as he changed his tunics. He also remembered that April had told him it was Wu Lien who had betrayed her husband, David, into the hands of the Empress.

"Yes," Wu Lien said, frowning. "The young traitor has grown into a man." He bowed slightly, but not low enough for it to be a compliment. "If the great Dowager Empress were alive today I would be forced to detach your handsome head from your shoulders."

"Our cousin," Leon said, "was a madwoman."

Wu Lien's hand snatched up the gleaming dagger he carried hidden in his waistband.

Ke Loo stepped between them. "We must not fight among ourselves," he said, giving Leon a fierce look. "Wu Lien has come to help defeat Sun Yat-sen and his republicans." To Wu Lien he said, "My son was too young to know the consequences of his disobedience to the Empress. He is still, however, my son and heir to the Manchu throne. There will be no quarreling between you."

Wu Lien bowed low. When he looked at Leon, Leon saw the threat. It was obvious that Wu Lien liked violence for violence's sake, on whichever side he found it. They would eventually clash and one of them would die—this Leon saw in Wu Lien's steady, cold stare.

"Your sister, April?" Wu Lien asked, feigning a pleasant smile. "She is well?"

"She is well," Leon answered curtly.

"Another who betrayed her obedience to the Empress." He turned to Prince Ke Loo. "It seems you have sired a litter of jackals."

Ke Loo merely smiled a malicious smile. "If you are so concerned about obedience to a dead woman, I wonder why you have crawled on your belly to reach my camp? You accuse my children of disloyalty to that woman, knowing full well I was the most disobedient of all. Mark me, Wu Lien. I know you well. Any tricks from you will cost you your life. You may rely on that. Come now," he said in a lighter tone, "we shall have rice wine and talk of our plans."

As evening drew nearer, the smell of the orchids and jasmine mingled with the delicious warmth of the late afternoon. Leon was awakened from his nap by the harsh, loud voice of Wu Lien, followed by a cry from Ohlan, Leon's wife. Leon pushed himself off the pallet and threw aside the bamboo screen to see Wu Lien holding Ohlan's wrists and trying to kiss her.

Leon grabbed Wu Lien's shoulder, pulled him around and smashed his fist into Wu Lien's face. The Chinese staggered and fell onto the mat floor. He lay there, rubbing his chin and glaring up at Leon who stood, fists clenched, over him. Of a sudden Wu Lien chuckled.

"Forgive me, cousin. Prince Ke Loo poured too freely of the wine. I did not know the woman was important to you."

Ohlan clung to her husband. "She is my wife and of high Manchu family," Leon said. "If you ever try to disgrace her again I will kill you."

Wu Lien was unimpressed. "I was looking for Mei Fei. Your father told me she lived near. I mistook your house for hers."

"Get out."

Slowly he got to his feet and adjusted his tunic. He bowed to Ohlan. "We will meet again, pretty one."

"Get out!" Leon repeated more sharply.

Outside, Wu Lien staggered away, his head reeling from the force of Leon's punch and the quantity of wine he'd drunk. He stumbled on into the thicket, feeling a sudden need to relieve himself. He went along the path a goodly way until he found a place suitable for his needs. As he urinated he heard the sound of a woman laughing. It came from somewhere up ahead.

Wu Lien shook off the last drops and tucked himself away, then started in the direction of the laughter. He staggered forward for almost a hundred or more yards before coming to the end of the thicket. He found himself on a rise overlooking the bleached sands and the blue waters of the lagoon. He recognized Mei Fei at once. Wu Lien frowned at the familiarity she displayed toward the Hawaiian native with whom she was frolicking.

He watched as Tehani dunked her head under the water. Mei Fei came up sputtering and laughing and began making for the shore. Tehani dove down and Wu Lien watched as Mei Fei was again pulled below the water. Again she came up squealing with delight and trying to get away from Tehani. When he tried to grab her again she splashed water in his face and swam for the sands.

It was when Wu Lien saw how awkwardly she swam that he remembered her severed hand, the hand he'd suggested the Dowager Empress cut off and send in a velvet box to April as a reminder of April's promised loyalty.

Mei Fei's right wrist was empty of a hand as she ran across the beach to where her muumuu was draped over a bush. Wu Lien hurriedly circled so that when she came into the concealment of the thicket he was there waiting for her. Her perfect nakedness made the blood pulse through his veins as she stooped and started to refit the sculptured hand to her wrist.

His hand clamped over her mouth before she could scream. In an instant he threw her to the ground and fell on top of her. He lost no time gaining his advantage. With a quick sweep he exposed his long, thick penis and thrust it hard up inside her. Mei Fei, her eyes wide with fear, screamed into his hand. When she felt the thrust of him she bit into the flesh, drawing blood. Wu Lien growled with pain and the instant his hand was removed Mei Fei screamed and screamed.

Tehani came across the sands like a charging bull. In a flash he was on top of Wu Lien, pounding his fists into the Chinese's back, shoulders, face—anything he could hit. Wu Lien struggled for his dagger, but Tehani was too quick. He snatched up a handful of dirt and threw it into Wu Lien's eyes, then grabbed a flat rock and struck Wu Lien's temple.

When Wu Lien gained consciousness a little while later he

found Mei Fie and Tehani huddled together. Wu Lien's dagger was in Tehani's hand.

The throbbing pain in his head was almost unbearable, but Wu Lien refused to acknowledge it. He glowered at Tehani, then at Mei Fei. "You will tell this Hawaiian peasant who I am, Mei Fei."

"Tehani is my husband," Mei Fei spat.

"Have you forgotten that you are still betrothed to me, Mei Fei?" Wu Lien reminded her.

"That was the Empress's decree, but not my wish, Wu Lien. This is not China. I am not the young, docile girl you knew. Tehani has taught me to be of my own mind."

"You married a native? Surely Prince Ke Loo did not sanction this."

Tehani said, "No, you will be happy to know we do not have Ke Loo's blessing."

"And do not need it," Mei Fei said. "We are not in your homeland, Wu Lien. This is Tehani's country, my country now. You do not belong here, but if you stay you had better remember that this is Hawaiian soil, not Chinese."

"I am royal while he is a peasant. Regardless of what dirt is beneath my feet, that fact cannot be changed."

"Do not cause trouble, Wu Lien. My husband's people do not take kindly to anyone who disturbs the peace of their islands."

Wu Lien laughed. "Peasants," he spat. "If that is what you want, welcome to them, but I will one day bring you to your senses, Mei Fei, even if I must do it by force."

"My people are as royal here as yours are in China," Tehani said. "And if you resort to force be assured that we are not unaccustomed to force ourselves."

# CHAPTER FIVE

Lorna MacNair had never ventured to the islands of Hawaii; she never entertained the remotest interest in the place. To her it was all grass huts and ukuleles played by half-naked savages, despite its popularity with American profiteers. San Francisco was the only civilized place to live and she seldom left it.

Age had agreed with Lorna, though her husband still did not find her attractive sexually. For Peter that attraction had always been her family's money—her money, now—and he didn't try to hide that fact. He still needed her financially or he would have left her long ago.

Lorna didn't care what reason Peter gave for living with her. She continued to thrill at the sight of him—broad in the shoulders and boyishly slim in the hips, always walking with the sexual movements of a graceful animal. His body never failed to stir her blood.

He did not touch her in a sexual way anymore, but Lorna often lost herself in her fantasies, remembering how she had writhed and clawed and screamed aloud during those earlier times when Peter used her for the demands of his young, potent body. She had never lost her need for sex.

Lorna never considered Mr. Ramsey as her lover despite the fact that for years now she'd had sexual relations with him whenever he demanded it. Blackmail was what she called it; Ramsey only laughed at her and told her she enjoyed it as much as he did. Neither of them wanted it any other way, Lorna admitted to herself. Ramsey was at least a release from her frustrations.

He sat across from her now, crossed-legged, thick and male and powerful, puffing on his ever-present cigar. She found her eyes moving carefully to his crotch and felt a stirring within her loins, visualizing the length and hardness that she knew only too well.

With a quick shake of her head she scowled. "I've told you not to smoke when you are in this house, Ramsey."

He laughed. "You've been telling me that for twenty years," he answered, puffing smoke at her. Mimicking Lorna's voice he said, "Peter will smell the smoke and demand to know who was here." In his natural voice he added, "For God's sake, Lorna, Peter ceased caring about what man you entertain long, long ago."

She winced but wouldn't show the hurt. "If he isn't concerned, he never mentioned it to me."

"Believe me, he isn't interested in what you do." He enjoyed the way she tortured herself.

"What do you want this time, Ramsey?"

He threw his cigar into the dead fireplace and got out of his chair. Moving toward her, he pulled her into his arms when she tried to back away. "You know perfectly well what I want," he breathed as he caressed her breasts and ran his hands down over the curve of her hips and buttocks. "I've had an erection all morning thinking about you."

"Don't be vulgar." She struggled to get free. his hardness made her struggles weaken. "No, not here. The servants...."

He kissed her hard on the mouth. "Screw the servants."

"No," she protested.

He slid his hand between her thighs.

Lorna hated the heat that was welling up inside her. To hide it she raised her hand and slapped his face.

He slapped her so hard she staggered back. "Don't look so horrified, Lorna—you love it when I get a little rough with you."

She held her hand over the stinging of her cheek. There was a mixture of loathing and desire swirling through her that she couldn't understand—never did. "Please, not here," she breathed, seeing his determination.

"Get your wrap. We'll go to my place."

"I can't. Not right now. I'll come later."

"Very well," he said, going back to his chair. "Now that that's settled, I have some news."

"News? About little Adam?"

"No, about April Moonsong."

Lorna's look soured.

"I believe we'll have little trouble with her once your grandson is found."

"If he is found," Lorna said dejectedly. "I honestly have given up hope, Ramsey." She sighed. "What about the child's mother?"

"From what I've been told, she's getting balmier every day. Naturally I've had her watched. She's prone to fits of rage and relapses into such deep melancholy that it takes days for her to come 'round. Sometimes, my agents report, she isn't even coherent. At least that's what they heard from the Nightsong servants. With all the old evidence we uncovered concerning her moral character It will be a simple matter to have her declared an unfit mother."

"Do you really think there is a chance of ever finding Adam?"

He shrugged and lit another cigar. "From the first day I became a detective I found that there is no such thing as a case that can't be solved."

"If you hadn't bungled the whole thing at the very start I'd have had the pleasure of raising my grandson."

"So I made a mistake."

"When you stole the child out of the crib why didn't you stick to the plan and deliver him to me? I never could understand why you had to deliver Adam to that woman in Sausalito."

"Listen, Lorna. Don't make me out as some dolt. I've been in the business far too long not to know how the police think and work. You were in on the snatch from the beginning. You agreed it had to look like a real kidnapping, so I hid the kid with Sylvia for a few days, intending to have one of my men 'accidentally' find the lad and bring him to you. How in hell did I know that crazy woman would bolt with the kid." He ran his hands through his thinning hair. "She was sickly at the time, out of her head with a fever or something, the neighbors told me, though they made no mention of seeing her with a child. Sylvia and the boy might both be dead by now."

"Don't say that."

"Well it is a possibility. I want to know as well as you. If they're dead, then you can stop wasting your time and mine fretting over the child."

"I never saw the reason for you keeping Sylvia a secret from me. I knew a man like you would have to have a wife some-where."

Ramsey chuckled. "I couldn't very well have my wife spying on you and me now, could I? Besides she'd always been sick and never strong enough to be a proper wife to any man. She'd always wanted a kid, too. Maybe she and the boy are living together somewhere out there. Nah, impossible," he decided. "I've made a thorough search, as have the police. They're dead, I tell you."

"I won't believe that. Ever." She turned on him. "And if you're proven right, Ramsey, so help me God I'll—"

"You'll what?" he asked, threateningly. "You were as much a part of the kidnapping as me. Don't you forget for an instant that paper you signed."

Lorna crumbled into a chair. "How can I forget it? You've been holding it over my head for decades."

"And I'll continue to do so until I get tired of fucking you.

Lorna jumped to her feet, her face red with rage. "Don't you ever use such language in my presence," she stormed.

Ramsey started to say something, but they both froze when the door to the library opened and Efrem started into the room. When he saw his mother and Ramsey his eyes widened. "Ramsey," he gasped. He stood staring at the man as if he were seeing an apparition.

"Efrem," Lorna said, feeling awkward. She patted her hair

self-consciously. "What are you doing home so early in the day."

Efrem didn't move. He kept staring at Ramsey.

"Hello, Efrem."

Lorna looked from one to the other. "You two know each other?"

"In passing," Ramsey said as he reached for his hat. "I must be going, Lorna. Don't forget to keep that appointment. Good-bye, Efrem. Nice seeing you again." He gave an insidious chuckle as he stepped around the younger man. To Lorna he said, "I know my way out."

A silence descended in his wake. Lorna studied her son's white face. At thirty-four Efrem had the appearance of a man twice his age. His once soft, near-feminine beauty had sagged into a grayish gauntness. The large, bright eyes now lay sunken and dead in his head, his body thin and frail. He was still her favorite child but years before something had happened in Efrem's life, something that caused him to slam a door in her face, shutting her out completely.

She'd never since—hard as she'd tried—been able to unlock that door.

Lorna wondered why the terrible fear in Efrem's face. "You know Mr. Ramsey?"

"Oh, God," he moaned, like a soul in torment. He turned abruptly and rushed up to his room. The door slammed shut behind him. Efrem hurried toward the cabinet against the far wall, took a bottle of whiskey from the shelf, pulled the cork, and took a deep swallow. The liquor burned his throat and started a familiar fire in the pit of his stomach. A sting of pain shot across his chest. He quenched it with another long drink from the bottle and collapsed on the bed.

"God," he breathed, putting his arm across his eyes. "He didn't tell her. He promised he wouldn't tell her," he cried. He thought again of putting an end to it all by slashing his wrists. The tears came all too quickly as he remembered his cowardice the last time. He'd thought his heavy drinking would have killed him by now, but God didn't want him either, he knew.

Efrem took another long draught from the bottle just as Lorna came into the room, not bothering to knock. Efrem made no move to hide the almost empty quart of liquor.

"We must talk," Lorna said in a stern voice.

"Leave me alone, Mother. There is nothing I want to talk to you about."

"Ramsey. How do you know him?"

Efrem's spirits lifted. Her question meant that Ramsey hadn't told her what he'd discovered about him and Leon Nightsong—how Ramsey had just happened to discover Efrem climbing into Leon's bed.

"I just know him, that's all. Let's leave it at that."

"No, we will not leave it at that. Mr. Ramsey is hardly a man with whom you'd be acquainted."

"I might ask, then, how you come to know him," Efrem shot back, taking another drink. He saw his mother's face grow red. Efrem narrowed his eyes and pressed his advantage. "What in hell was he doing here in our house?"

Lorna fumbled with the lavaliere on her blouse. "If you know anything about him, then you know he is one of the most capable detectives in San Francisco. I've been retaining him to find little Adam."

"He seemed to me to be very much at home here."

Lorna lost patience. "Mr. Ramsey is employed by your father and me. He reports almost weekly on his investigation."

"Oh, come off it, Mother. Ramsey isn't a detective anymore. He's given up that practice long ago."

"He's sold his agency, yes," she admitted. "He keeps working for us, however, on a personal basis."

"He drives the most expensive automobiles and wears diamond rings big as pears. You must pay him well." Efrem's sarcasm was cutting.

"How do you know so much about him?"

Efrem took another drink. "As I said, I just know him, that's all." He was tempted for a moment to tell his mother all about Ramsey and how he'd forced Efrem to cooperate in smuggling opium into the country under the cover of MacNair Products, through Efrem's department. A tiny voice told him to blurt it all out and get it over with. Let Ramsey tell everything he knew, but Efrem would have some telling of his own. It meant prison for them both. The thought terrified Efrem.

He drained the bottle, got off the bed, and staggered to the cabinet for a full bottle.

"You're killing yourself with drink."

"Didn't you know that's my intention?"

"Oh, Efrem," Lorna said, going to him and trying to embrace her youngest son.

He shoved her rudely away.

"Let me help you, darling. Whatever it is can't be all that awful."

He drank and said nothing.

"Please, Efrem. I love you. Your father loves you. We won't let anything happen. Just tell me what sort of trouble you've gotten mixed into."

"Oh, leave me alone, Mother. I'm not in any trouble. I just like to drink. It makes me feel good. So go away and let me feel good all by myself."

"No," she said angrily, and snatching the bottle out of his hand, she smashed it against the fireplace and grabbed Efrem's shoulder. "You are going to tell me what's eating you alive if I have to shake it out of you."

He was a rag doll in her grip. "Leave me alone," he said in a tired voice.

"I will not leave you alone. I've left you alone far too long, thinking you'd snap out of whatever has been gnawing at you. I've been negligent as your mother. I intend to correct that, starting right now."

"I am not a child, Mother. For God's sake I'm thirty-four years old. My problems aren't yours anymore."

"Yes they are. You are still my son."

"I'm no one's son," he said dropping back on the bed and covering his eyes. "I'm not even...." He bit off his words.

"You're not even what?"

"Nothing." He fought back the tears.

Somewhere below they heard the front door slam and Peter shouting Efrem's name.

"Please, Mother, I can't face Father," Efrem pleaded.

She started for the door. "All right, Efrem. I'll intercept him, but just remember that our conversation is far from finished." She hurried out to head off her husband.

"Where's that no good little—?"

"Peter," Lorna scowled. "Leave the boy alone. He's upset. I won't have you raging at him."

"He's upset? Did he tell you what he's doing home?"

"No."

"The entire shipment of oils from Hawaii—that little no-good son of mine refused the whole lot. He ordered the customs office to ship it all back, that it wasn't what we ordered. How in hell am I going to develop the new perfume without that oil? He's fouled up the whole damned production operation. Those petal oils were expected weeks ago as it is. God only knows how much this is going to put us back."

"I'm sure he had a good reason."

"He was obviously drunk—as usual."

"Peter," Lorna said softly. "We both know Efrem has problems. We are equally guilty in closing our eyes to his behavior. We should have made an issue of it long before this, but we must rectify it now."

"He's just a lazy, damned drunkard who refuses to help himself. And if he won't do anything about his habit no one can do it for him."

Lorna wasn't convinced of that. As she led Peter back down the stairs she thought of her meeting with Ramsey. She recalled the frightened look on Efrem's face when he found Ramsey in the library. She also recalled Efrem's remark about Ramsey's expensive cars and his jewelry. Mr. Ramsey was living very high, higher than he'd ever lived before as a detective.

An idea occurred to her. Perhaps it was time their roles were reversed and she became the detective. She decided she'd do a little checking up on Mr. Ramsey, if for no other reason than to find out why her son was so afraid of him.

Peter smelled cigar smoke as they went into the library, but he made no comment. He knew Lorna entertained some man. It didn't bother him. Actually, he was glad she had someone.

He poured himself a brandy. "I revoked that cancellation of Efrem's, of course, but I don't know how long it's going to take now for the customs people to get it back to us, if they haven't already rerouted it back to Hawaii." He took a sip from the balloon glass and set it aside. "I'm going to Europe," he said. "I sail from New York in ten days."

Lorna picked up a book and started back out of the room, trying to ignore the smell of Ramsey's cigar. "Yes, you told me," she said. "England, isn't it?"

He merely grunted and started sifting through some papers on the desk.

# CHAPTER SIX

The fountains of Blendmoor Manor sparkled under the lights of the lanterns that were strung throughout the courtyard of the country estate. Adam pulled his little roadster under the portico and handed it over to the liveried footman.

"I feel like a fish out of water," Adam said.

Pamela laughed, seeing the disapproving look on the footman's face as he got behind the wheel and steered the sporty little auto toward a solid bank of sleek limousines and handsome carriages at the edge of the drive. "Dressed as fine as you are, you could have at least called for me in a golden coach." She laughed again.

"It might turn into a pumpkin and then where would you be?" Adam limped up the long flight of stairs flanked by uniformed attendants.

"Are you managing all right, darling?"

"The leg's throbbing a bit from that damned bullet wound, but not as much as to keep me from escorting you to this do."

"I shouldn't have allowed you to talk me into it, King George or no King George."

"And let you come with that scurvy Jeremy Slyke? Not on your bottom buttons, old girl."

"I'd never have come with Jeremy. You know I wouldn't have."

"You look smashing. Have I told you?"

"Yes, and you'd better keep telling me because Father had a fit when he saw the bill for the gown."

"I think I'll keep you in white satin for the rest of your life."

"I'll look rather silly being your housewife dressed all day in white satin."

"My housewife? Have I asked you?" he joked.

"No, but I intend asking you if you don't get around to it soon."

The major domo in royal blue with silver and gold braid took their engraved invitations, loudly announcing their names: "Master Adam Clarendon and Miss Pamela Albright."

Adam tried not to limp too noticeably as they made their way down the short steps to the ballroom beyond. An orchestra was playing Franz Lehar's new Merry Widow Waltz, which made Adam's expression change.

Pamela noticed. "You look rather odd of a sudden."

"The waltz," Adam said in a low voice. "Isn't it rather tactless to be playing The Merry Widow in view of the fact that King Edward just died and Queen Alexandra is in bereavement?"

Pamela tilted her head up to him. "I—yes, I suppose you have a point, but judging from everyone else's expression, no one seems to mind."

Adam watched the dozens of handsome smiling couples spinning and turning across the polished marble floor. "I suppose you're right. Still, the King and Queen will be coming later; shouldn't I mention the indiscretion to someone? The Queen will certainly notice; she's quite the stickler for propriety, I understand."

"Mention it to your mother. She'll know what to do, if anything." She scanned the room. "I don't see your parents. Mine are over there near the entrance to the solarium." She raised her fan to acknowledge her father's bow of invitation to join them.

"Let's find Mother and Father first and get this waltz thing out of my system. It's bothering me."

"You're really becoming quite a fussbudget, Adam, do you know that?" she asked, grinning up at him.

"I'm a proper Englishman. Is there anything wrong in that?"

"You're an Englishman, I admit, but proper—?" She covered her laugh with her fan.

They found Lord and Lady Clarendon in a circle of conversation. Mrs. Asquith, the Prime Minister's wife, was among them and was quick to agree with Lady Clarendon when she told her of Adam's concern about the waltz. Mrs. Asquith hurried off to correct the inappropriate choice of dance music.

Lord Clarendon said to Adam, "The leg giving you any trouble, my boy?"

"It's a bit ginger, Father. I'm afraid I'll not be doing any dancing tonight, Merry Widow or no Merry Widow."

"I'm certain Pamela will not lack for partners."

"That's what I'm afraid of."

Pamela had joined the ladies' conversation, giving Lord Clarendon the chance to ease Adam slightly away from the others' hearing.

"The Slykes are here, of course," he cautioned his son. "Now I want no trouble."

"Why should I cause trouble?"

"Jeremy is most assuredly going to ask Pamela to dance. You are not to interfere. Do I make myself quite clear?"

Adam bit his lower lip. "That, of course, is for Pamela to say, Father. If she refuses to dance with Jeremy, I'll support her refusal, of course."

"Then you must convince her not to refuse. I had my say with Jeremy's father and the Slykes will go to any extreme to provoke me. Just be careful and try not to let that temper of yours get out of hand."

"Temper? Me?"

Lord Clarendon laughed. "Yes, you, my boy. I never did figure out where you got it, but it's the temper of a Scotsman that bursts out of you every so often. Must come from your mother's side of the family. There's Scottish blood somewhere 'way back."

Oddly, the mention of his Scottish temper made him think of an old dream he'd once had frequently, though now only occasionally. He dreamed he was a great lord in an oriental palace, surrounded by his samurai legions in their shining metal suits of war. He could see the smoke and fire billowing from his mouth as he ordered his men away to fight some ferocious enemy and steal away the beautiful maiden imprisoned in the ivory tower. His anger was always that of an oriental—Japanese, Chinese. He made no differentiation as to which.

His father touched his arm, pulling him out of his thoughts. "As you know I had a face-to-face with Tom Slyke," he said, pleased with himself. "I gave that old fool what-for. And you know, my lad, he had the audacity to laugh when I accused his son of firing on you. He neither denied it nor admitted it. He merely said Jeremy had always been a poor shot; never could hit anything he aimed at. Well, I gave him fair warning that if the Slykes want trouble they'll get it from me."

"I told you, Father, that you shouldn't have gone to the Slykes. We don't know for certain that Jeremy shot me.

"You know it and I know it, so why pretend we don't. I wanted to put the scare of God in them, that's all."

"You only angered Tom Slyke all the more by your accusation."

"Speaking of the devil," Lord Clarendon whispered when he saw Jeremy Slyke coming in their direction.

The young Jeremy Slyke had wavy black hair, a pencil thin moustache, and oily manners. It always surprised Adam that girls found him so attractive. Women doted on him. Even Pamela had once remarked on how good-looking Jeremy was.

"He's a marvelous dancer, too, and a perfect charmer," she'd continued until Adam had cut her off with some sharp remark and had stormed away.

Adam and Jeremy had never liked each other. At school they fought over the same seats, the same positions on the teams, the same books. And, of course, they'd fought over Pamela from the first day the three met accidentally at the horse show in Brodgenbrook.

Jeremy hesitated when he saw Adam and his father. Then,

his eyes moved to Pamela and Jeremy walked purposefully toward Adam.

"I heard of your bad luck, old chap. Surprised to see you here."

"Nothing fatal," Adam said, trying to be affable.

"Too bad," Jeremy answered, grinning. "You won't be dancing, obviously."

"Not unless I choose to."

Jeremy bowed slightly to Adam and his father, then walked to where Pamela was chatting with the other ladies. He touched her arm. "Miss Albright," he said sweetly.

"Hello, Jeremy."

He extended his hand, inviting her to walk with him. Pamela ignored it and glanced at Adam, who was watching them closely.

"May I have the pleasure of a dance then, Pamela?"

Pamela hedged. "We've only just arrived, Jeremy. I really should search out some friends and let them know I'm here."

"Of course. I can understand their concern when you're being escorted by Adam Clarendon."

Pamela fluttered her fan. "My family and friends happen to like Adam very much and they trust him implicitly." She glanced again at Adam. "It's his motorcar Mother was anxious about."

"Then let me escort you home. It will put your mother's mind at ease."

"Adam will take me home."

Jeremy tugged the lapels of his evening jacket straighter. "I trust you will allow me to sign your dance card?"

When he reached for the embossed white and silver card dangling from Pamela's wrist, she snatched it up. "I doubt if I'll be dancing this evening, Jeremy. I'd prefer staying with Adam."

"You'll damned well dance with me," he snarled. Several of the women turned toward them.

"Please, Jeremy. Don't insist. Now please excuse me." She glanced hopefully toward Adam. Two rather stout gentlemen had struck up a conversation between the space separating them, blocking Pamela's view of Adam.

"I will not excuse you," Jeremy said harshly as he took her wrist.

She began to tremble at the thought of his creating a disturbance. She knew the ease with which Adam flew off the handle at anything that concerned her and Jeremy Slyke. To avoid any possible unpleasantness she handed Jeremy her dance card.

"The next waltz, Jeremy. I'll be with my parents over near the solarium."

"The next waltz," he repeated smugly as he signed the tiny card. Just as he was doing so the two stout gentlemen moved off in time for Adam to see it. The glower that creased Adam's brow made Jeremy smile. With a jaunty cock of his head Jeremy Slyke moved along into the crush of guests.

In a flash Adam was beside her, his hand tight on her arm. "You've permitted Jeremy Slyke a dance?"

"I had to, Adam," she said, keeping her voice low. "He threatened to make a scene. I believed it to be the simplest way to avoid one. After all, it's only one dance. The rest I've saved for you—sitting down," she said with a laugh.

Before the concert master had time to raise his baton for the Strauss waltz, Pamela found Jeremy beside her. He looked defiantly at Adam. To Pamela he said, "My dance, I believe," and extended his arm.

With a nervous glance at Adam, Pamela slipped her arm in Jeremy's and let him escort her onto the dance floor.

It wasn't that she so much disliked Jeremy Slyke, it was just that she liked Adam far more. There were times when Adam upset her with his moods and tempers, but there was something far more sinister and frightening about Jeremy. Still, on those instances when she'd been alone with Jeremy—before she'd gotten serious about Adam—she'd enjoyed herself. Jeremy was an excellent conversationalist and she rather enjoyed his reckless manner, always thinking up something new and exciting to do.

She began to relax in his arms as the waltz continued. He was, indeed, a superb dancer. And perhaps his wickedness only added to his attraction.

When she found Adam watching them she felt guilty for enjoying the waltz.

"You're not going to marry Clarendon?" Jeremy said, making it sound like the most incredible thing imaginable.

"He hasn't asked me."

"He won't either. I've heard stories, you know."

"What kind of stories?"

"Just stories."

"Now don't annoy me, Jeremy, or I shall walk right off this dance floor and leave you standing like a stump in an empty field." When he hesitated she demanded, "What stories?"

He put his lips close to her ear. "Adam can't ask you to marry him for fear the truth will come out."

"What truth?"

"He's not their real son, you know."

Pamela stared up at him. "Not their son? You must be mad."

"He's not. If you don't believe me, ask for his birth certificate. Chances are he'll put you off or produce some phony old piece of paper his father arranged for."

"You are beginning to aggravate me, Jeremy. I don't believe a word of what you're saying."

Keeping his lips close to her ears he said, "I heard my parents talking of it one evening when they didn't know I was in the next room. It seems Lady Clarendon was always rather sickly—you know, always in bed—right after she married Lord Clarendon. Her husband hustled her off to doctor after doctor and though she got stronger there was something odd about her. She never liked being out in company and they kept to themselves almost exclusively."

He turned her expertly. "Then someone who knew her family in Devon told my mother that Lady Clarendon had a crazy sister in an institution somewhere in America. Chicago, I think."

"Jeremy," Pamela snapped. "I do not want to hear this." She found, however, that she could not move away from him. A part of her held her solid in his arms as they continued to turn and swirl around the room.

It was as though she hadn't spoken. "One day Lord Clarendon and his wife announced to one and all that they were going on a world cruise. A year or so later they returned with a small tyke who anyone could tell was three or four years old. My folks swear the Clarendons weren't away that long."

"Your parents were obviously mistaken."

Jeremy shook his head. "I doubt it. That beau of yours is the son of the Lady's balmy sister."

Pamela gave a little gasp. "You're talking rubbish."

"The sister had the baby in the insane asylum and sent word to Lady Clarendon to come and raise it as her own." He gave her a wink. "The sister had no one else to turn to, it seems, not even a husband." He smirked. "He'll never ask you to marry him."

The waltz ended. Pamela found herself staring at him. Her eyes were wet with tears. "I don't believe a word of it," she said. She'd heard gossip of the sort before, but it was all too ridiculous to even listen to.

When Jeremy led her back to where Adam was waiting, Adam immediately saw the tears Pamela was trying to hide.

"You're crying." He scowled at Jeremy. "What did you say to her?" His voice raised, turning a few heads.

Pamela put her hand on his arm. "I'd like some punch, Adam. Please. I'm quite dry."

There was something infuriating in Jeremy's smile as he walked away.

"What did he say to you?"

"Nothing." She fought back the tears. Surely Jeremy was lying, but something was now goading her on, egging her to ask Adam if she was right in not believing Jeremy's story.

"You don't come off a dance floor in tears without a reason," he said as he accepted two glass cups of champagne punch from the liveried servant and steered Pamela toward the terrace.

The night had grown darker. The electric lights inside the lanterns had been dimmed, lending a more romantic color to the garden below them.

"Tell me, please," Adam implored.

"You'll only make a scene."

"No I won't."

"I know you, Adam. Besides, it was nothing. Jeremy made some remarks that upset me. It has nothing whatever to do with anything."

"He said something about me, didn't he?"

"No."

He cupped her chin and forced her to turn and look up at him. "He did. I can see it in your face," he said when she refused to look at him. "What was it?"

"Nothing," Pamela insisted.

Adam put his punch cup on the balustrade. "Well," he fumed, "If you won't tell me then I'll get it out of Slyke."

Pamela tried to stop him. He brushed her aside and pushed his way into the ballroom just as the major domo rapped his staff at the doorway of the room.

"Ladies and gentlemen," he announced. "Their Royal Majesties have arrived in the anteroom. I suggest you all prepare yourselves for presentation."

The guests began to take up their places, forming an aisle at the bottom of the stairs where they would curtsy and bow as the King and Queen passed amongst them.

Adam was too obsessed with finding Jeremy Slyke. He saw him with his father. They were moving into position at the bottom of the stairs, tactfully elbowing others aside so theirs would be the first bows the King and Queen would acknowledge.

Adam grabbed Jeremy's shoulder and spun him around. "What did you say to Pamela?"

"My dear boy," Tom Slyke said, aghast at Adam's intrusion and obvious rudeness.

Adam ignored him. "I want to know why you made Pamela cry."

"Their Royal Highnesses," Tom Slyke reminded Adam.

Adam refused to listen to anything but his inner rage. He

grabbed Jeremy by the front of his evening jacket and shook him violently. "What did you tell her?"

"Please," someone to the left of Adam whispered.

A second later Adam heard his father's voice next to his ear. "Adam, you're creating a disturbance."

"I don't care," Adam snapped.

Again he shook Jeremy as hard as he could. The lapel of his jacket ripped. Jeremy's temper grew.

"I told her the truth, damn it," he shouted in Adam's face. "That you're a bastard!"

At the top of the stairs the major domo tapped his staff. "Their Royal Highnesses King George and Queen Mary." Trumpets blared.

As the royal couple started down the steps, Adam pulled back his fist and smashed it squarely into Jeremy's face, sending him sprawling and bloody at the very feet of the royal monarchs.

Lord Clarendon grabbed his son and pulled him away just as Adam was prepared to pounce on top of Jeremy Slyke. He struggled with Adam and with the help of others succeeded in getting him out of the ballroom—but not before looking at the face of King George and knowing that the Clarendons were henceforth ostracized from polite society.

# CHAPTER SEVEN

In New York City, Caroline Andrieux and her grandmother boarded the British luxury liner *Mauritania* at the Fourteenth Street pier. As accustomed as she was to the lavish world of the very rich, to Caroline it was like stepping into a dream palace.

"Oh, Grandmother, it's absolutely the most beautiful thing I've ever seen," Caroline said, gaping at the grandiose design and opulence of the beautiful steamship.

Lydia was too occupied scanning the crowd to see if she could spot Peter MacNair. He'd promised to join them at the gangway, but the "All Ashore" had sounded and Lydia was becoming anxious.

They were crossing the promenade deck toward their first-class center-ship cabin when she felt him beside her.

"Hello." He pretended to sound surprised.

"Peter. I thought you'd—" She realized their meeting was supposed to be accidental and glanced quickly at Caroline, then at Peter. "I thought you were planning on staying in New York."

"Mr. MacNair," Caroline cried with delight. "Oh, now I know the trip will be perfect." She'd always liked Peter MacNair. To her he represented what a very successful and sophisticated man should be. Caroline had bemoaned the fact that the MacNairs and the Nightsongs were supposed to be sworn enemies. Often in the past she had run into Susan MacNair at various functions and up until the time Susan married and moved east she thoroughly enjoyed her, and got the impression that Susan liked her as well. Caroline had been rather looking forward to seeing

Susan on their arrival in New York, but unfortunately Susan and the children had left for San Francisco the day before Caroline and her grandmother arrived.

"Beautiful, isn't she?" Peter said, looking around the steamship. "Come on, let me give you your first tour. I've sailed the *Mauritania* before and you won't be sorry you chose her."

He sent the steward along with the women's hand luggage and escorted the ladies forward. Caroline marveled at everything she saw: The library, the writing rooms, the drawing rooms. She gasped when they started down the grand staircase that led to the embarkation hall, dining room, on aft to the main lounge, the smoking room, and ending with the veranda cafe.

The grand salon gave a lavish impression of quiet eloquence on a massive scale. Its panels of polished mahogany each were lit by encircling moldings of gold light and interspaced with tall, slim pilasters of lilac-colored marble with caps and plinths of ormolu.

Out of all the lavishness, Caroline was most intrigued with the veranda café, complete with rush matting laid directly on the deck, potted palms, and white wicker furniture suggesting balmy nights and hot sunny days.

"How lovely it will be to sit here and sip a beverage and watch the promenade of passengers," she said to Peter as she sat down in one of the wicker chairs.

"Don't delude yourself, Caroline," he answered. "It's all show. This is something Mr. Cunard included solely for the travel brochures. He wanted everyone to think the voyage across the Atlantic is all sunshine and summer weather. We'll be fortunate if we sit comfortably on deck two afternoons during the entire crossing. Passengers seem to forget this is the North Atlantic, not the Mediterranean. That's why the interior is so luxurious as well as cozy. It was purposely designed as an indoor refuge from the ocean's cold unfriendliness."

Caroline was visibly disappointed.

"Buck up, young lady," Peter said. "There will be more than enough enjoyment for you during the crossing. The ship is packed stem to stern with good-looking young men, I'm sure. It usually is this time of year." He shook a finger at her. "No shipboard romances, however. They're very disappointing once you've reached where you're going." Peter smiled at Lydia. "But I'm sure your grandmother has already given you a list of the do's and don'ts."

"Yes," Lydia agreed. "However, young ladies tend to be more heedful of admonitions when they come from a man." To Caroline she said, "We've occupied enough of Mr. MacNair's time, dear. We should go to our cabin and begin to unpack. They've taken up the gangway."

"Would you both join me for dinner?" Peter asked. "The first night out is informal, you know."

Caroline jumped at the invitation, for which Lydia wanted to hug her.

"I'll wait for you in the lounge at seven."

A little before seven o'clock Lydia entered the lounge alone. When Peter saw her he rose slowly, dazed as always by her beauty. She wore a black dress cut fashionably low and with sheer sleeves. Her tight-fitting skirt was decorated with heavy fringes of beads and she wore simple white paradise feathers in her hair, a white chrysanthemum corsage at her cleavage, and carried a silver fan. To set off the entire ensemble, a brilliant amethyst sash girdled her slim waist. People stared—the men longingly, the women in envy—as she started toward Peter's table.

"You are positively ravishing," he said, pressing her hand hotly to his lips.

She thanked him and sat down. Peter asked the steward to bring two martinis, very dry with twists of lemon.

"Where's Caroline?"

"Still dressing. She's fussing as though this were her first date." She looked apologetic. "I'm sorry to disappoint you by not coming alone, Peter, but as I explained over the telephone in New York, it might look less suspicious our meeting aboard the same ship."

"It's perfectly all right. We'll have plenty of time to be alone. I'll see to that. I'm the one who should be apologizing. I know we'd planned on spending a little time alone while we were in New York, but Susan and the children were in such a flurry about leaving for California—and to tell the complete truth I came down with the most godawful cold." He felt sudden beads of perspiration on his forehead and blotted them with his linen handkerchief. "I still haven't shaken it completely."

She frowned. "You do look a bit piqued, Peter. Are you certain you're feeling all right now?"

"Perfectly," he lied. "It's breaking up," he said, but that wasn't true either. He hadn't felt well in a week. The doctor had feared influenza at first and ordered him to bed. Peter certainly did not listen to that advice, but purposely refused to let Lydia see him looking so bad.

"Still," Lydia said, "I think you'd better take advantage of this crossing and rest as much as possible. Now that I look at you more closely there is a definite pallor in your cheeks."

"Stop it, Lydia. It's just a ridiculous chest cold. I am fine, really I am."

The steward placed their cocktails in front of them. When he'd gone Peter leaned forward and whispered, "I have no intention of your using my chest cold as an excuse not to visit my cabin."

Lydia smiled seductively. "I can't think of a better excuse to give Caroline than that I'm sitting up with a sick friend."

"Speaking of Caroline," Peter said as he got up, "she just came in."

She looked lovely in her voile dress with its subtle blue and green floral design. The slim skirt with flared frills at the hem was trimmed with white lace. Like all the fashionable ladies, she wore white feathers in her beehive coiffeur and carried a fan.

Caroline extended her hand as she greeted Peter and her grandmother. Peter bent over it and kissed it softly. "Lovely," he said as they settled themselves. "There isn't a young man in the room whose eyes aren't riveted on you, Caroline."

"Yes," Lydia agreed, "you look absolutely charming, my dear. I'm glad you decided on the print. It adds a touch of spring to the room."

"You don't think it makes me too young-looking, Grandmother? I certainly don't want anyone to think I'm just a teenaged girl."

Lydia patted her hand. "Never stop wanting to look like a teenaged girl, darling. Age is only too anxious to take care of that all by itself in due time."

"Pardon, sir," the steward said as he offered Peter a note on a tray. "The Captain's compliments."

Peter read the invitation. "I'm to sit at the Captain's table tomorrow night," he said, slightly displeased. He wanted to be with Lydia every second.

"Lovely," Caroline said. "We'll be dinner partners."

Lydia asked what she meant.

"While I was getting dressed—after you left—an invitation came from the Captain asking us to join him at dinner tomorrow evening." She looked at Peter with a flush of embarrassment. "I didn't want to say anything about it when I arrived for fear of making you feel slighted."

An ancient scene crept back into Lydia's mind as she remembered her crossing from Shanghai to San Francisco with April. She'd been bestowed no honors then; in fact, just the opposite. She and April were not allowed to associate with anyone aboard, neither crew nor passengers. And because of some innocent scandal their baggage had been confiscated and they'd been put off the sailing ship without money or luggage.

"Grandmother?"

Lydia passed a hand over her eyes. "Oh, I was only thinking of another voyage I made with your mother that was far more uncomfortable than this." She forced back the dreary past and finished her cocktail. "I think I'll have another, Peter, and then we'll go in to dinner."

Dinner was sumptuous yet not as grand, Caroline found, as

the dinners that followed as the ship sped across the Atlantic. Everyone seemed to be getting the feel of the voyage by the second night, all busy making arrangements, introducing themselves, choosing the best possible company for the ten-day crossing.

"Ten days," Caroline said. "Isn't it extraordinary?"

"It may take longer if the weather turns against us. I do hope you don't get seasick," Peter said as they finished their coffee and started back to their staterooms.

"Not I," Caroline said bravely. "I've sailed on various sailboats and yachts often and am an excellent sailor."

"Good for you." Out on deck Peter looked up at the four high, black stacks of the *Mauritania* looming masterfully against the sky. "The *Mauritania*'s sister-ship, the *Lusitania*, made the crossing in a bit less than ten days. There's a friendly battle being waged between the two captains." He studied the line of the rail. "I haven't sailed the *Lusitania* and I doubt if I will. There's a lot of superstition in the navy and talk is that a woman stowed aboard when she was launched."

"So?" Caroline asked indignantly. "Why should that be so terrible?"

"A bad omen among navy men. They called this old girl Cunard's Golden Ship; they never gave the *Lusitania* a pet name. It's as if the older ship—although only three months older—was an unwanted child that wasn't destined to live for very long."

"*Lusitania, Mauritania*—I understand the British are to launch another, to be called the *Aquitania*. Why the penchant for 'ia' endings?"

"A phobia of Cunard Board members. They favor names of Roman provinces. They represent strength and endurance."

"The Romans didn't endure," Caroline argued.

"Long enough," Lydia said. "Longer than this lovely thing will last." She stopped and leaned against the rail, watching the sea, ignoring the bite of the night air.

Peter put his arm around her, and suddenly remembering Caroline, put his arm around her as well. "Cunard has three more liners on the drawing board. I hear they've run out of Roman provinces that are suitable. These three new ones are to be called the *Olympic*, *Titanic*, and *Britannic*."

"Sounds very Germanic to me for some reason," Lydia said, yawning. "Dear me, this sea air is making me sleepy." For two days she'd wanted to be alone with Peter, but could not tactfully send Caroline away.

It was Caroline who read her grandmother's mind and said, "I am going back to the lounge for a bit." When Peter moved to go with her she added, "No, stay with Grandmother. I'm too old to need a chaperone."

The lilt in her eyes told Lydia that Caroline was well aware their meeting Peter MacNair had been no accident.

"My cabin?" Peter asked the second they were alone.

Lydia simply nodded anxiously. He slipped his arms about her waist and they hurried out of the cold of the night.

Once inside his cabin Peter took her in his arms and kissed her passionately. "Oh, dear God, how I've been aching to do that," he murmured softly over her parted lips.

To Lydia his body felt hotter than usual. And there was a liquid quality about his eyes that disturbed her. She reached up and laid her hand on his cheek. "Peter, you're burning up."

"I always burn like this when I hold you in my arms," he smiled.

"No, seriously, darling. You're feverish." She forced herself out of his arms. "I'm going to have the ship's doctor check you."

He grabbed her and pulled her back into his embrace. "You are going to do no such thing except get undressed and climb into bed with me."

She wanted him as badly as he wanted her. She didn't put up too much argument as he began unfastening the hooks of her gown but once she was naked and lying next to him, she realized Peter's whole body was wet with perspiration. Peter suddenly began to shiver.

She threw back the coverlet and quickly pulled his dressing gown around her. "I'm calling the ship's doctor." It was an ultimatum and Peter was shivering too violently to stop her.

She made the urgent call and hurriedly slipped back into her clothes, helping Peter into a nightshirt. By the time the doctor arrived with his nurse, Peter and Lydia looked like two old friends who were the epitome of propriety.

"He had a cold," Lydia explained. "I thought it nothing serious, but his temperature shot up and then he began shivering."

The doctor took Peter's temperature while the nurse fussed about laying out completely useless instruments in an attempt to look efficient as well as busy.

"One hundred and two," the doctor announced. "A bit too high." He put a stethoscope to his chest and listened. "And I don't like that rasping, Mr. MacNair." He listened again for a longer time, moving the stethoscope to different locations. "Smoking too much, I'd say."

"Probably," Peter admitted.

"Here," the doctor said, handing him a small vial of pills. "Take two of these every three hours until the fever goes down. I suspect there's nothing serious the matter with you, but just to be on the safe side get yourself checked over completely when you get to wherever you're going."

The nurse began gathering up the neat design she'd made of instruments.

"I'll check on you tomorrow. Stay in bed." He looked at Lydia. "I'll hold you responsible, Mrs. Nightsong," he said jovially and left them alone.

Despite Lydia's admonitions, Peter refused to stay in bed. His fever dropped and he made the concession of resting all the next day, but he refused to have dinner alone in his room.

"I'm joining you and Caroline and that is that," he told Lydia. She knew better than to argue when Peter was determined.

At dinner Caroline whispered to Lydia, "He really does look a bit under the weather."

"I'm rather concerned. But I've known Peter long enough to know he'll do precisely what he wants to do."

"Who's the gentleman seated to the left of Peter? I've gotten the names all mixed up after we were introduced. Is he Mr. Bolter or Mr. Wells or Mr. Cartwright?"

There were ten at the table. The introductions had been simple, just names were given.

"Edward Wells. It rings a bell of sorts, but I'm trying to figure out where I've heard it. Oh, of course."

The gentleman next to her turned and asked, "I beg your pardon, Mrs. Nightsong, did you say something?"

"No. Yes. Oh, I'm sorry, Mr. Bolter, I was speaking to my granddaughter." She inclined her head and gazed, with a hint of a smile, at Edward Wells. She waited until he found her looking at him.

She said, "We have a friend in common, Mr. Wells."

He looked uncomfortable but he smiled and said, "Yes, I was thinking the same thing. 'Nightsong' is not a typical name, but I can't remember where I've heard it before."

"You were acquainted with my daughter in China. She mentioned you were to be our new charge d'affaires in London."

"Your daughter?" He continued to look blank, but behind that blankness Lydia was sure she saw a hint of displeasure.

"April. You may have known her as April MacNair. She tells me you helped to spirit her out of China when you were attached to the embassy in Peking."

"April. Of course." He glanced at Peter. "I thought the name MacNair sounded familiar also. I was about to ask you, Mr. MacNair, if you were in any way related to the lady, but then 'MacNair' is not all that uncommon a name."

Peter said, "Mrs. Nightsong's daughter married my son in China."

Eddie Wells sipped his wine. "Dear April. How is she?" He tried to sound enthusiastic. Lydia saw he wasn't the least interested.

"She's well," she lied.

"And the boy? She had her son with her when we had our little adventure. And quite an adventure it was," he went on, addressing everyone at the table. "The Dowager Empress would not permit the girl and child to leave Peking. We almost caused a small war. Unfortunately, the Empress's soldiers caught us and they would have slaughtered the lot of us if Mrs. Nightsong's daughter hadn't prevented it."

He saw the ladies blanch at the mention of slaughter. Eddie cursed himself for his lack of tact. "I'd heard she arrived safely in San Francisco," he added quickly. "I've always meant to contact her but—well, the State Department gives us little time to pursue our own pleasures."

Seeing him, smug and well turned out, Lydia did not believe this for a moment. Edward Wells was not the sort of man who put duty before pleasure. He was handsome, she had to admit, but ageing badly.

"The boy should be all grown up by now," Eddie said.

"Unfortunately," Peter said. "The boy disappeared shortly after April brought him to America."

"Disappeared? Oh yes, how clumsy of me. I do recall reading about it." He shook his head. "It seems so long ago. I'm afraid I was far too young to remember the details."

What an utter fool, Peter thought. He noticed that Caroline didn't share his opinion. She was gazing at Eddie Wells in that special way women had that said, "Please, look at me."

# CHAPTER EIGHT

The crossing turned out to be a painful one for everyone except, it seemed, Caroline and Eddie Wells. The seas were like mountains, rough and high and craggy. Most of the passengers were seasick or caring for those who were. Peter had another attack of fever and Lydia insisted he stay in bed. Though she herself felt queasy, she did not feel ill and spent most of her time nursing Peter.

By the time they reached Liverpool the 'Golden Ship' of the Cunard Line had almost lost its spare anchor on the fo'c'sle, several promenade deck windows had been shattered, and the teak rails of the monkey island—the lookout point on top of the bridge—had been twisted and battered as the *Mauritania* fought the grim realities of the North Atlantic for twelve long days and nights.

A dismal mist, cold and penetrating, greeted their arrival in England. Peter was looking very pale, whereupon Lydia decided that they would go directly on to London where he could get proper medical attention. She took complete charge without a single objection from Peter, oddly enough, which made her realize that he was more ill than he would admit.

At the Claridge, she booked adjoining suites after trying to convince Peter to go into hospital, which he adamantly refused to do. The doctors diagnosed his malaise as nothing more than an unidentifiable germ that would need time to work out of his system. They prescribed pills and after the second day in London, Peter was beginning to get back his color, as well as his normal disposition.

"You are making a gigantic mistake, Lydia, by permitting Caroline to see so much of that strutting Mr. Wells," Peter fumed as he fussed with the bedclothes.

"Calm yourself," she said as she brushed back the stray lock of hair that insisted upon falling over his forehead. "You sound like her parent."

"I feel like it," he admitted. "I'm extremely fond of that girl and I will not see her consorting with the likes of that fop."

"He's only taking her to another party. And she is enjoying meeting so many important people."

"Has he taken her to bed?" Peter snapped.

"I doubt it," Lydia answered unconcerned. "I know Caroline. She knows her values. She just wants to flirt and have fun. I'm allowing her to do just that."

"Typical."

"What is that supposed to mean?"

He threw back the covers and started to get up.

"Stay in that bed," Lydia ordered.

"I'm sick to death of this bed. I'm getting up."

"You are staying in bed even if I have to call the porter to help me tie you into it." She tried to push him back. He grabbed her and pulled her down on top of him, skirts flying.

A moment later he was kissing her hotly on the mouth and throat. She could feel the hardness of his desire. Peter started to undo the buttons of her shirtwaist, but she slapped his hands.

"No," she protested weakly.

"Yes," he murmured.

She couldn't disguise her need for him. "Someone may come in," she breathed.

"I'll lock the door."

Later as they embraced, Peter kissed the disarray of her hair. "I really should be up and about that Waterford business before they change their minds."

"I've already taken care of that."

He pushed himself up. "You've taken care of it? Since when

did you come to work for MacNair Products?" he joked.

"Since someone had to. I feel if you have a fifty percent hold on my company it's only fair that I have the same on yours. I mean to speak to an attorney about it."

He saw she wasn't serious. Her eyes were laughing at him.

Lydia said, "That will always be a bone of contention between us, Peter."

"I'd give you the entire corporation if you'd marry me."

"You can't give me something that isn't yours," she said, untangling herself and starting to put on her clothes. "MacNair Products belong to your wife. It's her money that keeps it alive."

He glowered. "Everything is in my name to do with it what I wish, but please let's not start up on that again."

"I have no intention of doing so. I just wanted you to know that after all this time, Peter, I'm still not completely susceptible to your Scottish charms. I love you desperately, but both of us know we want things just the way they are. Far, far down inside us is the need to be rivals."

"Independents, you mean."

She adjusted the neckline of her dress. "I've checked out the Waterford people for you. They're just as anxious for your business as ever but their prices are completely out of line, Peter. Now I've taken the liberty of having a law firm here in London do some checking around locally. There are two rather highly respected glass manufacturers not far from London who run in competition to each other. They piqued my interest because from what everyone says the relationship between the two companies isn't unlike ours."

"What are their names?"

"Clarendon Foundries and Slyke Glassworks, Ltd. They blow glass for just about any purpose and their charges are far below Waterford's. I can't honestly vouch for the quality because I haven't been in touch personally, only through the solicitors, so I haven't had the opportunity to make a comparison. I thought I'd wait until you were up and about so you could do that yourself."

Lydia took up her parasol and came over to the bed to kiss him on the mouth.

"Where are you going?"

"Out. Caroline wants to do some shopping and you are to get some sleep. I'll be back in time for cocktails and dinner. Oh." She fumbled in her bag and handed him a card. "Here are the names of the solicitors I've hired for you. They are waiting to hear from you. Call them."

He read the card and put it aside. "I'm not eating dinner in this room again."

She grinned. "No, I believe you've proven to me that you are strong enough to make it downstairs to the dining room." She laid her hand on his cheek. "You are looking so much better," she said.

He took her hand and placed it over his erection. "One hell of a lot better," he said and tried to pull her back into bed.

This time she resisted. "Later." She kissed him again and hurried out.

Lydia had almost forgotten her own reasons for coming to Europe. As she started toward the lift the man standing in the corridor looked so much like Raymond that she stopped and stared at him. When he turned and she saw his full face she breathed a sigh of relief, but a sense of foreboding gripped her, reminding her that her idyll with Peter and her concern for his enterprise and health would have to take second place to her own business troubles.

Caroline was seated at one of the writing desks in the lobby, addressing postcards. She saw her grandmother and shuffled them into a stack and shoved them into her handbag.

"You're a trifle late, aren't you?" Caroline said with a sly look.

"Peter and I got involved in some business. I'm sorry."

"Business, I bet," Caroline said with an accusing smile.

"Stop it." By the blush Lydia felt in her cheeks she knew she wasn't deceiving this wise young lady.

"Look, I'm all for it, Grandmother. I think you should have

married that man a long time ago."

"Unfortunately, I never had the chance." To change the subject she asked, "Where do you think we should go first— Harrod's?"

"No, I heard of some rather chic little shops near Bond Street. I do so like the new tailored look they're featuring this year. And would you think me completely scandalous if I bought one of those higher hemlines? I have the ankles for them," Caroline laughed. "Or so I've been told."

"Caroline, honestly, sometimes I can't be sure when you are being serious. Where have you been showing your ankles, pray tell?"

The pretty young woman linked her arm in Lydia's. "Nowhere improper, Grandmother." She gave her a little squeeze. "No one seems to want to see them yet."

"Not even Mr. Wells?"

"Not even Eddie Wells."

"Peter is rather concerned about your relationship with that man."

"There is no relationship. He's fun and is always going somewhere rather classy."

"Does he ever speak of your mother?"

"Never. I really think he'd rather not be reminded that he's old enough to be my father."

"Be careful, darling. Men who think themselves still young usually are as brash as youngsters."

"I can take very good care of myself, thank you. And you've known since I was a tot that I never do anything I don't want to do. I am no different when I'm with a man. Though I suppose I had better start paying more attention to my dates; all my school chums are thinking of me as a spinster."

"The right man will come along. I never did approve of girls marrying when they are scarcely into their teens." She remembered with horror that first night with Prince Ke Loo and how violently he'd taken her.

It started to rain just as they stepped into the portico where the hired car and chauffeur were waiting.

"Oh, dear," Caroline said, "I do hope the rain doesn't last through the evening. Eddie is taking me to a very fancy party. Royalty and all sorts of important people are going to be there. I don't want to arrive all damp and mildewed looking."

The rain lasted until early evening, stopping just before Caroline answered the telephone in their suite and was told that Mr. Wells was waiting in the lobby.

Caroline wore white satin, pearl eardrops, pearl necklace, and diamond and pearl pins scattered through her lovely new coiffeur. She looked ravishing. Eddie made a promise to himself that he was going to fuck her tonight. He'd waited long enough.

He gave the address of the house on Grosvenor Square and settled beside Caroline in the back of the limousine, taking her hand and pressing it to his lips. "You are the most stunning creature I have ever seen."

She saw the lust in his eyes and decided she'd best try and cool his ardor as quickly as possible. "I would wager anything that you've said those very same words to hundreds of women, including my mother," she added with a sweet, lilting laugh.

Unfortunately, hard as she tried during the entire evening, Eddie would not be discouraged. The party was glamorous beyond Caroline's dreams, with princes and princesses everywhere, dukes and earls and barons elbow to elbow. The house was a palace in comparison to the mansion she knew on Nob Hill. The entire Nightsong house, which she had always considered the last word in elegance, would easily have fit into the main ballroom with room to spare.

Much as she enjoyed the people, the music, the glitter, there was something stiff about it all. There was laughter, but not the hearty American kind—loud and a bit rough—to which she was accustomed. Everyone was overly polite, especially the men whom Caroline thought were almost effeminate in their speech and mannerisms.

Eddie knew everyone, of course. She danced until she thought she would drop. Her good spirits sagged, however, every time she looked at Eddie and saw the wanton lust in his eyes. She dreaded the party's ending. By the time it drew near, however, Eddie was drinking heavily. Perhaps he'd drink himself into a stupor. She prayed that he would.

He didn't. As the first guests began to leave Eddie found her on the terrace speaking with a young French viscount.

"Ah, there you are, Caroline."

"Edward. You know Viscount Chamberet?"

"Yes, in fact it was you I came to seek out, sir. Baron Fromme was asking about you. Something about you're going with him to the palace tomorrow."

"Oh yes, I'd forgotten," the Frenchman said. "We were to make arrangements before leaving this evening. Excuse me, Miss Caroline. I would much prefer your conversation, but the Baron is easily annoyed if he is inconvenienced in the slightest. You know how the Germans are."

She didn't, but she reluctantly let him take his leave, knowing she'd be left with Eddie. The time for all her strategies had come.

"Finally, I have you all to myself. You've been very popular this evening," Eddie said as he reached for her.

She let him embrace her, but when his mouth searched for hers she forced a laugh and playfully pushed him away. "I'm having much too good a time to be serious," she hedged.

He grabbed her arm and pulled her hard against him, smashing his mouth over hers. Caroline struggled as she felt his tongue trying to probe between her lips. She clenched her teeth and tried to pry herself loose. He was too strong and too determined to be denied. Caroline resorted to a defense she'd perfected over the years when in an impossible situation—she kicked him square on the shin.

Eddie yelped and Caroline pushed herself free. "You deserved that, Eddie. I do not appreciate your taking liberties."

"Liberties. Hell, Caroline, why have you been leading me on if you never—"

"Never what?" she snapped. "Never intended going to bed with you?"

"Precisely."

"When I go to bed with a man he'll be my husband."

"Oh, stop with the pure and innocent bit. You aren't a blushing sixteen anymore, Caroline. You are a very sophisticated woman. The delicate virgin role doesn't suit you."

"I find it very ungentlemanly of you to speak to me like that. If you feel I've led you on, I'm sorry. I have no intention of ever giving myself to you and never will. I thought we had fun together, nothing more."

"I can have fun at an arcade."

"Good night, Eddie. I'm leaving."

"Not without me you aren't. You came with me and I'd be humiliated if our host and hostess found you've rejected my escort home."

Caroline hesitated, thinking of the snobbish British protocol. "Very well. Let me get my wrap. We'll say our good-nights together, but please do not try pressuring me afterward."

He said nothing.

Caroline knew Eddie meant to have her before the night was over. Protocol or no, she went up the stairs to the powder room and retrieved her wrap from the maid in attendance, whom she asked, "Is there a side entrance by which I may leave? There's a rather persistent gentleman I'd prefer to avoid."

The maid looked surprised, but she remembered what the other servants said about the brash, outspoken Americans.

"This way, miss."

She showed Caroline to a private lift that deposited her in a wide hallway leading to the side portico. Once outside she had not the slightest notion of where she was or where to go. There were only the attendants at the main entrance of the house who would be in a position to help, but she couldn't chance meeting up with Eddie. He'd be furious by now and there would be no chance of her avoiding an ugly and eventually disastrous scene.

A long, curved walk took her to a grilled gateway. She swung it open on its well-oiled hinges and started away from the house, moving in the opposite direction of its lighted windows.

At the end of the gaslit street she came to a narrower street that wasn't very well lighted. She hurried along, her heart thumping nervously. Up ahead there was what looked to her to be a more brightly lighted street, which meant traffic and taxis and hackney cabs.

"'Ello, luv." A rough-looking type stepped from a dark doorway and reached for her.

Caroline gave a little cry and began running toward the lights up ahead.

When she reached the corner she stopped and leaned against the lamp post, catching her breath. After a moment she looked back along the dark street to make sure she wasn't being followed. Still looking back, scanning the dark, she unconsciously stepped off the curb.

Someone shouted and horses whinnied and reared as their driver reined them hard to prevent their trampling the girl in the white satin evening dress who'd so blindly walked out into the street.

Caroline screamed up at the slashing hooves of the two horses, throwing herself backward. She fell, cringing on the cobblestones as the horses were brought under control.

A young man in evening clothes jumped from the carriage and hurried toward her.

"Are you all right?"

"Yes," Caroline managed, her breathing labored.

"Here, let me help you up. You didn't break anything, did you?" he asked as she got carefully to her feet.

"I don't believe so. My dignity, perhaps," she said, trying to laugh.

"That's easily mended. But you really should be more careful before stepping into the street."

"Some strange man had approached me. I guess I was just overly anxious to get away from him."

"There are some undesirable types lurking about. What in the world were you doing out in the streets alone?"

"I'd been to Duke Edmond's gala. Were you there?"

The young man shook his head. "I'm afraid royalty and I are not on speaking terms for the moment."

Caroline suddenly winced when she took a step. "I'm afraid I did sprain something."

"Lean on me. I'll take you home." As he helped her toward the carriage he asked, "You're an American, aren't you?"

"Yes. I'm from California. San Francisco, to be exact."

"You were fortunate I wasn't driving my motorcar instead of the carriage."

"I suppose I am. The way the motorcars speed about these days I'm surprised no one has been run over by one by now."

As they settled themselves in the carriage the young man said, "I suppose we should introduce ourselves."

Caroline put out her hand in a typical American manner. "Andrieux. Caroline Andrieux."

"What a lovely name. French?"

"On my father's side."

"I'm Adam Clarendon." He took her hand and raised it to his lips. "Delighted to meet you, Miss Andrieux."

Their eyes were locked in mutual attraction. "Likewise, Mr. Clarendon.

Caroline suddenly felt at long last she'd met the man she wanted to marry.

# CHAPTER NINE

Lydia finished writing the cable and handed it to the desk clerk. "Would you have this sent off as soon as possible please?"

The clerk glanced at the cable. "But you forgot the name and address, madam."

"Oh, I am sorry. I was so concentrating on the message, I forgot. To Monsieur Raymond Andrieux," she dictated, spelling the last name. "Hotel Georges Cinq, Paris."

He stopped writing. "May I suggest, Mrs. Nightsong, that perhaps it would be more expeditious to telephone Paris. The service is quite excellent."

She did not want to speak with Raymond until absolutely necessary. "M. Andrieux—my husband," she explained, "is frequently not at the hotel. The cable is the best assurance I have that he'll learn of my arriving."

"I'll have it sent at once."

"You may put the charge on my account," Lydia said as she went toward the lift. She felt a quick, strong urge to turn back and destroy the cable but she steeled herself against it. The showdown with Raymond was inevitable. Much as she preferred staying in London with Peter, she had to be about her own affairs. The week she'd allowed herself before facing Raymond had helped put her thoughts into proper order. She had no idea what exactly she'd say to him, but it would be threatening. All she needed now was to think of some threat that would keep him in line and at the same time keep him reproducing the Nightsong perfume.

Paris. It had been a long time since she'd been to Paris. Except for the business with Raymond, she was looking forward to seeing the lovely City of Light, as everyone was now calling it. Idly, she wondered of a sudden if perhaps the cable had been too curt. She'd made the message brief. Maybe too brief, she thought, frowning.

\* \* \* \* \* \* \*

"Arriving Paris Tuesday next. Lydia," Raymond Andrieux read, and smiled. This time she hadn't recalled him home for the scolding; no, this time she was coming to him. Raymond put the cable down on the desk and went toward the windows. Below, the Avenue Georges Cinq was milling with early morning traffic. Taxis hooted, carriages clopped as they scurried along the cobblestoned street, the drivers shouting, waving their fists at everything that annoyed them. Raymond loved the sights and sounds of Paris. To him, no other city existed.

He heard Yvonne call to him from the next room. He caught his reflection in the mirror as he turned toward the bedroom door and paused, liking what he saw. He thought he looked the same as he had when Lydia had first seen him; certainly he did not look his fifty-nine years. His barber saw that his hair was kept the same black as it had been in his youth, adding a touch of gray at the temples to soften the faint lines of age in his face, which the most skillful of his cosmetic surgeons had said were impossible to erase. He'd watched his diet and had a daily massage to keep his waistline trim.

He straightened his cravat and smoothed the lapels of his dressing gown.

"My wife must be desperate," he said to the young girl sprawled naked on the bed, her hands behind her head, her thighs indecently parted, a cigarette dangling from between her painted lips.

Her black hair fell loose over her shoulders, accentuating the olive complexion. She wore a hard expression, yet there was something pathetic, pleading about the way she looked at Raymond—like the eyes of a hound that was used to being kicked and mistreated by its master.

Raymond did not particularly care for the girl's face, but the type of sex she offered him negated any thought of replacing her with another mistress.

"Your wife?" the girl asked. Her French had a hint of a southern drawl, though she told everyone she had been born and raised in Paris.

"Yes." Raymond took off his dressing gown and cravat. He stood naked beside the bed.

Yvonne stubbed out her cigarette and watched him.

He enjoyed the way she admired his body. An expression of total submission came into her eyes whenever she looked at his thick, long, heavily veined member. She was a slave to it. It was this that made Raymond's need for her so great—this and the fact that she was so very young, only eighteen and with the appetite and morals of a gutter rat.

She reached for him and began fondling him, feeling him grow in her hands, petting it as one would stroke a cat.

Raymond's eyes narrowed. He raised his hand and slapped her viciously across the face, sending her backward across the bed.

"When you want to touch me you will ask my permission," he snarled.

Yvonne rolled onto her stomach and crawled toward him, her blood racing, her sex suddenly wet. "I want you, please."

"No," he said, taunting her as he stood with his feet planted wide apart, his hands on his hips, his phallus jutting straight out in front of him.

Yvonne slid from the bed and knelt at his feet. She pressed her lips to his toes and began running her tongue into the crevices, working her way slowly upward.

As she licked and kissed his smooth muscled thighs Raymond thought again of Lydia's cable and he found himself going soft. Lydia had been the only woman he'd ever wanted and had never succeeded in having. He'd married her daughter only to hurt her. He'd blackmailed Lydia into becoming his wife after divorcing April. Still, Lydia eluded him. She gave her body, but never herself.

"Merde," he cursed as he shoved Yvonne's head away just as she took him into her mouth. He picked up his dressing gown and put it on.

"Please, Raymond," Yvonne whined. "I want you. I need you to hurt me."

"Get dressed and get out."

Her whining turned to anger. "Out? Out where? You told me this was my home now."

"Go shopping or something. I have thinking to do."

"About your wife?" the girl asked with a petulant curl of her mouth.

"Yes."

"You do not love her. She does not love you. You told me so many times."

"Be quiet," he barked. "Love has nothing to do with why she is coming to Paris."

"I will scratch out her eyes when I see her."

He glanced at the thin, frail little thing at his feet. "If she doesn't scratch yours out first," he said, wishing Lydia would do just that but knowing she never would. He hated her for that. He wanted her to want him. Instead, she felt nothing but indifference toward him, which was worse than feeling hated or loved.

Yvonne lit another cigarette and curled up on the bed. "Why is she coming to see you?"

"Business."

"This business. It is hers that you run?"

"A partnership arrangement."

"But you are spending more than a partner's share, no?"

Raymond grinned. "How sly you are, my pet. What would make you say that?"

She looked around the expensive bedroom. "You like to live very well. These rooms cost a small fortune, I know. The

Georges Cinq is not á bon marché. You spend all your days at the racing tracks and your nights in some casino or expensive night club. You are free with money and do little or nothing to earn it. I would not like you as a business partner," she said boldly, knowing by his eyes that she was making him angry.

"Do not be too observant, my little one. It is a costly mistake many women make."

Yvonne would not be put off. "I do not like this wife of yours."

"I don't much care for her myself," he lied.

"No. I think you do not care for her so far as the money and business are concerned. As a woman, 1 think you like her too much."

"You're wrong." He turned away.

"Well, if you do not like her, why do you stay married to her?"

"For business reasons, of course."

"But if you had your preference you would like to be rid of her." Her voice took on a soft purring tone.

Raymond shrugged. "I would like Empress Cosmetics to be mine to sell if I chose, yes. Unfortunately, it is not."

"Ah, mais mon cher, it could be."

He frowned. "What do you mean?"

Yvonne blew smoke through her nostrils and looked coy. "I know I tell everyone I am Parisian, no? You know I am not. In Tourmainne where I come from, the people are poor; there is much land but it is owned by a few rich families who control everything. When something or someone does not please the wealthy owners, they get rid of them."

Raymond's frown deepened. "What are you trying to say? How do the landowners get rid of them?"

Yvonne moved an indifferent shoulder. "They just get rid of them. Easy."

"My wife is not a woman so easily gotten rid of," he said, hoping Yvonne wasn't implying what he suspected. He knew the Tourmainne region and its reputation. It was what some called the Sicily of France and the landowners were the equivalent to the Italian Dons, ruthless and bloody.

"Everything is easy for the right price," she purred, again stomping out her cigarette and extending her arms to him.

He came into them, feeling that he was letting the gates of hell trap him.

"Kill her," Yvonne whispered against his ear. She felt him stiffen and start to draw away, but she held him tighter. "It can be easily arranged. I will do it only too gladly. You have but to ask me."

"You are speaking nonsense," he answered. Still, he did not move away. His heart was beginning to pound.

"Do you love her?"

He searched for an answer. "Yes," he admitted finally.

"Enough to have her control you for the rest of your life?"

"She doesn't control me. I do as I wish."

Yvonne laughed softly. "And that is why she comes to Paris? To let you do anything you wish? Oui?"

Raymond found his mind floundering from thought to thought, none of them in any way clear. How many times, he asked himself, had he wished Lydia dead? As much as he cared for her she was an annoyance—and she hated him, he knew. Life would be so much simpler without her harangues, her constant cutting of the purse strings.

Murder, a voice inside his head said. No, never. Besides, you aren't capable of it.

"You would never be suspected, even involved," Yvonne continued. "We would arrange a perfect alibi for you when it happens."

"We?"

"Friends," she said without elaborating.

"The idea is preposterous," he said. Again he made a move to turn away, but she pulled him back. She slipped her hand inside his dressing gown and began smoothing his hairy chest.

"I could arrange everything and then Yvonne would be yours forever afterward." Her hand moved downward.

"But—"

"Ssssh," she crooned, working loose the sash and slowly moving her fingers through the crisp thick pubic hairs at the base of his fast-hardening penis.

"How?" With that simple word he knew he'd showed his weakening. He was repulsed and intrigued at the same time. He also felt that his simple question had committed him.

"My brother made a rendezvous with his wife," she said, telling a story. "He did not keep the rendezvous. Everyone said it was unfortunate because if he had, the accident would not have happened."

"Accident?"

"His wife. She fell into a brook and drowned. They say her head struck a rock." She started to massage his cock, moving her hand slowly up and down the turgid, silky shaft.

"Drowned?" His breathing was faster.

"My brother's mistress, she was very sorry, but that did not keep them from marrying—after a respectful period of mourning, of course. His mistress was the daughter of the land-owner. My brother thought himself very lucky for so unfortunate an accident to have happened." Her words were like oil, her hands like flames.

"Never," Raymond said, trying not to feel the excitement that was rushing through him. The horror, the brutality of it excited him, however.

What sweet revenge he would have on April, whom he'd had to beat into submission, though she never submitted. What sweet revenge indeed on those who'd snubbed him, even on Lydia herself who treated him as an employee, a tool that she used to make her millions. It would be what they all deserved and he, as her husband, would wind up with everything. He'd see them all in the poorhouse—even his own children, who April and Lydia had turned against him.

"Your wife," Yvonne went on. "She has made you beg and crawl. Never would she grovel at your feet, begging to be kicked, spat upon, beaten. That is what you must have, my darling, and only by getting rid of her will you ever be completely free to have it with me."

Her hand was working faster on the shaft that pulsed and throbbed in her fist.

"God," Raymond gasped.

He felt the leaden feeling building up at the base of his pounding erection. He put his mouth over her nipple and sank his teeth into it.

"Hurt me," Yvonne begged as the pain shot through her. "Make me bleed."

He bit harder as she masturbated him faster and faster. The taste of her blood sent flashes of fire shooting through his entire body as he stiffened, shooting bolt after bolt of sticky semen from his engorged shaft.

Yvonne screamed in pain as Raymond's teeth bit deeper into her flesh. A torturous heat was burning her insides, scorching her flesh as wave after wave of rapturous convulsions threw her from spasm to spasm.

They sat, clasped together like jaws of a vise. The last jolting convulsions escaped him and Raymond began to relax. He exhaled a deep, contented sigh and fell back.

Neither spoke for a long time. The only sound was the tick, tick, tick of the ormolu clock on the mantel, then the striking of a match as Yvonne lit another cigarette. She held the cigarette between her teeth and searched in the drawer for a swatch of cotton, which she laid over the bleeding nipple.

As if in a dream Raymond asked, "How will you do it?"

"As my brother did," she answered quite matter-of-factly. "Late one afternoon you will ask your wife to meet you at the new restaurant on top of the Tour Eiffel. You will not show up for the rendezvous. She will wait and will receive your message that you have been detained on a business matter. You say you will call her later at her hotel. She will start to leave. I know a man who will push her from the tour and escape without being recognized, or even noticed. It will all seem accidental."

"The price for this man?"

"Not too much. It is his business. One thousand francs should be more than enough."

Raymond took the cigarette from between her lips and sucked on it. "And your price, Yvonne?"

She laughed. "Only marriage to you. After a respectful period of mourning, of course." Again she laughed and Raymond found himself laughing with her.

# CHAPTER TEN

In Peter MacNair's suite at the Claridge Hotel, London, Lydia howled with laughter when Peter pulled up his trousers and found he'd put them on backward. "You haven't been ill so long that you've forgotten how to dress yourself?" she chided.

"I'm just anxious to be about that business with the Clarendons and the Slykes. This damned bug that's been tying me down has put me way off schedule." He corrected the trousers. "I do appreciate your wet-nursing me, darling, and for the work you've done with the solicitors. You are coming with me to see the Clarendons this afternoon?"

She'd put off as long as possible having to tell him she was going to Paris. The time had come and she knew how disappointed he'd be. They'd worked well as a business team during the past few days. She had always put herself in the background, where she knew he wanted her to be.

"Sorry, Peter," she said trying to sound casual. "I'm afraid I'm off to Paris on my own affairs."

"Oh?" His disappointment made her glow with happiness.

"You can do very well without me hanging over your shoulder."

"I always have," he said petulantly, trying to hide his displeasure.

"Now don't be mean, darling." She took the tie he was trying to tie and made an expert knot. "I won't be away very long and you'll have Caroline for company."

"Caroline? She isn't going with you?"

"No, I'm leaving her here to make sure you don't get snatched up by some English beauty."

"I'm too old to need a watch dog and I rather like the idea of being ensnared by an English beauty."

"Well, it won't happen. Caroline has promised me she'd see that it didn't." Lydia went serious. "Actually, I'm a little mystified about Caroline."

"How so?" He inspected himself in the full-length mirror and what he saw pleased him. His color was back and his eyes were bright and shrewd and alive again.

"She's so secretive about where she goes and how she's been spending her time away from me. If I didn't know better I'd say she has a lover."

"Edward Wells?"

"No, Caroline told me about a rather unpleasant evening with Mr. Wells. He very definitely is off her list. She even refuses his telephone calls and never acknowledges his messages."

"So she met a young man." He gave her an admonishing look. "You should be pleased. Caroline is all grown up and overripe for a husband."

Lydia looked puzzled. "It isn't like her to keep a new beau a secret from me. She always tells me everything. These past several days, however, she has been as mute as a stone."

"Maybe she's gotten herself active in that Emancipation of Women movement that is so popular over here now. My Susan got all strange and secretive when she became involved with those suffragettes back home."

Lydia shook her head. "No, she'd tell me. It's a romance. I'm certain of that. I can tell by the way she's always so bubbly and constantly humming to herself."

"She'll tell you when the time comes." He turned around for inspection. "How do I look?"

He was wearing a dove gray suit with a pale blue shirt and printed waistcoat. The silk tie was a darker shade of blue than the shirt. The way he stood exaggerated the tight cut of the trousers, accentuating the length and shape of his manhood.

Lydia felt a pang of envy, knowing any sane woman would find it difficult not to be attracted to this handsome man. "Very dashing," she said, going to him and kissing his mouth. "I just want to warn you again that I expect you to behave."

He took her in his arms and kissed her deeply. "I adore you, Lydia."

"And I you." She eased out of his embrace when she noticed the time. "I must rush. I shouldn't be in Paris for more than a day or two. You will look after Caroline for me, won't you?"

"Of course. Don't worry about either of us. We'll be fine, darling."

Peter took up his walking stick and hat and they left the suite together. As Lydia stopped at the door to her suite the door opened and Caroline started out.

"So there you are," Caroline said. "I was just coming to look for you. You'd better hurry if you intend catching the steamer to Calais. Your train leaves in an hour."

"I'm all packed, except for a few things."

"I was wondering, Mr. MacNair, if you'd mind terribly if I accompanied you this afternoon."

He and Lydia exchanged looks.

"Of course not," Peter said, "but I can't for the life of me see why you'd be interested in sitting in on a business meeting about bottles and flasks." He eyed her suspiciously. "Or is this part of your promise to your grandmother to keep an eye on me?"

"No. I've heard both the Slykes and Clarendons glassworks are in Darthshire. They say the landscape is extremely lovely and it's a delightful day for a drive in the countryside."

"Slykes and Clarendons?" Lydia asked, arching an eyebrow. "When have you taken an interest in the manufacturing of glass?"

"I haven't," Caroline said. She knew she was blushing, but couldn't stop. "I just overheard you two mentioning the names at dinner the other evening and happened to notice them on a tour map I'd been poring over." She hated the lie and wondered if it showed in her face.

"I have no objections whatsoever," Peter said. He gave Lydia another baffled look.

"I'm off to Paris," Lydia announced. "You two are on your own." Lydia openly kissed Peter on the mouth. "Good-bye, darling. I'll be back as soon as I can." She kissed Caroline on both cheeks. "You take care of him, dear. He thinks he's as strong as an ox, but then all men think only we women get sick."

"I'll see to it that he doesn't overextend himself, Grandmother."

After Lydia went into her suite, Peter offered Caroline his arm. "You may be fooling your grandmother, young lady, but I have the feeling there is more to your sudden interest in glass-works than you're letting on."

Caroline smiled coyly. "If there is, Mr. MacNair, I'm not telling."

They waited for the lift.

"Your grandmother is a little concerned about you these past few days."

"Me?"

He studied her. "I can see why. There is something rather impish about you, like you know some wonderful secret you're dying to tell, but are a bit leery about how it will be received."

The lift arrived, giving Caroline the chance she needed to wrestle with the urge to talk to someone about the wonderful younger man she'd been with several times. Knowing Adam was younger than she, Caroline wasn't all that certain anyone—especially her grandmother—would approve. A man might, she decided, as the lift operator pulled open the grilled doors. On an impulse she decided to take a chance with Peter, though she knew well his views on the woman's place in life.

"You don't approve of voting rights for women, do you Mr. MacNair?" she asked when they were in the hired car outside.

"Some women should have it; most should not, simply because they aren't as interested in politics as men are and, therefore, are less informed."

It was a useless track and Caroline abandoned it now that she'd used it as a springboard to what she really wanted to talk about. "Women then, in your opinion, should content themselves with being wives and mothers."

"The majority, yes. There are a few who have special talents in the arts and sciences, but if you will notice, even these few eventually graduate to their born roles as wives and mothers."

Caroline sat for a moment, carefully arranging her next question. "Why do men usually marry women younger than themselves?"

"Because a man must earn a livelihood good enough to support himself and a family, which takes time. So when he's reached that stage he usually wants a younger woman whom he is sure will be able to give him a large family. With an older woman, a woman his own age, childbearing is often limited."

"Suppose the woman is financially secure and more than capable of contributing to the expense of running a household and helping provide for a family?"

Peter recalled his own youth and his marriage to Lorna, a woman almost his own age whom he'd married because his ambition needed her money.

"Just what are you getting at, Caroline?"

"I was just wondering why it is socially acceptable for a man to marry a woman younger than he, but not for a woman to marry a man younger than she."

A smile played at the corners of his mouth. "And just how much younger is this man who's captured your heart?"

Her face burned. "My question was purely hypothetical, Mr. MacNair."

"Stuff and nonsense. Who is he? Lydia is certain you've been seeing someone and she knows it isn't Mr. Wells. Come on, Caroline. You can confide in me. If you don't want your grandmother to know, cross my heart I won't breathe a word." He made an X across where his heart was.

She sat for a minute, deliberating. Finally, she said, "He isn't all that much younger than me, only a year and a half, perhaps. Maybe two years," she said offhandedly, and quickly added, "But he looks much older."

"And if I may make a wager, I'd venture that his name is either Slyke or Clarendon."

She hadn't meant to tell, but her heart was bursting with pride. "Clarendon," she said as if it were the most beautiful name in the world. "He'll be a Lord one day."

"And you think you would like to be a Lady?"

She fidgeted again, feeling the color rise in her cheeks. "Oh, we don't know each other all that well. We've only seen one another a few times." She leaned her head back against the seat. "He is so handsome," she sighed.

Caroline glanced at Peter. "He reminds me a lot of you in a way. In fact, he even resembles you, now that I notice." Her eyes moved away. "But then perhaps I'm only imagining that because I so approve of you and grandmother. You are so beautiful together."

Peter felt uncomfortable. "You are far too worldly for your own good, young lady." He glanced at his watch, wanting to change the subject away from an open discussion of his scandalous affair with Lydia, a subject that he felt was improper to discuss with his lover's granddaughter. "Your grandmother should be leaving the hotel by now if she intends making her train."

"Grandmother is always well organized. She'll make her connection."

Lydia almost did not make her connection. The car wasn't waiting out front when she came out of the hotel and the train was just getting ready to leave Victoria Station when she arrived. She boarded with only seconds to spare.

She still hadn't decided precisely what she planned on saying to Raymond. Even by the time they reached the French coast and she was on the train connecting Calais to Paris, she still had no clear-cut speech prepared. Somehow she had to make him realize his own folly. Without the continued success of Empress Cosmetics they were both doomed.

Surely he knew that, she told herself as the train pulled into the station. He was a cruel, selfish man, but certainly not a stupid one. He'd be obstinate and rude; she expected that. Regardless, she would make threats and try to make him see reason somehow.

It surprised her, however, when she called Raymond from her hotel to find him sounding genuinely pleased to hear her voice.

"Darling," he boomed. "When did you get in?"

"Half an hour ago. I must be back as soon as possible, Raymond. I'd like to leave tomorrow if it can be arranged. We—"

"Nonsense," he said, ignoring her coldness. "It's been ages, Lydia, since you and I have been together in Paris. I won't hear of your running back so soon."

It had been a long time. Almost twenty years. When April abandoned them all and fled to China, Lydia remembered how vulnerable she'd been, how she thought then that Raymond was her only solace. How very wrong she'd been.

"No, Raymond. I really must—"

"I said I will not hear of it." He paused. "You must be exhausted after the trip over, darling. Why not get yourself settled in and have a nice hot bath. Unfortunately, I was just on my way out to a dinner engagement. A business appointment I cannot get out of. Have a quiet dinner in your suite. I'll telephone you first thing in the morning. You'll be rested and I'll show you Paris again. It's more beautiful than you remember it."

She was tired, too tired to argue and not too anxious yet to have their confrontation. "Very well, Raymond. Until tomorrow then."

Lydia knew he was more than likely going to dinner with another woman. She didn't care. Actually, she was just as pleased. She took his advice and had her bath and a quiet, excellent meal, then retired early. It astonished her somewhat to find that she felt herself falling asleep so quickly.

The jangle of the telephone roused her from a sound sleep.

"I woke you," Raymond said.

"As a matter of fact you did. What time is it?"

"Ten o'clock. Time for you to put on something ravishing and meet me for lunch. I'd call for you, darling, but I'm all tied up with appointments until twelve-thirty." He didn't give her the opportunity to answer. "There is a marvelous new restaurant on the top of the Eiffel Tower. I'll meet you there as close to twelve-thirty as I can." His voice turned syrupy. "I can't wait to see you, love. Too bad it has to be somewhere so public, but then we can rectify that afterward."

"Raymond, really. I did not come to Paris—"

"I can't talk, darling. A business client just walked in. See you at twelve-thirty." He rang off.

Lydia sat holding the dead receiver. She stared at it for a moment and slammed it down. She didn't want a charming lunch and to have to listen to his glib talk. She came to have it out with him and she wanted it done and over with in the privacy of his office.

She took up the receiver and with some difficulty with the French-speaking operator, placed a call to Raymond's office at Empress Cosmetics.

Lydia ignored the secretary's questions when she asked, "Who is this calling, please?" in fractured English.

"I must speak with Monsieur Andrieux immediately."

"He is not here, madame. He has not been in today and is not expected. He is in Lyon on business."

Lydia broke the connection. She thought for a moment and again picked up the receiver. If she could not have her face-to-face with Raymond at his office she'd have it at his home. He most definitely was not in Lyon, she knew. She placed a call to Raymond at his suite at the Georges Cinq.

When Yvonne answered, Lydia slammed the receiver into its cradle and muttered an angry curse. As usual, things were to be as Raymond wanted them. He'd carefully seen to that.

With a sigh of resignation she slipped out of bed and started to ready herself for her luncheon date with Raymond on top of the Eiffel Tower.

She decided to stroll for a while, noticing that she was early leaving her hotel. It was too bad, she told herself, that her visit was being spoiled. Paris was more enchantingly beautiful than she remembered. Everyone was so bright and gay—even the noise was more music than dissonance. The smell of pine and wild flowers drifted across from the Bois de Boulogne. Bright posters were plastered on the quaint kiosks, luring customers to every imaginable kind of entertainment.

She walked a good distance, never tiring, and was surprised when she found herself at the Place de la Concorde with its terraces and fountains. Directly ahead rose the impressive Tour Eiffel, which public outrage had almost dismantled rivet by rivet.

Having started out early, Lydia arrived, however, at the tower entrance ten minutes late. The changing of elevators between the various levels made her twenty-five minutes late by the time she reached the restaurant. Tourists crowded every observation platform. She was not pleased when she noticed how crowded the restaurant was.

She gave Raymond's name to the maître d' and was more displeased when he said, "I am sorry, madame. There is no reservation for Monsieur Andrieux."

She fumed at his forgetfulness—or was he simply being his usual rude self?

"There is a small waiting pavilion just over there, Madame, if you'd care to wait. I will hold for you the next table that becomes available."

She thanked him and moved to the area he indicated, a spartan little platform, obviously an area to which the decorators had decided to give their final attention. A few couples walked about carrying their aperitifs or demitasse. Lydia felt the sway of the tower as a wind came up, but she'd been here before on that night so many years ago when she and Peter had stood almost on this very spot and toasted Paris, toasted this impressive tower and flung their champagne glasses over the railing into the velvet night. The restaurant had only been a makeshift bar then, set up for the opening ceremonies of the Exposition.

But, she noticed, what with all their improvements, nothing had been done to replace the low, rather useless looking guard rail that ran around the rim of the level. She remembered her quarrel with Peter that night, and the memory faded.

A page called her name several times before she realized that she was Madame Andrieux. He handed her a note on a silver salver. She gave him a gratuity and read, "Sorry, darling, held up on business. I'll phone you at your hotel. Forgive me. Raymond."

She crumpled the note, not seeing the man in the broad-rimmed hat and smock who was fumbling with setting up his easel and canvas quite nearby. Her anger seethed, slowly building to rage. With a furious swat at her skirts she turned and started back toward the lifts.

There was a crush of people waiting to descend. Lydia's exasperation grew as she tried to decide whether to wait for a table or join the queue. The maître d' hurried up just then, and decided for her.

"I will have a table for you, madame, if you can be patient for one moment longer. Le garçon is clearing it for you now."

"Very well," she said begrudgingly and walked, without purpose, back to the rail where she stood staring out at the loveliness of Paris, far, far below.

She noticed that the artist wasn't at his easel. Lydia's sidelong glance took in the unattended easel and she wondered what style of art he'd chosen for his eagle's nest view of the city.

She moved sidewards toward the easel and sensed rather than saw the man rush toward her. She screamed. The man charged at her but her move to the side had spoiled his aim. He hit her shoulder, knocking her to the floor but his momentum sent him into the railing and toppling, head over feet, over it. He screamed in anguish as he fell.

People pressed forward to watch the screaming man fall to his death. Lydia lay as if paralyzed, nearly fainting. Slowly, but with some difficulty, she recognized the maître d'. His imperious expression had been replaced with one of sheer horror.

A young antiseptic-smelling man waved essence of ammonia under her nose, causing her to cough and sit up, pushing away the vial.

"You should rest a while, madame," the young man said as he put a cap on the vial and replaced it in his medical bag.

"No, I'm all right," Lydia put her hands over her ears and tried to shut out the lingering echoes of the man's screaming.

"I saw," the maître d' gasped, his face a mask of white. "The man. He intended to push you over. I saw it all."

Lydia looked at him sharply, remembering everything that had happened. He was right. It was her body that was meant to be lying on the concrete below.

Shakily, she got to her feet, fighting back the dizziness. Raymond had meant to kill her! The horror of it was almost incomprehensible. Surely his thirst for money wasn't so great that he'd kill for it?

"Madame," the young doctor said. "Please rest for a while. You have had a terrible shock."

"No," Lydia said, determined. She took a few steps. *Raymond wanted her dead.*

She began to teeter as the blackness closed in on her again.

# PART TWO

# CHAPTER ELEVEN

Susan MacNair had changed little since leaving San Francisco to marry Sean Dillon; but San Francisco, she noticed, had vastly changed. Susan was still a slim, tailored beauty despite having borne three children, all of them herded about her as she went up the steps to her parents' new Nob Hill townhouse. Even when she was a child herself she'd resembled her father in looks, with brownish-red hair, thick and unruly; green shining eyes; and the silken smooth skin of a Scottish lass. At thirty-eight she'd become his mirror image in woman-form.

Lorrie, her oldest child and only daughter, took after her grandmother—dark hair, haughty brows, and eyes as sharp as razors. She was a beautiful girl of twelve, with the regal carriage of a princess. David was nine. Peter was seven. No one could mistake them for anything but brothers. Though named for their mother's relations, they had the same coloration and expression as Sean Dillon, their Irish father—both with thick black hair, blue eyes, and indecently handsome faces.

Marriage hadn't changed Susan's ways. She was as strict and as staunch a supporter of women's right to the vote as ever. Sean, her husband, had helped the suffragettes' cause, which is where she met and fell in love with him. They were raising their children to be like themselves, fair and equal and independent freethinkers. It was too early to tell how the boys would turn out; Lorrie, so far, was a failure. Like her grandmother, the girl had no interest in anything except social position. Even at twelve she was already a bit of a snob. Her brothers were like their father, rough and tumble types.

It was so like mother not to greet them at the door, Susan thought as the maid answered their ring and told them that Madame would "receive" them in the drawing room. Susan made a face, drawing her lips into tight lines.

"Ah, there you are, my dears," Lorna said as she put out her arms and remained seated in the high winged-back chair.

"Hello, Mother." The boys held tight to Susan's skirts, awed by the stern, imposing grandmother who could produce thunderbolts in a mere glance.

Lorrie went to Lorna and curtsied, then kissed her grandmother's cheek.

"Darling," Lorna said giving the girl a smile and a hug. "You have been away far too long."

The boys continued to huddle around Susan as she went to kiss the cheek her mother offered her.

"Peter, David," Lorna said putting her hand on top of their heads.

"He's Peter, I'm David," the oldest boy corrected. He reached up and smoothed his hair, though it hadn't been rumpled.

"Well," Lorna said, "I presume you had a pleasant journey? How long can you stay?"

"A few weeks," Susan answered. "The children must be back in time for school."

"You've enrolled them in a public school, if I recall," Lorna said, showing her displeasure by the tone of her voice.

"Yes. Sean and I thought it best they learn to cope with all classes. They seem to like it."

"I don't," Lorrie put in. To her grandmother she said, "It's very common, Grandmother. I really hate it."

Susan frowned at her. "You don't hate it, Lorrie. You just don't get your own way at times."

Lorna looked horrified. "Susan. If the child is unhappy she will never learn. There is much to be said for private tutoring. If it's a matter of money...."

"It isn't money, Mother. Sean and I are quite capable of

handling just about any expense."

"What then? The girl should be in a private school."

"No." She was adamant.

"Perhaps if Sean objects, Lorrie could come here and stay with me and attend my old alma mater."

"Oh, could I?" Lorrie whined.

"No," Susan said flatly. "And it isn't only that Sean objects to private schools—I object as well." She gave her mother a frosty look. "And I will not have you encouraging the child, Mother."

"I am not a child," Lorrie insisted.

"You behave like one," Susan reminded her.

The maid come to the door of the drawing room and announced tea.

"Tea?" David said, crinkling his nose.

Susan laughed. "Go and give your grandmother a hug, you two." Reluctantly they did, but held themselves as stiff as possible, ready to bolt away at the first sign of a threat. "We aren't very formal at home, I'm afraid," Susan said as the boys came back and stood beside her. "Sean—"

"Sean," Lorna said staying her with a move of her hand, "was not my choice of a husband for you."

"Nor would you be a choice of wife for him," Susan said defiantly.

There was a heavy silence as the two women glared at each other.

Of a sudden Lorna sagged, letting her eyes close and heaving a heavy sigh. "We mustn't be cruel, Susan. I realize you have always been your own woman."

"As you have been yours."

"True," Lorna admitted, but unwillingly. She put on a more agreeable face and got out of her chair. To the boys she said, "You'll enjoy tea; it's milk and sandwiches and cakes and cookies. I had cook make lovely things for you to eat. It isn't a bit formal and stuffy as your mother makes it out to be." She took Lorrie's hand. "Take off your wraps. Hannah will see to them. You must all be famished. First we'll fill your stomachs and then you can all have a nice rest."

To Susan she said, "This isn't the same house you grew up in, dear, but after the earthquake there was nothing left that could be salvaged. However, I've had the house laid out very much as before, so your room is overlooking the side terrace again. I've put the boys where David's old room used to be. And as for you, young lady," she said to Lorrie, "I've had a lovely new room made up just for you. It is right next to mine. Pink is still your favorite color, isn't it? I hope it is."

"Oh, yes," Lorrie beamed.

"When last I saw you," she said to the boys, "you were just tiny little things. My, how you've both grown. You are practically little men."

She settled them around the table. "Peter and David," Lorna said, nodding to them in turn. "See, I've gotten you all straightened out now." She made a helpless gesture. "You must forgive your old grandmother. It has been a while since I've seen you last."

"Petie," David corrected, still a little wary of the old woman. "He likes to be called 'Petie.'"

Petie bobbed his head, smiling admiringly at the courage of his older brother.

"Then Petie it shall be," Lorna said, trying to win the boy's good graces.

Tea was what their grandmother had promised, but it was still too stiff what with all the heavy silver and the fragile china and glassware. The boys were only too glad when it was over and they could escape their sister's constantly correcting them on their manners and posture and their grandmother's scrutiny.

"How's Father?" Susan asked when the children were excused and she and Lorna lingered over their teacups. "Have you heard from him yet?"

Lorna shook her head. "You know your father was never one for letter writing. As in so many other ways, you take after him on that score." She sipped her tea, refusing to acknowledge her daughter's scowl. "I suppose he's the same as when you saw him in New York." She looked over the rim of her cup. "You did see him in New York?"

"Yes, of course. He had a rather nasty cold. I wasn't all that keen on his going on the ocean voyage, but neither Sean nor I could talk him out of it."

"No one could talk him out of going anywhere whenever that Nightsong woman is involved."

"Mother," Susan admonished.

"Oh, I'm very well aware that Lydia Nightsong sailed on the same steamer."

"Still checking up on him, I see."

"Someone must. No one tells me anything. I wouldn't be the least surprised if you and Sean didn't entertain that woman while she was in New York."

"We didn't," Susan said, "But only because I wasn't aware that Mrs. Nightsong was there. Honestly, Mother, I do wish you would get rid of this hateful resentment you have against Lydia."

"If Lydia, as you so familiarly call her, were constantly trying to steal your husband and destroy your family, you'd resent her also, I'm sure."

Susan's laugh infuriated her. "If father had wanted Lydia Nightsong I'm certain he would have had her, knowing him." She poured herself another cup of tea. "I know all the gossip, Mother, and I also know Lydia Nightsong. She's a very charming woman."

"She's a viper and I absolutely forbid you to take her part over mine."

"I am not taking her part, Mother. I just happen to like the woman."

She thought back on how Lydia had come to the rescue when Peter disappeared, how Lydia had prevented him from becoming a derelict, how Lydia had consoled and advised Susan when Susan wanted to break with her own family.

She glanced at her mother. If only she knew how responsible Lydia Nightsong had been for keeping the MacNair family together. Susan had admired Mrs. Nightsong from that first frantic meeting; she also remembered, a little shamefacedly, how she used to follow Leon Nightsong about, how her heart gave little tugs whenever she saw him, how envious she'd been of Leon and her brother's friendship.

"How is Efrem?" Susan asked, pushing away her memories.

"No better, no worse," Lorna said with a sigh. "I'm afraid he's locked himself into his own private world. He won't let anyone near him. Oh, he eats his meals with us and says good morning and good night and goes to your father's factory every day like clockwork, but he is completely empty inside. I've tried reasoning with him, cajoling him. Nothing works. He is a complete stranger to me now." She felt the tears building up and could do nothing to stop them. She hastily groped in her sleeve for her handkerchief. "His whole life seems centered on whiskey bottles. The more I find and smash, the more appear as if he were manufacturing it in his room." She dabbed away the tears. "Then there is the business with him and Mr. Ramsey."

"Mr. Ramsey?"

"You remember," Lorna said, slightly uncomfortably. "He is that detective I retained, the one who got the proof that April Nightsong's son is my grandchild."

"What does he have to do with Efrem?"

"That's just it, dear. I have no idea, but they know each other." She told her about Efrem finding Ramsey and her together in the library. "Mr. Ramsey was here to give a current report on his search for little Adam and when Efrem saw him he acted as though he were seeing a ghost. He went stark white and later when I confronted him Efrem went into a complete collapse. He looked as if he wanted to kill himself."

"Oh, dear," Susan gasped as she put her cup in its saucer.

"I've hired someone to see if they can find a connection between Efrem and Mr. Ramsey, but no one has come up with anything whatsoever."

Susan said, with a try at levity, "If it weren't for you, Mother, the San Francisco detective agencies would be out of business."

"This is a serious matter, Susan," Lorna fumed.

"Yes, yes, of course. I know it is, darling," Susan said, patting her mother's hand. "I'll talk to Efrem. He used to confide in me."

"He won't now."

"Anyway, I'll try."

Susan was aghast at the way her brother looked when he came home late that afternoon. He was gaunt and pale and pounds lighter. Efrem greeted her cordially enough and seemed genuinely glad to see her, but he excused himself almost immediately and went up to his room.

It was Susan who volunteered to go up and fetch Efrem for dinner half an hour before it was to be served. She found him asleep, fully dressed as he had been earlier, with a half empty bottle of scotch on the floor beside the bed.

Tenderly, she laid her hand on his shoulder and shook him gently. "Dinner, Ef," she said softly.

He opened his eyes briefly and closed them again. "I'm not particularly hungry," he answered, and rolled away from her.

She smelled the liquor on his breath. "Mind if I have a drink? I know Mother thinks it very scandalous for ladies to drink hard liquor, but it's becoming very popular in New York."

"She doesn't approve of anything," Efrem mumbled.

"Want one?" Susan asked as she went into his private bath and got a water glass. When she returned he had propped himself against the headboard and was rubbing the sleep out of his eyes.

"Hard day?" she asked, pouring some scotch into her glass.

"Not any different from all the others." He took the bottle from her hand and took a swig.

"You look terrible; you know that, don't you?"

"Who cares?"

"I do."

"I don't."

"Why?"

He looked flustered for a moment but a moment later his expression was frightened and defensive. "That's none of anyone's business."

"I think I know."

He had the bottle halfway to his lips. His hand stayed and he narrowed his eyes. "What do you mean?"

Susan sipped the scotch and felt it burning its way down her throat. It was strong. Her eyes began to water. She made an excuse to turn away by pretending her shoe felt uncomfortable and kicked both off, then sat on the bed beside her brother.

His eyes were wide. "Did Mother's bloodhounds tell her anything? Oh, I know she's having me watched. I'm not blind."

"No, Mother knows nothing and suspects nothing."

He eyed her warily. "And I suppose you do?"

"I think so." She sipped her scotch. This time it felt only warm and less biting. Susan leveled her eyes on Efrem and said, quite casually, "He's married, you know."

He stared at her for a moment, then hid his fears by raising the bottle to his lips. "I don't know what you're talking about. Who's married?"

"Leon Nightsong."

Efrem choked on the liquor and sloshed some down the front of his shirt. His face was a picture of utter terror. "What—?"

She silenced him brusquely. "I've known about your friendship with Leon for some time. I also knew it was more than friendship, at least on your part."

"Shut up! Get out of here and leave me alone."

"Darling," she said gently. "I have always been a very freespirited woman. I'm going to tell you something no one else knows. I suppose it was the crowd I hung about with in New York that taught me the more sordid aspects of life, but regardless of what you may think, there isn't anything wrong with loving another person regardless of who it is."

When she went to touch him he cringed away.

Susan decided on a tactic she thought might work. She would create a kindred spirit with whom Efrem might confide. She'd make up something that might win his trust. She'd lie.

"When I was in my teens you remember the ruckus father made when I got involved with Susan Anthony and her followers? Well, I would have done anything for her then. Anything," she emphasized. "I had the good fortune of meeting Sean Dillon and I grew out of my girlhood crush. Unfortunately, you haven't yet been as fortunate."

"Good God," Efrem stormed. "What in the devil are you trying to say?"

She soothed him with a look. "I know, because I was there, Efrem."

His fears grew. "There? Where?"

"I'd been curious about Leon when you first introduced us. Remember? We all happened to be at the restaurant down at the wharf. You were with Ellen Stanton and Leon was with her sister, Alice."

"So?" His face was whiter.

"It didn't take a genius to see the way you looked up to him, the way you leaned on his every word."

"You're talking rot." He tried to quiet a sudden trembling that was spreading through him.

"You know I've been a friend of Mrs. Nightsong's. Through her I've written to Leon from time to time and he's written back." She noticed his terror. "You were never mentioned in our letters, other than in passing. He is very happily married, but he hates Hawaii. He only stays because of his father, he told me."

Efrem drank from the bottle, hiding the way his hands were shaking.

"I don't think Leon went to Hawaii because of his father, Efrem. I think he went because of you."

"I said to shut up!" He raised his hand as if he meant to strike her.

Susan didn't flinch. "I was in the front sitting room the night before Leon left San Francisco. I saw him bring you home drunk. I also saw what happened." She couldn't bring herself to tell him she'd seen him kiss Leon's mouth or the way Leon had so forcefully shoved him away.

Efrem became unglued. The tears poured from his eyes. "Will you get the hell out of my room and out of my life," he sobbed, turning away from her.

"Is that what this Mr. Ramsey knows?"

"Get out!" This time he struck her across the face. "Get out and leave me alone, goddamn it." He curled himself into the pillows and started to cry.

Susan put her hand on the sting of her cheek. She calmly put her glass on the night stand and stood up. She slipped her feet into her shoes and stood for a moment looking down at her brother.

At the door she paused. "I'll tell Mother you won't be down for dinner. I'll see that Hannah brings you a tray. But please, Efrem, let me help."

"Go away!" He threw himself up and flung the whiskey bottle, smashing it against the door as Susan ducked out.

Her mother met her on the stairs. "What's going on?"

"I'm afraid I've upset him," Susan said. "He's a very disturbed man."

"But why? That's what I've tried so hard to find out."

"I don't know," Susan hedged. She knew for certain she was on the right track. Efrem had reacted too violently, as one does when a nerve is hit. It was the matter of this detective, this Mr. Ramsey, that she did not understand. Where did he fit into Efrem's problem?

Blackmail? Perhaps, but if money were involved surely that would have been discovered by a simple check of Efrem's finances and her parents would have known—especially her father, who had confidants everywhere.

Susan decided that despite her mother's probing, she would check out this Ramsey on her own. She suddenly wished that Leon Nightsong were here to help.

Or would he make matters more complicated, she wondered.

# CHAPTER TWELVE

Leon lazed in the shade of a breadfruit tree, trying to delay for as long as possible his scheduled meeting with his father and his cousin, Wu Lien. Overhead some multicolored, adventurous birds pecked at the breadfruit on the crown of the tree. There was the smell of a squall in the air and not far away he heard the agitated waves of the ocean. On the lanai the children were listening to Leon's wife telling an age-old story of how the God Ora had forged the islands of Havaiki from lightning bolts.

There was a softness all around him, a melding of color and an aroma so delicious it captured his brain, intoxicating him into a calm he never thought possible.

The swing of the hammock gradually stopped as Leon's real desires moved foremost in his mind. Hawaii reminded him too much of his youth in China, years he had then thought beautiful but now knew for their true cruelty. He wanted, of a sudden, to go back to the fast, glaring sights and sounds of San Francisco, knowing that serene beauty was nothing but a veil that hid evil. Only his sister, Mei Fei, and his little family made Hawaii bearable for him.

He loved the bustle of San Francisco, that magnificent city that sat like a rock beside the bay. When he'd heard news of the earthquake years earlier he paid it little mind. He had no idea of the extent of the quake's damage. Tremors were common enough to Hawaii, small quakes that shook people from their drowsy life and frightened them only for a moment.

It had been only after a long time, when he'd received his

mother's letter, that he'd learned of the terrible damage left by the earthquake. But they had all escaped injury, Lydia had written, which meant Leon hadn't needed to rush across the seas.

Idly, he wondered if Efrem were safe as well. He would have heard if anything had happened to him. "Efrem."

The children's shrieks made him look toward the house, breaking off the painful reminders that were beginning to grow inside his head.

"Ohlan," he called. "Stop frightening the children with those demon stories."

She gave him a petulant look. "They should learn the island's history."

"You give them nightmares with stories about bloodthirsty gods. Besides, the islands' history should not concern them. They are not Hawaiian, they are Chinese," he reminded her.

He loved Ohlan, though he wished he could make her forget she'd been tutored by the Polynesians as a child and be more aware of the modern ways in which they lived now. Progress didn't lay in the hands of old legends, and since the United States had annexed Hawaii, progress was everything, except to Ohlan. She chose to cling to the old.

"Your father, Prince Ke Loo, is awaiting you," Ohlan said.

"Yes, I'm going." He swung his feet to the ground, girded his lavalava tighter about his waist, and started toward his father's house, the largest in the compound.

Ke Loo paced impatiently on the veranda. Leon's cousin, Wu Lien, lounged in a chaise, chewing on a slice of coconut. When Prince Ke Loo saw Leon he stopped and put his hands on his wide hips. "You have kept us waiting."

"Excuse me, Father, I'd forgotten the time."

"You have been forgetful of everything lately."

"My mind is elsewhere."

"I hope not with that abominable mother you seem to miss so much."

"Yes," Leon admitted. "I only wait for the time when all is

done here and I am able to go back to San Francisco."

"You will never go back. I have told you your place is beside me as Royal Prince of all China."

Leon caught Wu Lien's contemptuous glance. "My cousin, Wu Lien, would occupy that place far more comfortably than I."

"You are my son, not Wu Lien," Ke Loo reminded him, but he smiled at Wu Lien. "You, Wu Lien, will have everything I have promised: Power, money, comfort beyond any you have dreamed of."

"If I am to have it, then we should be about getting it," Wu Lien said.

Ke Loo settled his great bulk into the rattan peacock chair with much effort. "The time is now," he said gravely. "You both will return to China. All is ready for Dr. Sun Yat-sen to be punished for betraying me. He still believes us loyal to him, but is not aware that I've been told of his deceit. You will kill him. That is your first duty, so paving the way for me to ascend the throne. The child emperor will prove no hindrance, I'm assured."

"Both of us?" Leon asked, his heart sinking.

"Of course. If you are to be a future emperor, you must earn the privilege. You will go with Wu Lien."

"But—"

Wu Lien sneered. "Afraid, cousin? Perhaps I should take your sister, Mei Fei, instead."

"Stay away from Mei Fei, Wu Lien. You have caused trouble enough there. And as for me, I have never known fear," Leon said. But he did not want to go back to China. It was only that much farther away from his mother and America.

Rather than argue, however, Leon decided upon a reasonable excuse. "If I do return with Wu Lien and we are not successful, you will have no heir. You should not take the chance of sacrificing both of your line."

Ke Loo thought for a moment. "There is something in what you say, but I do not expect you will fail." He made a temple with his fingers and propped his ample chin on it. "Still...."

Wu Lien was quick to see a chance to place himself in greater favor. He knew Ke Loo. Much as he put importance on bloodline, he'd always distrusted his son. Leon had abandoned him once before; he could do so again.

Wu Lien threw away the uneaten coconut and picked his teeth. "I can do what must be done alone. Besides, our forces in China know me. They may not trust your son. They, too, remember," he said slyly.

Ke Loo silenced him with a look. He thought a moment longer. "You are right, of course, Wu Lien. You will go and muster our forces and dispose of that republic-making traitor." He clapped his hands for a servant. "It is settled. A steamer will be here tomorrow night. It will anchor beyond the reef. At midnight it will sail. You will be ready, Wu Lien."

"Yes, Prince Ke Loo." Still smirking at Leon, Wu Lien got up from the chaise and went into the house. He asked that rice wine be brought to his rooms where he threw off his clothes and lay naked on the bed. He would be glad to be back in China. The singsong girls of Hong Kong would be a welcome change to the dreary, brown-skinned girls he'd had to use for his pleasures here.

"Mei Fei," he murmured as he ran his hands over his smooth, muscled body. He felt his penis begin to lengthen as the want for her stirred his loins. When the servant brought the wine he did not bother to hide his erection. He was tempted to grab the Hawaiian girl, but instead his mind suddenly grasped onto another idea that excited him more. The idea so intrigued him that he started to laugh. It would all be so simple and he'd have the leverage he needed over both Ke Loo and his weakling son.

Wu Lien put his idea into motion the following night. Ke Loo had arranged a small feast to celebrate the success of Wu Lien's venture. Wu Lien did not take part in the arranged orgy that followed the feast. Instead—and to Ke Loo's astonishment— Wu Lien retired to his rooms and stayed there until he knew the prince and his whores were asleep.

Carefully he made his way out of the compound and went

toward the lagoon. The steamer was anchored beyond the reef as scheduled and there was a longboat and oarsmen waiting for him on the beach. When the steersman saw Wu Lien approach alone he said, "We were told there would be two passengers."

"There will be. I go now for the other." He glanced toward the steamer. "The tide will hold?"

"For an hour, no more."

"I will be back long before that."

Wu Lien put his small knapsack in the longboat and started off along the beach toward the hut of Mei Fei and Tehani. Everything was as black as onyx; even the moon had hid itself behind a cloud, as if not wanting to witness the foulness of Wu Lien's plan.

As he reached the hut a dog barked a warning. Wu Lien threw a stone at it, sending it scurrying off. Inside, everything was quiet. In the alcove he saw Mei Fei and Tehani fast asleep on their down-filled mattress. Carefully he undid the stopper of the tiny vial he'd slipped into his waistband earlier. Silently, he crept toward Tehani's the side of the bed. Tehani lay on his back, mouth slightly agape, breathing deeply. Wu Lien held the vial under Tehani's nostrils. For a brief moment Tehani stirred, but the powerful narcotic made his senses spin and he dropped, almost immediately, into a deep slumber.

Wu Lien poured some of the liquid from the vial onto a kerchief and made his way around the bed. He knelt down beside Mei Fei, feasting his greedy eyes on her nakedness. He leaned close until his breath was directly over her mouth.

Mei Fei's eyes flew open. For a moment she could see nothing, but sensed a dangerous presence. Before she could utter a sound Wu Lien clamped the cloth soaked with morphine over her mouth and nose. She didn't struggle long. In a moment she was limp and vulnerable in his arms.

Wu Lien started to lift her up, but a diabolical thought teased his lust. To have her in her very bed, beside her husband, gave him perverted pleasure.

His passions burst into fire as he began tearing himself out of his clothes. Uncaring, reckless, he threw himself on top of Mei Fei. He shoved her thighs wide apart and pushed his turgid penis deep inside her. He took his time, savoring the heat of her, the softness of her body. Slowly he stroked in and out, concentrating on the revenge he was reaping on the Hawaiian husband she'd chosen over him.

Wu Lien didn't bother to stifle his moans, his grunts, as he pounded unmercifully into Mei Fei's softness. With every stroke he buried himself to the hilt, jarring her body. He grabbed her ankles and spread her legs in a wide V, giving himself deeper access to her core.

"Easy, easy," he cautioned himself as he slowed his thrusts almost to a standstill. He was getting too close and he wanted it to last longer.

Then with a violence that he knew might tear her apart he pressed down tightly and shoved his entire weight into each mighty stroke. A gasp caught in his throat as he felt the leaden feeling beginning to build up inside him. His cock throbbed violently as his body jerked uncontrolled. A flood spewed from him as he ground himself hard against her inert body. Spasm after spasm wracked him as his passions erupted. With a groan he felt life being sapped from his veins. He growled out the last of his lust, then collapsed on top of Mei Fei. It was as if they were three dead bodies lying on the mattress.

Wu Lien lay quiet until his breathing returned to normal. Only then did he leisurely lift himself up, dress himself, and look around for something with which to cover Mei Fei. He found a muumuu on the peg and struggled to slip her into it.

Tehani stirred but his eyes stayed closed.

Taking Mei Fei's limp body into his arms, Wu Lien made his way out of the neat little hut and started back toward the beach and the waiting steamer.

\* \* \* \* \* \* \*

A terrific pain at the back of his skull was the first thing

Tehani felt. He was drifting through some terrible hell. With an effort he opened his eyes and tried to sit up, but his strength left him and he fell back.

"Mei Fei," he moaned as he searched for her with his hand. The slight movement brought on a wave of nausea. He tried to shut out the pain, the sickness, and dropped back into the black hell from which he'd fought to escape.

The heat of the sun woke him sometime later—or was it the sound of someone calling his name? When he forced open his eyes he found Leon bending over him, shaking him gently. He was grinning.

"It's not like you to sleep the entire day away," Leon said.

"What?" Tehani tried to sit up again and this time succeeded, but his head was pounding.

"Ke Loo wants to see Mei Fei about something, but no one knows where she is."

The awful realization of what happened shot throughTehani. He vaguely remembered the shadowy figure that had bent over him and the sweet, acrid smell of something being held under his nostrils. He'd thought it all a nightmare; now, he knew it had been real.

"Mei Fei," he said, groggy and slurred.

Leon frowned. "What's wrong with you?"

Tehani tried to forget the pain, the nausea. "Mei Fei," he said again, a little clearer.

"Yes. Where is she?"

Tehani cradled his head in his hands and tried to think. "Drugged," he managed. "Someone drugged me. My head...." He rubbed at his temples.

"God, no," Leon breathed as he remembered his father complaining about Wu Lien stealing off without a word to anyone. "Tehani," Leon said sharply. "Was Wu Lien here last night?"

"Wu Lien?" He tried to think. "I don't know. Someone. Something."

"You must try and remember."

"Mei Fei, she and I went to bed. Something happened. I don't know what. I dreamed."

Leon looked around, searching for some clue, hoping his fears would not be realized. He saw spots of blood on the linen where Mei Fei had slept. "Christ," he muttered. He moved around the bed and stepped on the small vial. It didn't break. He raised it to his nostrils and smelled the morphine. "Get dressed, Tehani," he ordered. "We have to go to Ke Loo." He didn't wait for Tehani. Leon raced toward his father's house.

Ke Loo was in the peacock chair on the veranda. A small girl in her preteens was fanning him with laced palm fronds.

"That bastard abducted Mei Fei," Leon shouted.

Ke Loo scowled. "What are you saying?"

"Wu Lien. He went to Tehani's and drugged him. He's taken Mei Fei."

Ke Loo looked unconcerned. "Better she be with one of her own than with that common native."

"You mean to do nothing?"

"What do you want me to do, swim after them?"

"She must be brought back."

"Why?"

"Don't you realize that if what I fear is true, Tehani and his family can cause a great deal of trouble. Mei Fei took the vow of allegiance to her Hawaiian in-laws. She became Hawaiian when she married Tehani. We are foreigners here. If they think you and I were accomplices to this abduction there will be hell to pay. You'll never get anyone to do your work—if, that is, they let you live."

For the first time Leon saw his father's eyes move nervously. "I had nothing to do with whatever Wu Lien did."

"These people won't believe that."

Ke Loo relaxed back into his chair, his eyes steady. "Let them believe what they wish."

Tehani came running across the compound looking weak and pale. "Where is my wife?" he demanded of Ke Loo.

"I know nothing of Mei Fei." Calmly he added, "If you were

a proper husband you would know where she is."

Leon put his hands on Tehani's shoulders and peered into his face. "Look. My cousin Wu Lien sailed last night for Hong Kong. I believe he drugged you and made off with Mei Fei."

"No!" Rage creased his face.

"It is the only answer. Everyone has been looking for Mei Fei since early this morning. It is the only thing I can think."

"I'll kill him." He turned on Ke Loo. "You did this," he threatened.

"No," Leon said gently. "I don't believe my father had anything to do with it."

Ke Loo sat smiling.

"He did," Tehani insisted. He leveled a finger at Ke Loo. "My people will make you pay dearly for this."

"Please, Tehani. Don't stir up your people. My father will send me after Mei Fei. I will bring her back." He turned to Ke Loo. "Prove to Tehani that you are blameless by sending me to bring Mei Fei home."

Ke Loo continued to look unconcerned. "If you wish," he said. "The next freighter will not be here for a week. You may have trouble finding them. Hong Kong is very large and you have not been to China for many years."

"I will find them," Leon swore.

"Do what you must," his father told him. "I had wanted you to go to China originally. If you had obeyed me this would not have happened."

What the old man said was true; it made Leon feel responsible. To Tehani he said, "I will go on the next ship. I will bring Mei Fei home to you or I will die trying."

"I will go with you," Tehani said.

"No. I can travel better alone. You do not know the language or the country. Stay here. Keep your people calm. I will bring my sister back, my friend."

It seemed forever before the freighter arrived on its way to Hong Kong. During that time Leon had a thousand misgivings about his pursuit. The last thing he wanted was to go any farther away from San Francisco.

By the time he was ready to leave it was with a sinking heart. He watched Tehani wave to him from the shore as the longboat pulled away. When Leon was on deck on the freighter Tehani was still a tiny figure standing on the sands, peering across the waters at him.

Leon leaned heavily on the deck rail and watched the land slowly disappear. He wished with all his heart that the ship was taking him in the opposite direction. He was very worried, of a sudden, about April. He had received his mother's letter—mailed from San Francisco weeks before—saying all was not well with his sister; that April had taken to strange moods and lapses of memory. She had never accepted the passage of time; she thought of her lost son as still a little boy, the same little boy she'd fled with from the Forbidden City.

"Beautiful April," he sighed as he pushed away from the rail and started toward the cabin. He wondered how long it would be before he saw her and his mother.

Perhaps never, he thought. He shuddered. "No," he said slamming his fist into his palm. He'd be back and he would go home where he belonged, he swore.

# CHAPTER THIRTEEN

April sat in the turret window of the Nob Hill mansion gazing down at the street. Her lovely hair was disheveled, her dress rumpled from having slept in it all afternoon. She saw no reason to keep herself tidy. After all, who was to see? There was only one pair of eyes she longed for and they had been stolen from her. First her husband had been beheaded while she was forced to watch. Then her son was kidnapped. Was it any wonder people thought her strange? She was empty inside and lived without a purpose, except for little Adam. If he didn't come home soon she knew she would not want to go on living.

Marcus had given her a glimmer of hope. He'd told her of the news he'd heard, of a young boy who had been found somewhere in the east. Indiana, she remembered correctly. A foundling who'd been abandoned at a railway station.

Marcus had said he was leaving to see if it might not be Adam, but that had been weeks ago and Marcus hadn't returned. Every day she sat in the turret window and watched the street.

Her heart gave a tug when she saw an auto taxi come up the hill and stop in front of the house. Marcus stepped from it. She gave a cry of joy and jumping from her seat, ran down the winding stairs to the front door.

"What news?" she cried before the door had even shut behind Marcus."Did you find the boy? Was it Adam?"

He put his ulster on the chair and set his small valise down beside it. "I'm sorry," he said, unable to look at her. He shook his head sadly. "It was a fruitless search."

He felt guilty now about telling the lie that he'd invented about a foundling in Indiana. It had been a cruel thing for him to do. The truth was, he'd gone to Indiana, to the city of Indianapolis, but not on the trail of Adam. All the time there he'd been involved in the inaugural races of the new auto speedway, something his grandmother had absolutely forbidden. His guilt gnawed at him, but even now, standing shamefaced and uneasy, he knew he'd do it again. There was nothing in his life more important than racing machines.

"But you said—" She broke off as the tears choked her.

"I'm sorry, Mother." He felt terrible. In all his twenty years he'd never felt so despicable. Yet the excitement of the races still roared in his ears.

"But you sounded so sure. When your grandmother warned you of making a long, useless trip you assured us you knew the facts, things that made you certain it was Adam. You remember how she wanted to cancel her trip to Europe and go with you? Remember how I pleaded with you to take me?"

His guilt made him impatient. "And do you remember how I insisted you not get your hopes us? That was why I wanted to go alone. A long, empty trip back would have been a terrible ordeal for you."

"And waiting for you wasn't a terrible ordeal?" Tears streamed down her cheeks. "Oh, Marcus. I'd so prayed you'd find him. Are you sure you checked thoroughly?"

He struggled to find his voice. "Yes," he stammered.

She clung to him when he turned away. "You didn't, I know you didn't. I should have gone. I was a fool to listen to you. You are only a stupid boy yourself. What do you care about finding my son?"

"Mother."

She turned her back on him. "I am going to Indiana myself."

"Please."

"Tell me what you heard. How did you learn of this boy?"

"It's useless. I've checked," he said but with little conviction. "It would be wasted effort for you to go there."

"Wasted effort," she shrieked, her eyes wild. "Wasted effort, to search for my son? You more than likely squandered your time in dance halls and God only knows where else. You left us as if you were going on a holiday." Her eyes narrowed. "Oh, I saw your face when it was agreed you should go. You didn't do anything to find Adam."

"Mother, please, you are working yourself into another of your spells."

"Tell me. I want to know what sent you? Who gave you the news of this boy? I demand that you tell me."

He stood, dejected, arms hanging limply at his sides. "You're right, Mother," he finally admitted, knowing he had to tell the truth. "There were no clues about a foundling."

She stared at him.

"I'm sorry. I know it was cruel of me, but if grandmother knew the truth she would never have permitted me to go to Indianapolis."

"The truth? What truth?"

"There were no reports of a boy resembling Adam. I made it all up. You see," he stammered, "there was this new auto racing speedway."

"Auto racing speedway?" She looked uncomprehending.

"I had to go. I made an excuse."

"Excuse?" She stared, not believing her ears. "You dared do this to me? How could you be so cruel?" She slapped him hard across the face. He stood without moving and let her slap him again and again. "I hate the very sight of you."

"Mother, please."

"I am not your mother, Adam is my only son. Adam would never have hurt me the way you have." Contempt riddled her words. She looked him up and down with disgust. "But then why should I have expected anything decent from a bastard son like you. Yes," she said, laughing at his astonishment. "You heard me. Bastard! That's what you are. You are no son of mine. You belong to that bitch of a woman you call 'grandmother.' She's your mother, not I. And you are exactly like her. A carbon copy of a vain, selfish woman who lived for herself. Oh, I know only too well what you're like because you are precisely like her and that despicable father of yours."

Marcus couldn't speak. He simply stared, his face a mask of incredulity.

"You don't believe me?" April said, her head thrown back, fire in her eyes. "Peter MacNair is your father, not Raymond Andrieux. Only he doesn't know any more than you did. But it is the truth, I tell you. You were born as a result of your grandmother's whoring with Peter MacNair."

"Mother, I...."

"Don't you ever call me that again. Get out of my sight. I have only one son and he was stolen from me." She went to claw his face but he grabbed her wrists. "I hope to God that one day you'll suffer as I have suffered. I will pray for that day."

"You don't know what you're saying. You're upset."

"Upset? You despicable boy. Don't touch me." She wrenched herself free, rubbing her wrists where he'd held them. "I hate and despise you just as I hate and despise your mother. She was never anything but an evil woman. Do you know she kept me as a servant when we came to this damned country? Me, a princess of the Manchus, daughter of a noble prince. I have royal blood in my veins, not the blood of a common slut."

"Stop it. You don't know what you're saying."

Drawn by the ruckus, Nellie, the housekeeper, appeared at the servants' entrance below the stairwell. Marcus saw her and said, "Nellie, you'd better phone for Dr. Hammond. I'll take Mother up to her room."

"Don't come near me, either of you," April shouted, retreating toward the stairs. "I don't need a doctor." Suddenly she let out a bloodcurdling scream and tore at her hair. "I want my son. I want little Adam."

Nellie managed to put her arms around April. "Come, child. Nellie will put you to bed and sit with you just like when you were a little girl." She expected April to fight her off, but she didn't. Her strength was spent.

Marcus made a move to help, but the old housekeeper sent him away with a quick shake of her head. He watched them go up the stairway. He'd never felt so horrible in all his life.

Gradually what April had shouted came back to him. Could it all be true? He knew she'd abandoned him and Caroline when they were children. Their grandmother had told them April had been called home to China by her father, the mandarin prince, but Marcus had learned the truth about her running off with David MacNair when the scandal erupted after Adam's kidnapping.

But what had she said, about his grandmother being his real mother? It was impossible to believe. He fell into the chair, crushing his ulster, and put his head in his hands.

She didn't know what she was saying, Marcus told himself. The word 'mad' filtered back to him, but he waved it away. His mother was overly distraught; she'd apologize when she was rested and rational.

Still, was it vaguely possible that she had spoken the truth? Was he his grandmother's son? His mother had never taken a real interest in him. Ever since a boy she had always treated him like a stranger. Memories from his childhood drifted in and out of his brain.

Marcus rubbed his temples and tried to think. His father. Yes, his father would surely know the truth. But his father was in Paris, thousands of miles away.

He needed to talk to someone. Despite his tiredness, his disheveled clothes, the long train trip from Indiana, he had to get out of this house, someplace where he could sort out his thoughts.

He got to his feet and pulled on his coat. There was only one person in whom he felt he could confide. Amelia Wilson loved him, as he loved her. She would tell him what he should do, if anything.

Amelia Wilson was one of the loveliest girls in San Francisco. They'd met at one of the Stantons' parties where his grandmother had taken him. Marcus would remember that evening as long as he lived. The moment he walked into the ballroom and saw Amelia, he knew he loved her.

As he made his way out of the Nightsong mansion and down the hill toward the house on Powell Street, he could still see Amelia seated beside the potted palms, her parents standing protectively beside her. She'd only been fifteen then, and he eighteen, but one exchange of looks was enough for them to know they were meant for each other.

When Lydia had introduced him to Mr. and Mrs. Wilson he only remembered seeing Amelia's smile, her raven hair, her fabulously beautiful face, her gentle, blue eyes, the faint flush on her cheeks. She'd been wearing a white chiffon gown over a pink taffeta lining. Her hair hung down her back, almost to the waist, tied with a broad, bright white ribbon. She was enchanting.

Now that Marcus thought of it, he had Efrem MacNair to thank for enabling him and Amelia to be alone together that night. Efrem had been the escort for Ellen Stanton, who followed him about like a puppy while Efrem got drunker and drunker until he'd caused a scene that sent everyone scurrying into the salon, leaving Amelia in Marcus's care.

He told her then that he loved her. She'd blushed scarlet, but didn't let go of his hand. During the days and weeks that followed they saw a lot of each other and Marcus found, much to his joy, that Amelia was as interested in motor cars and speed almost as much as he. It bound them together forever, he felt.

They would have been married by now if her parents hadn't insisted on taking Amelia on a world cruise so that she could be certain she loved Marcus Andrieux enough to become his wife. Then, when they returned, her mother became ill and was bedridden for a very long time before she mercifully died. There followed the long period of mourning.

Soon they'd announce their engagement.

Now, however, if what his mother had charged was true, Amelia's father—fair and broad-minded a man as he was— would not want his daughter subjected to another scandal, especially if the MacNairs were involved. Mr. Wilson had never forgiven the MacNair family for the disgraceful incident their son had caused at the Stantons, even though it hadn't been in his own house. Fair as Mr. Wilson was, he was a stickler for protocol and good taste. He still, to this day, muttered his disapproval of how the Stantons tolerated their daughter's dotage on that drunken Efrem MacNair.

Amelia was crouched by the rose bushes in front of their house, pruning away dead stems. "Darling," she called when Marcus started up the steps.

He ran to her and took her in his arms, not caring about the frowns of the two matrons who were passing by.

Amelia put her face up to his. "Kiss me or I'll scream 'masher.'"

He laughed and kissed her hotly on the mouth.

"Your letter said you'd be home tomorrow."

"The train was early. I made very good connections. I got in only an hour ago."

She looked at his wrinkled clothes. "You look it. Haven't you been home?"

His expression changed. Amelia frowned up at him. "What is it, Marcus? Something's the matter. The races?"

"No, nothing like that. The races were magnificent. Next time I'll take you with me."

"You'd better, because next time you go I have every intention of being there to root my husband on."

"If they'll let me race. Ray Harroun wouldn't even let me sit in his Marmon, let along drive it around the course."

"You'll have your own racer when you go again."

"I must talk to you. That's why I came looking the way I do."

"Of course, darling." She took his hand. "Come inside. Father is at the office. We have the place to ourselves. I may even lure you up to my boudoir." She giggled but when he didn't smile back she knew something serious was troubling him.

Amelia led him into the solarium and they settled themselves on the wicker settee. "Now," she said, holding his hand. "Why are you looking so grim?"

He made a futile gesture, a little shake of his head. "I don't know what to say."

"Say what's bothering you."

"Mother," he started.

"Oh, dear." Amelia let her shoulders droop. "She doesn't much care for me, you know. What trouble has she brewed up this time?"

"It's not you, Amelia." He screwed up his courage by taking a deep breath and blurted out, "My mother says I am not her son, that I am...a bastard."

The sun filtered through the delicate leaves of the tall ferns, making long patterns on the floor.

After a moment she said, "Your mother says wild things, Marcus. Everyone knows that."

"I know," he admitted without looking up. "But somehow this time I think she spoke the truth. You should have seen her. Besides, she doesn't much like me, either. She never has, if I'm to be honest."

"But that certainly doesn't mean you're not her son."

He lowered his eyes. "No, I think she's telling the truth. When I told her why I had gone to Indianapolis she acted like a woman gone mad."

"Your mother was upset and angry. We women often say terrible things when angered or disappointed."

"Still...."

Silence fell between them.

Amelia's curiosity got the better of her. "Well, if she's not your mother, whose son does she claim you are?"

Marcus swallowed hard. "My grandmother's and Peter MacNair's."

"Good heavens." To his utter surprise she laughed. "You do have Mr. MacNair's wavy hair."

"Be serious," he moaned.

"Listen, if you really believe there is any truth in what she said, ask your grandmother." She bit her hp. "I forgot, she's in

Europe with Caroline. So, then, ask Peter MacNair."

"You are crazy. What am I supposed to do, walk over to the MacNair house, ring the bell and say, 'Hello, there, Mr. MacNair. Are you my father?' "

Amelia tittered. "Why not?"

Marcus turned angry. "You are taking this all as some kind of lark. Do you realize what your father would say if he found out I was illegitimate? He'd never allow us to marry."

"You leave father to me. He likes you more than you think. Besides, we Wilsons aren't so high up in society that we're total snobs, as father likes to pretend. Now if you want my advice, darling, I'd let it all roll off my back like so much water. Forget it."

"I can't. I honestly believed her when she said those things."

"Then the only thing left for you to do is to find out for sure. Come on." She got up and pulled him after her.

"Where are we going?"

"To the telephone. You're going to call Peter MacNair and make an appointment to see him."

"Amelia, no. Mother said he doesn't know."

"If he's your father he must know." He started to argue, but she refused to listen. She picked up the telephone and asked the operator to connect her with the MacNair residence. When the connection was made she handed the telephone to Marcus.

"He doesn't know," he insisted. Helplessly, he took the telephone. When someone answered he started to stammer but he managed to ask for Mr. MacNair.

"Which Mr. MacNair do you wish to speak with?" the maid asked.

"Peter MacNair."

"I'm sorry, sir, Mr. Peter MacNair is in Europe."

The word Europe hit a nerve. His grandmother was in Europe. His mind began to spin around in a confusion of suspicions. He didn't want to think that his grandmother and Peter MacNair were together, but it was all he could think of.

"Well?" Amelia asked, watching his stunned expression as

he hung up the receiver.

"He's in Europe with my grandmother."

She stared at him. "Oh, Marcus, surely they didn't tell you that."

"They didn't have to." He walked aimlessly toward the door.

"Where are you going?" Amelia asked. He turned back, his face creased with doubt. "I think I'm going to go to Europe to see my father—whoever he is."

# CHAPTER FOURTEEN

Caroline was relieved when they left the clamor of London and started out into the countryside. Peter MacNair had been poring over some papers he'd spread on his lap while she marveled at the beauty of the English landscape. Everything was so tailored and neat, as though cut by one of those expert drapers on Bond Street. Green, lush fields stretched for miles, crowned by ridges of shimmering trees that swayed elegantly and proudly in the afternoon breeze.

She heard Peter shuffle his papers together and stuff them back into the leather case on the seat.

"Who do we see first?" Caroline asked, trying not to sound too anxious. "The Slykes or the Clarendons?"

"You'll be pleased to know, the Clarendons," he said with a gleam of a smile. "We are going to the estate. Lord Clarendon's secretary said he does all his business in his home study and seldom goes to the glass foundry."

She tried hard to hide her excitement. "He doesn't sound like a very good businessman to me."

He chuckled. "Englishmen don't conduct business in the same way we do back home. They're gentlemen, you must remember. I'm surprised he isn't seeing me at his club."

"Are they rich?" Caroline asked cautiously.

Peter shrugged. "I haven't met an Englishman yet who'd admit to being rich. Money is something they pretend doesn't exist."

The chauffeured motor car moved smoothly round a stand

of trees and Caroline gawked at the beautiful country estate nestled in a formal garden at the bottom of the rise. "Is that the Clarendons' place?" She gave a very unfeminine whistle. "They have money."

"Seems so," Peter agreed. "They must have inherited it because according to what your grandmother and I dug up their glass works isn't all that productive."

"The place must have a hundred rooms." She marveled at the turrets and towers and sprawling wings of Clarendon House.

Lord Clarendon himself was standing at the wide arched doorway waiting to welcome them. He wore the clothes of country gentry, tweedy and casual. Peter liked him instinctively. Caroline was looking behind him to see if his son were there, too. Much to her disappointment, he wasn't.

After the initial formalities, Lord Clarendon said, "I had no idea, Mr. MacNair, that you were bringing along such an enchanting business associate."

Peter grinned. "Miss Andrieux came along to see some of your countryside."

"Then by all means she shall see it while you and I sequester ourselves in my study. To a manservant he said, "Find Master Adam and send him to me."

Caroline's pulse quickened.

As Lord Clarendon ushered them into the mansion he asked Peter, "I do hope you weren't inconvenienced by my asking you to come here. Offices are sometimes rather depressing, don't you agree?"

Peter didn't, but smiled and said, "I do, of course, want to see your foundry."

"Naturally. It's not all that far from here, closer to London."

Caroline had seen pictures of castles and palaces, but until she was standing in one she never before really grasped their enormity.

Adam started down the staircase and her heart stopped. He was dressed for riding. His fawn britches and shiny boots accentuated his manliness. She thought him more handsome than ever here in his own surroundings.

Peter glanced up at the boy and did a double take. His breath caught in his chest. It was as if he were seeing the ghost of his dead son, but this ghost was alive and breathing and moving. His walk was the same; his face, his hair were exactly as David's had been. Peter rubbed a hand across his eyes and found himself rooted to the spot, unable to move.

"May I present my son, Adam," Lord Clarendon said. Adam put out his hand to Peter.

For a moment Peter was paralyzed. "Adam." He breathed the name as though it were something sacred.

"Adam, Mr. MacNair, the gentleman I mentioned to you."

"Honored, sir."

Except for the smooth British accent, it was David's voice.

Peter forced himself to respond. "How do you do," he managed, taking the boy's hand. He saw Adam frown at him when Peter kept Adam's hand in his. "Oh, please, excuse me for staring," Peter said. "But you remind me of my...of someone I used to know very well."

Lord Clarendon said, "Miss Andrieux, this is my son, Adam."

"We've met," Adam said, grinning sheepishly. "I'm very happy to see you again, Caroline."

Lord Clarendon was slightly flabbergasted. "Well, how very pleasant," he said.

Peter could only look at Adam Clarendon.

"Yes," Caroline answered extending her hand. "Your son rescued me from a very near collision with a team of galloping stallions."

Adam brought her hand to his lips. "I'm sorry I had to leave London without seeing you again. You got my note?"

"Yes," she said, knowing she was blushing.

Only belatedly did the nature of the conversation intrude on Peter's thoughts. He forced himself to concentrate on where he was and what was being said. So here was the young man Caroline was so hepped up about. But if his suspicions were right, Adam Clarendon was the last man in the world for

Caroline. There's wasn't the glimmer of doubt in Peter's mind that this Adam Clarendon was her stepbrother. He was a twin to his dead father, David. But how could it be? How did Adam come to be here, the son of an English lord?

Lord Clarendon clapped his hand on Adam's shoulder. "Miss Andrieux has come to admire our countryside. Be a good lad and show her about."

"My pleasure." Adam gave Caroline a warm smile. "Would you care to take a drive in my roadster, Caroline?"

"I'd adore it." She looked at Peter, who continuing to gaze at Adam. "Will that be all right, Mr. MacNair?"

"Yes, of course. Lord Clarendon and I have some lengthy business."

Lord Clarendon said, "You'll stay for tea, of course." To Adam he added, "Have yourselves back in time, dear boy."

"Yes, Father."

Lord Clarendon motioned Peter toward the study. Peter carefully weighed the questions he meant to ask.

"Fine-looking boy," he said to Lord Clarendon.

"Our utter pride."

"Your only son?"

"Alas, yes, Mr. MacNair."

"You'll excuse me from saying so, Lord Clarendon, but he must take after your wife's side of the family. The boy looks more Scot than Briton."

The slight widening of Lord Clarendon's eyes didn't escape Peter. He wondered if he'd struck a nerve or whether Lord Clarendon was annoyed by his brashness.

"A great disappointment," Lord Clarendon said affably. "But my wife is overjoyed. She's Scottish; that is, her ancestors are."

But when Peter met Lady Clarendon at tea her coloration was as different from Adam's as her husband's. Adam Clarendon was not their son; he was positive of that.

And Lady Clarendon looked extremely nervous.

While Caroline and Adam spoke low to each other, their heads close, Lady Clarendon asked Peter, "You haven't visited our competition as yet, Mr. MacNair?"

He sipped the tea and wished for something stronger. Every glance at Adam made him want to cry out and tell the boy who he really was. He smiled at Lady Clarendon, but it was a forced smile. "No, I had it on good reference that Clarendon's glass was far the superior of the two. After my conference with your husband, I'm beginning to believe that advice was right. He's a clever and fair businessman."

And Lord Clarendon had been, much to Peter's surprise, more than knowledgeable about his glass production. This soft spoken, proper Englishman had the business insight and cunning of the best tycoon in America.

He changed the subject back to where he wanted it. "Your husband tells me you are from Scotland, Lady Clarendon."

"Dear me, no, Mr. MacNair."

He saw the quick shake of her husband's head and his glance toward Adam, who was enthralled with whatever Caroline was saying.

"That is," Lady Clarendon added quickly, "I myself am not from Scotland, but my family originated there."

"I'm Scottish myself," Peter said proudly, and boldly looked at Adam. "I had remarked earlier to your husband, Your Ladyship, that Adam has the look of the Highlands about him. He reminds me so much of my own family."

Lady Clarendon took an involuntary intake of breath and fumbled with the long strands of pearls that hung from about her neck.

Lord Clarendon give a little start at the remark, as though he suddenly remembered something unpleasant he'd long ago forced himself to forget.

Lady Clarendon said, "Adam is the image of his great grand-father. There's a portrait of him here somewhere in the house."

"I'd like to see it," Peter pressed.

Lord Clarendon hurriedly corrected his wife. "The portrait, my dear, was stored away when we remodeled the grand hall."

"Oh, dear me, yes. I'd forgotten."

Peter wanted to pursue the matter, but his manners forbade it.

"My wife and I were away on a rather extended trip," Lord Clarendon explained. "We'd lost our firstborn and I had the workmen redo the old place to help remove some rather sore memories we both associated with those earlier days.

Peter leaned back and eyed them doubtfully. "Did you, by any chance, visit our country?"

"America? Oh my, yes," Lord Clarendon said with enthusiasm, trying hard to disguise his utter discomfort. "Beautiful country. We saw all of it."

"Then you saw San Francisco before the earthquake?"

"San Francisco?" She gave her husband a quick glance, then a vague one to Peter. "No, I'm afraid not. We toured the west coast toward the end of our trip.

I'm afraid our train stopped only briefly in San Francisco."

"Is that where you are from, Mr. MacNair?" Lord Clarendon asked. He was looking pale. "I received the impression from your London solicitors that you were from New York."

"No, San Francisco."

"The earthquake must have been a nightmare for you," Lady Clarendon said, trying to sound casual. She was tugging so hard on her pearls that Peter was sure they'd break. "I remember that lovely Victorian railway station. Was it completely demolished? It was so very quaint."

Peter nodded, his brain clicking. So that was it, he decided. Their train had stopped in San Francisco the night Adam disappeared and somehow, whoever snatched Adam came in contact with these two. Surely, his better side reminded him, this gentle, charming pair didn't knowingly steal his grandson.

Lord Clarendon hastily changed the subject back to his competitor, Tom Slyke.

"If you mean to confer with Mr. Slyke I warn you to be cautious. He's a very devious man."

Peter was of the opinion that people often see their own faults in their enemies. Perhaps Lord Clarendon was the devious one.

Lady Clarendon gave him a soft smile. "More tea, Mr.

MacNair?"

He wanted to linger over this game of cat and mouse, but knew the hour was getting late. "Thank you, no, Your Ladyship. Caroline and I should be starting back to London." He looked over at Caroline and Adam, who obviously were lost in each other. "Caroline."

"I'm sorry," she said, unconsciously putting her hand over Adam's. "Did you say something, Mr. MacNair?"

He checked his watch and gave her a tolerant smile. "I think we should be getting back to the hotel. We are having dinner with the Andersons this evening." He looked at Lady Clarendon. "Mutual friends who Caroline ran into by happenstance."

Reluctantly, Caroline began gathering herself together. "Yes, of course." She stood up when Peter did.

"Until Thursday then," Peter heard Adam say as he took Caroline's hand and again kissed it.

Peter hid his disapproval by turning to Lady Clarendon. He expressed his pleasure in having met her and thanked her for the lovely tea. He shook hands with her husband and promised to be in touch within the week.

At the door he turned to bid Lady Clarendon goodbye. He gave a little nod of his head. "Perhaps you shouldn't have packed away your Scottish heritage. Being a Scot myself I rather like to flaunt it."

He saw her flinch. He turned away before she could see his smug grin.

Lady Clarendon felt the anger building inside her, anger and uncontrolled fear. She held herself stiff until the car moved off down the drive and out of the courtyard. When the car was out of sight, she turned her anger on the one her eyes fell on first.

"How could you fawn over that American as you did?" she said to Adam. "Where is your loyalty to Pamela? Honestly, Adam, you behaved like one of them, a crude, unprincipled barbarian."

He was taken aback. "Really, Mother, I was just being civil."

"Civil?" She threw the word at him like a javelin.

"Millicent," her husband said, placing a consoling hand on her shoulder.

She could not depend on her own rationale. "We must speak in private, Basil."

"Yes." His simple answer told her that he, too, was afraid. "Adam, be a good lad and see to that new stallion the groom brought over from Brentenwoods."

Adam knew he was being dismissed. "I was only being polite."

"Later, my boy," his father said kindly.

As he walked away Adam felt a strange uneasiness. Was mere politeness the reason for his attention to Caroline? He knew better. His mother was right. He was being disloyal to Pamela by wanting to see so much of Caroline; yet, he could not help the attraction he had to her. She was so different from the other girls he knew, and especially different from Pamela.

He felt ashamed, but it didn't dissuade him from looking forward to seeing Caroline again on Thursday.

"He knows," Millicent gasped when she and her husband were alone in the library. She went directly to the wall safe behind the portrait of Queen Victoria and took out the small metal box.

The clippings were crisp and faded. She unfolded them carefully and began scanning the names, the old story that she and Basil had kept carefully out of mention for more than fifteen years.

"MacNair," she said as she read. "The father's name was MacNair." She fought for control. "Dear God, when I heard the name I made no connection," she said refolding the clippings. "Basil, why did you encourage this man's business?"

He fell heavily into a chair. "I had no idea. I never guessed there was a connection. MacNair is not a particularly uncommon name."

"What are we to do?" she wailed.

He fanned out his hands.

"You are to have nothing more to do with him. Tell him to

take his business to Tom Slyke," she insisted.

"That would only arouse his suspicions all the more. And," he added, giving her a stern look, "that is all it is, suspicions. He has no proof of anything. We have the documents I procured from the British consul in New York, the false birth certificate. For all anyone knows, you gave birth to Adam while we were traveling in America."

"Faked passport, false birth certificate. Oh dear, how criminal you make it all sound."

He was about to remind her that it had been a criminal act they'd committed, but saw no reason to upset her any more.

Lord Clarendon said, trying to sound encouraging, "Let Mr. MacNair check about all he likes. Adam is our son. No court of law would dispute that."

"Court of law?" She broke into tears.

"There, there, my dear. Calm yourself. You did right to admonish Adam for his attention to the Andrieux girl." He stood and put his arms around her. "We will continue to remind him of his duties toward Pamela. I heard Adam promise to see the American on Thursday. We will discourage that."

She leaned against his chest and sobbed bitterly.

* * * * * * *

Friday morning Peter was stretched out on the lounge beside the windows overlooking the park. He'd spent the past two days dividing his time between business and discretely checking records at the various offices of registry. Businesswise, the Clarendon proposal was far superior to Tom Slyke's. So far as the matter of Adam was concerned, everything proved he was indeed the son of Millicent and Basil Clarendon, born in America almost twenty years before.

Despite the records, things did not gel. Lady Clarendon had mentioned the quaint Victorian railway station in San Francisco. The station was built only fourteen years ago. He remembered that distinctly because he'd been one of the principal contributors to the expense of building it. It had been referred to as an architectural marvel that would stand for centuries and yet was the first building to topple that morning when the quake struck.

Something was amiss. Still, he could not bring himself to believe that Millicent and Basil Clarendon knowingly stole Adam.

A tap on the door roused him and Caroline came in.

"Am I disturbing you?" She was wearing a traveling suit.

"Come in. I was only drowsing. I could use some bright conversation."

"You have been looking a bit peaked again, if you don't mind my saying so."

"You sound like your grandmother."

"Speaking of whom, I am a little concerned about her. She said she'd be back from Paris in a day or two, but I received a cable saying she is extending her trip. No reason given."

"Your father is more than likely being his usual disagreeable self, I imagine."

"Well, I suppose there is no need for my being concerned, but I can't help it."

"I've been giving some thought to going over to Paris myself. Business, of course."

"Of course," she said with a sly grin.

"You'll come as chaperone, then."

"Can't. I'm off to the Clarendons for the weekend."

He looked up sharply. "The Clarendons?"

"Yes. Adam invited me last night after the opera. He almost didn't make it. Some kind of a mix-up in engagements at home. I think his parents dislike the idea of his going about with an American."

"And still they invited you for the weekend?"

"They don't know I'm coming. That is, they didn't know until today. Adam said last night he'd tell his mother and father he'd invited me."

"Don't be too surprised if you receive a call giving some excuse to postpone the visit."

"Why?"

He was sorely tempted to tell her of his suspicions, but reminded himself he had absolutely no grounds for them except the very marked resemblance between Adam and David.

Peter shrugged. "They're titled people, Caroline. We may have money, but our blood isn't blue enough for their son."

"Fiddlesticks," Caroline scoffed. "Adam isn't a bit pretentious about things like that."

"Oh?" He arched his brows.

"He told me he's been ostracized for causing a scene in the presence of the King and Queen." She giggled. "He hit a fellow and knocked him sprawling at their feet as the royal pair entered a ballroom." She waltzed toward the window humming an air from La Traviata. "I don't think Adam much likes the idea of someday inheriting a title."

"Well, well," Peter mused, his mind racing. "Perhaps...."

"Perhaps what?"

"Nothing," he said dismissing it with a wave of his hand. The idea hit him hard. Perhaps it might be an excellent idea for Caroline to spend time with the Clarendons. She might uncover information he'd never be privy to. Carefully, he asked, "Does Adam ever speak about his childhood?"

"His childhood? Why on earth should he?"

"I was just wondering about something."

She saw how sober he looked. "What are you thinking? You have a foxy glint in your eyes, Mr. MacNair."

The telephone rang, rescuing him from giving an answer. "Yes?" He listened. "Yes, she is." A pause. "Tell Mr. Clarendon she will be right down." He hung up. "Your young lord awaits in the lobby, m'lady," he said grandly.

"See, I knew his parents wouldn't mind after all." She started out.

"Caroline?"

She stopped and turned back.

"Get Adam to talk to you about his schooling and how he was brought up."

"Why?"

"I'm a businessman. If I am to do business with the Clarendons and something ever happened to the lord, I'd like to know a little about his heir."

"Men," she scoffed, smiling. "Is that all you ever think about, business?"

After she'd gone he sat a long time thinking. He remembered the strange way the Clarendons had acted when he spoke of Adam's birth, their visit to America. He was positive he had hit a nerve. Still, if they were aware of his suspicions why would they invite Caroline for a weekend? Surely she wasn't walking into some danger. Or perhaps, they wanted to pick Caroline's brain as he had wanted her to pick Adam's.

He got up and gazed down at the street. Adam was helping Caroline into his roadster. Peter's eyes only saw his son, David, cranking the motor and driving off. He watched until they were gone, then decided he'd pack a few things and go to Paris. Between them, he and Lydia would find some way to unravel the mystery.

Peter stopped halfway across the room as a strange tingling sensation ran up and down his arms. His head became light. The dizziness made him stagger toward the chaise and throw himself down. Nausea rose inside him. He fought it back, clenching his fists, pinching shut his eyes. Sweat was pouring out of him.

He lay for a long while, refusing to admit that he wasn't well. He could not move either arm to mop away the perspiration that ran down his face.

Then it passed. The room stopped turning and the sensation gradually crept back into his arms. Carefully, he opened his eyes and lay breathing heavily. After a moment he pushed himself up and started to get on his feet, but his legs were weak. He sat back down, rubbing his face with his hands.

"Damn."

A sudden homesickness for San Francisco swept through him. He wished he and Lydia were back there where they belonged.

Lydia, he thought. He had to get to her in Paris and speak to her about Adam Clarendon. Determined, he got up, ignoring the fact that he had to support himself between chair and table, door frames and bedstead.

He started to pack.

# CHAPTER FIFTEEN

In San Francisco, Susan MacNair linked her arm through Ellen Stanton's and steered her out onto the terrace. "I have got to talk to you, Ellen."

Ellen was a plain-looking girl with a boyish face and unstylish bobbed hair, but Ellen didn't care much about fashion; she never had. Despite her family's money and position, she liked ordinary things—tailored clothes, neat and without flounces and ruffles. All her life she'd been called a tomboy. She wished she'd never been made to grow up and become a woman.

"I really should keep an eye on Efrem," Ellen protested.

"Mother's here. Efrem will behave himself."

The Stanton party was going well, though everyone had reservations when Efrem MacNair arrived with his mother and sister. His drinking problem was the talk of San Francisco society and except for his family's position and Ellen's insistence, Efrem's presence there would never have been permitted.

Ellen was five years younger than Susan, but her almost boyish plainness made her seem much younger. She leaned against the balustrade overlooking the garden and waited for Susan to speak.

Susan chose her words carefully, but directly. "You are in love with my brother, aren't you, Ellen?"

Ellen laughed, but it was an unhappy laugh. "That is no secret. Everyone says I'm making a fool of myself, the way I throw myself at him." She put her elbows on the balustrade and rested her chin on her hands. "I've always loved Efrem. I suppose I will always love him. Of course, he doesn't know I exist."

"He has a serious problem. You realize that."

"Everyone knows that."

"People who drink have a reason for drinking. I've read some papers on alcoholism. It's a real sickness, something the person cannot help."

Ellen shook her head. "I just don't understand any of it. Efrem hated alcohol when we first started going about together. Of course, I won't say how many years ago that was."

"Something happened to him that forced him into it," Susan said. "I've tried talking to him about it, but he has shut me out completely."

"Shut you out. He practically tears my head off if I so much as mention the subject."

"When did it all start? Do you remember?"

Ellen straightened and creased her brow. "I've thought about that. The nearest I can come up with is that it started shortly after Efrem went to work for your father."

"Then it must be his work."

"No, I don't think so. He seemed happy enough at first. He used to rattle on about how well he was doing and how much he enjoyed it, especially his father's compliments on his work. Then out of the blue everything changed. He tried to hide it, but as time passed he made no secret that he carried a flask in his breast pocket. I complained once that I thought he was getting the habit and he flatly told me that if I didn't like it I could stop seeing him."

Susan watched her. Knowing Ellen most of her life, she knew her to be an aggressive and assertive individual. Even knowing this, however, Susan picked her way cautiously. "You and Efrem more or less grew up together. Of all the people in San Francisco I think you know him better than anyone, including us, his family. Has he ever confided in you?"

Ellen turned. "What do you mean?"

"Has he ever mentioned a man by the name of Ramsey?"

"Ramsey? No, I don't think so. Who is he?"

"A detective here in San Francisco, or at least he used to be, according to what I've found out. He's the dark, mysterious type man women are supposed to swoon over in those lurid dime novels."

"Dark, mysterious type," Ellen reflected. She brightened. "Wait a minute. I do remember Efrem speaking with such a man. Yes, that was the name Efrem used. We'd been to a dance. Efrem was on his very best behavior until he saw this man. Dark and mysterious, as you say. He was with some rather loud people and when Efrem saw him he actually turned white as a sheet. He said the man's name and pushed away from me. Then he proceeded in getting staggeringly drunk. Later, when I pleaded with him to take me home I distinctly remember him looking frightened and asking, 'Is Ramsey gone?' I thought it very odd." She peered anxiously at Susan. "What does this man have to do with Efrem?"

"That is what I'm trying to dig up, but so far without any luck. Mr. Ramsey is at the root of Efrem's problem, of that I am certain."

"A detective? You don't think Efrem is involved in anything illegal?"

"No, I'm certain he isn't," she said, giving Ellen an assuring pat on her hand.

"What then?"

Susan thought of Leon Nightsong. It was possible that she wasn't the only one who'd seen Leon's and Efrem's parting scene. The more she mulled over that possibility the more she was convinced that had to be the answer.

Prudently, she asked Ellen, "I know I'm being very brash, Ellen, but I must ask you something."

"Ask away."

"You won't get angry?"

"I haven't heard your question yet."

Susan paused, letting the clicking of the crickets and the breeze wafting through the trees still her anxiety. "Have you ever been to bed with Efrem?"

"Susan MacNair!" Ellen said with feigned indignity. "I see living in the middle of that New York fast life has had its effect on you." She laughed.

"Have you?"

"Alas, no," Ellen said with a dramatic sigh. "Much as I have wanted to. As far as I could say, Efrem is still ignorant of the fact that there is a difference between the male and female anatomies. No, I believe Efrem and I are the only two virgins in San Francisco." After a quick, sidelong glance she added, "He's terribly shy, you know."

"Perhaps, in that case, he needs to be seduced."

Ellen turned her whole body. "Just what on earth are you getting at?"

"Merely that I believe Efrem, deep down, is very much in love with you," she lied. "Sometimes a woman needs to take a situation such as yours into her own hands."

"Are you suggesting I seduce your brother? I realize this is the twentieth century, but really, Susan, I don't see myself as the femme fatale type."

"Efrem might," Susan said, refusing to let go.

"You're impossible."

Efrem came out onto the terrace, drink in hand. "So there you both are," he slurred, teetering slightly but not dangerously so.

Ellen never noticed the sallow complexion, the hollowed cheeks, the thin, gaunt frame. To her Efrem MacNair was still the quiet, handsome boy she'd remembered from her school days and, to her, he would never be anything else.

"You're drinking," Susan scolded. "Efrem, you promised."

"Promises are supposed to be broken." He took a deep swallow.

"You will have Mother in a rage."

"Never mind," Ellen said sweetly. "The party needs a little livening up."

"Please, Ellen, don't encourage him."

"Why not? It's the only pleasure he seems to have." She put her arm around Efrem's waist and led him back into the party.

Susan stood on the terrace watching them go. A wicked, devious plan occurred to her. "Why not, indeed?" she asked herself as she followed them in.

During the rest of the evening Susan watched Ellen doting on Efrem's every move, every word. When he wanted another drink Ellen glared back at those who looked disapproving and saw to it that Efrem got his drink.

By the time it came for them to leave, Efrem was quite drunk, seated in a corner with Ellen, both of them giggling like two young girls.

Susan saw him lean close to Ellen and whisper something. Ellen got up and helped Efrem to his feet. Susan saw her mother glowering at them, but everyone else was pretending they weren't there, not even when Efrem bumped into a pedestal and sent a vase crashing to the floor.

Ellen steadied him as they went through a door toward the guest bathroom just beyond the foyer. Susan made an excuse and went after them. She found Ellen leaning against the door jamb after having helped Efrem inside.

"He's had too much to drink to be able to make a graceful exit," Susan said in her ear.

Ellen looked blank.

Susan glanced toward the stairs. "Perhaps we'd best help him up to one of the guest rooms. I'm sure your father will understand and let him stay the night."

"You have a crafty gleam in your eyes, Susan MacNair."

"It's simply an earnest interest in keeping face. Mother would be humiliated if she had to help her son stagger out of here. We can have one of the servants put him to bed here and say he wasn't well, though everyone will know the truth." She winked. "It's easy to seduce a man when he least expects it."

The Stantons and their guests, particularly Lorna, were only too willing to accept Susan's excuse that Efrem wasn't feeling all that well and Ellen had taken the liberty of having him put to bed in one of the guest rooms. It was as if a pall had been lifted from the party. The guests became merrier. Even Lorna started to enjoy herself.

Ellen, however, couldn't wait for everyone to leave. From time to time she'd trip upstairs and peek in on Efrem, who her father's valet had undressed. Efrem was lying flat on his back under a light sheet. He was sound asleep. The sight of him in bed, beautiful and vulnerable, was almost too much for her to stand.

When the house finally did quiet down, Ellen could not sleep. All she could think of was her conversation with Susan and the fact that the object of all her physical desires lay on the other side of the dividing wall.

At first it was only her need to want to lie beside him, feel his body next to hers, touch her mouth to his full lips. As thoughts of him whirled about inside her head, however, her body seethed with more passionate desires. Her hands itched to caress his bare chest, feel the press of his naked thigh against her own.

Her room grew stifling hot as she threw back the sheet and lay, luxuriating in her erotic desires. Almost without knowing how she'd gotten there, she found herself before his door, turning the knob and quietly slipping into the bedroom. A shaft of moonlight spilled his face.

This was insanity, a voice in her head said; but there was another voice, a stronger one urging her to take what she wanted, just as her father did. Why should she deny her most basic needs because of stupid convention?

As she stared down at him, his naked body outlined invitingly under the sheet, the stronger voice took over. She let her eyes feast on him as she undid her robe and let it fall in a heap on the floor. With trembling fingers she undid the tie at the throat of her nightdress, lifted it over her head and cast it aside. She felt the coolness of the air on her skin, but the heat inside her brought out tiny beads of perspiration. She took a step closer to the bed.

She carefully inched the sheet down over his body. God, he

was beautiful, she thought. His skin shone like satin, his boyish muscles filled her with blinding excitement. She could feel the wetness seeping from her as she looked at the flaccid penis, large and thick, lying heavily between his parted thighs. Thousands of electric sparks raced through her.

Efrem gave a little moan. Ellen stiffened, waiting for him to open his eyes but he gave a heavy sigh and went back into his dreams.

She could not take her eyes off his penis. She'd never seen a man's penis, only in drawings and the medical books her girl-friends had sneaked from various home libraries.

Ellen knelt down beside the bed and carefully laid her hand on Efrem's chest. She told herself she mustn't do this, but there was no way she could stop herself. She was like someone in a trance, acting against her will.

Slowly her hand moved down over his body, as if on its own accord. It seemed like hours before her fingers reached his abdomen. She was on fire. She had never felt anything so exciting as his smooth, silky skin, almost like a woman's; but the stomach was hard with a fan of hair starting at his navel and trailing downward, spreading at the base of his phallus.

When her fingers touched his pubic hairs, exquisite jolts of electricity shot through her. She was sure she would awaken him because her hand was trembling so. She waited, listening to his breathing. After an eternity of silence she moved her hand again. Her fingers crept through the thick, springy dark pubic hair. It felt fantastic.

Of a sudden her fingertips touched his penis. Slowly, tenderly she put her hand on it and closed her fingers around it. It was the most delicious moment of her life. She could not resist stroking it. The flaccid column started to pulse and grow. Horrified, she yanked away and stared again at Efrem's face, waiting for him to wake up and swear at her.

Efrem muttered something that Ellen thought was her name. She watched with utter amazement as the penis began to harden and grow longer. She had never seen a more exhilarating sight.

It pulsed to full erection, standing straight and rigid from his groin. She had to touch it, feel its strength—and be damned the consequences.

Again her hands encircled it, but she kept her eyes glued to his face as again she stroked the erection. She thought she saw his eyes flicker, but she wasn't sure. His long, graceful lashes rested softly on his cheeks. He gave no sign of being aware of what she was doing.

Reluctantly, she let go of his erection and eased herself onto the bed beside him. Ellen curled up next to his handsome body and rested her head lightly on his shoulders. Again she reached for him.

He breathed a word. She thought it had been her name, but his slurred, drink-laden voice made it come out sounding like "Leellonn."

The sound gave her the last bit of courage she needed. She put her lips lightly against his as she moved to straddle him. Regardless of the consequences, she could not stop herself.

Again, he breathed what sounded like her name as she fitted him against her seeping vagina and impaled herself on his throbbing penis. She felt her hymen tear. The pain was fleeting, followed by the most exquisite pleasure she'd ever experienced. He filled her with such bliss, such heat she reached her climax almost at once. Gasping and on fire, she could not bring herself to release the fullness inside her. She rose and lowered herself, reveling in the most delicious sensations.

"Lee-onn."

Ellen drew him deeper inside her and when she felt his penis jerk and his lips lurch upward, his semen pouring into her, she climaxed again and sat on him with all her weight.

Now she didn't care if he was awake or not. She fell on his body, panting heavily and wrapped her arms around him, kissing him full on the mouth.

His eyes stayed shut. Ellen rolled exhausted and spent to his side and lay for a long time fighting off the need to sleep.

"Efrem," she whispered as she raised up and touched her

mouth to his again.

His eyes opened, but he looked at her as if he saw no one. Like a child he smiled and curled himself into a fetal position and went back into his dream.

Ellen got up, knowing she could not risk being found asleep in his arms. She quickly slipped into her nightdress and robe and stole quietly back to her room.

Back in her own bed she could sense the heavy wetness of him inside her womb. She didn't give a thought to her shattered hymen, the need to bathe herself. Sleep was paramount.

With a contented sigh she pulled the sheet over her and drifted off into what she prayed would be the same dream as Efrem's.

She hadn't a single regret.

# CHAPTER SIXTEEN

Discord and regret were rare in Clarendon Hall.

"It's dangerous having that Andrieux girl here for an entire weekend, Millicent. It was very foolish of you," Basil said.

"What else could I do? If I had flatly refused Adam when he told me of his invitation, I would have been unable to give a reason. Good manners demanded that I give my consent."

He saw he'd upset her. "I'm sorry, my dear, it is just that—"

"I know, Basil," she said in a low wail. "But surely the girl knows nothing."

"Unless Mr. MacNair sent her here purposely to spy on us, try to find out things."

"What things? There is nothing she can find out. Adam is our legal son. He doesn't remember anything from before coming here."

"Some children hang onto old memories, even when they think they've forgotten. Remember how he called out that Chinese name in his sleep? The newspapers made mention of it. She'd been his old nurse."

"That was years ago. He's forgotten."

Basil Clarendon was not convinced. "Children remember," he repeated. He rubbed his chin. "We must be certain this friendship between Adam and the American doesn't blossom into something serious."

"Adam is simply fascinated by a woman from a different culture. I've taken the liberty of inviting Pamela for the weekend as well. Our son will quickly forget this infatuation."

"You've invited Pamela?" Lord Clarendon asked

"Of course. I know it wasn't exactly cricket to promote competition, but if Adam is smitten by the American I think Pamela should have full opportunity to work her wiles. You'll see. In the end Adam will prefer his own kind."

"That's just the point, my dear. Miss Andrieux is his own kind. He's an American too, remember."

"Caroline Andrieux is his half-sister, if you recall the newspaper clippings."

"Good Lord, I'd forgotten that. Heaven help us; we must do something drastic to stop the relationship if it comes to anything," Lord Clarendon said, his expression alarmed. "And from the way I've seen Adam look at Caroline I'd say he wants more than a friendship with her."

"Basil, he is just a boy."

"He is almost twenty, which makes him a man."

"Listen," Lady Clarendon said, cocking her head. "There's Adam's motorcar now. They're here."

Together they went toward the main hall just as Adam and Caroline entered.

"My dear," Lady Clarendon said. "We are so pleased to have you. I do hope you won't find our countryside too boring after London."

"I think I've fallen in love with it already, Lady Clarendon."

Millicent and Basil exchanged glances.

"Miss Andrieux," Basil said, taking her hand.

"Caroline, please," she corrected.

"Well," Lady Clarendon said motioning toward the staircase. "Let's get you settled in. Have Robbins put Miss...Caroline's luggage in the rose room, darling," she said to Adam.

"I'll do it myself," he volunteered.

"No." She spoke too curtly. "Pamela's coming for the weekend also. I'd almost forgotten I'd invited her. She rang up earlier and I volunteered that you'd drive over and collect her."

Adam looked crestfallen. "Pamela? But—"

His mother gave him one of those looks that was easily interpreted. She took Caroline's arm. "You'll like Miss Albright. She and Adam are more or less engaged."

Adam stood helpless. He watched Caroline's smile fade as his mother led her up the broad, curving staircase.

Caroline, however, did like Pamela Albright though she resented the proprietary way in which Pamela treated Adam.

And Pamela liked Caroline. "She's very nice," she told Adam when Caroline had left to dress for dinner. "For an American, that is."

When Caroline reappeared looking ravishing in a silver and white dinner gown, Pamela felt a twinge of resentment. She didn't like the way Adam stared at the American. She had been suspicious of a rival; now, she knew she had one.

And a formidable rival, Pamela told herself looking at this stunning woman as she walked into the drawing room. Caroline's gown was of Chinese silk, with a high waist, low décolletage, and soft puffy sleeves. It made Pamela look like what she was—a simple country girl in a plain, dowdy dress of drab pink.

"You look beautiful," Adam breathed.

Pamela knew then she might lose him to this American. She wouldn't permit that. "You do indeed, Caroline," she said sweetly. "Is that something you bought in Paris? I suppose our London shops are a bit conservative for you."

"No, Pam, actually, I bought this in New York, It's by an American designer "

Pamela hated to be called 'Pam,' even by Adam. It made her feel like a child.

"Some sherry?" Lord Clarendon offered.

"Thank you."

There were only the four of them for dinner. Afterward, however, Mr. Plimpton arrived looking for a game of bridge. Caroline loved playing and eagerly volunteered to be the fourth. After committing herself, however, she was sorry. It left Adam and Pamela to themselves.

"She's charming," Pamela said as he brought her a demitasse

and mints.

"Yes, a real stunner."

"Is she coming with us to the dance at Ravencourt tomorrow night?"

"Oh dear, I'd forgotten that was this weekend. I suppose I will have to take her."

"Don't make it sound like such a chore, Adam. You're not fooling me for one moment. You're quite taken with her."

"I am not," he lied.

Pamela smiled. "I'm not a bit jealous, darling. She is far too old for you."

"Caroline? She's my age."

"Years older. Thirty, I would say," Pamela said coyly, sipping her coffee.

"Nonsense. It's her dress. It makes her appear more mature."

"Americans," she scoffed.

"What's wrong with Americans?"

"Oh, I forgot. You're supposed to be part American, aren't you? That is, if what Jeremy Slyke says is true."

"Pamela," he fumed. "I thought you promised me you'd never bring up that tripe he told you. It isn't like you to be so heartless."

She put her hand on his cheek. "I'm sorry, darling. It was cruel of me. Of course I didn't believe what Jeremy said. It's just, well, it's just that I don't like the way you look at Caroline."

He smiled into her eyes. "Do you like the way I'm looking at you now?"

"Do you know, Adam Clarendon, if I didn't know you better I'd say you were a cad."

He winked. "I am."

Adam told himself a dozen times the following day that he was indeed being a cad. He kept dividing his admiration between Pamela and Caroline, unable to decide which of the two he cared for most. Caroline was so mature and sophisticated; Pamela so demure and innocent. They were in sharp contrast to one another.

"Where's Pam off to?" Caroline asked, interrupting his struggles with his conscience.

"Oh." He got up quickly from the terrace chaise, feeling as though she'd been listening to his thoughts. "Father is taking her home. She wanted a different gown for the ball this evening. I'm afraid you put everyone to shame in that lovely dress you wore to dinner last night."

"Dear me," Caroline said, genuinely contrite. "I didn't mean—"

"It's all right, Caroline. Sometimes, out here in the country, we don't always keep up with fashions, especially the women. Even mother remarked about how handsomely you dressed."

"I get the impression that your mother doesn't particularly approve of me."

"You're imagining it. Except she does so dislike being trounced at bridge."

Caroline laughed. "You should have told me. I would have played badly if I'd known." She looked over the side terrace. "What's that?" She pointed.

"The maze."

"How delightful. I've never been in a maze before."

"Then come on. I'll show you."

"I'll get lost."

"I'd never permit that."

Purposely he did let her get lost, however, and rescued her at the last minute when her calls to him became frantic. He led her around the angles of hedge and down long manicured lanes until they came to a little pavilion of white lattice, the center of the maze.

"It's enchanting," she breathed, "but a bit frightening too. Don't let me wander in here alone. I'd never find my way out."

"You would. I'll show you the secret markings on our way back."

She laced her fingers in her lap and said, "I'm supposed to ask you all about yourself."

"Beg pardon?"

"Peter MacNair, the man who is dealing with your father, he said he'd like to know more about you."

"Me? Why?"

"Because, as he said, if anything happens to the father, then he must deal with the son and likes to know everything about who he's dealing with."

Adam laughed. "Father will live to be a thousand."

"Still, I do have to bring back some sort of report." She didn't care about Peter MacNair; she wanted to know all she could about this handsome young man for selfish reasons. She knew she was falling in love with him. It was wrong, of course, but she couldn't do anything about it.

"Well, I was born in your country for starters. I don't remember too much about that." He grinned. "There's gossip that my real parents were American gypsies and my parents kidnapped me from Chicago gangsters who bought me from the gypsies."

"Be serious."

"Let me see. Mother had me when she and father were traveling in America. I was sent to school at Weddington and I'll go to Oxford next quarter, I suspect. That was father's school."

"Are you looking forward to it?" She didn't like the reminder of the differences in their ages.

"I suppose so."

"You don't sound overly eager."

"Oh, I am, but—"

"But what?"

He leaned forward, resting his elbows on his knees. "I'm not too keen about taking over Clarendon Foundries. I find glass-making extremely uninteresting."

"Mr. MacNair won't like hearing that."

"I'm sorry. Father has tried to interest me in the foundry and running this estate but it all seems so—so inactive."

"What would you prefer doing with your future?"

"Travel," he said with enthusiasm. "Especially to the Far

East. China fascinates me. I've read all I can about it. I got the highest grade I ever received at school on an examination dealing with the history and geography of China." He lowered his eyes. "My parents thought it frivolous and insisted I concentrate on English history, which bored me."

"China," Caroline mused. "My mother is half Chinese. Her father was a Mandarin prince. A Manchu."

His eyes lit up. "How positively exciting. Really?"

Caroline nodded. "My grandmother was the daughter of a missionary couple, but when they died, she was forced into marriage to Prince Ke Loo. She took the name 'Nightsong' when she brought my mother and herself to America."

"Nightsong. Fascinating."

"People usually laugh at it."

"I'd like to meet your grandmother."

"She's absolutely my favorite person in all the world."

"Not your mother?" He acted surprised.

Caroline shifted on the seat. "Mother is rather erratic at times. She still acts like a princess, all demanding and imperious. We never got on very well, I'm afraid."

"And your father?"

"Wait a minute. I'm supposed to be questioning you."

He took her hands. "I want to know everything about you. You are the most—"

"No," Caroline said. She stood, withdrawing her hands tactfully, reluctantly. The way he was looking at her made her heart pound. She purposely looked up at the darkening sky. "We should be starting back. Pamela will be looking for you."

He didn't move. "You know, when I was small I had a recurring dream about being in a Chinese palace—or temple, I can't remember which. I was dressed in this heavy little robe, all embroidered with dragons and horses. There were soldiers leading me down a long, long corridor to huge golden doors." He shook his head. "I don't remember anything after that. I usually wake up."

"You still have this dream?"

"Oddly enough, I do. But not as often as I did when I was a lad."

"You're still a lad," she reminded him.

"I am not." He stood. There was defiance in his eyes. "We're the same age. Do you consider yourself a girl?"

He was inches taller than she and when she looked up at him she felt a melting feeling inside her. "No, of course not. I'm sorry, Adam." Her voice was shaking. "I think you'd better take me back."

He reached for her, but she slipped away. "Come along," she said, skipping ahead of him. "If you lose me this time I'll likely wind up as some wandering spirit who'll haunt your maze forever."

It took a tremendous effort to walk away from him. She knew he wanted to make love to her. She wanted him to. Pamela's pretty face kept flashing at the backs of her eyes. She dared not interfere. She was suddenly sorry she'd come. If she had known about Pamela she'd never have done so. Oh well, she told herself as they started back along the confusing paths, tomorrow she'd make an excuse and go back to London. She knew she should make that excuse now and leave today, but she couldn't bring herself to do it.

* * * * * * *

"I'm afraid you may find our country balls a little dull," Pamela said as they started off for Ravencourt. She was beautifully dressed in a ball gown of blue crepe de chine and chiffon. Her hair was piled high and held by pins of sapphire. The innocent girl of the night before was gone. This evening she was every inch a woman.

Earlier, Caroline had come out of her room just as Pamela was going down the staircase looking regal and mature. Caroline knew she was doing wrong, but went back into her room and changed her elegant yellow, bugle-beaded gown for one less sophisticated, a simple trim-skirted gown of mauve and pink with a chemisette that fitted close around her neck. She let her hair fall more loosely and wore no jewelry except for an amethyst broach high under her chin. A beaded bag to match her gown dangled from her wrist.

Despite deliberately dressing herself down, however, when they entered Ravencourt Hall Caroline could tell by the glancess that she looked more as if she belonged here than did the regal Pamela Albright.

There was something about the ballroom that made Caroline uneasy. Unlike the clean, classic lines of Clarendon Hall, this place, with its heavy beams and horsey paintings, made her uncomfortable. It held a sense of foreboding, something dark and dire. An English murder mystery came to mind. Despite the gay music, the happy guests, she had the notion that the evening would not go well.

Adam danced first with Pamela, as was expected of him; but it was clear he'd have preferred to hold Caroline in his arms. Even as he and Pamela whirled about the floor, his eyes kept searching for Caroline.

"Remember me?" Pamela asked as Adam and Caroline exchanged smiles yet again—it seemed like the hundredth time.

"What?"

Pamela pouted. "You can't take your eyes off her. Really, Adam, you are being most annoying. If I didn't know any better I'd suspect you'd prefer her to me."

"You're talking rot."

The music ended and they started to leave the floor. Pamela said, "Two can play the same game, remember."

"I don't know what you mean."

She saw Jeremy Slyke enter the ballroom. She decided to snatch the chance of getting Adam's full attention. She caught Jeremy's notice and flashed him an inviting smile.

"Pamela," Jeremy said as he came up to them. He ignored Adam completely. Adam noticed that his bruised face had mended. "You look positively ravishing."

"I'm pleased someone noticed." She gave Adam a withering

look. Adam was glowering at Jeremy.

The music started.

"Dance with me?" Jeremy invited.

"I'd love to."

"Pamela," Adam warned from between clenched teeth.

"Excuse me," Pamela said as she took Jeremy's arm and flounced off.

Caroline tapped his shoulder. "Who's the smooth, handsome gentleman dancing with Pam?"

"He's no gentleman."

"He is very good-looking."

"He's a rotter."

"Oh my, do I detect a note of jealousy?"

He forced a smile. "Jeremy Slyke has been trying to take Pamela away from me since we were children."

Caroline nodded toward the laughing couple that danced by. "By the way she's enjoying herself, your Mr. Slyke may be succeeding." The name suddenly registered. "Slyke. The same Slyke who is in competition with Clarendon Foundries?"

"The same. He's Thomas Slyke's only son and heir. Dance with me, Caroline."

Adam felt as if he were being torn in two as the evening progressed. One minute he was blissful at having Caroline in his arms, feeling her full soft breasts against his chest. Then, glimpses of Pamela being monopolized by Jeremy made him boil with resentment. The greatest hurt was that Pamela was ignoring him, dancing almost every dance with Jeremy.

Toward the end of the party Caroline found herself in the arms of a charming retired major who was brimming with amusing stories of his military career. She saw Pamela and Jeremy and looked for Adam. She found him standing on the sideline glaring at them.

On the next turn around the floor, however, Caroline found Pamela and Jeremy gone. Adam, forced into a conversation with his host and a group of friends, hadn't noticed. As the major waltzed her around the second turn of the floor Caroline saw Adam turn and search out Pamela. His face grew red with anger. He slammed down his punch cup on the buffet and rudely pushed his way through the dancers toward the open doors leading into the garden.

There would be a brawl, Caroline was certain. She tried to find some tactful way of going off after Adam.

The waltz finally ended. Caroline excused herself and hurried into the garden. She hesitated, not knowing which way to go. The night was black with huge stars but no moon showed her the way.

She heard Pamela's muffled scream and ran toward it. Her slippers soaked up the dampness from the grass as she went quickly across the lawn and brushed through high rhododendrons bursting with flowers.

Suddenly she saw Jeremy Slyke lying on the ground beneath a tall sycamore tree. Adam stood over him, fists clenched, a smear of blood at the corner of his mouth. Pamela pressed back hard against the trunk of the sycamore tree, her hands to her mouth.

"I'll kill you if it's the last thing I do," Jeremy swore, wiping blood from his mouth.

"If I don't kill you first," Adam growled.

Slowly Jeremy got to his feet. He crouched like a caged animal, glowering at Adam.

Adam said, "Go home, Jeremy. Don't make me knock you down again."

"You've humiliated me for the last time." From the side pocket of his trousers he took out something long and thick. Caroline heard the click and saw the sharp deadly knife blade shoot out from its handle.

"No." Caroline yelled and rushed toward them.

Adam moved so quickly no one knew rightfully how it happened. One minute the blade flashed, the next Adam had caught Jeremy's arm and twisted it hard, sending the blade into Jeremy's shoulder.

# CHAPTER SEVENTEEN

Lydia found it inconceivable that Raymond would actually hire an assassin to push her from the top level of the Eiffel Tower, but that was surely what he had done. Who else had a motive for wanting her killed?

She did not tell the police of her suspicions when they questioned her. Why, she could not say. Even after the victim had been identified as a notorious hired killer she could still not bring herself to point an accusing finger at her husband.

Lydia had been told by his secretary and by the concierge of Raymond's hotel that her husband had left Paris. She had every intention of waiting for him to return, despite her yearning to be with Peter in London. She was tempted to call Peter and ask him to join her in Paris, but she knew of his complicated business transactions and did not want to interfere. Besides, Peter was not well. That thought disconcerted her more than her husband's attempt to murder her.

Lydia almost fainted with joy when she opened the door of her suite and found Peter MacNair standing there. He was pale and unsteady with beads of sweat dotting his forehead. She cried his name and wanted to throw her arms around him, but was afraid that he looked too frail.

She kissed him lingeringly, softly. Under the yellow pallor in his eyes, she saw sparks of excitement.

"Darling," she said, pulling him into the room. He kissed her again, more passionately.

"If I didn't have the most fantastic news I'd rip your clothes off before telling you."

"I think you'd better sit down. You don't look well."

"It's that damned fog crossing over. It brought on the sweats again."

"You shouldn't have ventured it."

"I couldn't stay away." He sat wearily in a chair. "Aren't you interested in my news?"

"It must be about business; I know nothing else that makes your eyes dance. A drink?" she asked holding up a decanter of brandy.

He nodded. "It isn't business this time." He waited until he had her full attention. When she handed him the balloon glass he said, "I've found Adam."

The glass she'd filled for herself almost dropped from her hand.

"Well," he added with an apologetic little wave of his hand. "I think I've found our grandson."

Lydia couldn't speak, except in monosyllables. "Where? When? Who?"

He sipped his brandy. "His name is Adam Clarendon."

"The Clarendon Foundries?"

He nodded. "When I met Lord Clarendon's young son, I almost dropped. He's the spitting image of David. The same hair, the same eyes, the same face. He walks like him, talks like him—except for that blasted English accent."

"But how? I don't understand."

"I need proof, of course." He hurriedly told her of everything he'd found out. "The Clarendons admit that Adam was born in America," he ended.

She lowered herself carefully into a chair. "But that doesn't mean—"

"I know, I know. I have no proof whatsoever that he's our grandson, Lydia, but I swear to you when you see him you will be as convinced as I am."

"It makes no sense. Surely Lord Clarendon and his wife didn't steal the child."

"I'm certain they didn't do so personally. Something happened when they were in America that put Adam into their hands."

"The kidnapping was too well publicized for them not to know who Adam was," she argued.

"They took him, I tell you. Their son is our grandson. I know he is."

"But you said you checked the records."

"Records can always be doctored, as we both know from personal past experience. That boy is Adam MacNair."

Lydia toyed with her glass, wondering if Peter's illness was making him desperate.

"Come back with me, Lydia. When you see for yourself you will know Adam belongs to us."

"I can't, Peter. Not just yet."

"Trouble with your husband?" He emptied the glass and went over to the liquor tray and refilled it.

"Serious trouble, I'm afraid." She fought back a sudden flood of tears. "Dear God," she said remembering the horror of that afternoon on top of the tower.

Hurriedly, he put aside his glass and knelt beside her, seeing her fear. "What is it, Lydia?"

She never thought she could get the words out. They choked her. "Raymond tried to have me killed."

"What?"

In stammering, broken sentences she told him about the man in the floppy hat and artist's smock who'd hurled himself instead of her over the railing of the platform. "I know Raymond was responsible," she finished.

"You've proof?"

She shook her head and blotted her tears. "No, but who else would benefit from my death?"

"That dirty son-of-a-bitch," Peter breathed. More gently he asked, "Have you informed the police?"

She shrugged and twisted the handkerchief in her hands. "Like you with the Clarendon boy, what proof have I?"

Peter got up and resumed his seat. He gulped more brandy. "I knew the man was a lunatic—but this!"

"He's obviously desperate," she answered fighting to keep her composure.

"And they say we Americans are barbarians."

"So you see, Peter, I can't let this thing go unresolved. Raymond is away from Paris, God only knows where. I must stay and have it out with him."

"Not you," he corrected. "I'll deal with your damned husband."

"No." The word was emphatic. "You must stay out of this."

"Why?"

"Because I know your temper and I know Raymond's sadism. You'll end up killing each other." She got up and splashed more brandy into her glass. "I've dealt with Raymond before. I know I can handle this myself."

"Strange. The last confrontation we three had was when you sided with that bastard and leveled a gun at my head." He was smiling.

"That was a long time ago. I'd prefer to forget it."

He put aside his glass again. "I do not intend leaving you here alone, Lydia."

"I don't know if Raymond is aware that his fiendish plot has failed. He may still think me dead. The sight of me will throw him off balance. I'll make my threats and he'll listen. I know he will."

"Threats?"

She made an offhand gesture. "I've lied before. I'm an expert at it when I have to be. How can Raymond be certain that poor devil didn't speak to me before...." She blotted out the memory. "I'll let Raymond believe we tussled and the man gloated about his intentions."

"Raymond won't believe that."

"He's a vain, stupid man, Peter. And very easily intimidated. He'll believe me. I can be very convincing when I have a mind to be."

"If he tried once and failed, he may try again. Have you thought of that? You must not stay here, Lydia. Give the bastard the company. Let him run it into the ground if he wants to. Your life isn't worth losing for Empress Cosmetics and Nightsong Perfume."

"I've been through too much to toss it all away at this point in time. I have the children to think about. I owe it to April and Leon, as well as to Caroline and Marcus. No, Peter, Raymond will never get the better of me. He's shown his hand. I'm on my guard now."

Peter saw she was determined. "God, Lydia, please be careful. I wouldn't want to live if anything happened to you."

The sincerity of his voice brought back her tears. "Oh, Peter, I love you so," she cried as she went into his arms.

"And I adore you."

They kissed. Lovingly he cupped her breasts. He reached for her hand and placed it on his hardening erection. "I need you," he whispered.

"And I you."

They rose and went toward the bedroom.

\* \* \* \* \* \* \*

Sometime later the telephone on the night stand jostled Lydia out of her sleep. Peter merely moaned and turned over.

It was the concierge of Raymond's hotel. "You asked me to telephone you, Madame, when Monsieur Andrieux returned. He came in a short while ago."

She thanked him, then rested herself back against the pillows, gathering up her willpower. Quietly she slipped out of bed, brushed her hair, put on the first dress she touched, and slipped from the darkened room.

Half an hour later she pressed the door buzzer of Raymond's penthouse suite.

"You!"

Lydia smiled and waltzed past him into the room. "Yes,

Raymond, it's me. I'm not a ghost." She offered him her arm. "Would you care to feel me? It's flesh and blood and bone, be assured."

He only stood there gaping.

"Close the door," Lydia ordered. "We have things to discuss."

Raymond nervously cleared his throat and fiddled with the ascot he wore under his lounging robe. He shut the door and when he turned to her he was beaming. He rubbed his hands together and said, "This is indeed a surprise."

"I'm sure it is."

"I'm sorry about our luncheon date, Lydia. Some rather pressing business came up that took me out of Paris."

"Stop it, Raymond. If it wasn't for me, it would have been the inspector of police ringing your door bell."

"What do you mean?" She was pleased to hear the note of fear in his voice.

"You know perfectly well what I mean. That unfortunate sham artist was too proud of his previous successes not to gloat when we grappled together on that platform. He even told me how much you were paying him to push me over. Unfortunately," she said, tossing her gloves on a table, "he did not reckon with my determination to stay alive."

"But...."

"The police have my account. I told them he lost his balance and fell instead of me. They knew him. A hired assassin, they told me."

"You told them what he said to you?" Raymond asked, his words tumbling together.

"As I said, if I had, the police would be here, not I."

He stared at her. Gradually his composure returned. "No one would believe you."

"Why not? Who else would want me dead? You'd have a lot to gain if I'd stumbled over that railing."

"What do you want?"

She lost patience with him. "You know damned well what I want. I want a divorce, for starters, and I want you to start producing Nightsong again. You know you are the only one in the world who has the nose to duplicate it. The company is going bankrupt, thanks to you. I want that stopped."

"Blackmail."

"If that's what you want to call it, so be it." She glared at him. "Do I get what I want?"

To her amazement Raymond laughed. "There for a moment you almost had me fooled. Hired assassins do not gloat about their accomplishments."

"This one did."

"No, Lydia, you are lying."

The door behind him opened and Yvonne swept into the room. When she saw Lydia she froze. "Who is this woman?" she demanded.

"Yvonne," Raymond said with a casual wave, "May I present my wife."

"Your wife? I thought—"

"You thought I was dead," Lydia finished. She studied the rather plain young woman. "Your taste in women is slipping, Raymond. After my daughter and myself I thought you'd have learned to be more discriminating."

Yvonne flung herself at Lydia's throat. Raymond grabbed her wrists and shoved her back.

Lydia remained unruffled. She picked up her gloves and went toward the door. "Remember what I said, Raymond. Either you give me what I ask or I will go to the authorities."

"The authorities?" Yvonne gasped. "She knows?"

"Shut up."

"So you are in on this together," Lydia said. "In that case I trust you have things to discuss between you so I'll take my leave."

"Wait a minute, Lydia," Raymond said. "You aren't frightening me. I have every intention of taking every cent out of Empress Cosmetics. There is to be no more Nightsong."

"You are as big a fool as I thought you were. Without Nightsong where would you be? Where would any of us be? Be sensible, for God's sake. Let's all forget this disgusting affair, give me a divorce, and go back to making this perfume that lines both our pockets."

"No. I want nothing more to do with being your 'nose.' "

"What do you want?"

"As I said, everything. Every cent."

"And when that's gone?"

"By the time I spend all I make from selling off the shares in your company—our company—I'll be too old to worry about it."

Lydia remembered something and smiled. "But you don't own all the shares in Empress Cosmetics."

"As your husband I do."

"No, Raymond. I myself don't own all the shares."

He watched her warily. "Now what lies are you concocting?"

She took her hand off the door handle and came back. "Many years ago, a man by the name of Walter Hanover financed my start with Empress Cosmetics. He owned fifty percent and gave me the other fifty percent. Mr. Hanover was not a gentleman. When the company collapsed that first time he skipped out, leaving me with a mountain of debts, which I eventually paid off. When Empress Cosmetics made its fortune he turned up like the proverbial bad penny and laid claim to his fifty percent. Peter MacNair bought that fifty percent from Mr. Hanover."

"Peter MacNair?"

Lydia nodded. "Your old adversary. So if you think you can sell off all the shares of Empress Cosmetics, you'd better consult with Mr. MacNair first. I don't believe he'll permit it."

"You are a bitch."

"A live bitch. No thanks to you."

Yvonne clutched his arm. "But you told me there were no other shares of the stock except what you controlled."

"There aren't. She's lying. Lydia knows as well as I the stock records show a one hundred percent holding."

"Peter never laid claim to his half, but he has the paper to prove his claim. All he needs to do is file it in a court of law. Oh, there would be another Nightsong scandal, as the newspapers like to call them, and there have been enough of those not to faze me at this stage of my life. But think, Raymond. I'd have to testify about that little incident on top of the Eiffel Tower. You'd be surprised at the number of people who'd believe me and I'm sure a thorough investigation by the police would turn up your connection with that man. And if not yours, hers," she said, pointing at Yvonne.

"Impossible," Yvonne blurted.

"I think not. It makes no difference to me which of you goes to prison, young lady. I'd prefer it to be you, of course, because I need Raymond's talented nose for business purposes." She looked from one to the other. "Think about it. I will expect to hear from you tomorrow and no later."

She went to the door and opened it. "Au revoir," she said, smiling, and left.

# CHAPTER EIGHTEEN

Marcus hadn't told his mother—if April was his mother—that he was leaving San Francisco for Paris. She would have forbidden him, just as she forbade everything that had to do with his father—if Raymond Andrieux was his father.

His mother's ravings had swept an entire world out from under him. Marcus wasn't sure where he belonged when he got on the steamship in New York. The more he thought of what she'd said, the more convinced he was that there could be an element of truth in it all. She had never much cared for him. His earliest memories were of an aloof, cold woman who frightened him with her dark eyes and strange moods. His grandmother had always been more of a mother to both him and his sister, Caroline. He never thought of himself as Marcus Andrieux, but as Marcus Nightsong, though his grandmother wouldn't permit him to use her name.

He'd never understood how his father could be married to his mother at one time and then to his grandmother at another. By the time he was old enough to ask questions, he was too embarrassed and put it out of his head. This wasn't too difficult because his father was seldom there, always traveling or living in Paris.

Caroline and he were close, yet even she, as they grew up, put a distance between them. Or had he been responsible for that distance? The first time he saw a racing machine it took over his life. Nothing mattered much, not anything except motor cars and Amelia Wilson.

"She's common," his mother had said, which made Marcus love Amelia all the more.

His grandmother, on the other hand, was fond of Amelia.

When Marcus disembarked at Le Havre, the first thing he noticed in the customs shed was a poster advertising an automobile race in Paris. Mercedes, Delage, and Peugeot had machines in the race. Marcus passionately wanted to see them. He hadn't been looking forward to arriving in Paris; now his meeting with his father didn't seem all that terrible.

He had no trouble with customs and managed to make an early connection with the boat train to Paris. Surprisingly, his high school French came back to him in phrases, then sentences; he managed rather well, except he was glad when he found so many people spoke English.

Settling himself in a compartment, which he had to himself, he opened his carryall and took out a science journal that contained an article about Henry Ford's new engine. He was engrossed in the article when the door slid open and a young girl came in, slammed shut the door, and dropped onto the seat opposite, muttering a word Marcus knew but thought nice girls never used.

*"Merde."*

He glanced up and found himself staring at her. Despite the angry scowl, the fiery eyes, she held a remarkable resemblance to Amelia.

*"Qu'est-ce qu'il y a?"* she spat.

"Excuse me." He went back to his article.

He heard her heavy sigh, then the drumming of her fingers on the wooden arm of the seat. Marcus glanced up. Their eyes met again.

*"Avez-vous une cigarette?"*

*"Je regrette."*

*"Merde."*

He grimaced, but could not help being attracted by her resemblance to Amelia. *"Avez-vous relatives en Amérique?"* he asked.

*"Pardon?"*

He repeated his question.

She laughed at him. "Speak English. Your French is terrible."

"I'm sorry." His face flushed. He hated it when anyone laughed at him. At least he was trying; to him that counted for something. Besides, the customs officers and train depot people had all understood him.

The girl said, "I made you annoyed, yes? I am sorry."

"That's all right. I know my French isn't all that good."

Her voice softened. "It will get better. To answer your question, no, I do not have relatives in America. Why?"

The sweetness with which she spoke encouraged him. "You are a dead ringer for someone I knew very well."

"Dead ringer?" she asked, making a sour face.

"Sorry. It's American slang for the exact copy, a mirror image."

"Ah, une jumelle."

"*Oui*. I mean, yes."

"She is pretty?" she asked with a coy smile.

"Very pretty."

"Then it must be that I am very pretty, no?"

"Very," he said. The science pamphlet fell forgotten to the floor.

She sighed. "My boyfriend, he does not think I am pretty. He said I am too old."

Marcus figured she could be no older than Amelia, younger even. Perhaps eighteen, he decided.

"Your boyfriend is blind."

Fire danced in her eyes. "My boyfriend is not blind! I, Denise Ambroise, do not have to go with blind men."

"It's only an expression. It means that he doesn't know real beauty when he sees it."

She thought about that, her finger dragging down a corner of her mouth. "That is true." With a hurt look she added, "He prefers that fat beast of a wife to me. Me! Imagine that. And his wife is old. She is thirty, maybe more," she stormed.

Marcus lowered his head and moved it sadly from side to side, suppressing his smile. When he looked up the smile was gone. Gradually he realized what she'd said and it embarrassed him. "You should not go with married men. A young pretty girl like you could have her pick of eligible bachelors."

"Bachelors. Bah! Young single men have no money to afford Denise."

"What about love?"

"Love. It is word, that is all. Where I come from, there is no place for love, only money."

"Where do you come from, Denise?"

"Paris, of course. But my friend, he lives in Le Havre in a big house with many servants. He furnished an apartment for me overlooking the bay. It was very beautiful. It had many rooms. I had even my own maid." Again the scowl returned. "Then that bitch of a wife made him throw me into the streets."

His face was burning. "I'm sorry."

"Oh, I suppose everything will turn out all right. I was getting tired of him anyway. I am missing Paris. It will be good to get back. He gave me plenty of money." She gave him a quick, side-long glance, realizing her mistake. "Not a lot of money, just enough to go back and to find myself a tiny room somewhere."

"You have no family?"

"Yes, I suppose I do. Somewhere," she said indifferently. She brightened. "Perhaps I can stay with you, no?"

He was taken aback. "Me?"

"You said I was beautiful, no?"

"Yes, very beautiful, but—"

"You have a mistress of your own?"

He couldn't answer. He merely lowered his head.

*"Alors?"*

"I am going to be staying with my father, I think."

"Does he have a mistress?"

Marcus had to smile. "Probably."

*"Quel dommage."*

The porter interrupted, announcing the dinner servings.

Denise said to Marcus, "You will take me to dinner with you? All Americans are rich so I know you can afford it." The porter looked disapproving.

"Yes, of course."

To the porter she said, "We will sit for the first service. A table for two only," she emphasized.

The Frenchman made a note and bowed to Marcus. "In fifteen minutes then, sir," he said and left.

"I hope you are not annoyed with Denise. I am very hungry. I did not eat before." She pouted. "I was too upset."

"It's all right. I'm hungry myself."

"*Bon.* Of course, I will repay you later."

He squirmed slightly, yet the thought of what she inferred made his penis begin to throb. He quickly covered it with the magazine when he picked it up from the floor.

The dining car was practically empty, for which Marcus was grateful. Denise ate like a field hand, wolfing down everything that was placed before her and demanding more. What she could not manage with knife and fork she ate with her hands. Marcus fidgeted, looking around to see if others were watching.

He was glad when she finished her third glacé and leaned back, rubbing her stomach. "Ah, now I feel alive again," she said smacking her lips. "A cigarette. Ah, but you do not smoke cigarettes. I forgot." To the passing waiter she said, *"Garçon, apportez mois des cigarettes."*

The waiter frowned and glanced at Marcus, who gave a helpless little nod. *"Oui, madame."*

"See," she said in a burst of fury. "He called me *madame.*" Then she pouted and sighed. "Albert was right. I am old. I am no longer *une mademoiselle.*"

Marcus smiled, but said nothing.

"You agree?" she asked in an angry voice.

"No, of course not."

The waiter brought the package of cigarettes and laid them beside Marcus's plate. Denise snatched them up and put them in her purse.

"I will not smoke here where the servants believe me to be a madame," she insisted for the waiter's benefit. "We will go to our compartment." To add to Marcus's discomfort she said with a loud laugh, "But I do not even know your name, monsieur."

He didn't answer. He put the necessary franc notes on the tray and stood up, thankful to be away from the disapproving eyes.

"Now," Denise said after settling herself in the compartment and lighting a cigarette. "We are alone."

He unconsciously glanced toward the glass doors.

"Ah, but if you are modest and want privacy, that is easily accomplished."

He started to protest but the girl quickly pulled down the shades and threw the latch. "Voilà. We are now private." She curled up on the seat beside him and toyed with the shaggy hair at the back of his neck.

He jumped as though an electric spark had touched him.

"Relax, *mon cher*. I will not eat you." She giggled and moved closer. "Or perhaps I will. You look, how do you say, delectable."

Marcus tried to clear the lump in his throat. He stretched at the collar of his shirt. The compartment was suddenly uncomfortably warm.

He wasn't totally ignorant about sex. He'd visited the sing-song girls in Chinatown once or twice with some of his friends. Once, after a heavy petting session with Amelia, he'd gone alone.

"Tell me again about this girl who is my dead ringer?" Denise cooed. "See, I learn American slang fast, no?"

He coughed as she blew in his ear. "Well," he started, trying not to let her notice how aroused she was making him. "She is very beautiful."

"Like Denise." Her voice was like cream.

"Yes." He closed his eyes and saw Amelia's lovely face. Amelia was nothing like this tart; he saw that now, but that did not prevent his penis from jumping to erection as her hands moved across his thigh.

With the tip of her fingers she outlined his length through the material of his tight trousers.

"You are large," she said in a low, hypnotizing voice. "I like large men."

He could not bring himself to stop her.

One by one she began undoing the buttons on his trousers. His body started to shake.

"Denise will do everything. She will show you how a frenchwoman shows her appreciation."

A gasp jolted him as she fumbled with the opening of his underpants and wrapped her hand around his engorged penis. She used both hands to free it.

"But—" Marcus said, a little frightened as again he looked toward the door.

"We will not be bothered. Paris is still a long way."

He could not resist the need that she was creating. His legs were parted and spread out in front of him as he slumped on the seat.

He turned his head to kiss her mouth, but she wagged a finger at him as she continued to stroke his penis. "French girls do not kiss strange men."

When she lowered her face to his lap it took every morsel of his strength to keep from crying out. He felt her hot breath on the glans of his erection and then the fleeting touch of her tongue. She kissed the head, holding the shaft with both hands. Slowly her head descended. She took the head of him into her mouth.

Marcus groaned as every fiber in him stiffened.

Slowly she sank to the base as though it were nothing at all. Little rivulets of saliva seeped from between her lips as she moistened the shaft, making soft sucking noises as she moved carefully, slowly up and down.

"God," Marcus breathed as strange new sensations coursed through him. He'd heard about things like this, but not even the singsong girls of Chinatown had created such ecstatic pleasure.

He couldn't help himself. He felt the telltale feeling building up at the base of his shaft and knew it would all be over far too soon. Agonizing little moans escaped his lips as Denise worked more frantically, massaging him with her hands as she sucked, swallowing him deeper and deeper into her throat.

Marcus's whole body went taut and he jutted upward with his hips. He didn't care whether he strangled her or not. The flood gates collapsed and the rush of semen bolted forth in thick, gushing streams.

Denise sensed the explosion and pushed him all the way into her throat, holding him there until the last of his spasms settled away.

Marcus was too spent to remember much afterward. Vaguely he felt her tuck him away and rebutton his trousers, then curl next to him. He heard her murmur something and then go across to her own seat.

It wasn't until the train pulled into the Gare de Nord in Paris that he opened his eyes and found he was alone. At first he thought he'd dreamed it all. On the platform, however, his dreams came hurrying up to him through the crowds.

"Hello," she beamed. "You snore. I could not sleep so I rode in the other compartment."

Marcus turned beet red.

"Be a nice boy and give Denise some money." She said it in a voice accustomed to asking such things without a care about who overheard.

Marcus nervously reached for his wallet and took out several hundred francs. He handed them to her. She made a face. He couldn't tell whether she was pleased or not.

"*Au revoir, mon cher.* If you want to see me again come to Madame Claire's. Everyone knows where it is." She threw him a kiss and disappeared down a stairway.

Marcus picked up his carryall and started toward the exit. Suddenly he found his steps lighter and he was grinning to himself. He started to whistle "*La Marseillaise*".

He hailed a taxi and gave the driver the name of the hotel

where his father lived. Paris moved around him like a flowing tapestry of texture, color, and sound. It was so strange, yet so familiar. He remembered, out of nowhere, that he'd been born here, according to his birth certificate. Remembering that, he sat straighter in the seat as the taxi honked and shook its way along Rue de Madeleine. Raymond Andrieux was surely his father, he decided. His mother had only lied to him because she had been upset.

He began to feel that the trip was a senseless waste of time. A smile touched his mouth as he remembered the pretty prostitute, Denise. Not a total waste, he told himself.

The taxi stopped under the porte cochere of the Hotel Georges Cinq. Marcus fumbled with the unfamiliar currency and paid the driver; too much, he thought, when the man grinned, tipped his cap, and sped off. A porter started toward him, saw his single carryall, and turned back.

When Marcus rang the buzzer of his father's suite he thought at first there was no one inside. He heard no sounds and had to press the button a second time. Still no one; but the desk clerk had assured him Monsieur Andrieux was at home.

Finally, tousled-haired, weary looking, Raymond opened the door. It took a moment before either of them recognized the other.

"Father?"

Raymond frowned. "Marcus. What in blazes are you doing here? What is this, some kind of family convention?"

Marcus didn't understand.

"Oh, forgive me, boy," Raymond said, forcing himself to smile as he ran his hands through his hair. "I've been having a bad day. Come in. Come in. What brings you to Paris? Did you cross over with your grandmother?" Raymond left him standing just inside the door and walked over to a smoking stand and lit a cigarette.

"No, I came on my own. Have you seen Grandmother?"

"Unfortunately, yes." He glanced at Marcus, who was shifting his weight from one foot to the other. "I am being rude," he said.

"Come. Sit down. I cannot give you much time, my boy. I was just getting ready to go out. Business," he added lamely.

"Of course. I only want a moment. If it's inconvenient I can come back."

Raymond didn't want to be forced into the position of host. He wanted Marcus away, back to wherever he'd come from. "No, I can spare the time. What is it you want? Money?"

"No, nothing like that."

"A place to stay?" He didn't let Marcus answer. "You can't stay here with me, unfortunately. I...."

"No, that isn't it."

"What then?"

Marcus fiddled with the straps of his carryall. "Father," he said hesitantly.

"Yes?"

"Are you really my father?"

"Am I—?" He shut his mouth. He looked at the boy and suddenly saw him as a possible threat he could hold over Lydia's head. She'd taken a great deal of pain and effort to hide the fact that Marcus wasn't her son by Peter MacNair. The truth would ruin Peter's marriage and everyone in the industry knew he depended on his wife for his finances. He could not afford to lose her and he might if she knew Lydia had borne Peter a bastard.

Lydia would never chance it, he decided. He smiled at Marcus and decided he'd play for time. "Of course I am your father. Who else?"

Marcus falteringly told him what April had said.

"Your mother is a lunatic." He made little circles at his temples. "You were born not far from this hotel. I know. I was there." It was no lie.

Raymond was buoyant. He was anxious now to keep his rendezvous with Lydia. "Now, if there is anything else you want of me, it will have to wait." He glanced at the clock on the wall. "I am late as it is."

"No," Marcus said as he started out. He felt disappointed and never realized how much he wanted what his mother had said to be true. "I'll be going."

"Are you staying in Paris very long?"

"No. I think I'll track down Grandmother and Caroline. You said you saw Grandmother?"

"Yes, but she was only here for a short visit. I believe she went back to London," he lied. He didn't want Marcus seeing Lydia just yet.

"Then I'll go over to London before going home."

"You do that, my boy. I only wish you and I could spend more time with each other but business...." He made a helpless gesture.

"Of course."

As Marcus left the hotel he had no idea where to start looking for passage to London. He walked aimlessly. He felt tired and didn't like the idea of again having to sleep on a train.

The train gave him another idea. On impulse he hailed a taxi and asked the driver to take him to Madame Claire's.

The driver grinned and made a U-turn in the middle of the street.

# CHAPTER NINETEEN

On the other side of the world, rickshaws and yellow skinned Chinese mingled easily with the governing English of Hong Kong. Wu Lien glowered at the way his countrymen kowtowed to the foreigners. He had been in Hong Kong too long, living in hiding in a squalid shack down near the waterfront. For fear of anyone recognizing him for who he was—a Manchu royal— he'd been forced to keep himself and Mei Fei out of sight during the daylight, venturing into the city only under the cloak of darkness.

Ignoring the humid, sticky night air, Wu Lien made his way along the crowded street, searching out the shop he'd visited before on his first night here, the shop of Wang Seng, dealer in imports and exports. Every night he came; every night it was dark and locked. This he thought peculiar, especially since Wang Seng had been so enthusiastic about putting Wu Lien in touch with Sun Yat-sen. Since their initial talk in Wu Lien's shack several weeks before, Wang Seng's shop was always empty. This annoyed Wu Lien, but he supposed it took time for Wang Seng to make his contacts and that he had to travel in order to do so.

There was no reason to distrust Wang Seng; he'd been a loyalist to the Dowager Empress, to whom he owed everything. The fat old man was a master of intrigue and treachery, but would never betray his own kind. Wang Seng was a Manchu through some obscure relative, Wu Lien reminded himself. The man had nothing to gain by siding with the republicans.

Wu Lien's anxiety to be about his business of disposing of the republican's leader made him impatient. He hurried across the street, edged his way through the shadows toward the rear of the shop. Three taps, then two. He waited, expecting again to receive no reply. This time, however, he heard a sound and a moment later the door creaked open and Wang Seng's face appeared in the light of the crack. The lizard eyes, hooded and black, had a hungry look about them.

Wu Lien was admitted into a large hot room overcrowded with priceless antiques, bronzes, ivory inlaid furniture. A huge pair of golden foo dogs guarded a doorway that led to the front room of the store.

"Where have you been?" Wu Lien asked.

The fat Chinese wagged his head. "These things cannot be hurried. Our mission is a delicate one. It was necessary that I travel north to make certain my information was correct."

"Then you have learned of Sun Yat-sen's headquarters?"

"His headquarters are common knowledge. It was his private residence I had to find. You would never reach within one hundred feet of the man in his headquarters. Your face is too well known, as are your intentions."

Wu Lien froze. "They know I am here to kill him?"

"They know you are Royal Manchu. They think you are in Hong Kong. They are not stupid men, Wu Lien. A Chinese republic is the answer to their prayers. Not a man among them would hesitate to cut you down on sight if he ever set eyes on you. You are a threat to their dreams."

"Fools. There can never be a republican government in China. This is my family's land and will never be anyone else's."

Wang Seng motioned for him to be seated and settled his corpulent body into a high-backed chair, giving him the look of an emperor. It angered Wu Lien that this merchant was seated higher than himself, but he needed the man's cooperation. There would be time enough later to deal with his imperiousness.

Wang Seng clapped his hands and a servant padded in carrying a lacquer tray with porcelain tea service. Wu Lien fidgeted while the fat Chinese served himself, then offered tea to Wu Lien, who shook his head.

"What have you learned?"

"Patience, Wu Lien. First we must speak of how you intend disposing of the great doctor." The flabby lips curled in a malicious grin.

"Knife, bullet, what does it matter?"

"Silence is a preference to sound. The knife, I think, which means you must be close enough to throw it, but in so doing you will not be absolutely certain he will die. Of this you must be sure."

"Tell me where I may find him and you need have no fears of his being alive after our meeting."

"Good." He set aside his teacup and unfolded a piece of paper he'd tucked into his sleeve. "This is where he sleeps. It is guarded, of course."

"No matter. I will manage." Wu Lien memorized the directions.

"Do you know the place?" Wang Seng nodded to the paper.

"It is to the northeast. Yes. I know it."

Wang Seng rose with some effort. "Then it is best you start out. The sooner this is accomplished, the better." He bowed, but the lizard eyes kept themselves fixed on Wu Lien. "I will take back the paper," he said, "lest it be found and I am implicated by my clumsy penmanship."

Wu Lien gave him the paper and quickly left the room.

No sooner had the door closed than Wang Seng clapped his hands again. The servant appeared. The lizard eyes moved toward the door. "Lose no time in dealing with this," he said. "If the Manchu succeeds we will be back to being mere merchants."

"Yes, master." The man bowed low and started out. Wang Seng stopped him with a word. "Wait. Did you find out where the Manchu is staying?"

"No, Lord."

"You've had him followed, of course."

"Yes, master, but he has been cautious."

"Search every shack on the waterfront. The ship captain said Wu Lien came with a woman who wore an ivory hand. It can only be the Princess Mei Fei. See that she, too, meets her ancestors."

"Lord," the servant said with a bow and slipped out the door.

Outside he stopped and made a quick jerk of his head. Two men, barefooted and in black, stepped from the shadows. The servant moved his eyes in the direction of the street. "You saw him?"

"Yes."

"That is the man you want. Do not lose him as did the others. He may make contact with a woman, a Manchu of the royal house. She too must be dealt with."

The two men gave grim nods and slipped back into the shadows.

A distance ahead Wu Lien started back to his shack, keeping under the cover of the night, hiding himself from patches of moonlight and lanterns. Halfway there he stopped, fingering the long dagger in his belt and wondered why he was wasting time on Mei Fei. He was sorry now that he had taken her. She did nothing but weep and moan and claw at him. He was tired of her body, so cold and unresponsive.

"Let her stay where she is among the rats and garbage," he decided. He turned back, not seeing the two men with the skinny eyes who ducked out of sight.

Wu Lien decided the deed must be done now. Afterward, perhaps, he would return for Mei Fei, if the mood pleased him. If it did not, she could rot where she was. She was in truth just another stumbling block to his own succession to the Manchu throne. Prince Ke Loo would be none the wiser. It could easily be explained. An unexpected separation. It was simple to lose someone in teeming Hong Kong. If she managed to survive, he would have an excuse ready.

He hurried along the street until he came to the road that led to the northeast toward Guangzhou. It was a long walk but the thought that within the next few days the leader of the rabble army would be dead made his steps quicker. After he killed Sun Yat-sen he would communicate with the Manchu generals and tell them to prepare for Prince Ke Loo's return. The generals would have their final confrontation with the republican rabble, but a peasant army without a leader or a purpose was no match for the Prince's soldiers.

Wu Lien smiled to himself as he reached the woods and broke into a run. "Ke Loo," he said. "I will deal with you after you have gotten China for me."

He did not know what hit him. A sudden stabbing pain scorched his back, as if a huge bee had stung him. He tried to clutch at the pain but it was too high, too well centered between his shoulder blades. He stumbled on, the pain spreading. A strange nausea seized him as a thick, heavy sweat broke out all over his body. Wu Lien staggered to a tree and leaned heavily against it.

Two black figures with yellow eyes, like those of starved leopards, came at him in a rush. He felt the bite of their knives rip open his stomach and slash upward, spilling his guts onto the ground. His eyes rolled in his head as he toppled forward. He rolled to one side, still trying to clutch at the pain in his back, not realizing he was already dead.

With a shuddering gasp he sprawled on his back as the last of his breath left his body. His bowels relaxed to relieve their waste.

"What do we do with him?" one asked.

"Drag him deeper into the trees. The forest animals will make their dinner on him tonight."

"And the Manchu woman?"

"She must be somewhere near the wharf," the older man said. "We should have no difficulty in locating her." He gave a soft laugh. "And now that we have fed the animals with this one, we will feed the fish with her."

His companion laughed and clapped his friend on the back. They pulled their weapons from Wu Lien's body and dragged it deeper into the tangled forest.

* * * * * * *

It had been four days since Mei Fei had seen Wu Lien. She did not know whether it was fear or relief she felt. Afraid to make inquiries, she kept inside the shack, never venturing out except at night to forage for food. She tried not to think of Tehani or the luxuries of her early years. The memories were too painful. She scraped through the rubbish and sniffed at discarded food, testing its degree of rot, like an experienced animal.

The waterfront was swirling in pockets of mist. In them Mei Fei found safety as she moved from alley to alley, trash heap to trash heap. Fog horns belched their sad drones. Dockworkers and deck hands, made ghosts by the ever pervasive fog, shouted to one another.

Mei Fei chased off a rat before it could attack the hunk of bread she'd spied, and heard voices from beyond the shadows that hid her. "Ivory hand with a pearl and jade ring," someone said. She instinctively pulled her hand into the sleeve of her dress. She inched forward and peered around the corner. Two men, young and rough, dressed in black tunics and trousers, were standing in the light of a street lamp talking to a man Mei Fei recognized as the one who dumped the uneaten food in the alley.

She saw him finger his scruffy beard and shake his head.

Her hunger was forgotten, displaced by terror. Someone wanted her found. Not Wu Lien, she told herself, else the men would have come directly to the shack. She could only suppose that the men were her enemies, revolutionaries who sought to destroy all Manchus. Wu Lien had warned her of the dangers of their being in Hong Kong. But only Wu Lien knew she was here, except for the ship's captain and his crew. As she looked at the men, intuition told her something was wrong. Wu Lien was not coming back; his mission had failed.

Where could she run? How could she escape? She had nothing except the dress she wore and her pearl and jade ring. A thousand times she'd been tempted to bribe passage back to Hawaii at the expense of the magnificent ring. Each time, however, she balked, telling herself that the ring only confirmed her royal bearing, which would betray her. Contrarily, if she tried to pawn it, someone might suppose she had stolen it. Either way it could mean her death.

She fought back the tears and the frustration and stepped deeper into the shadows, watching the two men move off down the waterfront. She knew it would be but a matter of time before someone would lead these men to the shack she and Wu Lien had occupied. She could not chance going back there, whatever the cost. Where, though could she find a refuge?

Unconsciously, she bit into the chunk of bread and tried to think more clearly. The bread was stale and tasteless and made her mouth dry. When she saw the men go into one of the saloons that lined the wharf she hid the uneaten bread in her sleeve and moved quickly in the opposite direction.

Wang Seng. The name came to her out of nowhere. He was the man Wu Lien said he must see and she remembered the fat, aging Chinese from long ago when he was the only food merchant trusted to bring provisions inside the Forbidden City. Surely if he had once earned the confidence of the Empress she could rely on his help.

Where to find him was her new problem. The chance that it was Wang Seng who'd betrayed Wu Lien occurred to her, but she had no one else she could turn to without even greater risk. Besides, unlike Wu Lien, she was here against her will and posed no threat to the republican insurgents. Wang Seng's appetite for rare and expensive things was known to her. She would buy his help with her prized ring of pearl and jade.

Mei Fei found new courage now that she had a goal. She remembered Wu Lien leaving at the first signs of night, saying he was going into the city. It was there, Mei Fei told herself that she must begin her search. The thought that she was being looked for on the waterfront made the business streets of Hong Kong more danger-free.

It was as she started away from the waterfront that her heart gave a little lurch when she saw a familiar figure. The man had his back to her and had stopped to light a cigarette. He exhaled smoke and rubbed the back of his neck. Then he turned back toward the far end of the wharf.

His name caught in her throat. She dared not call out for fear she was mistaken. Stealthfully, she followed the striding figure in the American clothes. When he walked toward the gangway of a freighter half obscured in the fog, he stopped again. Someone on board the freighter called to him.

"Leon!" Mei Fei cried and ran toward him.

Tears were streaming out of her eyes as she threw herself into his outstretched arms.

Leon spoke her name softly as he kissed her hair, her face. "Dear sister," he breathed. "Thank God. Thank God."

She didn't hear him. All the pent-up horrors of the preceding weeks swept through her. Her body sagged, her eyes closed and she fainted in his arms.

When she again opened her eyes she was lying on a clean white sheet, a light coverlet tucked securely around her. Leon was sitting anxiously on a stool beside the bunk.

Mei Fei flung herself into his arms again. "Oh, Leon," she sobbed. "Leon."

"It is all right now, Mei Fei. I'm taking you home. Wu Lien will not harm you again."

"Wu Lien is gone. I don't know where."

"Good. I hope hell has swallowed him up. But even hell is too good for him."

"Tehani?" Mei Fei asked.

"He is worried, of course. But you will be with him soon. This ship sails on the morning tide. I was going to stay until I found you, even if it took all my life."

"Oh, Leon, my sweet brother. You are a gift from heaven."

"You look as though you could use some food. Are you strong enough to go with me or shall I bring you a tray?"

"Don't leave me alone," she sobbed, clinging to him, her eyes wide with fear. "I am so afraid."

"I will never leave you until I have seen you safe in the arms of your husband. Come, let us go to the galley. The cook will get us something."

As Leon watched Mei Fei eat, looking like a starved kitten, he said, "I assume Wu Lien abandoned you."

She shook her head and bit off a large portion of roasted chicken, her ivory hand lying heavy on the table. "I do not know where he is. I have not seen him for four days. He went to see Wang Seng and never returned." She told him about the men she'd seen who were asking about her.

"Wang Seng?"

"You remember him from Peking? He provisioned the empress's storehouses. He was to tell Wu Lien where to find Sun Yat-sen."

"Even I know where to find Sun Yat-sen," Leon said.

Mei Fei looked up sharply.

"He is in Peking. The news is that the young emperor's reign is in its last days. It is only a matter of a short time before China becomes a republic. The news reached the islands just before I left."

"Then Wu Lien is dead."

"Let us hope so," he said without regret.

"And our father?"

Leon shrugged. "He is, of course, angry, but still blind to failure."

"But with China becoming republic how will he manage his opium trafficking?"

"Opium trafficking?"

She saw his astonished expression. "You did not know? All these years, our father has kept you, too, ignorant of what he was doing in Hawaii. Even Tehani did not know. The opium trade is how Ke Loo raised money for Sun Yat-sen, who was supposed to put Prince Ke Loo on the throne. After Sun Yat-sen betrayed our father, Prince Ke Loo used the money to finance his own soldiers. Wu Lien told me everything. Prince Ke Loo was exporting opium out of China and arranging for it to be sent into America under the disguise of cosmetics for some large company in San Francisco."

"MacNair Products," he said, trancelike as he recalled the name on the bales marked "Attar" and "Talc" that he'd helped load into the longboats.

"Wu Lien said an agent in San Francisco received the bales and then passed them on to another distributor."

"Damn," Leon swore.

"What is it?"

"I know the MacNair company. Peter MacNair, reprobate that he is, would never get involved in such an illegal operation."

Mei Fei shrugged and went on eating. "It is what Wu Lien told me."

Of a sudden Leon remembered Efrem MacNair. He worked for MacNair Products now and his sister's not-too-frequent letters mentioned how concerned the family was about Efrem.

"Surely not," Leon said, thinking out loud.

"What is it?"

"Nothing." All he wanted now was for the morning tide to roll in so they could be away from this damnable place. Once in Hawaii he had to go to San Francisco and speak to Efrem.

On the one hand the prospect of seeing Efrem again elated him; on the other hand, his suspicions made him terribly afraid.

# CHAPTER TWENTY

Fear was the last emotion Peter MacNair felt. His rage surmounted everything as he paced the sitting room of his Paris hotel suite. Lydia sat complacent and pale in a chair beside the fireplace.

"Let me understand this, Lydia. You mean you have agreed to that bastard's demands?"

She studied her hands in her lap. "I had no other choice."

"No other choice?" He broke into a wracking cough.

Her patience snapped. "Peter, please try and calm yourself. Look at you. You are as weak as a rabbit. Get back into bed. I'll get the medicine the doctor left." She got up and started toward the bedroom.

"To hell with the medicine. I'm mad, Lydia, damned mad. How could you agree to Andrieux's terms? How could you? Tell me."

Lydia ignored him as she went to the night stand and picked up the brown bottle and a spoon. When she came back into the room Peter was in a chair, wiping the sweat from his face.

"Get into bed," she ordered.

His anger seethed, but a terrible sick tightness clamped across his chest like a band of steel.

Lydia poured out a tablespoon of medicine and held it in front of his mouth. Peter frowned at it for a moment. Feeling another urge to cough he opened his mouth and let her feed him the foul-tasting stuff. He made a face and wiped the back of his hand across his lips.

"I just cannot understand you, Lydia," he said.

"I told you, Peter. Raymond's threats convinced me to give him what he wants."

"You mentioned his threats, but what threats?"

She tried to hold herself in control. "I think the threat of being murdered is quite reason enough."

"Jesus Christ!"

"I'm sorry, Peter." She became irritated. At all costs she had to keep Raymond from telling Peter about Marcus. "I happen to want to live a few years longer and die in a comfortable bed and not from accidental drowning or a fall under the wheels of a motorcar."

He made a sound of disgust. "Since when have you been afraid of assassins? They didn't seem to bother you much when that crazy empress had her henchman trying to run you down or strangle you in your own bedroom."

"I was younger then. I am not anymore and I want to enjoy what years I have left."

"You're insane."

"Leave it alone, Peter. I have already told Raymond I would give him control of Empress Cosmetics and he can run it into the ground for all I care. I have more money than I'll ever need, so what can it matter?"

"Just hand over everything you've stolen and fought for?" He shook his head. "No, it isn't like you, Lydia. You were never one to give in so easily and you are the same woman you always were."

"I am not. I'm tired. That's all."

He watched her for a moment. "You're not telling me every-thing. There's something that louse is holding over your head and it isn't a hired assassin. Now what is it?"

"It's nothing," she said impatiently.

He got up and grabbed her, turning her to face him. "Look into my eyes and tell me there is no more than what you've told me."

She looked away. "Oh, please, Peter, leave me alone."

Lydia's head ached. If she told Peter about their son, Marcus, he'd hate her for having kept that secret from him all these years, hate her for having the selfish pleasure of raising a son that belonged to them. When Marcus was born they had been enemies, she and Peter. He would have taken Marcus from her, brought up her scandalous life, and would have taken Nightsong as well. Nightsong had been his only reason for wanting her back then. She couldn't lose Peter's love now after fighting for it for so long. And now, today, knowing about Marcus, Peter would leave his wife for Lydia and their son. If he did that, Lorna would destroy all of them with her money and influence. No, she decided, steeling her spine, Peter must never know.

"You are not telling me everything." His jaw tightened as he looked toward the door. "If you won't tell me what in hell is going on, then I'll make him tell me." He flung her aside.

"Peter. No."

He got as far as the bedroom doorway before the dizziness took hold of him. He braced his weight against the jamb and rubbed his eyes.

"You're sick," Lydia said. "Get into bed this instant."

"I'm all right." He knew he wasn't. The room was spinning again and it was all he could do to reach the bed and sit down.

Lydia eased him back, resting his head on the pillows, lifting his feet. He didn't have the strength to stop her.

Sleep came easily and when he awoke the room was dark. Lydia was naked beside him. He adjusted his eyes to the dark and tried to remember what it was he had to do.

"The bastard," he muttered under his breath as he carefully got out of bed and started to dress. Quietly he crept out of the suite and went down the corridor.

The mirror near the lifts reflected a man he didn't know. He peered at the face until he realized it was his own. The eyes were sunken and hollow, the cheeks pale and drawn. He could look at the reflection only long enough to straighten his tie.

Thinking of Lydia's husband made him angry and his anger put new strength back into his body. He tugged at his lapels and left the hotel.

* * * * * * *

Raymond had Yvonne spread-eagled and naked on the bed. "Well, little slave," he said. His voice was husky, devilish. "What game shall we play tonight?"

Yvonne trembled as he forced two fingers roughly between the lips of her vagina. He bit hard into her nipple. She choked back a cry of pain and writhed under the cruel way he was fingering her. Her thighs spread, urging him deeper, wanting his whole fist if she could take it.

"Shall I tie you up?"

"Please." It was only a whisper.

Reaching into the bottom drawer of the small chest he took out manacles with which he slowly fastened her wrists to the brass bedstead. His breathing was heavy and rapid as he shackled her ankles with silk cords to the bottom posts.

He stood, vicious smile curling his mouth, his eyes lusting over her vulnerability. He lit a candle and tilted it close to her nipple, letting the hot wax drip slowly, painfully onto the taut, rigid flesh. Yvonne cried out in agony as the wax seared her skin. He moved the flaming candle to the left breast.

Yvonne twisted and tugged at her bonds as the candle came closer, the wax hotter, more scalding.

A banging on the door froze his hand. "Merde!"

"Ignore whoever it is," Yvonne begged.

Raymond ignored her. He wanted full concentration now that the game had begun. Quickly he snuffed out the candle and put it on the stand.

"Please," Yvonne begged. "Don't stop now. I need you."

"Wait." He adjusted his straining erection and pulled on a dressing gown. "I will get rid of whoever it is."

It took a moment before he recognized Peter MacNair. When he did he grinned. "I was wondering when I would hear from you."

"Bastard," Peter snarled.

Raymond laughed. "You don't look well, my friend. Perhaps you had better say what you have come to say. But first you had better sit down before you fall down."

"I can say it on my feet. You're a prick, Raymond. You have always been a prick."

"Perhaps that is why women find me so appealing." He shrugged. "But then perhaps you do not know of such things; perhaps you don't have a prick, Mr. MacNair." He opened the door wider and let Peter into the suite.

"What did you say to Lydia?" Peter demanded, ignoring the insult.

From the other room Yvonne called, "Raymond. Who is it?"

"I'll only be a moment, my dear." To Peter he said, "You see, my prick is being called for, so I would appreciate it if you would make your visit brief."

"I want to know what you said to Lydia."

Raymond shoved his hands into his pockets of his dressing gown. "My conversation with my wife is personal. Of course, if she chooses to tell you, then that is a different matter."

"Damn you. You know perfectly well I wouldn't be here if she told me what rotten threat you're holding over her."

"Threat? I made no threat. I merely reminded her that she was my wife and that husbands and wives share secrets."

"What secrets?"

"It is her secret, my friend, and therefore up to her to divulge, if she wishes."

Peter clenched his fists and tried to fight back the perspiration that was beginning to drench him.

"Sit down, Peter," Raymond said, smugly solicitous. "You don't look well."

A strangling tightness ran across Peter's chest. He found it difficult to swallow. He waved Raymond off. "I feel fine."

"A drink?" Raymond went to the cabinet and poured some liquor into a glass. When he offered it to Peter, Peter slapped it from his hand.

The insult angered the Frenchman. "Look, my friend, you and I have nothing to say to one another. What is between Lydia and me is none of your business."

"It is very much my business that you intend destroying an empire in which I hold a fifty percent interest."

"Oh, that." Raymond grinned. "Lydia mentioned something about a claim you have to Empress Cosmetics. Frankly, it doesn't bother me. If you wish to take me into the courts, please be my guest. I'm certain, however, that Lydia would never permit it." He narrowed his eyes. "And from what I understand, you do just about everything my wife asks you to do. Strange, isn't it, Peter, how things turn out. I remember you as a man who was just that, a man. You never allowed anyone to control what you wanted, especially a woman."

"Bastard." Peter lurched forward but his legs were too weak. He grabbed a table for support.

"Sit down, for God's sake, or better still, get out."

Yvonne called Raymond's name again.

"Coming, my dear." He leveled his eyes on Peter. "As I said, I am not alone, so if you came here with any intention of doing me harm, you had best think twice. But look at you, you are in no position to trample a bug."

"You son-of-a-bitch." Peter lurched again but as before his strength abandoned him. His knees buckled. The sweat was pouring out of him. His head dropped, his shoulders went limp as he dropped to the floor. He stayed there, kneeling trying to get his body to respond.

When he raised his eyes, Raymond was standing over him, his hands on his hips. He threw back his head and laughed. Sadistic bliss engulfed him as he looked down at the helpless man. "Finally comes the day when the great Peter MacNair kneels at my feet." He had an irrepressible urge to revel in his warped pleasure. "You called me a prick," he said, undoing the sash of his dressing gown and opening it to show his naked body. "As you can see I am very much that, my friend. I have never found men interesting, but now I have a strong desire to feel what a man's mouth is like." He moved closer.

Peter's disgust built up. He fought back the nausea as he hung his head and tried to speak. Even his voice was numb with revulsion and hatred. When he sensed Raymond's closeness some unknown force tightened his muscles, stiffened his bones.

"Here," he heard Raymond say and he knew, without looking, what Raymond was fondling.

"Filthy pig," Peter roared as he summoned all his strength and threw himself at the man standing over him. Peter knocked Raymond backward, sending him sprawling on his back.

"Raymond!"

Peter, blind with rage and disgust, put all his weight on top of Raymond's chest, straddling him, planting his knees on Raymond's upper arms, holding him helpless. He grabbed Raymond by the hair of his head and using every ounce of strength he began banging the back of Raymond's skull against the white marble floor. "Pig," Peter snarled as again and again he smashed the head down on the marble. "You rotten, perverted pig."

"Raymond," Yvonne's voice grew frantic, hearing the commotion she couldn't see.

"I'll kill you," Peter snarled in blind rage. Harder and harder he banged the head on the marble, scarcely hearing the crunch of bone, the shattering of the skull, or seeing the dead eyes staring up at him.

He didn't stop until the last of his strength abandoned him and he fell limp and unconscious to the side of Raymond's dead body.

Peter didn't know how long he lay there. Far off somewhere in the distance a woman was yelling words he could not make out. Gradually his eyes opened and he stared up at a pale blue ceding, a suspended chandelier that twisted and spun like a crystal top. He lay wondering why the woman's voice stayed so far away.

He became aware of a stickiness on his fingers. He raised them to his face and saw the blood, still wet and warm. It all came back to him then in such vivid horror that he was incapable of turning his head toward the dead body next to him.

Peter covered his eyes with his arm and rolled onto his side. He curled into a fetal position, trying to ease the wrenching pain in his chest and stomach, deafening his ears to the woman's frantic cries. Gradually the pain began to lessen, the power seeped back into his muscles. With an effort he pushed himself up, noticing the smudges of blood his fingertips left on the white marble.

Once on his feet he took a step, testing his legs. Every part of him ached; the worst was the excruciating stabbing in his chest. Sweat poured into his eyes as he staggered forward, bracing himself, grabbing the edge of the table to prevent his falling.

His face was hot and wet, his hair plastered to his scalp. Reason told him to get away. He could hardly move, let alone run. Water. His mind craved for something cool and clean and wet, something with which he could cleanse himself, wash away the bile that coated his tongue and throat.

Cautiously he staggered toward the bedroom, searching for a basin, a faucet. When he appeared framed in the doorway, Yvonne screamed. She yanked and pulled at her shackles. Her wrists and ankles were already raw and bleeding from her desperate struggling.

"Who are you? What have you done to Raymond?" she shrieked.

Peter saw the open bathroom door and staggered toward it, propping his way, leaving bloody prints wherever his fingers touched the wall or chair or dresser top.

He turned on the tap and splashed water into his face, gulping down the cool liquid he scooped up in his hands. The woman continued to yell and sob but he scarcely heard her.

When he felt slightly refreshed he straightened and looked at his face in the glass over the sink. His eyes closed on the horror of the sight. He turned quickly and started back out of the room. For a moment he stopped and looked at Yvonne.

His crazed expression, the deadness of his eyes froze her

blood. She stifled another scream as his eyes moved over her.

A voice kept telling him to leave, to get far away from this depraved place. Seeing the way she was tied to the bed only sickened him all the more. He swallowed the vomit that crept into his throat and made a lunge for the doorway.

He moved as a blind man finding his way through blackness. Raymond's body was lying as before. Peter would not permit himself to look at it. The man was dead, of that he had no doubt, and he had murdered him.

Fear and disgust propelled him out of the suite and into the corridor. He groped his way toward the elevators just as their doors slid open.

"Peter!" Lydia gasped as he teetered toward her.

"Lydia." It was as if he had said a prayer. He started to fall.

"Help me," Lydia cried to the lift attendant. "He's been ill. I must get him into a hospital."

Between them they got Peter to his feet and onto the elevator. In the lobby the lift attendant barked French to his superior. There was a scurry of people. Peter was only barely conscious that arms supported him, that people were talking, that he was being forced to move.

When the fresh air blew over his face through the open taxi window he opened his eyes. The scent of Nightsong filled his nostrils. For a moment he thought he was back in China, in Lydia's arms, in that crude shack with its painting of a nightingale a plum branch singing to the moon.

Lydia stroked his hair, rocking him gently as the taxi jostled them through the busy night traffic in Paris.

Peter heaved a desperate sigh and straightened his head. "Lydia," he sighed.

"Hush, darling. You are going to be all right."

"The hotel," Peter managed. "Take me to the hotel. We must leave here tonight."

"You are going to a hospital," Lydia said firmly.

"No. You don't understand," he said in desperation. He put his lips close to her ear. "Raymond is dead, I killed him."

Lydia's eyes widened.

"It's true. I killed him. We have got to get out of Paris tonight."

# PART THREE

# CHAPTER TWENTY-ONE

She believed him. No man on earth could look as haunted as he and not be speaking the truth.

Somehow she got him back to their hotel and up to his suite. Peter fell exhausted on the bed. With an effort she got him to take some medicine and let him sleep as she hurriedly crammed his belongings into his suitcase. Every sound, every flap of the draperies gave her a start. Any moment she expected the door to crash open and the police to rush in and arrest them both.

No one came.

After she finished emptying his wardrobe and bureau drawers she hurriedly cleared the bathroom of his toilet articles, then, checking to be certain he was fast asleep, she reluctantly rushed to her suite and began packing her things, not bothering about neatness or even items she decided to abandon.

Lydia phoned the desk clerk and inquired about a boat train to Calais. There was one at eleven that made a channel connection. The next wasn't until six the following morning.

"Peter," she urged, shaking him gently, then more roughly when he refused to open his eyes. "Peter!"

She couldn't rouse him no matter how hard she shook him. Almost to the point of hysteria, she splashed cold water on his face. Still he did not stir.

An agonizing fear clutched at her heart. She sank down on the side of the bed, resigning herself to the inevitable.

But still no one came. The room was dark, the curtains moved softly as the night air drifted through the windows.

Hours passed. No one came.

Lydia stood braced against the framework of the French doors, watching the chinks of dawn break into the night sky. She turned sharply when she heard Peter moan and move on the bed. She rushed to his side.

"Darling," she said in an urgent voice.

He opened his eyes. He held his arms out to her.

She threw herself into his arms; their feel and comfort swept away the terrible night she'd paced through, not daring to close her eyes.

"Peter. We must leave. There is a boat train at six. We haven't much time."

"Leave?" His mind was groggy, his eyes not fully in focus.

"The police."

Peter pushed himself up on one elbow and looked around. He saw the suitcases sitting beside the door.

"Dear God," he breathed, rubbing his hands over his face to blot out the sudden image of Raymond's smashed skull, the accusing eyes, the pool of blood.

"Can you stand?" Lydia coaxed.

"Yes. I'm all right now." He swung his feet over the side of the bed and started to get up. He wobbled and fell back, putting his hands over his head.

"Just take it slowly, darling. Come. I'll help you. Lean on me."

"It's all right, I'll manage. Christ," he said shaking his head slowly from side to side. After a moment he looked up and saw her tears. "I'm sorry, Lydia. I lost control. There was a scuffle. Raymond fell. He hit his head."

"Please, Peter. Don't think about it. We must be away before anyone finds out. You were seen and will be recognized. It's only a matter of time."

"I know, I know." He got to his feet unsteadily.

"I've packed for both of us." She went to the phone and asked for a porter and a taxi to be waiting to take them to the railway depot.

Through the whole mad-dash trip to Calais and after, Peter could not bring himself to tell her the truth of what had happened in Raymond's suite. The sound of Yvonne's voice, her tortured face haunted him whenever he closed his eyes. More haunting still were those lifeless, staying eyes peering up at him from that white marble floor, stained indelibly with Raymond's blood.

As for Lydia, a hundred times she started to ask what he and Raymond had said, but she could not bring herself to ask. The fact that Peter made no mention, not even the slightest hint about Marcus, assured Lydia that Raymond had kept his part of their bargain—at the cost of his life, she reminded herself.

No good would come of any of it. She knew that as well as she knew the channel steamer was bumping the pier at Dover. At least they'd gotten safely out of France. Deep down, she knew Raymond's ghost would never let them forget him. Peter could be identified by any number of people. They should go home to America as soon as possible, she decided.

As she looked at Peter dozing beside her, a sharp pain stabbed at her heart. He was far too ill to attempt so long and damp a trip yet. She had to wait until he was stronger.

"Darling, we've reached England."

Peter's eyes shot open. He looked at her through a thin veil and when he saw her smile he rubbed his eyes, glad that she'd awakened him just before the nightmare started again.

Weak and tired, Peter managed to push himself up. His legs were like rubber but held him, much to his surprise. A happier surprise was that they had no problems when the customs officer checked their passports and cleared them without more than the perfunctory questions.

"I don't think it's a good idea to go back to the hotel in London," Peter said. Things were clearer in his mind now that he was rested. He remembered all the evidence he'd left in Raymond's suite, the fingerprints, the witness shackled to the bed, the desk clerk who'd given him Raymond's suite number, the elevator attendant who would remember, when questioned, the stains on his jacket and shirt front.

Lydia nodded, her brow creased. "I've been giving thought to that and I agree. Besides, you should be somewhere where you can get a lot of rest and quiet."

"No hospital," Peter said.

"No," Lydia agreed.

A porter tapped on the compartment door, asking if they would like lap robes or pillows.

"Yes, please," Lydia answered. "When we arrive in London is there a convenient doctor near the station? My husband is not feeling very well."

Peter smiled. He liked that: "My husband."

"There is a small clinic right in Victoria Station, ma'am," the porter told her.

"Excellent. Would it be possible to arrange for a wheelchair?"

"Lydia," Peter objected. She stopped him with a sharp reproving shake of her head.

"Of course, ma'am. I'll see to it."

"I'm not an invalid," Peter said when they were alone.

"The sooner you are completely well, the sooner we can go home." She wasn't thinking of that entirely, however; in the back of her mind was the thought that if they were looking for a man wanted for murder, they'd least expect him to.be in a wheelchair.

"Home," Peter sighed. "Yes, it would be nice to be in San Francisco now." He put his hands behind his head and conjured up the soft breeze that blew in from the Bay, the steep hills, the clanging trolleys.

"Adam," he said, suddenly remembering. "Christ, I'd almost forgotten."

"The Clarendon boy?"

"He isn't the Clarendon boy. He is our grandson, April's and David's child."

"Peter," she said patiently. "You can't be positive of that. He may resemble David, but that proves nothing."

"You haven't seen him. Wait until you meet him."

"Don't you think we had best forget about this boy under the circumstances?" She gave him an uneasy smile. "Think of your predicament. Until you have cleared yourself of Raymond's accident, you won't be able to move in this country, let alone start some scandal against Lord and Lady Clarendon. It would be wise for us to go back to San Francisco as soon as possible and let it be handled through the proper authorities."

"Proper authorities," he scoffed. "What will they do? Check the records—which have been faked—and we come up empty handed again. No, Lydia, this time I am going to do it myself."

"And if you do, you'll destroy the Clarendons, even if you still come up empty-handed. They are nice people, from all I've gathered."

"I'm a nice person and look what I did."

"All right. I agree the Clarendons may have taken the boy, but I am positive there were extenuating circumstances. They couldn't have known who he was."

"They knew. I saw the looks on their faces when I hinted about Adam. No, Lydia, they are guilty as sin."

"They are also not without influence and money."

"Influence, I won't argue. Money? I don't think they have all that much."

"We are still foreigners in their country. You haven't a prayer to win out over them. These people are still fighting the Revolutionary War whether they like to admit it or not. Public sentiments will favor the Clarendons and every possible stumbling block will be put in your path before the British authorities admit they did anything wrong."

Peter thought. "There's one item of proof that we must have that will settle everything."

"What?"

"The tattoo April described. The mark of the Manchu that devil of an Empress carved into the boy's thigh." His eyes shone. "That old devil. She finally did something of which I approve."

"And how do you propose finding out if the young man has such a tattoo on his thigh? You can scarcely ask him to remove his trousers to satisfy your curiosity. Remember what they did to Oscar Wilde."

"I'll think of something."

"You are going to rest for a week or two before you do anything." She glanced out of the window. "We're coming into London."

The wheelchair was waiting with a white-coated attendant. They had no trouble getting to the neat little clinic, all white and efficient. There was no doctor at the moment but the matron nurse took Peter's temperature, auscultated his chest, and checked his blood pressure.

"There is a fever," she diagnosed, "and a rasping in your husband's chest. I'm only a nurse, of course, so I'd suggest you have a doctor give him a thorough examination," she told Lydia after leaving Peter in the curtained cubicle.

"He's been very tired of late. I was thinking possibly of a resting-in place. Somewhere he could be kept away from business stress, somewhere quiet and remote but not too far from London."

The nurse wrote an address on a card. "This should be ideal. It's a small, private sanitarium but very highly regarded." She eyed Lydia's clothes. "It is not inexpensive, but I think it is precisely what you have in mind."

It was indeed what Lydia wanted. Nestled in acres of woodlands not far from the hub of London sat a picturesque Tudor mansion that looked nothing like what it was.

"Just rest, darling, " she told him when they had gotten Peter installed in a private room, "and try to think of nothing but getting better. I'll visit every day."

"You are not going back to the hotel?"

"Of course. Caroline is already worried about me. I'm sure."

"You were seen with me," he reminded her. "That elevator man will describe you just as he'll describe me."

"If anyone asks, all he can tell them is that I got off the lift and we both helped you to a taxi. Besides, whatever dangers threaten, I want to know of them. Someone has to keep a finger on the pulse of this thing and you are in no position."

He rested against the pillows, exhausted again. "I suppose you're right."

"Of course I'm right. You get well. That's an order." She kissed him gingerly on the lips.

He hated the idea of staying, but the pains burned inside his chest and he felt unnaturally weak. With a sigh he accepted the fact that it was best to stay quiet, at least for a day or two. Then he would find some way to prove Adam Clarendon was his grandchild and he'd take him back home where he belonged.

* * * * * * *

He wanted to kiss her. The desire pulsed inside him, the pressures kept building and building like a long dormant volcano that struggled for life.

Adam closed the top of the picnic hamper just as Caroline reached to do the same. Their hands touched, their eyes met, and each saw the other's desires. Without speaking Adam stood and stretched out his hand. She felt the heat of his body as he stepped closer. Her body trembled as he took her in his arms.

"Are you sure?" she whispered.

"Never more sure," he answered.

She wanted to remind him of Pamela but couldn't.

The kiss was hot and passionate. Neither could stop what was inevitable. For days, since Pamela was now refusing to see him, taunting him with a seeming preference for Jeremy Slyke's company, Adam countered her taunts by seeing Caroline at every opportunity. Being with Caroline made him forget Pamela, and holding Caroline in his arms, kissing her as he was doing now, Pamela disappeared from his thoughts completely.

"I want you." Caroline's bold whisper kindled the flame that burned hot in his loins. He loved her forwardness, the way she had of anticipating his thoughts, his needs, and taking control of them.

"Oh God," he breathed over her mouth. "And I want you, my darling." He fumbled with her blouse, one hand cupping her breasts. Never had he felt such wanton desire. He knew this inexperience made him crude, but her eyes spoke only of what she needed him to do.

"Not here," Caroline said, looking around at the pleasant meadow with a small cluster of sheep grazing at the far end, two young shepherds sitting, legs crossed, on top of a rise.

"Where?" He was breathless.

"Take me back."

The words shattered him. He gaped at her, feeling her slip from his arms. "But—"

"Grandmother is still in Paris." She walked quickly toward the roadster, her hips swaying provocatively. "Bring the hamper."

They spoke little on the drive into the city. Adam drove faster than he normally did, which was fast enough. His heart beat in his chest, his hands were tight on the steering wheel. From time to time he glanced sidelong at Caroline, who sat wedged in the corner of the seat studying his face.

"We shouldn't, you know," she said evenly.

"I know." It was all he could manage. After another mile of silence he asked, "Have you ever before?"

"Of course not." Another long pause. "Have you?"

He merely shook his head.

For one without experience, Adam astonished her with the way he caressed her body, kissed her breasts, moved his hands to precisely where she wanted them.

"Are you certain your grandmother won't come in?"

Caroline had to smile. "It's a bit late to be thinking of that now that we are both naked and in bed together."

"The maid?" he asked breathlessly as he let his eyes roam over her beauty. The sheen of her skin was like polished ivory, its softness made him tingle. He liked her total lack of inhibitions. She was so free, so open and honest. He didn't want her to be shy with him—and she wasn't. She had reached for him the moment their naked bodies pressed together, stroking his throbbing erection as if it were the most precious jewel in the world.

Caroline felt that she was drowning in the love that poured

from within her heart. She wanted to speak of her love but was afraid. He belonged to another; she knew that and chastised herself for having seduced him.

Dear God, she thought, I couldn't help myself. Adam Clarendon was all she had thought about since that first night he'd rescued her. There were worlds between them but none of it mattered to her as she felt his hands caressing her thighs, bringing her from one high pitch of ecstasy to another.

"Adam," she murmured into his shoulder as she clung to him, feeling him between her legs, probing, begging for admittance.

"Please," he gasped.

"Yes. Oh yes."

He loomed over her and sank deep into her warmth. She wrapped herself around him, pulling him deeper, blinding herself to the shame she knew she should feel.

The hardness of his body, the power of his thrusts drove her to the borders of insanity. The sharp pain of his first entry was supplanted by the most delicious waves of intense pleasure. She began to move, awkwardly at first, then with increasing urgency as he dominated every move of their bodies. She panted and gasped as he pummeled her harder and harder. For Caroline life didn't exist, only the tremendous need that itched at her. Faster and faster their bodies pounded together, their flesh melting into one. Flashes of brilliant light lit up her brain, shooting sparks through her as Adam began to moan softly, then more audibly as he threw back his head, pinched shut his eyes, and sank his long, thick penis all the way in to its hilt.

The room exploded in a searing burst of blinding sensations. It was as if their two sweating bodies were lifted high into a star-filled sky, offering themselves as sacrifices to unbearable ecstasy.

Far off somewhere distant she heard sobs and realized they were her own.

Adam rolled away and lay staring up at the ceiling. She nestled close to him, trying desperately not to let him see her tears. Accusing voices sounded in her ears, reviling her for her wantonness.

Adam's eyes were wet with his own conscience. A sheet of guilt and remorse pressed over him with almost unbearable weight. He closed his eyes tight when Pamela's face started to take form.

"Adam?"

He turned his head but did not look at her face.

"Are you sorry?"

"No. It was terrific," he said, smoothing her shoulder, caressing the nape of her neck. He gave her an encouraging hug.

"But I'm not Pamela, right?" Caroline said as she brushed away her tears and propped herself up.

"Stop that. I won't have you thinking like that."

Caroline went quiet as she studied his handsome body. "I'm not sorry," she said. "I don't want you to be either."

"I'm not. It was wonderful."

"And I don't want you thinking it makes any commitment on us."

Now he looked at her. "But I want a commitment."

"No. I think we should take things slowly. What we did we did because we wanted to. I wanted it as much as you and I have no regrets."

"Neither have I," he said giving her an encouraging kiss. The kiss was light, without warmth or feeling.

"We couldn't help what happened."

Suddenly Adam laughed. "We certainly could have, except we didn't want to." Suddenly he felt himself getting aroused again by watching the rise and fall of her breasts, the pouting nipples he so badly wanted to feel between his lips.

With an unexpected jerk he grabbed her and began tickling her.

Caroline squealed, laughing hysterically as his fingers teased her ribs. The foreplay turned more violent as they scrambled about on the bed, tossing in one direction, then the other until Caroline toppled to the floor.

She lay sprawled, laughing up at him. The moment went

serious as their eyes met and held. Again the surge of desire swept through her. She took the hand he held out and crawled back onto the bed. This time she took the initiative, arousing him with her tongue as she licked the muscles on his chest, her fingers toying with the wiry dark hairs that based his erection.

Caroline looked down at it, idly wondering how she could have accommodated so lusty a weapon without being ripped apart. As she looked her eyes moved down over his thighs.

The tattoo of what looked to be two open flowers caught her eyes.

"What is this?" she asked, tracing the design with her fingertip.

"A birthmark. At least that's what my parents said."

"How peculiar. It looks so perfect, as if it were put there on purpose."

"Here," he said, taking her hand and putting it around his eager erection. "This was put there for a very definite purpose."

"You're shameless," she said as she touched her mouth to his.

As it happened, Lydia took that precise moment to walk into the bedroom of their suite.

# CHAPTER TWENTY-TWO

Prince Ke Loo's peacock chair was empty. Leon pushed open the door to the dark inner room and found his father kneeling on a mat, his forehead touching the floor in obeisance to the golden idol on the altar before him. Leon had returned with Mei Fei only three days before. In those three short days the pompous, strutting prince, his father, had turned from a god into a feeble old man. His purpose for living was over. There would be no throne, no armies to direct, no subjects to rule. He'd been beaten, betrayed, and the defeat had sapped him of all ambition.

"The gods won't change anything," Leon mocked.

Prince Ke Loo did not move.

"I am leaving, father. I want no part in this opium traffic. Furthermore, I would suggest you look elsewhere for means of a livelihood because I intend going to San Francisco and exposing this entire filthy business of yours."

His father's deception had made him furious and desperate for revenge. Further, he was concerned about Efrem. The more he thought about what Susan had written about Efrem and the fact that their company was being used by Ke Loo for opium importing, the more Leon was afraid. He had to get to San Francisco as soon as possible, regardless of how much he dreaded confronting Efrem. Too much time had already elapsed; God only knew how deeply Efrem was involved, and Leon was convinced he was involved.

Prince Ke Loo straightened but did not turn his eyes from the golden idol. His lips moved, muttering some ancient prayer.

Prayer for what, Leon wondered? Tradition had taught him to revere his father, but Leon had broken with Chinese tradition long ago. As he looked at the old prince he couldn't bring himself to hate him—he only pitied him, which was far greater insult to the great Manchu prince.

"I'm going," Leon said.

Still Prince Ke Loo did not turn. He bent low and touched his forehead to the floor again.

Leon hesitated. "I wish you no harm, Father. It is just that what you are doing cannot continue."

Finally the old man spoke to him. "You disgraced your family before. You are no Manchu, no son of mine."

Leon turned quickly and went out.

He did not see Prince Ke Loo reach for the white silk robe with the twin poppies design embroidered down the back. Slowly, carefully he put on the robe and arranged it about his corpulent body, pulling the sash tight. He placed the dagger before him on the mat. Again he bent low to the idol, then straightened, lifting his eyes to heaven. Slowly he extracted the dagger from its sheath. He held it firmly with both hands and pressed the sharp tip of the blade against his naval. Some antique intonation moved his lips as he slid the dagger into his stomach, slicing upward, opening his stomach from navel to rib cage.

\* \* \* \* \* \* \*

Leon found San Francisco vastly changed. There were still a few scars here and there reminding everyone of the devastating earthquake. The new San Francisco excited him all the more with its modern, high buildings, its sleek newness, the bustling people all looking so anxiously forward to its future.

As he drove through the streets from the wharf he made a vow that he would return to Hawaii only long enough to gather up his family and bring them here where new horizons were opening up.

The house on Nob Hill was different yet oddly the same. He

had to smile as he looked at the turrets and spires, the Victorian trim for which his mother had such a passion. Determined and progressive as she wanted everyone to think she was, the old ways died slowly for her.

He would build his own house for Ohlan and the children, but not here on the hill. He wanted it overlooking the sea, a place where he could see the farstretching oceans and feel the freedom America represented.

April recognized her brother the minute he walked into the drawing room. She jumped from her chair, letting the book she'd been reading fall to the floor.

"Leon," she cried, throwing herself into his arms. "Oh my darling Leon." She kissed his cheeks and hugged him tightly. "You don't know how I have missed you."

"And I you," Leon said. He held her at arm's length and looked at her. She'd changed so much. There was no sparkle in her eyes and her hair was streaked with gray. She looked old. The black dress with its high neckline made her look older.

"You look wonderful," April said.

He returned the compliment but didn't mean it.

"What are you doing here? Why didn't you let me know?"

"It was a sudden decision. Things were not going well."

Her expression saddened as she moved away. "Yes, I heard of the news in China. That accursed Dr. Sun Yat-sen. And what of our father?"

"He's dead, April." His voice was flat. "Just before I sailed, Mei Fei told me his concubine discovered the body. He died honorably by his own hand."

April went limp. "So we are finished."

"We were finished many years ago. The republic was inevitable."

"No. Our blood will again rule China one day."

Her expression frightened him. He looked away. "The world is changing, April. We must change with it."

April drew herself up. "You were always the weak link in our family's chain, Leon. Never have you been dedicated to the

Manchu's supreme right. If you had not deserted the Empress and Prince Ke Loo for this American who is your mother, we would still be in power in China."

"Talk sense," he said, becoming annoyed. "What is a handful of Manchus against an entire nation that wants to rid itself of its bondage?"

"Wu Lien will do what you should have done. He will not let the Manchus die like old apples on a tree."

"Wu Lien is dead also. He was assassinated in Hong Kong. Word of it reached father before...." He let his words trail off.

"Assassinated?"

"Call it what you wish. He was betrayed by Wang Seng, Prince Ke Loo's trusted emissary."

"The snake," April hissed.

Leon glanced around. The deadly quiet of the house pressed against his ears. "Forget the old, April. It is passed and best stay in the past."

"Never."

He was in no mood to pursue the subject. "Where is Mother?"

She shrugged. "London. Paris. Who knows. Wherever it is, you can be certain she is up to no good."

"You shouldn't dislike her so much."

"I don't dislike her. I despise her for everything she's done to me."

"April, please don't start in on that again. As I said, can't you forget the past?"

"No. I am not like you, Leon. I will never forget who I am or where my loyalties lie."

His impatience grew. "Your loyalties lay with the woman who brought you into this world and protected you from a heinous father who would have had you smothered at birth or cast into the 'baby well' if your mother hadn't intervened. It was she who protected you from being poisoned by the Dowager Empress."

"Our mother is an empty foolish woman, ignorant of Manchu traditions and customs. How can you sympathize with her? She is a Caucasian. We are Chinese."

"Half-Chinese," Leon reminded her.

"I don't acknowledge that part of me. I am a princess just as you are a prince. Wait." She ran out of the room and up to her bedroom. A moment later he heard her tripping down the stairs. When she came up to him she was breathless with excitement. She held out a clenched fist and slowly opened it. Resting in her palm was a lovely jade and gold ring, handsomely etched with a twin poppies design.

"Do you know what this is?"

"Yes, of course. It is the emblem of the Manchu Dynasty."

"Only a royal Manchu dare wear it. I had the Empress's personal goldsmith make it. I wanted to give it to my husband. You are a Manchu Prince, the only living heir to the throne. You must wear it."

He tried to hand it back. "I am finished with all that."

She raised her hand and slapped him hard on the cheek. "Traitor." She suddenly broke into heart-wrenching tears.

Leon took her in his arms and soothed her. "All right, dear sister, if it will please you I will wear the ring. See, it fits perfectly."

Her tears were forgotten. "Of course. Now swear to me that you will never remove it. You are the true prince of China. No revolution, no world calamity will ever change that. And it is because of our loyal blood that our mother hates us."

"She does not hate us." The ring felt heavy on his finger.

"She does. Oh, you think she likes you. When it suits her she will turn on you as she turned on me many years ago. Don't you see, Leon, our mother will never accept our royal blood. She lives her life the way she was brought into it, by low peasant people who scratched out a living trying to force their god on others. Her entire life is plain because she is plain, all black and white, which is the way she thinks. I was never someone she wanted. I was forced upon her. How can she do anything but resent me? She is a hard, callous woman, vain and ambitious who lives to survive for her own pleasures." She turned aside. "She is old now. She will be dead soon. Good riddance."

"April."

"Leon, don't you understand that we have a family to preserve? We must overcome Prince Ke Loo's mistakes."

Leon stepped back, as if afraid her madness was contagious. To try and reason with her would be useless, he saw. It was far too late for reasoning.

"What about Caroline? Marcus?" he asked.

"Gone. Everyone is gone. Adam, David—everyone is gone."

Leon shifted nervously. "Listen," he said brightly, "as long as it's just you and I, why don't you get yourself all decked out and I'll take you somewhere elegant for dinner? To celebrate my homecoming."

"Your home is in China."

"Please, April. For me?"

Slowly she shook her head and sat in the chair next to the windows. She parted the curtains and stared out at the street. "I can never leave this house until he comes back."

"He? Who?"

She turned to him. "My son, of course. He is coming back. I have to be here."

"Yes, of course," he stammered. It was futile. If and when the boy was brought back, how would he accept this half-crazed woman as his mother? But perhaps with Adam back, April would return to her old, vibrant self.

"And when Adam comes home we will go to China, to Kalgan, to the home of his grandfather."

Leon turned from her and went up the stairs to where his room used to be. Knowing his mother, it would be much the same as when he'd left it. The thought made him pause. April wasn't all that different from their mother; they both clung hard to the old ways. The only difference was that his mother would not permit the old ways to obsess her completely.

He met Nellie coming out of his mother's bedroom. "Leon," she cried as she dropped the sheets she was carrying and hugged him. "Oh, your mother will be so pleased to find you home again."

"Hello, Nellie. Still changing linens?"

"You can't trust the help we get these days." She looked a bit embarrassed. "Your mother's away, but I still change the sheets regularly. Old habits, you know. And you know her, bound to come popping in without so much as a word."

"She's in Europe, April tells me."

"Business. She took Caroline along this time. Marcus went dashing off after them soon afterward." Her pleasant Irish face grew somber. "You've seen Miss April?"

"Yes. I found her in the drawing room when the maid let me in."

"Poor love," she said, touching the corner of her starched apron to her eyes. "Always sitting staring out at the street, waiting for the boy." She sniffed. "Ah, now here I am blubbering and you just arrived, starving as usual, I gather."

"I thought I'd eat out."

"Not as long as old Nellie is running the house in Miss Lydia's absence. I'll fix all your favorites meself, just like always."

Leon didn't relish eating dinner with his sister and Nellie read his thoughts. "Miss April eats in her room now—near the window where she can watch the street." She gave him a little shove. "Go wash the sea air off you. You smell like a sailor. Your room is where it always was and I've kept it ready for you, of course."

"Thanks, Nellie." He gave her a kiss. "You're a treasure."

"An old one," she laughed. "But antiques increase in value, they tell me."

"They do indeed." He started away. "Incidentally, the MacNairs? Is their house still up the street?"

"The old house was blown up like ours to make a fire break during the quake. They're in the same spot, though but they went modern and put themselves up one of those townhouses, they call them. Same lot. Right on the corner." She frowned. "What would you be doing wanting to visit the MacNairs? The man's away. Only Mrs. MacNair's there, and the son, of course. Oh, yes, her daughter and grandchildren are visiting from New

York, one of the maids told me."

"Susan's here?"

"Has been for a few weeks, I understand."

"I'll go up after dinner and pay my respects."

Nellie scoffed. "If Mrs. MacNair is home you'll not pay anything of the sort. She still carries her grudge against the lot of us."

"Well, let's hope the old firebrand isn't home." He paused. "Efrem?" he asked. "Susan's brother?"

The old woman made a face. "In the saloons I imagine." Then she laid a finger on her cheek. "But now that I think of it, one of the help was gossiping about his seeing a lot of that Stanton girl."

"Ellen Stanton?"

"The younger sister. Yes, Ellen's her name."

Leon started for his room; he found himself smiling.

"Dinner at the usual time," Nellie called as she gathered up the sheets she'd dropped and went down the hall. "I'll not forget the apple fritters."

# CHAPTER TWENTY-THREE

Not far from Clarendon Hall in the Slykes' mansion, Tom Slyke sat in the wing chair by the fire, swirling brandy around the bottom of the snifter. Jeremy, his son, was sprawled on the divan staring up at the beamed ceiling.

"They'll not get away with it," Tom Slyke swore as he raised the glass to his lips and drained it.

Jeremy knew what he meant. "Damned Clarendons," he muttered. "I'll settle my score with Adam if it is the last thing I ever do." He touched his shoulder where the knife blade had stabbed him.

"The son is not our immediate concern. It's the MacNair contract we've got to have. Basil Clarendon will never have it, that I can promise you."

"And how do you propose getting it away from him, Father? If Mr. MacNair hadn't skipped off to the continent they'd have the glass contract in their hands already. It's only a matter of the American coming back before it's settled."

"Which gives us time to do something to put a wrench in the cogs."

"Like what? That girl MacNair brought with him is in thick with the Clarendons, especially with Adam. And the great lord and lady will do anything that bastard wants."

"You've hit it on the noggin, my boy. That bastard," he echoed. He suddenly thought of something.

"Of course," said Jeremy. "I'm not complaining about the bastard's attention to the American woman." He laughed. "That ass left the door wide open for me. Pamela's practically fainting in my arms these days. She can't seem to get enough of me." He stretched his handsome frame, wincing at the pain from the stab wound. He touched it gingerly. "But I still have a score to settle with Adam, nonetheless. That boy has to be taught a lesson."

"You should have shot him when you had the chance."

"I didn't want to kill him. I could have if I had wanted to. Everyone knows there is bad blood between us. No, I have something else in mind for Adam."

"Like what?"

"Make him a cripple. Pamela would never want to be married to a cripple. Cut his balls off. Now that's really what I'd enjoy doing."

"How?" his father asked, unimpressed. His son, he'd learned long ago, was a lot of talk and little else. "He is not a stallion you can tether and slice."

Jeremy knew his dream was unrealistic. He shrugged.

"Ruin the grand lord and you will emasculate the son," Tom Slyke said.

"How?"

"Scandal, of course. Pamela's family wouldn't consent to a marriage to someone in disgrace."

"He's already in disgrace because of what happened at the party. He's been ostracized."

"Not really. The Clarendons have a lot of pull. They're royalty and after all the royals side with each other regardless of what."

"Then what would a scandal accomplish?"

"Discredit the heir. Without an heir who's to inherit?"

"Surely you aren't thinking of that gossip about Adam being the son of a mad woman? Everyone has heard that and has laughed it off."

"Still, there is something queer about the way the Clarendons suddenly returned from their travels with an heir. Deep down I know they're hiding something."

"You've checked into that long ago. Everything proves him to be legitimate."

Tom Slyke slammed his fist into his palm. "That's what rankles me. Everything is too perfect. Something is rotten about the whole affair." He leaned back, propping his chin on his fingertips. "I have been reading in the papers about those East End thugs who go about pressuring merchants into paying for protection. We might use that."

"Protection? I don't understand."

"You don't have to," his father answered, irritated. "I have a plan."

"What kind of a plan?"

"You'll see." He sat quiet for a moment. "I must frighten the Clarendons off. They're gradually reducing us to paupers what with their new glassblowing methods. Basil is getting too progressive for his own good."

"You really hate him, don't you?"

"He married the woman I once loved."

"Millicent Clarendon?" Jeremy said, surprised.

"Millicent Farnsworth then. Common, like myself, but the most beautiful woman in England. We were engaged—or practically so, until Basil Clarendon decided he wanted her. My family was no match for his."

"But if she loved you—"

"Millicent never loved anyone but herself. She was always a selfish, spoiled woman who got whatever she wanted. Oh, you wouldn't know that now by looking at her. She's all polish and refinement with an invented high Scottish family. She wasn't always like that. Common as us," he repeated, "and just as ambitious." He leaned forward. "I guess I couldn't blame her for trying to better herself."

"So she married a title."

He nodded gravely. "Without a glance backward."

"Do you still love her?"

Tom Slyke didn't hesitate. "I hate the sight of her. That's why I have no qualms about ruining them both."

"Is the Clarendon Foundries so stiff a competitor?"

His father scowled. "If you'd take an interest in your father's business you'd know the answer to that."

"Business bores me."

"It won't when you're put out into the streets."

"Bad as all that, is it?"

"Worse. The MacNair contract would put me back on my feet. Without it the glass works will have to close down and we will both have to find ourselves a job."

"A job? Father, you must be joking."

"No. I wish I were. I've made it possible for you to go to the best schools, even cut a niche for you in society, but we don't have a title, only a little money and that will soon run out. You'll find, my boy, that without money the Slykes are finished."

"But this house, the fortune you've made."

"Times change. I've put everything I have into the new machinery to try and keep in competition with Clarendon. If the glass works fail, we are destitute. This house is mortgaged; everything we have was put up as security with the banks in London."

"God, I didn't realize."

"I didn't want you to know. I've raised you to be a gentleman and a gentleman you shall be. Leave Basil Clarendon and Millicent to me. They'll not ruin me if it takes my last breath to prevent them. With them out of the picture, all their business will come to the Slykes Glassworks. We'll never have to concern ourselves again."

"I still don't see how you intend accomplishing that."

"As I said, I have a plan."

"Some bullyboy type threat won't frighten them."

"Basil runs like a hare when threatened. He's not a fighter, only a business man with foresight and luck." He got up. "Come along, we're going to pay a visit on Lord and Lady Clarendon."

"Now?" He glanced at the clock on the mantel. "I have a dinner party I'm taking Pamela to."

"You'll be back in time to dress. Our visit will be a short one, believe me."

\* \* \* \* \* \* \*

"I don't like it," Millicent Clarendon said to her husband. "Adam is spending far too much time with that Andrieux woman."

"All the better for business, my dear."

"Pamela is heartbroken."

"Not from all appearances. She's seen regularly on the arm of Jeremy Slyke."

"All the more reason for you to put a stop to Adam's seeing Caroline. Besides, she's years older than Adam."

"Caroline will be going back to America in a short time. Once the MacNair contracts are signed she'll go home with Peter MacNair and her grandmother."

"Grandmother? I've heard of her but I still have to see this grandmother. Frankly, I doubt if she exists. It's scandalous for Caroline to be traipsing about with an older man to whom she isn't slightly related. And as for Peter MacNair, I don't like that man," Millicent said.

"You don't like his questions about Adam."

"We both know who he is. It was in the newspapers. If Mr. MacNair suspects, he'll do everything to prove his suspicions correct."

"He will never prove his suspicions. I've seen to that. Just calm yourself, my dear. They will be gone soon and everything will be back the way it was, only better."

"I wonder. I feel afraid, Basil. Things could turn against us. If only Adam would come back from London. Why is he staying away so long? What if...."

The sound of a car pulling into the courtyard made her pause. She went to the mullioned windows and looked out.

"Tom and Jeremy Slyke," she said with astonishment. "What on earth are they doing here?"

Basil asked the Slykes the same question after the butler showed them into the study.

Tom Slyke bowed to Millicent. "This is not a social call," he said.

"I hardly expected it to be," she said

Tom Slyke turned to Basil. "I've come to discuss the MacNair contracts."

"There is not much to discuss, Tom. The MacNair contracts have nothing to do with you."

"They belong to me and I want them."

Basil raised his brows. "You want them, do you? Well, you'll not have them. Mr. MacNair gave us both equal opportunity. He happened to have chosen my foundries."

"Not because your glass is superior, surely?"

"You know it is. Oh, I'm aware of all that new equipment you've been installing but aren't you a trifle late, Tom? You've been so preoccupied playing the country gentleman that you've allowed your business to suffer. This is no time to do what you should have done years ago."

"As you did?"

"Yes. Mass production is the future for all businesses. Truthfully, I've shown MacNair that I can produce his perfume vials and cream jars faster and cheaper than anyone else."

"My new machines will do better," Tom Slyke argued.

"They are not even completely operative yet. The American won't sit on his hands waiting for you to prove yourself. You are a slacker, Tom Slyke. You always have been."

"And you are too ambitious for your own good." He spoke more to Millicent than to her husband.

She said, "If ambition makes my husband better at business than you, then he is indeed ambitious."

"He or you, Millicent?"

"Tom, please. Say what you have come to say and kindly leave. We have guests coming."

"I've said what I have to say, except...." He watched the wariness rise in their faces. "There is the matter of your heir to be considered."

"What does Adam have to do with any of this?" Millicent asked.

"He is not your son." Tom Slyke said coldly. "I am positive of that."

Millicent refused to be daunted. "Of course Adam is our son. What devious gossip are you hatching now?"

He grinned. "If I had proof that Adam is not yours, what would you exchange for that proof? The MacNair contracts?"

"Get out," Millicent ordered. "I'll not listen to a new pack of lies from the likes of you."

"I have such proof," he lied.

Jeremy, who'd been standing just inside the study door said, "But I thought...."

"Be quiet," his father barked. To the Clarendons he said, "Adam is not your son. I know he isn't."

Millicent calmed the beating of her heart. "You can't have any such proof because none exists. The birth record is on file for anyone to see."

"Records are easily falsified."

"Kindly leave, Tom. You're talking like a madman."

"I've made inquiries. I know Adam isn't yours."

Millicent threw back her head and laughed at him. "You know nothing."

"You'll not laugh when you're without a penny, without your precious title."

Basil said, "I don't know what deviltry you are up to, Tom, but I warn you to be careful." He went to the door and opened it. "I would appreciate it if you and your son left these premises. You are not welcome here. You never will be."

Tom Slyke motioned to Jeremy and they started out. As Tom got even with Basil he said, "I'll see to it that you are disgraced and thrown in jail for child-snatching. Then we will see who listens to me and who doesn't."

"Get out."

When the door closed after them, Lady Clarendon said, "What proof does he have?"

"None, my dear. He's only bluffing. He needs the MacNair contracts and will stoop to the lowest level to get them." He rubbed his chin. "It isn't Adam's legitimacy I'm concerned about now."

"What then?"

"That man is desperate. I know Tom Slyke. Desperate men do desperate things."

"But what can he do?"

"Nothing that I can think of, but Tom Slyke is a man in a corner. He's tried to ruin me before. He'll try again." He went to the windows and watched the Slykes' automobile start down the drive.

\* \* \* \* \* \* \*

When their car rounded the corner, out of view of the house, Tom Slyke braked and looked toward a small thatch-roofed building just beyond the hedges, almost adjacent to the left wing of the main house. "Odd, he said to Jeremy.

"What?" He looked about.

"That shed. It's new." Tom saw the head gardener pushing a wheelbarrow along the box hedge. "Shamus," he called.

The Irishman doffed his cap and came over to the automobile. "Good day to you, Mr. Slyke. Never thought I'd be seeing you paying a social call on his lordship."

"Business, Shamus. Something mutually beneficial which erases ill feelings." He glanced toward the shed. "That's new, isn't it? Are you sure it will stand up in a good wind?"

The gardener cackled. "Ah, it's a lark of his lordship's. He built it for ventilation, he said. His lordship keeps all kinds of bottles and kegs and bubbly stuff in there where he wants them kept dark, but cool and airy. God himself only knows what's in there. It has to do with the making of the glass, it does. That's what his lordship says, but as for meself, I think it's devil's work. Funny-looking stuff; all different colors, seethin' and foamin'." He shuddered.

"Most likely going to still his own whiskey," Tom joked.

"Not his lordship. Only the best liquor for him these days."

"Doing well, is he?"

"From the looks of it. He's even ordered a new greenhouse built—a solarium, her ladyship calls it. Supposed to be attached to the back of the left wing overlooking the lily ponds. A lot of nonsense if you ask me. Flowers are to be grown out in the air, not in a hothouse of glass."

"Well," Tom said grinding the gears. "I'll be seeing you, Shamus."

The Irishman tipped his cap as Tom drove on down the drive.

"Chemicals," he said to himself. "Well, now isn't that convenient."

# CHAPTER TWENTY-FOUR

By the end of the week Peter MacNair was feeling his old self again, or very nearly. Idleness was something that rubbed against his grain. Lying in bed only served to make him feel worse.

"What are you doing?" the stiffly starched nurse asked when she came in to find Peter buttoning his shirt and stuffing the tails into his trousers.

"Getting dressed, of course."

"Mr. MacNair. You are not to leave that bed for at least another week. Doctor's orders. So get yourself out of those street clothes and back into your pajamas."

"No way. I am going for a walk."

"You are going no such place."

"I might even motor into London."

"I'll fetch the orderly." As she started out of the room she met Lydia coming in. "Mrs. MacNair, will you kindly try to talk some sense into your husband's head? He's far too weak to be walking about."

"Peter?" Lydia said as she kissed him. "Are you sure you are strong enough to be up?"

"I won't get stronger by lying on my back all day."

Lydia turned to the nurse. "I'll see to him," she said. "You are looking so much better."

"I'm feeling it. Oh, my legs are not exactly the Rock of Gibraltar. All they need is some exercise." He put his arms around her. "I've got to get out of here, Lydia. This place is beginning to depress me. The only thing I like about it is that they call you Mrs. MacNair. It has a lovely sound to it."

"Yes, I know. I rather like it myself."

He kissed her mouth. "Now that you're here, that bed doesn't seem all that bad. Want to try it out, love?"

"Peter." She slapped his chest. "We are both too old and respectable to act like a hot blooded intern and a student nurse."

"Never. Every time I look at you I feel twenty again." He caressed her breasts. "Darling."

She felt herself melt against him. "No, Peter, please. Not here."

"Where?"

"Oh, I want to, darling, but I'm afraid it might tire you."

"Tire me?" he said angrily. "What do you think I am, some puny weakling? I'm as strong as I ever was."

"Yes, of course, you are."

He kissed her again. "If you're worried about my overexerting myself, you could do all the work and I'd just lie still and enjoy myself."

"You're incorrigible."

The nurse was back with a muscleman in white.

"It will be all right, nurse," Lydia said. "I have a car and chauffeur outside. I'll look after my husband. A Little fresh air might do him good. He isn't accustomed to being confined."

"The responsibility is yours, of course," the nurse said.

"And I'll gladly assume it."

Outside the air was crisp and clean and smelled of autumn. The leaves were beginning to turn and fall. The sky had a frosty tint to it though the day was warm.

"I am very concerned about Caroline," Lydia said as they settled themselves in the back of the towncar and drove off through the gates.

"You told her who Adam is?"

"No, I'm afraid I couldn't bring myself to."

"Damn it, Lydia, you must. They're brother and sister. What you walked in on was incestuous."

"I know. I've told myself a thousand times Caroline must be told, but truthfully, Peter, we have no absolute proof that Adam is who you think he is."

"You saw him. Is there any doubt that he is David's son? They're twins."

"Yes, there is a strong resemblance. It's just inconceivable for me to understand how the boy got to England. If he is our grandchild, how did they explain him to the immigration people?"

"Embassy connections, obviously. Lord Clarendon has a lot of influential friends. Old family and all that rot. His kind stick together like flypaper." He cranked down the window that separated them from the driver. "Drive into London," he ordered. "The Claridge Hotel."

"Peter, no."

"Yes," he said emphatically when the glass was up again. "If you won't tell Caroline, then I will."

"But if you're wrong...?"

"I am not wrong and I'd feel a lot happier if you'd come over to my side on this."

The car lumbered forward, whipping up dead leaves around it as it sped over the country road. When they reached the hotel Lydia asked, "Do you really think this is wise, Peter? I mean what with Raymond's death and all, people may be looking for you."

"No one has so far, you told me."

"True, but it will only be a matter of time before they make an identification. The sanitorium is where you should stay until I can get the Clarendon contracts signed and we can leave for home."

"How are you managing with that?" he asked, hedging her complaint.

"I haven't been in touch personally with Lord Clarendon. Your solicitors are handling it all but they're as slow as snails. I've tried hurrying them, which seems to make them all the slower."

"That's because they aren't keen on dealing with a woman.

I'll put a fire under them."

"Light the fire quickly, darling. I want to be away from here. I must get you and Caroline home."

Caroline was just coming from her bath when Lydia and Peter walked into the suite. She was rubbing her long, dark hair briskly with a towel.

"Peter," she cried as she went to him and kissed his cheek. "You look wonderful."

"I'm no less the worse for wear and tear." He pecked her forehead. "I could use a chair, however. My legs are still a bit shaky."

"Here, sit here," Lydia said. "I'll get you a brandy."

"A brandy," he sighed. "I'd almost forgotten there was such a thing. And I never want to see a glass of milk or a cup of tea again."

Caroline started for her own room. Peter stopped her. "I want to speak with you, Caroline."

"Oh?"

"It's about what your grandmother told me involving you and Adam Clarendon."

Caroline's face reddened. "Oh, that."

"Yes, that." He paused. "I don't want to embarrass you, my dear, but I need to know a few things."

"Here we go again," Caroline said, rolling her eyes. "You asked me once before to play Grand Inquisitor with Adam but you never explained to me why."

"I intend to now."

"Peter," Lydia protested.

"Let me handle this, Lydia. I am convinced that Adam Clarendon is your brother."

The color drained slowly from Caroline's face. "You must be joking."

"I only wish I were, Caroline."

"But that isn't possible."

Peter sipped the brandy and leaned back, crossing his ankles. He studied Caroline's shocked expression. "I am afraid I must ask you a most indelicate question. You remember, of course, that your mother lost a son some fifteen years ago?"

Caroline nodded slowly, apprehensively.

"His name was Adam. He was my son David's child by your mother."

"I know all about that," Caroline managed.

"Well, I think Lord and Lady Clarendon were the ones who took Adam from San Francisco and brought him here to England."

"Impossible!"

"Not so impossible. Their private railway car was at the San Francisco depot on the night Adam disappeared. They were traveling in America and on their way to New York and eventually home."

"Your fever has left you mad."

"No, my fever gave me a lot of time to think. I have no absolute proof, I admit. Only you can give me that."

"Me?"

"Here comes the indelicate part, my dear. I don't like prying into other people's private affairs, but this time I must. When you were in bed with Adam—"

"Peter!" Lydia cried.

He held up a restraining hand and started again. "When you and Adam were together in your bedroom, did you perhaps notice anything unusual on his body?"

Caroline's face was crimson. She couldn't speak. She looked helplessly toward her grandmother.

Lydia said, "You're mortifying the girl."

"I'm sorry. I must know, Lydia. Please, Caroline, it's important. Did you notice a tattoo on the boy's thigh?"

"Peter, this is most embarrassing," Lydia objected.

"No more so than for me. Well, did you Caroline? Two open poppy flowers surrounded by a wreath of dots, tattooed high up on his left thigh."

Caroline's eyes were wide and frightened. She braced herself against the table beside her.

"Well?"

She gave a quick nod. "Adam said it was a birthmark."

"It is a tattoo that the Empress of China implanted in his skin, the mark of the Manchu Dynasty. It was done when April and he were held prisoners in the Forbidden City. Your mother will tell you all about it, if you don't recall yourself the descriptions of Adam that were published in the newspapers."

"Dear God," Caroline sobbed. She did remember now.

"There you are, Lydia. Now we have the proof we need to confront the Clarendons."

Lydia was rooted to the spot. She saw Caroline's horror, her misery. Proof indeed, she thought, but at what a terrible expense. "What good will all this accomplish?" she asked Peter. She was thinking of Caroline and also of her half-crazed daughter, April, whom they'd give Adam to. April was hardly fit for the part of an ideal mother. Better she be left to dream and hope and live in the private world she'd created for herself.

"What good? If you don't want your grandchild, then I certainly can't understand you, Lydia."

"Of course I want him, but April...."

"April needs him more than either of us. From all you've told me she is living like a dead woman. Restoring her son will bring life back into her."

"Perhaps," Lydia said, but she wasn't convinced of that.

"My God," Caroline breathed as tears of shame rushed down her cheeks. She felt unclean, spotted, like a leper.

Lydia tried to console her. She put her arms around her granddaughter. "You had no way of knowing, darling."

It was little consolation. Caroline pushed herself away and fled into her bedroom, agonizing sobs tearing at her throat.

When the door slammed shut a heavy silence dropped over the room. After a moment Peter took another sip of brandy and looked up at Lydia. "Well, there it is. Adam Clarendon is our grandson."

"Oh, Peter, I don't know. Think of Caroline."

"As you told her, she acted in innocence. She'll feel terrible about it, naturally, but that can't be helped. We didn't put her in bed with him. She'll recover."

"I wonder—especially if you're wrong."

"Wrong? What more proof do you need? How many Adams are walking about with a Manchu crest tattooed on their thigh? Face facts, Lydia. Stop fighting me on this." He put his glass on the table and stood up. His legs were unsteady but they held him. "I'm going to the Clarendons."

"Now?"

"Yes, now. The sooner this thing is brought out into the open the better for everyone concerned."

Lydia sorted through her confused thoughts. She had to think more clearly; she needed time. "Perhaps you should go back to the clinic. This can wait another day or two. You are peaked-looking."

"I am feeling better than I have in months. He raised a questioning eyebrow. "Are you coming with me or do I go alone?"

Lydia knew she could not dissuade him. She picked up her gloves. "I'll come with you, of course."

\* \* \* \* \* \*

The late afternoon sun streaked the road as the motorcar pulled into the Clarendon estate. Caroline's desperate sobs coming from behind the closed door still echoed in Lydia's ears. One part of her wanted things to rest where they were; another wanted justice and her lost grandson.

"Peter?" she said, questioningly.

"I know what I'm doing, Lydia."

"But if it's true, if Adam Clarendon is April's child, think of all the others who will be hurt, even Adam himself."

"Call it selfishness, or whatever you like. I want that boy to know who he is. After that, the decision will be his to make."

"What will it accomplish?"

He gave her a hard look. "You astonish me, Lydia. Think of all April has been through. Knowing will give her peace of mind at least."

"I wonder," Lydia said as the door opened and the butler told them his lordship was in the drawing room with his wife having tea.

"Mr. MacNair," Basil Clarendon said. "How very nice. You're just in time for tea." He glanced at Lydia.

"May I introduce Mrs. Nightsong," Peter said. Out of the corner of his eye he saw Lady Clarendon stiffen in her chair. "Mrs. Nightsong is Caroline's grandmother."

Basil Clarendon was obviously shaken. "Yes, of course," he said in a stammer. "Charmed." He took the hand Lydia offered him. "I've heard Caroline speak of you, of course. May I present my wife."

The two women smiled and exchanged nods, but there was a touch of hostility in their smiles. It was clear that Lady Clarendon was upset. She may have not remembered the name MacNair, but she certainly remembered the name Nightsong.

"I'm happy to meet you, Mrs. Nightsong," Lady Clarendon said. "I've heard of you and your wonderful perfume, of course."

Peter saw she was terribly frightened. She hadn't even offered her hand to Lydia. He could see that Millicent Clarendon considered Lydia untouchable.

"Tea?" Lady Clarendon asked as she motioned toward the elaborate silver service.

"Thank you, no," Lydia said.

"Please, sit down."

"This is not a social call," Peter said as they grouped themselves around the low table in front of the fireplace.

"Then the contracts are all ready?" Lord Clarendon rubbed his hands together.

"No, that isn't why we are here either. We came to speak to you about Adam."

He heard Millicent's audible gasp and saw their quick exchange of glances.

"Our son?" Basil asked, falteringly.

"He isn't your son, is he?" Peter's voice was soft and gentle, like a parent coaxing the truth from a naughty child.

Millicent bristled. "I don't know what you mean."

"I'll try and make this as painless as possible, Lady Clarendon." Peter put his elbows on his knees and leaned toward her. "We have absolute proof that Adam is actually Mrs. Nightsong's grandson." He wanted to say "our" grandson, but didn't want to cloud the issue or make it any more unseemly than it was. He noticed Lydia's disapproval.

"To be truthful," Lydia said boldly. "He is our grandson. My daughter was married to Mr. MacNair's son."

"This is preposterous," Basil huffed.

"No," said Peter. "As I said, we have definite proof."

"What proof?" Lady Clarendon's voice was bitter.

"He has a tattoo on his left thigh. Twin poppies encircled by a ring of dots, the insignia of the Manchu dynasty. His mother's dynasty."

He saw them crumble. In a split second Lady Clarendon regained herself, her expression one of complete defiance and abhorrence. "It is a birthmark, nothing more."

"Then you admit such a mark exists?" Peter said, caging her in.

She grew flustered. Her face turned red. She put back her head, fighting off the threatening tears. When she could she said, "Adam is not Chinese." She slurred the word as if spitting out some foul poison.

Lydia was unruffled. The woman's defiance made her defensive. "I am afraid he is, at least partly." She saw Millicent's hatred. "We don't want to make this anymore unpleasant than it is. A scandal—"

"Scandal?" Lady Clarendon cried. "That, my dear, is something with which you are all too well acquainted."

It was Lydia's turn to become angry. "And I have no compunctions about becoming embroiled in still another."

Peter smiled, wanting to shout "Bravo!" This was the Lydia he so dearly loved. He saw the fire in her eyes and knew she was ready now for battle.

"We don't know how you came to kidnap our grandson," Lydia said, "but I am certain that a thorough investigation will result in many red faces in your group of peers. You have connections and influence, but we aren't without them either. And as you said, Lady Clarendon, scandal is not new to me. I am accustomed to it, while you...." Her voice faltered. "I am not certain you would be able to cope with the sordid headlines and the gossip that would come with them."

Millicent tried to reach for her teacup, but her hands were trembling badly. Suddenly, she broke into a torrent of tears and buried her face in her hands.

Her husband, seated beside her on the divan, put his arm around her shoulder and pulled her against him, patting her hair with his hand.

"It's true," Basil said weakly. "We took the boy."

"No!" Millicent wailed.

"It's senseless to carry on the charade under the circumstances, my dear. We don't want a scandal and besides, we agreed that we would tell Adam the truth when he reached his twenty-first birthday." He looked at Lydia, his eyes wet, his mouth turned down at the corners. "We aren't evil people, Mrs. Nightsong. We were traveling in your country visiting noted specialists who would, we hoped, be able to come up with some remedy for my wife's barrenness. Our train stopped in San Francisco. There was a woman on board with a child. The woman was extremely ill and we had the conductor bring her and the boy into our private car where she would be warm and comfortable." He heaved a heavy sigh, looking down at the tea tray without seeing it. "She died, poor thing."

"And you kept the boy," Lydia finished.

He nodded and let his head droop.

"Who was the woman?" Peter asked.

"We never knew. She was taken off the train in St. Louis, I believe it was."

"Surely you saw the newspapers during your trip across country. The kidnapping was headlined in every state."

"We saw them," Lord Clarendon admitted.

"And still you kept the child?" Lydia found that inconceivable.

"My wife could bear no children. To attempt having one would have killed her. She knew I wanted an heir. She swore she would give me one, one way or another, or die trying. I had no choice."

"But the boy's mother, his family. Surely you must have thought of the pain and suffering you'd cause them," Lydia said.

It was then Millicent lifted her head and glowered at Lydia. Her face was a mask of malice, hatred, and complete contempt.

"Family? I read of the poor child's family. Your chronicles were well advertised. A mother who had abandoned her husband and children to flee to that heathen country with a young man? Marrying that man under Chinese law without benefit or thought of legal divorce. A grandmother who'd whored herself into a perfume fortune?"

Lydia blanched, but Peter could see the smoldering behind her eyes.

"We could not bring ourselves to return that child to such an environment. His mother gave up her previous children, how could we be certain she wouldn't as easily abandon Adam? And you two. Who are you to think of yourselves as fit grandparents for the boy? Adulterers and God only knows what else you both are."

Peter curbed his fury. "He is still ours. You have no claim on the boy and if it takes a court battle we will have him back where he belongs."

"As I said, Mr. MacNair," Lord Clarendon said calmly, "we intended telling Adam in a year or so. Why not leave it at that and let him decide when the time comes."

"No," Peter said adamantly. "I want Adam told now. Today."

Basil saw utter defeat. "Very well. I suppose sooner is better than later. But you can be assured, Mr. MacNair, that Adam will choose to remain where he is when he is old enough to decide for himself. We have been loving parents. He'll not likely forget that."

"I am sure that he won't. However, let the boy decide."

"He's presently in London, staying with friends. We will tell him when he returns."

"See that you do. Otherwise he will hear it from me and my solicitors," Peter threatened.

Peter got up. He held himself straight and tall as he strode out of the room. He tried to hide the sweat that was beginning to bead his forehead. Once outside the cool late afternoon breeze made him feel refreshed, but inside the backseat of the automobile he grabbed his chest as a sharp pain stabbed him.

"Peter, are you all right?" Lydia asked.

"We did well," he said as the pain began to subside. He mopped his brow.

To the driver Lydia said, "Take us back to the sanitorium."

"No," Peter said in a tight voice. "The hotel is closer. I need to lie down."

"But—"

"Please, Lydia. Don't argue with me. I just want to sleep for a bit."

She didn't argue. What he'd set out to accomplish he'd accomplished. He deserved some rest. Still, as they drove away from the estate she wondered how it would all turn out.

# CHAPTER TWENTY-FIVE

The moon was full that night, making ghostly shadows of the trees, like silent sentinels swaying in the night air. Jeremy Slyke and his father parked their motorcar a good distance from the Clarendon postern. The rear of the house was dark, except for a single light that burned in one of the downstairs windows.

"The servants are all in town," Tom Slyke said. "There's only the lord and lady at home. We shouldn't have any problem with being seen."

"What about the old gardener? He waved to us when he passed us on the road."

"Shamus hasn't an idea that we're coming here. Come along, lad."

Jeremy picked up the two metal containers he'd taken from the boot of the car and doggedly followed his father's path through the shrubberies. They moved, crouched, among the topiaries and hedges until they reached the far side of the sculptured garden with its lily pond and tall cypresses. Just ahead was the thatched-roof building the gardener had told them about. Near it the wooden framework that served as the foundation for the newly planned solarium stood naked and stark in the moonlight, its thick, grainy studs jutting to the second level of the house. Scattered about were piles of slats and boards and braces meant to complete the intricate lattice work that would support the multiple glass panels under which the plants would teem with growth.

"An expensive whim," Tom Slyke commented as he studied

the half-finished addition. "The grand lord is spending money he'll never have." He laughed under his breath. "All the better. Come along." He moved closer to the little building with the thatched roof.

The heavily studded door was barred but not locked. He raised the bar with gnarled hands and carefully, silently lifted it out of its metal supports.

A sudden gust of wind came up, flipping Tom's broad-brimmed hat from his head, tossing it into a clump of leaves piled just beside the clapboard wall of the small building.

Jeremy reached for the hat, but another gust sent it flitting farther along the path toward where they'd left the car.

"Leave it. We'll get it on our way back."

Inside the air was cool, almost cold. The night wind, growing stronger, whistled eerily through the thatch.

Tables and shelves were stacked with jars and bottles and tins of every description. Jeremy clicked on his torch and focused the beam on one of the metal drums standing just inside the door.

"Silicon dioxide," he read aloud.

"Sandlike particles of hard stone," his father explained. "It's reduced to a salt which is fused at high heat to make glass." He was reading the various labels of the containers on the shelves. "All chemicals for producing color and texture," he said, speaking to himself.

"What?"

"Nothing. It's just that his lordship is planning a very ambitious project. Obviously the MacNair contracts call for some special craftsmanship. These are volatile materials which he apparently is experimenting with."

He picked up one particularly large vessel and held it to the beam of the torch. The grayish liquid swirled around inside its container as Tom spun it in a circle. "Odd stuff," he commented. He put the vessel back and kept looking at it. "Well, whatever it is, his lordship will have to do without it after we finish our business here."

"Suppose there are explosives in here?"

"Don't be daft. There's nothing dangerous in the making of glass if you know what you're about. These are just a special lot of supplies his lordship needs for the MacNair bottles. Without these he'll be badly delayed with no chance of catching up once I convince the American we can and will meet whatever deadline he's set. By putting this to the flame we will put Lord Clarendon where he belongs—out of the running."

Tom motioned to the two cans his son had set at his side. "Splash the petrol over the lot of it," he said, taking the flashlight from Jeremy. "And splash down the walls. We don't want a particle to be intact when the flames die down."

Jeremy uncapped the first tin and emptied it over the shelves and tables. He tossed the empty can aside and splashed the gasoline head-high over the walls.

"Good. Now get yourself outside," Tom ordered as he took some wooden matches out of his pocket. "We'd both best have a clear avenue of escape when I strike the match. The fumes alone could singe off our hair."

They moved to the door. Jeremy went outside after taking the flashlight from his father. He started scanning the ground for his father's hat. He didn't see it.

Tom stuck a match and tossed it toward the upper shelves. Immediately a high flash of flame began eating its way along the wood, hungrily devouring everything it touched. A second match he threw against the wall and quickly shut and barred the heavy door.

"Our work's done here," he said as wisps of smoke already drifted through the thatched roof, swept into a stream by the wind that blew from the north.

"The wind's changed," he commented, looking up at the sky.

"Your hat. I can't find your hat."

"Here, give me the torch." He took the flashlight from his son's hand. "There. Over by that pile of lumber." He started toward the flapping hat when suddenly the thatch ignited, sending flames dancing up into the air. A soft, far away sounding explosion sent another more powerful sheet of fire skyward, lifting a section of burning thatch, hurling it up and then downward in the fickle wind.

The bundle of thatch landed on Tom Slyke's back as he stooped to retrieve his hat. Immediately his coat caught fire as he gave out a yelp of pain. Jeremy whipped off his jacket and threw it about his father, smothering the flames, but not in time to prevent the fire from scorching his father's neck and singeing the thick gray mat of hair on the back of Tom's head.

"Lord Almighty," Tom groaned as the pain coursed through him. He grimaced as he turned to see the building erupt in a fireball. "Let's get out of here," he said, urgency blinding him to pain.

The two of them scurried through the shrubs until they reached the path leading to the postern. They ran hard. When they reached the motorcar Tom jumped into the front seat and switched on the ignition as Jeremy operated the crank. In a moment the car sputtered to life. Jeremy threw the crank onto the floor of the front seat as his father made a sharp turn and sped off toward their home.

When they were a good mile down the road Jeremy turned and looked back. "Good Lord, Father, look."

"Never look back, my boy."

"But the wind. It looks as if it's spread the fire to the main house."

"It's stone and mortar. No harm will come to it.

Tom Slyke was wrong.

In the shifting wind the flames spread quickly from the shed to the pile of lumber stacked beside the skeleton of the solarium. Dry leaves fell easy victim to the fire, burst into sparks, and drifted and flew in every direction. The aged, dry beams of the solarium caught easily.

On the second floor if the main house, in the master suite, Millicent lay peacefully asleep. It had taken two tablespoons of laudanum before she could fall asleep after their terrible conversation with Peter and Lydia. Basil, too, was sound asleep having drowned his sorrow and guilt with too many brandies, dreading the thoughts of morning and Adam's return home.

Neither of them heard the crackling flames that licked their way up the supports of the solarium and across the latticed ceiling. Smoke drifted in lazy waves through the half-open casement windows and across the floor. As the ceiling below became a solid sheet of fire, the floor of the bedroom became hotter.

Basil stirred, coughed, but did not wake up. He curled closer to his wife on the huge bed and buried his face in a pillow. Millicent lay flat on her back, an arm over her head, the other across her waist.

The crackling grew louder, the smoke more dense. The room was thick with the toxic smoke that seeped up around the bed.

Millicent's throat became choked as she tried to breathe. She fought to climb out of her nightmare, but the black phantom that was pursuing her was getting nearer until she found herself completely surrounded by its heavy cloak. She tried to scream, but the thick folds smothered her breath.

Lord and Lady Clarendon felt neither the heat nor the smoke as the floor gave out from under them, pitching them down into the killing fire.

# CHAPTER TWENTY-SIX

Adam could not understand why Caroline was avoiding him. Several times during the past days he'd tried reaching her both by telephone and in person. Each time he was told she was not in.

He felt guilty for wanting her as he did; but Caroline was able to give him something Pamela could not, or would not, give. His body craved for the sensations Caroline had made him feel. He longed for her soft wetness, the smell of her hair, the exciting ecstasy of his orgasms. Never before had he experienced such sublime bliss. Inexperienced as Caroline purported to be, she was as wanton as he when it came to the physical aspects of love. He wondered idly if Pamela would be able to excite him in the same ways.

That, he knew, he could only find out by marrying Pamela. She was far too staid and proper to entertain the thought of premarital sex. Now that Adam had the taste of it, it was all he could think about.

In fact, on that first day when Caroline could not be reached he found he could not bring himself to go home as promised. His glands overreacted and he found himself in one of those houses in Soho his friends had told him about. It hadn't been the same. Yet, Caroline's continued avoidance of him sent him back for entire days and nights. The thrills had not been the same at all. There had been no love, no tenderness at Mrs. Castle's, only sheer physical lust, the rutting of animals, nothing more. And he needed more, he told himself.

Adam shaved and bathed himself, soaking for a long time in the tub, scrubbing away the cheap perfume of Mrs. Castle's girls. The friends with whom he was staying in London had gone off for the weekend. Adam had told himself a dozen times to go home, to patch things up with Pamela and to forget Caroline. He could not. Some invisible force held him in London where he could at least be close to Caroline. Sharing the same city gave him a sense of hope.

He put on his new waistcoat and trousers and left the fashionable townhouse on Riverton Square and hailed a cruising taxi.

"The Claridge Hotel," he told the driver. This time he wouldn't inquire at the desk; he'd go directly to Caroline's suite and demand some explanation. Having her grandmother walk in on them, as she had, was certainly no reason for refusing to see him. He knew he should telephone home and tell his parents he was staying in London longer, but he couldn't face hearing their objections. They didn't approve of Caroline; he knew that.

He pressed the door buzzer of the second floor suite and waiting, expecting no answer. After several seconds he rapped on the paneled door. It opened and Caroline's grandmother was standing there, looking at him questioningly, as if she were seeing a stranger.

"Oh, Adam," she said. "I thought you'd be at home."

"I'd like to see Caroline if I may, Mrs. Nightsong."

It was obvious to her, by the look of him, that he hadn't heard the dreadful news of the fire at Clarendon Hall.

"Come in, Adam."

He noticed her lowered eyes, the paleness of her complexion. "What's wrong? Is something the matter with Caroline?"

"Caroline's gone," Peter MacNair said as he rose from the chair shadowed by the heavy draperies of the windows.

"Mr. MacNair." The man looked very ill, he thought. He was unsteady on his feet, his hands shook slightly.

"Hello, Adam. I take it you haven't been home?"

"No, I've been staying with friends here in London."

"I see." Peter motioned to a chair. "I think you had better sit down, my boy."

He spoke in that voice that people use whenever they're about to deliver bad news.

"Where did Caroline go?" Adam asked urgently, still standing. "If you're angry with me for what you stumbled upon, Mrs. Nightsong, I—"

"It isn't that, Adam. Sit down, child. Something has happened."

"Caroline?" He still remained standing.

"No, Caroline is all right. She has gone on a trip. She left a note saying she wanted to travel for a while."

"Travel? I don't understand."

"She has good reason."

"But that's ridiculous. Just because we—"

Lydia touched his arm. "Please, Adam. Sit down. I'm afraid we have some rather tragic news."

He saw the sad eyes that couldn't look at him. There was a sinking feeling in his stomach. "Tragic news?" The backs of his legs hit the edge of the chair. He lowered himself into it like a man suddenly blind. "What's happened?"

Peter said, "You haven't seen a newspaper either, I suspect."

"No. Why?"

Lydia said, "This is most difficult, especially since we are comparative strangers. Or perhaps it is better."

Adam didn't understand any of it. "Just what are you trying to say?"

Lydia took a deep breath. She forced herself to look deep into his eyes. "You must be strong, my boy." She took another breath and looked at Peter.

Peter said, "It's your parents, Adam. There was a fire at Clarendon Hall. I'm afraid they didn't survive it."

Adam merely stared. He heard the words but nothing registered. He frowned at Peter, refusing to let the words be true. "What?"

Lydia said, "I'm afraid they are both dead, Adam. They were asleep upstairs. The smoke...." She fidgeted with her handkerchief. "They never woke up."

"This can't be true!"

"I am afraid it is," Peter said.

Adam continued to stare. He still couldn't understand. Death was something that happened to other people, to strangers. Never to people one loved. It just couldn't be true.

"I'm sorry," Lydia said. "Mr. MacNair and I had called on them the afternoon before the accident."

"It was no accident," Peter said.

The shock had so stunned Adam that he couldn't cry. It was all too unbelievable for tears.

"No accident?" Adam said looking from one to the other.

"Please, Peter. The boy has had a shock. Let it wait."

Peter ignored her and handed Adam the morning newspaper. There on the front page were pictures of Lord and Lady Clarendon, taken years before, under the glaring headline: FIRE CLAIMS CLARENDONS.

As Adam studied the smiling faces it all began to register. He felt the stinging at the corners of his eyes and tried to sniff back the tears. He couldn't. They rolled down his cheeks unchecked as he stared at his parents' faces. He tried to read the words, but they blurred as the newspaper fell to the floor and he cupped his face in his hands. His body started to shake.

They let him cry. After several moments Lydia put her hand on his shoulder. "I am so very sorry, my dear. Is there someone you want us to call? Someone you'd like to be with?"

"I want to go home," Adam sobbed.

"Of course," Lydia said. "I'll have the car brought 'round. We'll drive with you, Adam."

"Please, Mrs. Nightsong. I want to be alone."

"I understand, of course."

When he left Lydia strolled toward the window and stood there until she saw Adam get into the motorcar and drive off. She turned and walked across the room and poured herself a drink to brace her nerves.

"We should have told him," Peter said sitting slumped in his chair, his arms hanging limp over its sides.

Lydia looked at him; her heart ached. His face was marked with hollows, his eyes were as dull as dead coals. "Not yet, Peter. It would have been too cruel to take his parents away twice at one time."

"They weren't his parents."

"He doesn't know that yet." She hesitated. "I still wonder if he should know now." She was thinking of April again. For the boy to lose so loving a mother and father only to be given over to an unstable woman who lived in dreams and fantasies seemed to Lydia senseless, if not heartless.

"I intend to tell him," Peter said.

Lydia sighed. "Yes. He'll be told, but not just yet, Peter. Let the boy have his grief and his mourning. There is ample time in which to tell him the truth."

He eyed her suspiciously. "You don't approve of his knowing the truth, do you?"

She moved her head slowly. "I was thinking only of April. All my life I've thought only of what was best for her. She never saw it in that light, but it's true. All I did, I did for April, even from the first day she was born when Prince Ke Loo ordered her killed."

"Having Adam back will give April only the greatest joy."

"I wonder," Lydia said and sighed again. "April lives in the past. She still thinks of Adam as a little boy of four. It's the child she wants. I don't know how she will accept him as a man, and a man who is a duplicate of the husband she saw beheaded in front of her eyes."

"I want my grandson."

"And I mine." She couldn't help herself. She burst into tears as she threw herself on the floor beside Peter's chair and buried her face in his lap. "Oh, Peter, every time I think of the horrible way those two poor, desperate people died...."

"They kidnapped our grandchild, Lydia. They stole away almost fifteen years of his life."

"Regardless, they deserved better. They planned on telling

him."

"Perhaps. Or perhaps they only said that to placate us."

"I believed them." She sat up and wiped her eyes. "But I was always too trusting, I suppose."

He felt the barb and realized that even still, after so many years, she'd never forgiven him completely for having betrayed her into Prince Ke Loo's hands. "Adam must be told."

"Yes," she said sadly. "I know. It's only that we may be depriving him of whatever benefits he will inherit from this horrible tragedy."

"Benefits?"

"He is Lord Clarendon's only heir of record."

"Good heavens, Lydia. As our grandson he will have more money than he'll ever need."

"You forget, Peter, Adam is, contrary to his true birth, an Englishman and will inherit Lord Clarendon's title and position. We can't offer him that and we will take it away from him if we make public what the Clarendons did. From a position of royal respectability we will reduce Adam to scandalous ostracism."

"Title, royal respectability. Who cares about that nonsense?"

"He thinks himself British. He has been educated to that role. We can't take it away from him. And what of Caroline? How will Adam cope with living in the same house with a woman he once bedded and who turned out to be his sister?"

Peter grew exasperated. "He is only a boy. Time will have answers for all those questions."

"You always did look at things through a simple glass."

"It is the only way to see anything clearly."

"Not always. Distortions must always be taken into consideration. "

He eased himself up. "I'm in no mood for your philosophizing this afternoon, Lydia. I think I'll go to my room and lie down. I'm feeling rather tired."

"Yes, of course," she said as she got to her feet. "It has been an exhausting day for both of us."

The sound of the buzzer made them both turn and look

toward the door.

"Now what?" Peter asked, disgruntled.

Lydia went to the door and opened it. "Marcus," she gasped as she saw their young grandson standing in the corridor, a carryall hanging at his side. He looked unshaven and extremely tired. "What on earth?"

"Hello, Grandmother." He tried to smile. It scarcely made a dent on his lips. "I've been in Paris to see my father."

"Come in, darling," she said after putting her arms around him and giving him a kiss on his cheek.

Marcus swayed slightly. He saw Peter and nodded. "Hello, Mr. MacNair."

"Hello, my boy." The two shook hands rather falteringly.

Marcus turned to Lydia. "I'm afraid I come with rather bad news, Grandmother. My father," he said. He swallowed hard. "He's dead. The police told me that he'd been murdered."

\* \* \* \* \* \* \*

When the motorcar pulled into the courtyard, Adam could not believe what he saw. The entire right wing was just a façade of blackened mortar and stone, looking like a scorched skull with large staring eyes that had once been windows. The central part of the house was untouched, as was the left wing. The lopsided mansion reeked of smoke and ruin. Several men were poking about in the rubble, none of whom Adam recognized. They appeared very official.

As he stepped from the back of the towncar Pamela ran out of the front door and threw herself into his arms, her face wet and swollen from crying. Framed in the archway behind her stood her father.

"Adam," Pamela cried as she smothered her face against his chest. He couldn't move, couldn't bring himself to embrace her. He only stared at the devastation, his mind numb, his whole being refusing to believe all this was really true.

Pamela clung to him. Unconsciously, as if some other force

moved his arms, he embraced her. He didn't try to hide his tears as he stared at the burned-out shell.

Her father came up to him and put a consoling hand on Adam's shoulder. "Dreadful thing," was all he said. "Dreadful."

"But how?" Adam managed as the sobs wracked him.

"Come inside," Mr. Albright said. "It was no accident, the fire warden tells us."

"That's what...." He cut himself off as he felt Pamela crying bitterly against his chest. He couldn't tell her he'd heard of the calamity from Mrs. Nightsong when he'd gone looking for Caroline. "The newspapers...," he stammered.

Mr. Albright said, "We've been trying to ring you up since yesterday." He fanned out his hands. "But perhaps it is better that you found out yourself." He patted the boy's shoulder. "Come inside. We could all use a touch of something."

The house reeked of smoke, so thick Adam began to cough.

"I've had the servants open all the windows. It is only sheer luck that the fire brigade saw the flames and arrived in time to save the rest of the old place. A pity they didn't get here sooner." He settled Adam and Pamela on the divan under the open windows and splashed some brandy into a glass. He handed it to Adam. "Drink this, Adam. It will help." He poured himself a snifter and took the chair opposite his daughter and Adam.

"It started in the chemical shed. The chief fire warden found evidence of arson."

"Arson?"

"Didn't you read the newspaper account?"

Adam lowered his head, feeling guilty. "I just saw the headline."

"Jeremy and Tom Slyke are responsible. They've already been taken into custody."

"The Slykes? But why?"

"Oh, I doubt if they intended to do anything more than a bit of mischief. It seems Shamus, your gardener, saw them driving here the night of the fire. Checking about, the authorities found two metal containers of petrol in the burnt-out shed.

Harry Wilkens, who runs the petrol station on Squire Lane, said he'd sold two gallon tins of petrol to Jeremy Slyke the afternoon before. The tins he identified as his own. His markings were on the bottom. Then, when Inspector Helms went around to see the Slykes he found Tom in bed with a badly burned back and scalp. They were questioned, of course. Jeremy broke down and admitted they'd only wanted to destroy the chemical shed to prevent your father from getting some important glass contracts. They meant no bodily harm to anyone."

"Dear God," Adam cried. Tears spilled from his eyes.

Mr. Albright reached inside his pocket and took out a sealed envelope. "Your father entrusted this to me many years ago. He gave instructions that it not be read by anyone but you and only in the event—if such an unfortunate incident as this occurred. I'm keeping that promise I gave him. I have no idea what his letter contains. I only pray it will help make your loss a little lighter."

Adam took the envelope and sat staring at his father's familiar scrawl. He started to unseal it.

"No," Mr. Albright said. "Your father said you were to read it in private." He glanced at his daughter.

Pamela put her hand over Adam's. "I think you'd better come and stay with us, darling. You mustn't stay here alone."

Adam shook his head sadly. "No, I'd rather stay here, Pamela."

"Adam should be alone if that is what he wants, daughter. Come along." He held out his hand to her. "The servants will see that he gets whatever he needs."

Pamela hesitated, then got up and went with her father toward the door.

"Remember, my boy," Mr. Albright said, "our home is yours whenever you want it."

"I appreciate that sir. Thank you. I just want to be by myself for a while. Perhaps I'll come later on. There are the arrangements...."

Mr. Albright stopped him with a move of his hand. "You are not to think about that. We'll see that everything is attended to properly."

When they had gone, Adam sat quite still, aware of nothing but the emptiness in his breast and the crisp linen envelope in his hand. Finally he ripped open the seal and removed the letter. Inside the folds of the letter was a yellowed newspaper clipping with a San Francisco, California, masthead and banner. He looked first at the clipping and saw the sketch of a four-year-old boy and the headline: NIGHTSONG CHILD KIDNAPPED.

# CHAPTER TWENTY-SEVEN

Walking up Nob Hill toward the new MacNair town-house, Leon had the oddest feeling of time-out-of-place. Here and there in his mind he saw archways and ornate fencing that were there before the earthquake.

The location of the MacNair property was the same; the house was entirely different. Gone was the sprawling, clapboard mansion with its fretted balconies and conical turret rooms. Instead, a tall, cold square edifice of stone and granite rose like some monumental tower with dull windows made heavy by ornate plaster moldings.

A maid in a stiff apron and lace cap answered the bell, curtsying respectfully to the well-dressed stranger who, to her, looked slightly Oriental and out of place in his well-tailored suit.

"Mr. Efrem MacNair, please," Leon said.

Efrem was not at home. "The madam is out as well," the maid told him.

"Who is it, Bridget?" Susan called, coming up behind the maid. When Susan saw Leon she let out a hoot and threw her arms around him. "Leon. Is it really you?"

"Every pound of me," he beamed as he hugged his old friend.

"You haven't changed a bit. Oh, perhaps a bit browner. But I suspect that's a result of all that Hawaiian sunshine."

"You look marvelous. I expected you to be fat and very matronly. After all, you did write that you were the mother of three now."

"That is not necessarily a prerequisite to becoming fat and

matronly."

"Susan," he said holding her at arm's length and admiring her beauty. "You are more lovely than I remembered."

"Come in," she said, pulling him inside.

The interior of the house was as sterile and cold as its façade. It was as if some faddish decorator had talked Mrs. MacNair into going modern and then, finding his efforts to her dislike, she'd heaped in mounds of old furniture to try and lend a bit of warmth to the rooms. The result was a stylistic disaster.

"Horrible, isn't it?" Susan said. "I so miss the old house, but Mother insisted that this is what she wanted. As for Father, he could care less whether she kept a pen of goats in the drawing room."

"How are your parents?"

"Fine. At least I suspect they are. Mother is out somewhere for the day. Father's in Europe on business. We won't hear from him until he's back. Truthfully, I don't believe he knows there are such things as personal letters. All business. And your family?"

"Wife and children all in perfect health. My father died shortly before I left the islands."

"I'm sorry."

"I'm not."

"Leon!"

He shrugged. "I never cared for him—ever. I can't be a hypocrite now that he's dead."

"And the others?"

"Mother is also abroad. April is—well, she is April."

"Poor April. She's had a terrible time of it these past many years."

"They've taken their toll." He hesitated for a moment. "Look, it's great to see you, of course, but I had hoped to speak with Efrem."

"He's at the office, I suppose. He doesn't confide his whereabouts to any of us, except possibly to Ellen Stanton. He's seeing quite a lot of her lately."

"He always did like her. Is he finally getting serious?"

"Let's hope so." The subject clearly made her uncomfortable. "A drink? Or some tea, perhaps." She went toward the bell pull.

"No, thank you, Susan."

She paused. "I'm glad you're going to see Efrem. I'm afraid he's in some sort of trouble."

"Yes, I know."

"What do you mean?"

"I mean, I think I know what the trouble is." Again he paused, searching her face. " I have no proof but perhaps between us we can make things right."

"Leon, you are speaking in riddles."

He took her hand and they seated themselves close together on the pillow-littered sofa. "The reason I came back to San Francisco is to stop something in which your father's company is involved. Something illegal."

"MacNair Products?"

He nodded. In a low voice he told her about his father's smuggling operation and the bales and crates all marked for delivery to MacNair Products.

"It can't be that Father is involved."

"I think Efrem is the one who is involved," he said glumly.

Susan lowered her eyes. "That would explain Efrem's strange behavior all this time. But why would he...?" She looked up sharply. "You and Efrem," she blurted out without thinking.

Leon's face turned purplered. She put her hand over his. "Please, Leon, I know it's embarrassing for you, but I happened to have been in my bedroom window overlooking the street the night you and Efrem parted. You left to join your father the following day."

Leon couldn't face her. "We were only boys, stupid and innocent."

"Please, you don't have to explain to me." She gave a half-hearted laugh. "If you remember, even as a girl I was always intrigued by the unorthodox." She stopped smiling. "The fortunate part is that you've grown up and put aside your boyhood;

unfortunately, my brother seems to want to hold on to his."

Leon's mind had latched onto something she said earlier. "If you saw us that night then it is certainly possible that someone else did as well."

She didn't want to admit that she'd thought the same thing.

"All the way over on the steamer I've been trying to figure out why Efrem would let himself become involved with my father's filthy business. I knew it had to be someone with authority in MacNair Products and was certain it wasn't your father. It isn't his style. Then I remembered that each bale being addressed to MacNair Products was printed differently, as if in code, although perfectly innocent-seeming. I came up with one answer. Someone at MacNair Products could identify by the way the parcels were addressed which contained the opium and which the actual cosmetic products. If it were Efrem, then he was being blackmailed into personally handling those bales that contained the opium."

"Blackmailed?"

"It all fits." His face turned red again. "As you said, you saw us together when we said good-bye. Someone else also saw us and then threatened Efrem. I would also have been a target, but I'd skipped to Hawaii."

"There is someone," she said hesitantly. "A friend of my mother's." She told of Efrem's reaction to stumbling upon Ramsey and their mother in the study—the story her mother had told her and of Efrem's fury at the mention of Ramsey's name. "I've tried to find out about this Mr. Ramsey, but only discovered that he was once a prominent detective, living now in retired luxury, apparently."

"Ramsey," Leon searched his memory but he did not recognize the name.

"Yes. I have his address. It's in one of the smartest parts of the city."

"Detectives don't earn that much, do they?"

"I wondered about that myself. And there is this connection between Mother and Mr. Ramsey. It's so inconceivable that she'd befriend someone of that caliber."

"She sees him socially?"

"I've done some sleuthing on my own. She goes to his place quite often. I've never questioned her, naturally."

Leon got abruptly to his feet. "I've got to speak with Efrem. He must talk to me and tell me just how deeply he's involved in this sordid business. Between us, Susan, we must get him out of it, regardless of the cost."

"I agree. But I don't think Efrem will volunteer anything, even to you."

"I think he will." He smiled and kissed both her cheeks. "I'll report back to you as soon as I can. Oh, say, would you have dinner with me this evening?"

"I'd love to."

"I'll call for you at seven."

"No, perhaps it best that I meet you at Mario's on the Wharf."

"At seven then," he said and hurried out.

He half dreaded his forthcoming meeting with Efrem and half looked forward to it. Over the years the boyhood love he'd once had for that timid, handsome youth had faded. He no longer was afraid of that love. A new love had taken its place; a proper love that men could be proud to show for one another, a love that came only from a profound and meaningful friendship.

\* \* \* \* \* \* \*

Efrem wasn't at the MacNair offices.

"Try Zinman's," one of his coworkers suggested drily. "He's usually there putting away a pint or two about this time every day."

When Leon did see Efrem he had to look twice to be certain he hadn't been mistaken. Zinman's was a fashionable enough establishment, all crimson and gold with tasteful mirror panels and dark mahogany. Efrem was seated slouched in a corner booth, his hands wrapped tightly around a tall glass of whiskey, his eyes staring straight ahead at the empty wall.

"Hello, Ef."

The dull eyes moved slowly. When they focused on Leon's face they clouded with tears. In an instant Efrem jumped to his feet, knocking over his whiskey glass, and threw his arms around his friend.

"Oh, God, Leon. How I prayed you'd come back to me." He started to cry.

Embarrassed, Leon tactfully freed himself from Efrem's embrace and slid into the empty seat, putting the table between them.

Efrem sniffed, shifted uncomfortably as he looked about, and sat back down. He wiped the tears away with the back of his hand. "This is fantastic," he said, half laughing, half crying.

A waiter came over to mop up the spilled drink, giving them both a moment to collect themselves. Efrem ordered another scotch. Leon asked for a glass of white wine.

"Oh, Leon," Efrem said He put his hand on Leon's and quickly removed it. "I'm sorry. I'm behaving badly."

"It's all right, Ef."

"You just don't know what hell I've been in since you left."

"I believe I do. That's why I'm here."

Efrem looked at him through wide eyes.

The waiter came back, setting their drinks on the table and left, but not before giving them both a rather fishy once-over with his button-brown eyes.

Leon took a sip of his drink and watched the waiter go to the bar and exchange whispers with the barman, who glanced in their direction.

"Let's get out of here, Efrem. We have to talk." He stood up and threw a few bills on the table.

Efrem didn't hesitate. He downed his scotch and followed Leon out the door, staggering ever so slightly.

"I'm a bit tight," he admitted as they started slowly down the street.

"You're always a bit of that, I hear," Leon remonstrated. He saw the injured look and put his arm protectively on Efrem's shoulder.

The mere touch sobered him. "You don't know how much I needed you, Leon. When you ran away, I—"

"I ran away for a very good reason, Ef. I did it as much for you as for myself."

Efrem nodded solemnly. "Yes, I know."

"I've never stopped being your friend, Efrem. I want you to understand that, and I never will."

"And I'll never stop—" He cut off his words. "The only time I'm ever happy is when I think of you and the hope that someday you'll come back."

"We can't go back, Ef. Ever." He spied a secluded bench hidden behind overgrown lilacs and hedge. He steered Efrem toward it.

Once seated Efrem groped for Leon's hand and squeezed it hard. Leon let his hand rest between them for a moment, then drew it away. "That's what I mean by our never being able to go back, Efrem. You must understand that."

"I know," Efrem said, rubbing his face with his hands. "It's just that...." He couldn't find either the words or the courage.

"I love you very much, Efrem, but I know it isn't the kind of love you think you want." He saw Efrem's expression grow sadder. "What happened that night in the Red Lantern sometimes happens between boys. We were only teenagers and anxious to experiment."

"It made me happy."

Leon picked up a handful of pebbles and began pitching them at imaginary targets. "Ef," he said finally, "I never thought I'd admit this, but if I ever loved another man and wanted him physically, you would be that man. But I have no desire for that kind of love. And you can't afford it, either. What we did wasn't wrong, it was just adolescent and stupidly innocent. Surely you know that by now."

Efrem heaved a sigh and let his shoulders droop. "You're right, of course. Ellen's always saying much the same thing."

"I understand you've been seeing Ellen Stanton. Anything

serious?"

"I see her regularly now. She's the only one who seems to understand my drinking. She doesn't encourage it, of course. I think she knows my problem, but she'd never talk about it."

"Do you like her?" Leon asked, feeling encouraged.

Efrem shrugged. "As much as I like any girl. No, that isn't true. I do like Ellen. She isn't like other girls. She grew into a rather plain woman, yet there's something absolutely beautiful about her. She's told me she's in love with me." He laughed a sweet, boyish laugh. "That's just like Ellen. She's like you in a lot of ways, Leon, always there to take charge and give me a good lecture when I don't behave." He shook his head. "I don't love her, naturally. I wish I could."

"You can if you want to. Maybe now that I'm back you'll realize that we have both grown up and out of our boyhood crushes."

"Perhaps." He sighed again. "Unfortunately, there are others who will never allow me to forget my boyhood crush, as you so delicately call it."

"Who?" When he didn't answer Leon said, "Mr. Ramsey?"

Efrem's head shot up. There was terror in his eyes. "How do you know about Ramsey? Oh God, Leon, he didn't trace you to Hawaii? He isn't—?"

"No, it's all right, Ef. I'm safe. So are you, now." He saw Efrem didn't understand. "I know about the opium shipments to your father's plant."

"You know?" Efrem's eyes grew wider and his face began to lose its color.

"I sent those bales."

"You?"

Leon made a self-conscious gesture. "Well, not me directly." He quickly explained his innocent involvement with his father's drug trafficking. "I didn't know until only recently what was going on." He half smiled. "Being Chinese I was taught never to question one's elders, especially one's father."

"You're only part Chinese," Efrem reminded him.

Leon laughed softly. "It was that part of me that surfaced in the end, when I rebelled completely and for always." He cast away the last of the pebbles he'd been holding in his hand. "Now tell me about this Mr. Ramsey. He forced you into this rotten business, I assume."

"Yes," Efrem admitted. "He was in that house with the sing-song girls the night I went crazy with drink and crawled into your bed. He saw it all. He made threats." The tears came but he hid his face. "I had no choice, Leon. I had to do what he wanted. He said he'd have me arrested as a...."

Leon put his hand on his friend's shoulder again. "He can do nothing, Efrem. I'll see to that."

"How can you? You're as involved as I am. Ramsey saw both of us."

"Opium trafficking and adolescent lack of discretion are two entirely different things." He patted Efrem. "Come on. Let me walk you home. Have a bath. Call Ellen Stanton and join Susan and me for dinner at Mario's tonight. Just like old times."

"Susan? You've spoken to Susan?"

"She's very worried about you, Ef, as am I. We care. We truly care. We both love you very much."

Efrem let the tears come.

Leon couldn't hold himself back. He hugged Efrem tightly against him, as one brother might hug another. "Come on, let's go home."

As they walked out of the square and started up the steep sidewalk toward Nob Hill, Efrem felt strangely alive. The mere presence of Leon beside him, tall and mature, made his steps more definite, his back straighter. There was a buoyancy inside him that he'd never known before. It was as if he'd stepped into a new world, one which had an exhilarating sobriety about it.

"Oh, damn," Efrem said as he remembered. "I can't join you and Susan tonight. I'm expected at the Stantons. Ellen would really be peeved if I failed to show up."

"Tomorrow night then. I'm most anxious to see Ellen again."

Out of nowhere Efrem chuckled. When Leon glanced at him

questioningly Efrem said, "I'm not a total virgin, you know. At least I don't think I am. I got drunk one night at a party at the Stantons. Mother and Susan were there. I think Ellen and Susan cooked it up between them, though Ellen denies that. Ellen insisted I sleep over. She seduced me."

"Good for Ellen," Leon said, clapping Efrem on the back. "I knew I always liked that girl."

"to be honest, I don't remember much, except that I thought it was you."

To his utter surprise Leon said, "Good. If that's what it takes to perform successfully, be my guest and think of me any time you like. There's nothing wrong in fantasizing. I do it myself sometimes."

"About me?"

Leon blushed. "At first. But in time the fantasies changed. You'll find that out for yourself. Next time, however, my young friend I think you should do the seducing."

\* \* \* \* \* \* \*

Susan was late. Leon sat anxiously fingering the jade ring April had given him, the ring he had promised never to remove. He was just about to order dinner without her when Susan came breathlessly into the restaurant.

"I'm sorry, Leon. I couldn't get away. Mother was going out again and she insisted she could not cancel her appointment. The servants were off. I finally found someone to stay with the children."

"You should have telephoned. I would have understood."

"No, I had to come. What on earth transpired between you and Efrem? He was actually whistling when he left for the Stantons' dinner party."

"We had a man-to-man. He told me everything. Ramsey is the snake behind the whole mess."

He ordered her a cocktail and another for himself, then told her what Efrem had said.

"Poor, poor Efrem. If only he'd confided in me."

"It is hardly the sort of thing a man admits to his sister. I'm surprised at my own admissions, but I suppose my being part Oriental makes me look at things differently. Efrem is deeply ashamed and frightened to death over Ramsey's threats. And you must give me your solemn promise that you will never tell Efrem what I just told you. He'd hate the both of us for the rest of his life. We'd always be a reminder of his shame. Let him work it out in his own way, Susan. And he will, I know he will."

"But what are we to do about this odious Mr. Ramsey? We can't go to the police. He'll implicate Efrem."

"I intend paying a visit to Mr. Ramsey. You said you had his address."

"Yes. I wrote it down," she answered, rummaging in her handbag. "I want to come with you."

"That may not be a good idea."

"Good idea or bad, I'm going to come with you."

He saw how determined she was. "All right, then let's order dinner and pay Mr. Ramsey a call. The sooner we get this over with the better."

Both were too keyed up to bother much about what they ate, though the food was superb and Leon insisted on a bottle of wine. By the time they finished they were in high spirits and eager for their adventure.

On the way to their rendezvous, however, both fell quiet. Leon kept turning the jade ring round and round on his finger as the taxi brought them nearer the address Susan had given the driver. A fog had moved in from the bay, adding an element of danger neither of them had given much thought to.

"There. That's the building," Susan said, seeing the house number on a brass plaque studded to the masonry.

"New and obviously very expensive," Leon commented. "It looks like an embassy."

"Mr. Ramsey, I've been told, enjoys living comfortably."

Leon paid off the cabbie. In this section of town he had no worries about return transportation. As a last resort, the trolley lines were within walking distance.

An old Chinese houseman answered their ring. He was in oriental dress, a queue hanging long down his back. "Mr. Ramsey in bed. No visitors," he said before either of them spoke. He started to shut the massive door.

Leon put his foot against it. He spoke harshly to the old man and spoke in Chinese. At the sound of his voice the Chinese man stared up at him. Leon unleashed another torrent of Chinese, none of which Susan understood.

The door opened a little wider. Leon pushed forward his fist, letting the light in the foyer catch the reflection of his jade ring. "Do you recognize this?" he asked in Chinese.

To Susan's astonishment, the man fell to his knees and touched his forehead to the floor. He muttered something distinguishable only to Leon.

"Come on," Leon said, leading Susan around the prostrate figure.

She followed Leon, hesitantly, up the curved marble staircase. "What was all that about?" she whispered.

"I'll explain later." He looked at the closed doors that lined the second-floor corridor, trying to decide which would be Ramsey's bedroom. At the far end he saw double doors with highly polished brass hardware. "The master suite, obviously," he said to Susan, smiling and nodding toward the impressive doors.

As they grew near they heard odd sounds coming from inside the bedroom. They weren't voices exactly, more like moans or sobs, Susan could not decide which. Then other sounds, feminine—but no less guttural and erotic.

"He isn't alone," Susan said.

"That can't be helped. We're here now and I am going to have my say to Mr. Ramsey tonight." He tried the knob. The doors were unlocked and swung open soundlessly.

Susan stifled a little gasp. Leon stared and looked away. But Susan could not take her eyes from the two naked figures on the bed.

The woman's head hung over the side. The lamp on the nearby table was lit. There was no doubt of who she was.

Lorna tightened her bare legs around Ramsey's waist as he plowed into her, jarring her body with every deep, violent thrust.

"Harder. Oh, God, harder," Lorna moaned as she felt her orgasm building higher. "Oh God, make it hurt," she groaned.

Urged on, Ramsey, his heavy hairy body glistening with sweat, pounded her unmercifully.

"More. More," Lorna pleaded as she clawed his back, drawing long scratches that oozed blood.

Susan's mind snapped. "Mother!" she screamed at the top of her lungs.

# CHAPTER TWENTY-EIGHT

In Lydia's suite at the Claridge, Marcus stood in front of his grandmother, looking lost and confused. Dark circles lay heavy beneath his eyes.

"Father told me you had been in Paris," he said glancing at Peter MacNair, who sat quietly behind Lydia.

"Yes," his grandmother answered. Her tone was light.

"Then you knew he was dead."

"No, of course not."

"But you don't seem surprised, even sorry," Marcus said.

"Please, darling, sit down. You look very tired." When he didn't move Lydia began fussing with the lavaliere at her throat. "Of course I'm surprised. As for being sorry, I will not say that I am. Your father and I were not on very friendly terms of late. You certainly are aware of that."

There was a heavy silence in the room.

"Was he my father?" Marcus asked, his words accusing.

Lydia drew in a sharp breath. Out of the corner of her eye she saw Peter mopping perspiration from his brow though the room was decidedly cool. He appeared completely unconcerned with everything except how badly he felt.

"Why on earth would you ask a question like that?" she hedged.

"Because my mother, April, told me she and Raymond Andrieux are not my parents."

"Your mother is not herself these days. Surely you know that."

Marcus would not be put off. "My father said much the same thing, yet somehow I had the feeling he was lying to me. Even when upset and a little unhinged, a mother doesn't renounce a son." He screwed up his courage. "When I was in Paris I went to the hospital where I was born and checked the records." He saw how nervous his grandmother suddenly became. "The records showed my parents to be April and Raymond Andrieux."

"So there," Lydia said, unable to look at him.

"But there was something else, something an expecting mother cannot lie about. The records showed that my mother was thirty-five years old. My mother—April, that is—just had her forty-first birthday this year. You're my mother, aren't you, Grandmother? What April told me is true. You and Mr. MacNair are my parents."

Lydia was saved from answering by a sharp rapping on the door. She hurried to open it, ignoring Peter's demands for her to answer Marcus.

A dour-looking man in a dark suit stood in the corridor, flanked by two men in police uniforms. "I am looking for a Mr. Peter MacNair," the man said, flashing a badge.

Lydia's heart leapt into her throat.

"He wasn't in his suite," the man said. "The chambermaid said he may be here with you, Mrs. Nightsong. You are Lydia Nightsong? Or should I say, Mrs. Andrieux?" He didn't wait for an answer. "I'm Inspector Dillon, Scotland Yard. I'm afraid we've come to ask Mr. MacNair some questions."

"Questions about what?" Peter demanded as he came up behind Lydia.

"About a certain Monsieur Andrieux who was found murdered in his hotel suite in Paris. We were led to believe that you might be able to shed some light on the situation. You did know Mrs. Nightsong's husband, I assume?"

"Yes."

"If you'd be so kind, Mr. MacNair, I'd appreciate it if you would come along with us down to the Yard."

"He can't," Lydia said. "He hasn't been well. He needs to be in bed."

"Well," Inspector Dillon said, "if it's a bed he needs, there are beds at the Yard."

"I object to this," Lydia said.

"It's all right, my dear, I'll be fine," Peter said. He looked at Marcus and started to say something, but decided against it. "If what your mother told you is true, I knew nothing about it." He glanced at Lydia, then back to Marcus. "Take care of your grandmother for me, my boy."

"Yes, sir," Marcus stammered.

He kissed Lydia on the lips. "Now don't fuss. Everything will turn out all right."

\* \* \* \* \* \* \*

But things were not turning out all right, Lydia found, as two days passed and she could get no information from anyone. Eddie Wells at the Embassy made inquiries, but all that he could tell Lydia was that Peter was being held incommunicado.

"Incommunicado, indeed," she said, slamming down the telephone receiver and going for her hat and gloves. "We'll just see about that."

On her way to Scotland Yard she tried to remember the inspector's name. It didn't come until she was approaching the sergeant's desk. "Inspector Dillon," she demanded. "My name is Lydia Nightsong."

"I'm afraid the inspector is out at the moment, ma'am. Perhaps I can help you."

"I'll wait," she said.

Almost an hour passed before the inspector walked through the door. She was on her feet and standing in front of him in an instant.

"Where is Peter MacNair?"

"Well, hello, Mrs. Nightsong," he said taking off his bowler and giving her a wry smile.

"I demand you permit me to see him."

The inspector made a little bow and motioned toward a hallway that led off to the right. "Come with me to my office," he said. "I'd like to talk with you."

The office was no more than a square box with a single window that hadn't been washed in years. There was a paper-littered desk and two straight, wooden chairs. An electric fan sat motionless on top of a battered file cabinet.

"Sit down, please, Mrs. Nightsong. Some tea?"

She shook her head impatiently.

Inspector Dillon took his time making himself a cup of tea, then settled his squat body in the squeaky swivel chair behind his desk.

"Mr. MacNair, I'm afraid, is in a great deal of trouble."

"It was all an accident," she said. "He told me what happened."

"Did he now? And why, then, did the two of you slip off so slylike to London? Why not report this 'accident' to the gendarmes?"

Lydia grew flustered. "Mr. MacNair was not well. I had to get him to a sanitarium here where we could speak and under-stand the language."

"Ah, I see." He put his fingertips together. "Did Mr. MacNair by any chance mention the fact that there had been someone else in Monsieur Andrieux's suite when the 'accident' happened?"

"Someone else?"

He consulted a dossier. "A young lady by the name of Yvonne Roget. She was in the bedroom at the time. She did not see exactly what happened, but she heard it all. She also saw Mr. MacNair when he staggered into the bathroom to wash the blood off his hands. She's identified him through passport photographs."

"Blood?"

Inspector Dillon rolled his eyes and put his hands behind his head. "I have no doubt that you are not in any way implicated, Mrs. Nightsong. The lift operator at the hotel confirmed that. You stepped off the elevator as Mr. MacNair collapsed in your arms." He paused. "Did you know Mr. MacNair was going to see your late husband?"

"No."

"I believe you. And I also believe that Mr. MacNair told you lies."

"Lies?"

"Oh, there was most certainly a bitter quarrel and Monsieur Andrieux did die from head wounds. Unpleasant as I must be, the man's skull was almost pulverized from repeated poundings against the marble floor. It was no accident, dear lady. Peter MacNair viciously murdered your husband."

"No." She felt herself begin to tremble. Terror gripped her like a vise.

"Yes, I'm sorry to say. He's told us the whole sordid story. If what he said is true, he had provocation to be angry enough to thrash the gentleman, but certainly not to murder him."

"Provocation?" She found she could hardly speak.

"Far too sordid for me to repeat to a lady." He moved his head sadly. "The French are a peculiar lot. Quite immoral," he said, remembering with disgust the story Peter had told.

"I don't understand."

"I hope you never do."

"Mr. MacNair. I must see him."

"Yes, of course. Unhappily I must report that you were correct. The man is seriously ill. At present he is in the police hospital."

"Take me to him, please."

"Of course. Come with me."

The room he took her to reeked of antiseptic and new paint. It was cheerless and dim with a wrought-iron bed and metal stand. Except for a chair, there were no other furnishings, not even a picture to lend a bit of color.

Peter lay beneath the white sheets, his face the color of ashes. His eyelids were closed, his arms resting at his sides. When Lydia spoke his name his lids flickered and slowly opened.

"You've come at last."

"They wouldn't allow me before now." She laid her hand on his forehead. The skin was dry and brittle. She smoothed his hair and smiled into his face. "How do you feel?"

"There's no sense in avoiding it, Lydia. I know I'm done for."

"Don't say that." She fought back her tears.

"It's just as well. If I recover they'll only hang me. I'm taking the easier way out."

"Oh, Peter." She threw herself across him and started to cry. "You mustn't lose hope. I've spoken to the consulate."

"There's nothing anyone can do, Lydia. I lied to you about Raymond."

She tried to smile. "It isn't the first time you've lied to me."

"It will be the last."

"Stop it, Peter. I won't have you talking like this."

He moved his hands to her face and slowly let his eyes memorize every inch of it. "You remind me of a frightened rain-soaked little girl I once met in a Chinese village. Still, the same lovely hair and eyes, the same nervous smile. You haven't changed, my darling." He kissed her mouth. "I love you very much, Lydia. I always have. I always will. There was never anyone else."

"Oh, my darling." She sobbed as she laid her head on his shoulder.

He let her cry for a while. "There are a few things I must tell you, Lydia."

"Lie still, Peter. There will be plenty of time later."

"No." He started to cough and groped for a handkerchief. Lydia got it for him and noticed there were splotches of blood on it.

When he was resting quietly again Peter said, "I have left everything to you."

"Please, Peter, don't."

"I must. MacNair Products is yours. You know my lawyers in San Francisco. They have access to all my holdings, including my fifty percent claim to Nightsong, which is all legally endorsed over to you. Lorna will raise hell, of course. But she'd only sell everything I've worked so hard to build up. She has plenty of money of her own. I don't want her to have anything whatever to do with my corporate affairs. I leave all that to you."

"I do wish you'd stop this talk."

"I'm just being realistic, Lydia. With Raymond gone there will be no more Nightsong Perfume. He was the only talent who could successfully reproduce it. Without him and Nightsong you'll need my products. Merge our corporations. You'll have the largest cosmetic empire in the world. And who knows, one day there may be another Nightsong."

"I hate it," Lydia cried, letting her tears flow freely. "I hate everything it's done to us. I should have known that horrible Empress would have her revenge."

"You're wrong. You've beaten her, Lydia. You'll always be on top."

"I'll be nowhere without you, Peter."

He patted her trembling shoulders.

"Marcus?" he said after a while. "Was he telling the truth about those hospital records? Are we his parents?"

She started to cry more bitterly. "Oh, dear God, Peter, forgive me. I never wanted you to know because I was afraid you'd hate me for keeping Marcus from you. We were enemies at the time. Afterward, it all became too complicated. I thought it best, for Marcus's sake, that I don't start up a new Nightsong scandal."

"I am angry with you; yet, I'm happy we have a son. He's a handsome lad."

"He takes after his father," Lydia said, trying again to smile. "I'm surprised you've never noticed."

"I would like him to know I'm his father," Peter said. "If he wants to keep it a secret, then that's for him to decide."

"I'll tell him, I promise."

"Don't tell him about what I did to Raymond. I don't want Marcus to remember his father as being a murderer."

"I refuse to let you call yourself that."

"Just tell Marcus I was taken in for questioning and became ill. He needn't know the rest of it."

"Oh, Peter."

He kissed her hair. A spasm of coughing came over him, wracking his whole body. Several drops of blood splattered the sheet.

Lydia's eyes widened in alarm. "I'll get the doctor."

"No," he said, taking her hand. "Stay with me." He coughed and grew quiet, lying back and breathing hard.

"Remember the painting in that shack?" he asked.

"The little bird on the plum branch singing to the moon."

"Strange," Peter said, "I can actually see it. I never did find out how it came to be on that peeling wall."

"Perhaps some young man, hopelessly in love, painted it for his young love." Her head rested on his chest as he smoothed her hair.

"It's all I seem to remember about China, except that lovely girl with red-gold hair and dark green eyes who came in from a storm. It's all I want to remember. Take Adam home," he murmured. His voice faded.

"Peter?" she said softly, her head pressed tightly against his chest.

She knew before raising her head that his heart had stopped.

# CHAPTER TWENTY-NINE

For the better part of a week, Lydia sat at the window of her suite looking out at the dreary London weather. She wore her hair pulled back and tied tightly with a black ribbon; a half-veil covered her eyes; a high-necked black dress made her look like an old woman. Marcus was in constant attendance, trying to tempt her with her favorite foods, even insisting on champagne whenever she did condescend to eat.

She told Marcus about Peter, that he was his real father and she his real mother. He hadn't been surprised and even seemed pleased.

"I liked Mr. MacNair," he'd said. "I'm not sorry he was my father, only that I didn't know before now."

He told her about his concern for the scandal the news would make and they decided between them that he would tell only Amelia.

"No one else need know," he'd said, "until such time as I feel I want them told."

Despite the possibility of a scandal, he started then and there to call his grandmother "Mother."

It was a wet Friday afternoon when Adam Clarendon came.

"Mother," Marcus said, laying his hand on her drooping shoulder. "There's someone here to see you."

She patted his hand without moving her head. "I don't want to see anyone, darling."

"I think, after all you've told me, you'll want to see him." He handed her Adam's calling card.

Lydia read the name and turned it over in her hand. "How very British," she commented, studying the card. She sighed. "Yes. I'll see the young man."

"How are you, Grandmother?" Adam asked, bending over the hand she offered.

Her eyes brightened as she smiled. "You've been told?"

"Yes. Father left a letter for me. It explained everything. I assure you, my parents meant no harm, Grandmother."

"You needn't call me that if it makes you uncomfortable, Adam," she said.

"It doesn't. I've never really had grandparents before—not that I remember. Mother's and Father's parents died when I was six. I scarcely knew them." He shifted his weight. "I suppose I'll always think of Mother and Father as my parents."

"It's only natural that you do. Sit down, please," Lydia said, motioning for Marcus to pull up a chair. "They were indeed more of a father and mother to you than my daughter and Mr. MacNair's son."

"I'm sorry about Mr. MacNair. It was in the newspapers, of course."

"You have your own personal sorrows to dwell upon, Adam. It is dreadful to discover on our first reunion that the only thing we have in common is mutual mourning." She turned toward the windows. "I would have attended your parents' funeral, naturally, but there were so many details to be attended to concerning your grandfather."

"I understand."

"Well," she said, letting out the breath she had been holding. "The dead are dead; we must go on with the living."

"Which is the reason for this visit," Adam said. He fished into his side pocket and brought out the letter Lord Clarendon had written to him. "I would like you to read this."

Lydia glanced at the letter, then motioned to Marcus for her reading glasses.

The letter was several pages and when she finished she unhooked her glasses and handed it back to him. "I admire your father his courage. He'd told Mr. MacNair...your grandfather and me that he intended telling you when you became of age." She touched his hand. "Now, what have you decided you want to do?"

Adam put the letter back inside his pocket. "No one, except you and I have read that letter. I am so very confused, Grandmother. Oh, it isn't Father's title and estates that I'm thinking about...."

"You must think about them," Lydia said sharply. "You have no idea of how you will feel toward your real mother. What your father said in that letter is all too true. My daughter was never a very stable woman. She gave in to every caprice. You must not deny what is your due, Adam. According to every record you are Lord Clarendon's heir. I advise you to retain that position, at least until you can decide for yourself what you want to do with your life."

"I've told Pamela," he said flatly.

"Oh yes, the young lady I was told about." She settled her eyes firmly on his face. "If you told her of that letter then I assume you are quite serious in your intentions toward her."

"But Caroline...," he stammered in despair.

Lydia hushed him with a look. She turned and said to Marcus, "Would you be a darling and leave us for a moment?"

"Of course, Mother."

When she and Adam were alone, Lydia gave him a stern look. "What happened between you and Caroline must be forgotten. She knows, naturally, and feels as guilt-ridden about the entire affair as you must feel. It was an innocent mistake, nothing more, but it is a mistake that must never be repeated."

"Of course it will never be repeated," Adam said, feeling hopelessly disgusted with himself. "But how can I ever face her? By going to America with you it's inevitable that we will meet again."

"You plan on going to America with me?"

"Yes. I've made that decision. I must at least get to know my real mother. Somehow I want to try and undo some of the wrong my parents did to her. During this past week I've been so confused. One moment I grieve for them so badly it pains me; then, thinking of how they actually took another woman's child makes me want to hate them."

"Stop it, Adam. I refuse to let you speak like that. I will not have you blame your parents. My daughter has suffered, that's true. She is also a woman capable of making others suffer. You said yourself, your parents meant no harm. They thought they were doing the right thing." She touched his arm again. "I know I sound like a disagreeable, heartless old woman, but the circumstances surrounding your disappearance were grim indeed." She sighed. "There are times when I think it was God's will that you be taken from April. I know I am being disloyal, but my daughter led the life she wanted to lead. Now you must do the same."

After a moment Adam said, "I still want to return to America with you."

"You are more than welcome, of course, if that is your decision."

"It is."

"Then I only stress that you keep the contents of that letter as secret as possible. If I were you, I'd destroy it. As for the problem of Caroline, you needn't see her, at least until you have made your final decision. She sends me word as to where she is and where she's going. She'll be traveling for several more months, perhaps longer. It will be some time before she returns to San Francisco."

"And if I decide to remain with my real mother?"

"We'll have to face that problem when and if it arrives." Despite his great loss, Lydia detected a boyish gleam for adventure. "You're still very young, Adam. America may seem a wild and glamorous place to you now. I can understand your enthusiasm as well as your curiosity, but you know only what you were brought up and educated to know. Here you are a titled gentleman. In America you will be a commoner, like the rest of us."

"I don't care about titles. Remember, I was born a commoner."

She gave him a faint smile. "No, in fact, you were born a prince of the Manchu Dynasty of China. Your real mother is a princess. That telltale tattoo on your thigh is the mark of Manchu royalty."

His early dream of the oriental temple and uniformed guards swept back into his memory. Now he wanted more than ever to see his real mother.

Lydia said, "I had planned on sailing on the *Mauritania* on Tuesday. I'm taking your grandfather's body home. However, if you are not ready to leave so soon, I can delay our departure."

"No, I'll be ready. I don't want to travel alone. For some reason, ever since I can remember, I've had a terrible dread of traveling alone."

\* \* \* \* \* \* \*

Pamela was in tears when Adam told her what he'd decided to do. "Please understand, Pamela. I must know who my mother is. I must see her."

"Adam, I'm so afraid you will never come back to me."

"If not," he said with boyish gallantry, "there is nothing to prevent your coming to America."

"Do you think you're doing the right thing? If you decide to stay in America you will forfeit everything your father worked so hard to give you."

Adam's adolescent enthusiasm burst from him. "My real mother is a princess."

"A Chinese princess," she reminded him. "Be serious, Adam. Honestly, I do believe you're taking all this as some sort of lark."

His smile faded. "April MacNair is my true mother, Pamela. I'd never be completely at rest until I've met her. It's strange, but I never really did feel as though I belonged here."

"That's nonsense. You're only feeling like that now because you know you weren't born here. But you don't know any other life than this one, Adam. You'll be miserable away from England."

"That is what I must find out for myself, mustn't I?"

Reluctantly, Pamela nodded. "I suppose you must. Go then, go to America. But I ask one favor, however."

"Anything."

"Swear to me that the letter your father left for you will remain a secret, at least until you're sure you know what you want to do."

"You're talking like my grandmother. She said exactly the same thing."

"Don't call her that, at least not to anyone here. If you decide to come home and claim your inheritance no one must know the truth except you and me. Having it made public that you are not a Clarendon will only ruin everything for you. Promise me."

"I promise."

"Now, we must think up some logical excuse for your going to America so soon after...I know," she said, snatching at an idea. "Mrs. Nightsong was here with Mr. MacNair to do business with the Clarendon Foundries. You'll say you are going back with her to conclude that business on behalf of your father."

He shrugged. "I suppose that will be as good as any reason."

"When do you sail?"

"Tuesday next."

"So soon?"

"I want to leave with grand...with Mrs. Nightsong."

"Very well." Pamela glanced at the little watch that hung from a pin on her lapel. "Goodness. Father and Mother are expecting us for dinner. We'll have to hurry. Now remember, Adam, let's for the moment forget all about the letter your father wrote. Tell Daddy it was just things about business affairs or something of that sort. And for goodness sake, make certain you ask him to oversee the repairs to Clarendon Hall. We want them to suspect nothing."

"You are already ordering me about like a wife does a husband."

"Perhaps you should begin thinking of me as one."

He smiled at that, but as they started across the garden and up the path to the manor house he suddenly remembered Caroline and felt a sinking sensation in the pit of his stomach.

# CHAPTER THIRTY

Caroline opened her grandmother's letter. She read it through quickly, then walked toward the window and looked down at the gondolas sliding smoothly over the waters of the Grand Canal. She loved Venice but it was a city for lovers, not to a wandering gypsy like herself. She sat down by the window and opened her grandmother's letter again:

"Forgive me, darling, for having to write so sad a letter, but I thought you should know that Peter Mac-Nair is dead. It's terrible of me, I know, to be so blunt, but sometimes bad news is best expressed that way. Marcus and I are taking the body home to America on Tuesday. You should also know that Adam Clarendon, or should I say Adam MacNair, is coming with us. He has decided he wants to meet his real mother. God only knows what the outcome of their reunion will be.

"I know how you felt about my darling Peter and would want to attend his funeral, but in view of Adam's being there, I heartily suggest that you stay away. I intend to do the same for Lorna's sake. I've caused enough grief to that poor woman, which I deeply regret.

"You have no doubt read of your father's tragedy. I'm beginning to think my entire life has been a tragedy, except for Peter and my darling children and especially you.

"You must forgive me if I can't write anymore just now. All I seem to do these days is cry. Please try to not feel guilty about what happened between you and your half-brother. Travel, my dear, and forget. Make your life as happy as you can. I love you very much and miss you dreadfully. Please write and tell me where you are.

"All my love,

"Grandmother"

Caroline breathed a heavy sigh and tried without success to hold back the tears. Peter MacNair was dead. "Dear, darling Peter," she said as she turned again toward the window. The tears ran freely down her cheeks. And Adam was going to San Francisco to see their mother.

"Damn it," she swore as she clenched her fists, pressing them hard against her eyes. "Adam is not my brother. He can't be. If it's the last thing I do, I'll prove that he isn't."

She was convinced that Peter and her grandmother had snatched at a straw out of their own desperate need to find their lost grandson. She loved Adam Clarendon, and he was a Clarendon, not a MacNair. She couldn't help the way she felt about him. She loved him totally. It just wasn't possible that he was her brother. God would never be so cruel.

There was a tap on her door, and when she opened it the page handed her a note on a silver tray, together with a single yellow rose. "Compliments of Count Cambruzio," the page said.

"Have dinner with me tonight," she read. "I will call for you at eight o'clock. Antonio."

She crumpled the note and threw it toward the waste-basket. The ego of Italian men was something she hadn't gotten accustomed to. They were all so convinced of their irresistible charms. She'd call him and tell him not to bother calling for her, that she had a previous dinner date. But as she smelled the lovely yellow rose and started for the telephone she hesitated. Count Cambruzio was young and handsome and delightful company. Besides, she knew he wanted to go to bed with her. Perhaps she would give in to him. The diversion might help ease the terrible need she had for Adam.

\* \* \* \* \* \* \*

After stumbling upon the indecent tableau in Mr. Ramsey's bedroom, both Leon and Susan had run from the house, forgetting completely, for the moment, why they'd come.

Susan ignored her mother for days, refusing even the slightest move on Lorna's part to try and explain.

"There is nothing to explain, Mother. I am making arrangements to go back to New York with the children. We will be gone in a day or two and that will be the end of it."

"Susan, dear—"

"Mother, please," Susan said, stomping her foot. "I do not wish to discuss it. The sooner I leave, the better."

The following morning Susan hid herself in the nursery with the children. David was being particularly peevish, which only made Petie peevish as well. Susan found her nerves completely frayed.

Though they were in a remote part of the house and behind closed doors, the piercing scream from the library sent Susan flying downstairs. She met the servants scurrying from their quarters, all wide-eyed with wonder.

Susan, with the others crowding behind her, opened the library door to find her mother in a faint on the floor. An elderly man was kneeling beside her, his face as gray as his suit.

"She's fainted," he said, rubbing Lorna's wrists.

"Call the doctor," Susan ordered over her shoulder.

Lorna's eyes fluttered open. She moaned and tried to sit up.

Between them they got her onto the divan and propped her against the bank of pillows.

"The shock," the elderly man said.

Susan looked at him, questioningly.

"Your father," Lorna sobbed as she put her arm across her eyes.

"What about Father?" Susan asked the question of the man.

"I'm afraid I brought dreadful news," he said. "I'm Charles Wilkinson of the British Embassy. I know your mother quite well. I thought the news best come from someone she knew."

"What news? What's happened to Father?"

"I'm sorry, my dear, I'm afraid he died in London. We just received word of it last evening."

Susan went quite pale and gripped the back of the chair. "Dead?" she gasped. The tears stung her eyes.

"Yes, I'm afraid so. Some internal infection that developed into a consumptive condition and then to pneumonia. It was all quite unexpected." He didn't give the more lurid details because it had been decided that none be made public. "Lydia Nightsong is bringing his body home."

"Lydia?"

"She was with him when he died, we were informed. It was a peaceful death. He didn't suffer."

"Father dead?" Susan said through her tears as she looked at her mother. The revulsion she'd felt for Lorna turned to pity. Somehow the dreadful news was penance for her mother's indiscretions with Mr. Ramsey, she felt. As she looked at her mother she saw the tears, but she saw something else: Anger, Susan decided. She wondered if Lorna was angry at having been deprived of her husband or the fact that he'd died in Lydia Nightsong's arms.

After Mr. Wilkinson left and the doctor ordered Lorna to bed, the house settled into that heavy hush that comes only with death. Everyone spoke in whispers and walked softly, like people do in graveyards.

It surprised Susan that her brother took the loss so hard. She'd always imagined Efrem as being indifferent toward his father. His tears, real and unashamed, puzzled her.

"If Father had only let me get to know him," Efrem cried as

he went slowly up to his room and shut himself in.

The outside world permitted the MacNairs a first day of private grief. On the second morning the parade began. Lorna saw everyone, like a queen holding court, reveling in self-pity and wishes of condolence. She wore her loss like a badge; a photograph of Peter, black-draped, sat prominently on the table beside her chair.

The following evening Leon arrived. The last of the well-wishers had trickled off leaving only Susan, Efrem, and Ellen Stanton sitting with Lorna.

"Are you all right?" Leon asked as Susan met him in the foyer.

"Yes, as well as can be expected. It was a terrible blow to all of us."

"I know your mother won't see me. I came only because April received a letter from mother. They arrive Saturday morning aboard the *Mauritania*."

Susan fought back her tears. "Thank you, Leon."

"There's more," he said. "Mother is bringing someone with her. Your mother should know." Susan looked through her tears, waiting. "Your father succeeded in locating Adam."

"Adam?"

"David's son."

Susan stared at him.

"Mother didn't give many details, only that they traced Adam to a titled family in England. They have definite proof that he is the child who was kidnapped."

"Dear God."

Efrem appeared in the doorway of the sitting room. "Leon," he beamed, shaking Leon's hand and putting a hand on his shoulder. In a low voice he said, "Mother sent me to see what all the whispering is about."

Susan hurriedly told him about Adam being found.

"You must tell Mother," Efrem said, pulling Leon by the arm.

"No, Ef. I doubt if she'll welcome even happy news from me."

He refused to be dissuaded. "It's about time mother realized who her real friends are. Come along."

Leon still balked. Susan said, "Efrem's right, Leon. After all, Adam is as much your relation as he is ours. It's time all old grievances be patched up."

Between them they took Leon into the sitting room. Ellen recognized him at once. "Hello, Leon," she said and kissed his cheek.

When Leon looked at Lorna her back straightened. She folded her hands in her lap and glared at him. "How dare you come here? You are not welcome in this house, Mr. Nightsong."

"I realize that, Mrs. MacNair. I only came—"

"Your reason, however well meaning, is also unwelcome."

"Mother," Susan said a little sharper than she'd intended. "Leon has news of Adam."

"My grandson?" Her scowl disappeared. She looked bewildered. "What do you know of Adam?"

"Only that your husband located him."

"How do you know this?"

He tactfully refrained from any mention of his mother's letter, even her name. "Adam is bringing your husband home."

"But how? Where?"

Efrem said, "All that matters, Mother, is that Adam's identity had been verified without a doubt. He's coming to San Francisco."

Lorna rested her head against the high-backed chair.

"My grandson to replace my husband." By the way she spoke they all glanced at one another, wondering if she meant it to be a fair exchange. Then Lorna's eyes narrowed wickedly. "Coming to his mother, I suspect."

Leon was rescued from an answer by the maid's appearance in the doorway. Like so many uncomfortable situations this one was made more uncomfortable by the maid's announcement. "A Mr. Ramsey is here to pay his respects," she told Lorna.

It was as if a switch had been thrown, plunging the room into a terrifying silence. Ellen Stanton was the only one to show any motion, her hands toying idly with the lace on her cuffs, her eyes moving from one to the other, wondering why everyone suddenly looked so frightened.

Lorna opened her mouth to say she was receiving no one further this evening, but Ramsey closed it for her when he stepped around the maid, hat in hand.

One sweeping glance took in the group, his eyes resting for a fraction of a second on each of the faces. He nodded to Ellen, the only stranger to him.

Ramsey went up to Lorna and took her hand from her lap. He raised it to his lips, but Lorna snatched it away. "I appreciate your coming, Ramsey, but I was about to go to bed."

Ramsey did something shocking. He laughed. "Run off to bed when we have such an excellent opportunity to satisfy curiosities?" He directed the last to Susan and Leon.

"Ramsey," Lorna said through clenched teeth. "This is hardly the time."

"What better time?" He went over to Ellen and put out his hand. "Manners seem to be lacking," he said. "My name is Ramsey."

Confused, Ellen took the hand he offered.

Efrem stepped beside Ellen and put a proprietary hand on her shoulder. "My fiancée, Mr. Ramsey, Ellen Stanton." He spoke with defiance.

"Fiancée? Yours?" Ramsey laughed again.

Ellen saw Efrem's frightened look. "It hasn't been officially announced as yet, under the circumstances," she said.

Ramsey saw from the other's surprise that this was the first they'd heard of the engagement. No one, however, said anything.

Efrem said to his mother, "We had intended waiting until next month to tell you."

With an evil leer Ramsey said to Efrem, "A wife won't solve your problems, boy."

Efrem clenched his fists and jutted out his chin. "You've threatened me for the last time, Ramsey."

"We'll see about that."

"Yes indeed, we'll see," Leon said, taking command. "I know of your hold over Efrem and I also know about what you've forced him into doing for you."

Ramsey was not taken aback. He merely grinned and rubbed his jaw. "You're being very brave, Mr. Nightsong. But I suppose that's part of your role as the boy's paramour."

Lorna gasped. Ramsey arched his eyebrows. "Surely, Lorna, you are aware of your son's deviation? You can't be all that blind."

Susan bristled. "You are a disgusting old man, Mr. Ramsey. You've frightened my brother into believing himself to be something he is not." She turned to her mother. "Your Mr. Ramsey has been blackmailing Efrem all these years for a boyish indiscretion that happened long ago. It was no more than that, an adolescent error in judgment. He's been threatening Efrem with scandal and arrest if Efrem didn't do what Mr. Ramsey ordered him to do."

Lorna stared; her speech was gone. Her world, she felt, was coming apart.

Ramsey's snake eyes darted from Susan to Leon to Efrem. "You are what you are, boy," he said.

Ellen stood firm, her head high, her mouth drawn thin. "He is hardly what you claim, Mr. Ramsey. If he were, he would hardly be capable of fathering the child I'm carrying."

There was a stunned silence.

"Child?" Lorna stammered. She fell limp in her chair.

"Yes." To Efrem Ellen said, "I didn't want to tell you like this, darling. In fact I hadn't planned on telling you at all. I felt it might have pressured you into proposing. It's true, though. The doctor told me last week that my tests were positive."

"Dear Ellen," Efrem beamed. He kissed her lightly on the lips. "I do love you."

Lorna dabbed her handkerchief to the corners of her mouth. Almost inaudibly she said, "I don't understand any of this."

In a quiet monotone Leon gently told her of Ramsey's smuggling of opium through MacNair Products. "He forced Efrem to cooperate in the operation."

"Opium?" Lorna cried, gaining her composure, letting her venom rise. "You spoke to me of this many years ago, Ramsey. I warned you then what I would do if you tried such a despicable thing. So you went through my son. How dare you?"

Ramsey shrugged.

Leon said, "I mean to make all this known to the police, Mr. Ramsey. That's what Susan and I came to tell you the other evening."

Lorna turned red under her anger.

"And if you do, Mr. Nightsong," Ramsey said, "you will, of course, implicate Efrem as well. I suppose you've given thought to that?"

"Efrem was a pawn. He will hardly be held responsible."

Ramsey remained unintimidated. He looked at Lorna's mask of hatred and disgust, knowing it was meant for herself as well as for him. "You certainly don't want another scandal, Lorna. There is so much more than can be brought out if any charges are brought against me. We go back a long way, my dear. If I am forced into becoming desperate, I'll have to resort to the business of your grandson."

"Get out!" Lorna cried.

"I'd think twice before casting your lot against me, Lorna. A cornered animal is always the most vicious."

Susan said to her mother, "What business about Adam?"

"It happened years ago," Lorna said, every muscle in her body felt tired.

"Be quiet, Lorna."

His rebuke only added to her strength. "I won't be quiet. I've been quiet for too long. You have held this family in your greedy hands long enough, Ramsey. Damned the consequences." To Susan she said, "It was Mr. Ramsey who kidnapped Adam."

"Not without your help," Ramsey reminded her, his voice like the sharp edge of a sword.

"You were to take the child to me," Lorna cried.

"Mother!"

Lorna began to cry, her body shaking. She leaned back against the chair, gripping its arms for strength. "We had agreed between us to take the child from his mother. I felt that I would be able to raise Adam in a healthier environment." She could not look at Leon.

"Lorna," Ramsey warned.

She ignored him. "The plan was to take the child, make it appear as a kidnapping that was made possible by the lax supervision his mother gave the boy. Ramsey was to conceal Adam and then, under the employ as my detective, find the child and deliver him to me. Something went wrong. The woman who was to hide Adam skipped off with him. We don't know why."

"Who was this woman?" Susan demanded of Ramsey.

He hesitated, then shrugged again. "As long as everyone is in such a purgative mood I suppose I might as well fill in the gaps. I had a wife in Sausalito."

Lorna closed her eyes.

"I gave the boy into my wife's care, believing I could trust her. Unfortunately, Sylvia was never a well person. My charwoman told me later that a woman fitting Sylvia's description came to my flat on the second night after Adam's disappearance. She had a young boy of four with her." He looked at Lorna. "It was the night it rained so hard, the night I was to fetch the boy. The weather was too bad. You and I stayed together most of the night."

Lorna kept her face hidden, a handkerchief clamped tight over her mouth holding down the bile, the humiliation.

"Sylvia obviously stumbled upon us, much in the same way you and Mr. Nightsong did the other evening," he said to Susan. "I don't know any more. Only that when I went to Sausalito the following morning Sylvia and the boy were gone. One of my agents said they were seen boarding an eastbound train, but no one could describe the pair with any certainty. The ticket seller said the woman was hidden in a shawl. He did not remember seeing any boy. We followed the lead but got nowhere." He breathed a sigh and made a helpless gesture, but he was still smiling. "So there you have it." He turned to Leon. "Go to the police, Mr. Nightsong. I assure you I will not be the only one arrested."

No one spoke. No one moved.

Ramsey made a move toward the door. He saw the determined fix to Leon's chin. Ramsey did not fancy the idea of prison, even if he did drag the others down with him. As he gazed at Lorna, limp and beaten, he could not help but feel the love he had for her.

"Tell you what," Ramsey said. "I've always been good at making deals, so I'll offer one that may save us all a lot of embarrassment." He waited. When no one spoke he went on. "I will leave San Francisco for good. I won't come back, ever."

He wanted Lorna to look at him, but she kept her eyes shut, the handkerchief to her mouth. "I'll do this only for you, Lorna. Despite everything, I do love you very much." When still she didn't speak Ramsey asked, "Agreed?"

Their mute faces unnerved him. He slapped his hat against his thigh. "Very well then, it's agreed," he said. He gazed for the last time at Lorna, then turned and walked out of the house.

* * * * * * *

Susan, Efrem, and Leon met the train at the Oakland Mole a week after the *Mauritania* had docked in New York. It was a strange reunion, Susan and Efrem attending to their father's coffin, Adam standing stiff and formal beside Lydia, Marcus accepting their handshakes and muttering words of welcome. No one seemed to have anything to say.

At last the group separated, Efrem and Susan going off with their unhappy cargo, the Nightsongs to the mansion on Nob Hill.

They rode in silence, Lydia worried about Adam's first meeting with his mother. Leon stared out at the streets. Marcus, sensing everyone else's edginess, grew edgy himself. All he wanted to do was be with Amelia.

Adam felt he must say something to relieve the tension that

was permeating the limousine. "You are with Grandmother's business, Leon?"

"Not at present," Leon said, glad for conversation. "I have been living with my wife and family in Hawaii. That, I intend to change, however."

Lydia smiled. "I'm very glad to hear that, dear."

"I don't know how Ohlan will like the idea of moving to San Francisco, but she was brought up in the old ways. In time she'll love this city as much as I do and it will be so much better for the children." He took his mother's hand. "I've spent some time of late with one of your chemists, Mother. We may have a surprise for you. It may even rival Nightsong perfume."

"Nightsong perfume is in the past, darling," she said sadly. "We will think of another name."

As the car pulled under the portico Lydia saw April's face peering out at them. Then the curtain dropped closed.

April was standing on the stairs as they came into the entry hall. Her eyes were wide, unbelieving. She stared at Adam. Lydia saw the wildness in April's eyes. Her worst fears were realized.

"David!" April cried, unable to move. "You're not dead." She flung herself down the stairs and threw her body against Adam, who stood confused and noticeably frightened. "Oh, David, my darling husband, you've come back to me at last."

"It's Adam, dear," Lydia said. "Adam. Remember, I wrote you a letter."

"Letter?" April tried to remember. Her expression turned angry. "Lies! You wrote me lies!" She turned to Adam, pleading. "They are always lying to me. Remember how they lied when you and I tried to elope, how your father lied to you in China?" She glowered at Lydia and Marcus. "You're alike, both of you." Her haunted eyes moved back to Adam. "They've stolen our son, David. You'll find him and bring him home, won't you?"

Adam's dreams of the beautiful princess who was his mother vanished. He was so embarrassed he couldn't find anything to say to her.

Marcus mumbled something feeble about being hungry and went off toward the kitchen.

Leon put his arm around April's waist. "He'll find him," he said softly. "Now you'd better come along with me and have your nap."

As he tried to lead her away she stretched out her arms to Adam. "David. Come with me."

"He'll come up presently," Leon said as he took her up the stairs. "You must rest, April."

"I'm sorry, Adam," Lydia said. "It's far worse than I'd feared. It is just that you look so much like your father, your mother became confused. Come with me. We'll get you settled in. She'll be all right after she has had time to think things out for herself."

Lydia had told him the grisly details of his father's beheading and had hinted at his mother's lapses into a private world of her own. Adam had no idea that her lapses were so extreme.

His felt as if his life was in shambles. As the days passed, he found that when his mother did not speak to him as her husband, she treated him like a stranger, polite and disinterested in anything he had to say.

He and Leon attended Peter MacNair's funeral; Lydia tastefully stayed away. But even with the MacNairs, Adam found himself uncomfortable. His grandmother MacNair kept looking at him as one might look at a reminder of their more grievous sins.

It surprised Leon that Lorna extended no invitation to Adam to come to the MacNair house, except a perfunctory one of coming to dinner so that they could all become acquainted. It was obvious to Leon that Lorna wanted nothing to do with Adam. He was living proof of her crime—and of Mr. Ramsey, Leon decided.

Adam accepted Lorna's dinner invitation but came back more confused than ever, finding that any mention of his mother was ignored by Mrs. MacNair.

As the days passed Adam realized he did not belong here. He

told Lydia so.

"I guess I'm just homesick," he said, skirting the real reason for wanting to go home.

She offered no resistance. "You must go where you will be happiest," she said.

"It's not my mother," Adam said weakly.

"You need make no explanation to me, Adam. We are strangers to you, as you are a stranger to us. It is only natural that you should be where you belong. To be frank, I had serious doubts about your coming here. But at least you know the truth about yourself and we, thank God, know that you are well and strong and will be happy."

They agreed between them that his departure would be low-keyed. "We needn't upset my daughter unduly," was all Lydia said.

Adam had been concerned about Caroline coming home unexpectedly. She didn't, for which he was glad. It wasn't that he was afraid of his feelings for her. Seeing her family, the disorganized way in which they lived—everyone so independent of the others—made him think of her only as a sad mistake he'd made.

Five days after he'd arrived, he was again packed and ready for the trip across the country and a ship back to England. Lydia bade him farewell with what Adam thought was welcome relief. He paid a short, formal visit to his grandmother MacNair, who sat alone in a high-backed chair with a black draped photograph of her husband sitting on the table beside her. The house was like a tomb.

"Susan left for New York only yesterday. You could have traveled together." It was all she said in parting.

The chauffeur was waiting with Adam's luggage when he returned to the Nightsong mansion.

"Good-bye, Grandmother." He kissed Lydia on both cheeks.

"Good-bye, Adam. You must bring your bride to see us one day."

"Of course. Pamela has always been anxious to see America."

She stood on the wide porch with its Victorian trim and

waved as the car pulled off down the street. When it was out of sight she went into the house and up the stairs to her daughter's room.

April was sitting in her usual place in the window seat. "Where is David going?" April asked, staring out through the curtains.

"He's going to find Adam," Lydia said. She blinked back her tears as she smoothed April's hair. "He'll be back in time."

# ABOUT THE AUTHOR

**V. J. BANIS** is the critically acclaimed author ("the master's touch in storytelling..."—*Publishers Weekly*) of more than 200 published books and numerous short stories in a career spanning nearly a half century. A native of Ohio and a longtime Californian, he lives and writes now in West Virginia's beautiful Blue Ridge.

You can visit him at http://www.vjbanis.com

www.ingramcontent.com/pod-product-compliance
Lightning Source LLC
Chambersburg PA
CBHW020644030726
47498CB00002B/364